Nothing Random

Shannon Plate

For Eileen Broderick, who spirited me to Ireland.

Give her eternal rest, O Lord, and may your light shine on her forever.

Introduction

I am not resigned to the shutting away of loving hearts in the cold ground.
So it is, and so it will be for so it has been, time out of mind
  Edna St. Vincent Millay

The day after her husband's funeral, Larkin May awoke. When she could, she got out of bed. Thinking back on it later, she was sure other things must have happened. Probably the phone rang. She hoped she'd fed the dog. A neighbor may have stopped by and in the afternoon the mail came, one could be sure (neither snow nor rain nor heat nor gloom of night...) but she remembered none of it. The days following were much the same until the tenth day when she woke up hungry. On that day she knew she wouldn't die.

Life returned to different parts of her body, slowly. For a time her feet felt numb and her hips wore bruises from bumping into furniture. Her hands were icy and uncertain and she burned herself without knowing, her fingers puffing at a touch in the oven. She had trouble buttoning shirts so she put them in the back of the closet and wore pullovers. On some days, eating was out of the question, her stomach frozen, but quietly she thawed from the ground up and finally even her shoulders lost their rigidity, and movement seemed natural instead of calculated.

After the accident, when it seemed months of rehabilitation would be necessary, she had taken a leave of absence from her job to be available for the care Pat would need. After he died she went back, not as an individual and group counselor but a receptionist, answering phones and making appointments.

A year to the day, she lay in bed and wished it over. She had dreaded this coming and knew it would exact its price. Anniversaries of almost any kind are counted in months until the first year, so now when people were brave enough or rude enough to ask she could say, "It's been a year," instead of seven months, or nine, like a proud parent or a newlywed.

There had been times this year when pain had seemed like a malevolent roommate, creeping up and blindsiding her in sneaky ways. She walked carefully through those months and had no curiosity for the unknown; she looked both ways, took up no new hobbies, and made no new friends.

So here was the day, stretched out in front of her like a snake over which she couldn't step. She dressed and drank coffee, grabbed her purse, and after a moment went upstairs and put on her wedding rings. They felt heavy on her hand and made that clinking metallic noise she remembered.

She drove to the store and bought toothpaste on sale and a towel to match her set that had been mangled in the wash. She went to another and bought 2 packages of 24 rolls of toilet paper and socks for all three of her next-door neighbor's children. She filled her cart, stood in line to pay, and was just another of the faceless crowd doing the same thing on this rainy afternoon. She didn't speak to the cashiers. They didn't know she was barely composed, they didn't know she wasn't really married; they didn't know anything about her and they didn't care.

Once home, she dumped one of the packages of toilet paper and all of the socks on her neighbor's porch. Everything else she took in and put away, then sat down to a movie she'd seen before with a pizza made in the microwave, her dog molded to her side. There were four messages on the answering machine that she ignored and mail she didn't open. She couldn't comfort or be comforted. The voice of her mother would salt the wound and the notes from friends would break her. It would wait. Tomorrow would be soon enough, but not today, not this day. In this way the hours passed, this black day that would mark her life as an anniversary she never wished to see, but the day after which she had told herself, quite sternly, she had no further excuse not to live.

1 . Two years later

Instead of pulling her car into her garage, Larkin parked in front of the main sidewalk dividing the two rows of town homes where she lived. It was June and the flowers in all the neighbors' minuscule front gardens were blooming and fragrant. Walking up the wide steps leading to the complex, she was glad again that she had been able to keep the house. She thought she'd have to sell after Pat died, but he had taken care of her once again and the property was paid off with the insurance he had argued for and that she had dismissed as a waste of money.

Reaching the top of the stairs, she paused. Gardening was competitive here and the result was mosaic, colors running down each side of the walk, some plots staying with the traditional geraniums and impatiens, pansies and petunias native to Illinois, and the inventive straying toward more exotic blooms -- pitcher plants from South America, orchids in pots, and Venus Fly Traps.

Directly across from Larkin's front door was Mr. Carney's garden. He was a purist, this old Irishman, and he grew only roses. One of the blessings Larkin counted was that she lived within wind of Mr. Carney's roses, for he was particular about not only the look of the blooms but also their fragrance. In times past, he had given away plants that didn't suit his nose or that took attention from the others by their scent.

"Roses are jealous flowers," he said. "You can't have a queen among them. They must all feel equal, or they'll pout and won't bloom."

When Larkin got to her unit, she reached for the mail, opened the door to let the dog out, and sat down on the step to sift through the bundle. The dog, a brown toy poodle, bounded around her, choosing between greeting her and nature's call.

"Go ahead, I'll wait for you," Larkin instructed.

As he watered her New Guinea Impatiens, she scanned the mail. Mostly junk, there were only bills and a short note from her mother to keep. In the note, her mother restated her views on Larkin's decision not to meet them for vacation in August at the lake, and vehemently encouraged her to change her mind.

Larkin's mother adhered to the thought that if she stated something with enough force, it would happen. Larkin added the note to the recycle pile. The dog, done with his routine, came looking for her.

"Hello, Bubba, how are you? Did you miss me? Did you miss me very much?"

The dog scurried round her legs as she talked, putting his paws on her knees and reaching up to lick her chin as she bent down, panting in her face. He did the same thing every time she returned to the house, whether she had been gone all day or on a quick run for Chinese. She bought an embroidered pillow once, a kitschy thing and unusual for her, but with a statement true to the bone: "Be the person your dog thinks you are."

She stretched out her legs and pulled her jeans up over her calves to catch the sun. The door to her right opened, and her next-door neighbor stepped out to hunt for mail.

"Hey, Larkin."

"Hey, Sukki."

Sukki had lived in the complex since its opening 16 years ago, her first husband moving them as a surprise when she was in the hospital producing their first child. Now divorced from her second husband, she paid the bills working as a graphic artist out of a home office. When that work was slow, she augmented her income with custom painting jobs, addressing wedding envelopes in calligraphy, and whatever else she could talk someone into paying her to do.

She was as resourceful a person as Larkin had ever known.

"Is today the day you see your friend?" Sukki asked.

"Late this afternoon. I pick her up at the Hyatt at four and I promised her dinner. Where should we go?"

"Don't go. I'll cook. I've got all kinds of stuff thawing and I'm in a cooking kind of mood. Anything she doesn't eat?"

Larkin thought. "She can't eat shellfish. Makes her tongue itch. And she won't eat sprouts of any kind after some vegetarian fiasco. Other than that, go to town."

"So much for "Brussels Shrimp Alfalfa.""

"Will you really cook?" Larkin looked at Sukki. "I thought you were up to your neck in invitations."

Sukki smiled. "Done and happy. It was a good job, but checking the spelling on 450 names got old."

Larkin stood and shook her jeans back down to her ankles. "I couldn't scrounge up 450 people to invite to anything." She opened the door, and Bubba went around her to get in. "What time for dinner?"

"Around six. Do you have any chicken broth?"

"I think so."

"Good. I'll send Errol to get it. I'll replace it next time I go to the store."

"Sure you will." Larkin grinned at her. Sukki never replaced anything she borrowed with the same item, but something that caught her eye she felt Larkin needed more, like plum sauce, or tiny ears of corn in a jar. Once, she borrowed a dozen eggs, but hard-boiled the ones she gave back.

Inside, Larkin walked downstairs to the kitchen, found the chicken broth, and waited for Errol to come get it. The lower level of the town home housed the kitchen, family room, laundry, and a huge walk-in closet. There was a light knock from the inside of the closet door.

"Come on in, Errol."

"Tee. Mom needs something you have."

"This is it."

"And she wants to talk to you. You're supposed to come back with me."

"Now?"

"I'll take you," Errol said, turning back into the closet. Hand in hand, they walked past winter clothes, Christmas decorations, and the desk where Pat used to do the taxes. Just past the desk was a door, a secret door Larkin and Sukki had put in to join their townhomes so they wouldn't have to go outside to get into each other's houses.

The door came about as the result of one of the hardest days after Pat's death. When it came time to do the taxes, Larkin was digging around in the desk looking for paperwork. She opened one drawer to find it filled with cards for her - greeting cards for future birthdays, anniversaries, Valentine's Day - and gifts. She opened all the boxes. There was a pair of earrings shaped like leaves, a tiny soft bunny, a small drawing pad with new pencils, and an empty journal covered with flowers. They were all well-thought gifts, personal to her likes, and finding them nearly broke her. She sat on the floor reading the cards, fingering the gifts, and rocking. At some point she gave way, laid on the floor, and wept. When she was spent, there was a soft knock on the wall beside her. Sukki's closet ended on the other side of the wall, and one of the kids had heard Larkin's crying and gone to get her.

"Larkin? Are you OK?"

"No, I am not OK; I will never again be OK."

"What happened?"

Larkin told her about the gifts and the cards and the realization once again that this was a fine man she had married, a man who could never be replaced, that she had loved him completely and now that he was dead, she couldn't see past it, couldn't get through the pain and loss of him. Sukki sat on the floor in her closet and they talked through the wall, Sukki soothing Larkin with her words as if she was next to her with a light hand on her back. Larkin talked about how dead she felt with Pat gone, of how thinking about being with another man made her sick to her stomach. She wondered if that part of her was forever gone. Sukki told her she thought Larkin would reach it again, this centering with a man, because of who she was, that there was a hope in Larkin, deep.

When they finished talking, each sat quiet on her own side of the wall. Then Sukki, because she was Sukki, said in a thoughtful voice that it would be nice to have a door here, nice to have a way back and forth without going outside. Wouldn't that be nice, she said to Larkin, and Larkin replied that it certainly would be nice, but how in the world would they do that, and would it be allowed by the association that set the rules for the complex, and what would happen when one of them went to sell their place?

"Larkin, you're borrowing trouble. I think I can do it. Are you busy tomorrow?"

The next morning, Sukki was ready with a Sawz-all, tape measures, a fat carpenter's pencil, and a leather tool apron strapped around her waist. She had made her calls, gotten a book from the library, and was quite ready to attempt something she'd never done before with large, noisy tools.

"You look like that annoying woman on TV, the one who can miter things." Larkin was dragging everything out of Sukki's closet, after having cleared her side. Sukki was measuring and marking the outline of a door on the wall.

"Miter, schmiter. Time to cut."

Larkin held her breath as Sukki banged a hole through the drywall with a hammer, then started the saw and touched it to the wallboard. Dust and particles flew from the blade, but Sukki was steady, and in little time, they removed a door-sized piece of drywall.

"Now, through the studs."

Those she cut one by one, and pried them away from the framing at the floor. Larkin had to go to work, but when she got home there was a door there, trimmed but not mitered at the edges.

"You have to draw the line somewhere," Sukki told her. "I don't change my oil, and I don't miter."

It was a good doorway, swinging level, with a lock on each side like adjoining hotel rooms.

"For privacy," Sukki said. "For days we don't want company, or for days we already have it."

Larkin laughed. "We're nuns, you and I."

"You won't always be like this. A woman like you, I'm surprised you haven't hopped the fence, already."

"What did you tell the kids about the door?"

"I swore them to secrecy. I told them if anyone found out, we'd have to build the wall back in, that it was this great secret we shared, and we all agreed - holding hands - that it was a special thing we didn't want ruined."

The door became a part of their days. Sukki's kids wandered in and out, showing Larkin school papers and projects and asking her opinion a variety of subjects. Bubba went back and forth and quickly learned there were treats next door he wasn't allowed at home. It turned out to be one of the things in life that was just as they'd hoped, and Larkin was grateful again for whatever it was in Sukki that made her act on her ideas and not just think them.

Holding Errol's hand, Larkin followed him out of Sukki's closet door and into her family room. Emmy, Sukki's daughter, waved from the couch with an IPod and a stack of cookies. Sukki's son lay in a semi-circle of books on the floor. Sukki had named him James for her father, not his, and would not hear him called "Jim." James' father was called Jimmy to this day - a fitting name, Sukki said, for a 40 year-old man still acting like a boy.

James looked up when they came in and grinned.

"Tee! You'll never guess what we did in gym today."

"Stay away from me." Larkin waved him off.

"No, really, you'll like this one." His class was in a unit on wrestling, and last week he'd come over to show her a new move, at one point heaving her off the floor in a surprising show of strength.

He twisted around to his feet. Moving behind her, he took her arms and brought them together in the middle of her back.

"See, you pin the guy's arms like this, and then sweep his feet out from under him..."

"No sweeping!"

"I won't, I won't. But see how it works? He has nothing to break his fall, goes right down on his face, and before he gets his head back, you pin him. Get it?"

"I've got it. Not that I'll ever use it." Larkin turned to Sukki. "What did you want me for?"

"Will you pick up a bottle of wine on your way back? Something white and crisp would be good."

"What are we having?"

"It's a surprise."

"Are you making it up as you go along? This should be good."

Larkin went home and readied herself to pick up Kate. She pulled on slim black jeans and a sleeveless cobalt shirt. It occurred to her it was the most she had been concerned about her appearance in some time, but seeing this old friend stirred her. She found silver earrings and a bracelet, and sprayed on perfume.

Kate was waiting outside the hotel in the sun. She spotted the car and came toward it, Larkin getting out and meeting her halfway.

"Larkin! Oh, it's so good to see you!"

They hugged, then held the other at arm's length and smiled.

"Come on, get in. Another 30 seconds, they'll tow the car. The bellmen are vicious here."

They picked up wine on the way home and pulled into the garage with a half-hour before dinner. The women took glasses and one of the bottles to Larkin's deck overlooking an open wooded area and settled in at the patio table.

Kate was enthusiastic. "This is such a great spot. You'd never know you were right in the middle of town."

"It's one of the reasons we bought this place." Larkin took a sip of wine. "The village owns that," she said, pointing to the trees, "so it will never be developed. It's protected wetlands, or something."

"Nice. Now, how are you? You look wonderful."

"Strictly for your benefit."

"Not just your clothes. Your face looks good, you look healthy."

"You're a dermatologist. What else would you look at? How is the convention?"

"Horribly boring. I thought from the brochures it was going to be something new and startling, but it's not. I'm pretty sure the best part of the trip will be seeing you."

Their conversation tripped along with knowledge shared only by people who had known each other since childhood.

Errol poked his head out the French doors to the deck.

"Tee. Mom says come eat."

"Is it six already? Errol, come and meet my friend Kate. We met when we were younger than you."

Errol came and plastered himself to Larkin's side.

"Kate, this is Sukki's son, Errol."

"It's nice to meet you," Errol said.

"And, you, Errol."

Errol looked sideways at Larkin. "Go ahead, Errol," she said. "Tell your mom we'll be right there."

Errol ran back through the house as the women rose to their feet and gathered their glasses and the half-full bottle of wine. Kate turned to Larkin.

"Tee? Is that what Errol called you?"

"Yes. It's a derivative of 'Auntie.' When the kids were small, Sukki decided she didn't want them calling me Larkin, and I didn't want them calling me Mrs. May. Emmy thought 'Auntie' would be a good choice, but James shortened it to 'Tee.'"

"It's a good fit. I'm glad you have people so close that care about you."

"You don't know how close. Will you open the closet door for me? My hands are full."

"Do you need something in there? Can I get it for you?"

"Nope, just walk."

"Why?"

"Just walk. It's Narnia."

2.

When Sukki really cooked, there was no stopping her. All she asked for her ministrations was that her guests bask in it all and compliment her.

It was, Larkin thought, a small price to pay.

She fed them well. Her main dish was chicken, sautéed in olive oil with garlic and thyme, and then sprinkled with lemon, the oil thickened with a bit of flour, and that sauce making magic of the mashed potatoes on which the chicken sat. She had a salad of unusual greens, mixed with vinegar so fresh and biting one would have thought she'd made it that morning. She'd made baking powder biscuits from scratch, adding cutout shapes on top of each one for effect, then brushing them with butter as they baked. She took broccoli, cauliflower, and sweet onion, swirled them in a pan with a bit of oil, and tossed it with kidney beans, coriander and a touch more garlic. For dessert, she'd made chocolate cheesecake sitting in a dollop fresh raspberry glace. Fragrant coffee, cut half with milk for James, finished it.

Larkin and Kate sat back in their chairs and rested their hands on their stomachs.

"I hope no one is expecting me to move," Kate sighed. "Does she feed you like this often?"

"Not often enough. I live on well-named but tasteless frozen entrees," Larkin answered.

Sukki brought the coffee pot to the table and faced the two women.

"I want some details," she said. "How long have you known each other? Were you neighbors? Went to college together? What?"

Larkin and Kate looked at each other and smiled.

Kate started. "We were neighbors from second grade on. We lived twelve houses from each other on a street that ended in a cul-de-sac. We about wore out the sidewalk between them. One year Larkin's dad made us stilts and we walked back and forth to each other's houses on them for an entire summer."

Larkin laughed. "I'd forgotten about the stilts. Whatever happened to them?"

"I kept them when you moved, don't you remember? My kids use them now, although not with the panache we did."

Kate went on to tell other stories that took them back twenty five years: kick-the-can in the dark, catching fireflies and letting them go, and listening to the hum of their parents talking, sitting on webbed lawn chairs with a Coke or a beer. She told stories of things they had gotten away with, things they'd gotten in trouble for; all the nooks and crannies of their shared experiences were spread out for Sukki to appreciate.

Larkin watched Kate's hands draw pictures in the air and get showy with the telling of those stories. She would know those hands anywhere. Her fingers were thin and straight with square nails, feminine working hands. Kate's whole family had the same hands and feet; they ran with them like blond hair or a strong forehead. It was a big family with cousins and grandparents that came to visit and eat ham-off-the-bone, different home-made pickles and olives from a divided tray. Kate's mother cut carrots in a way that made them look wavy, like French fries, and made radishes into roses.

Looking at the two of them, Larkin felt strong and connected to these women, one knowing her well for the first half of her life, the other for the second. She watched Kate draw Sukki in, Sukki properly amazed and amused at just the right times.

Larkin, sitting there with her feet propped on the chair next to her, could have nodded off had they not turned on her, all at once.

Kate started it off.

"So, Larkin, what is new for you this year? Are you traveling?"

"I don't have anything planned. There's no place I really want to go." Larkin shrugged. Vacation time had just been piling up since Pat died.

Both pairs of eyes trained on her, one hazel, one light brown.

"Might be a good idea to get away, to have some new experiences," Sukki said.

"Why? Do you think I'm getting boring?" Larkin laughed. Sukki was silent. Larkin turned and faced her. "What, you do think I'm getting boring?"

"Boring is kind of harsh. I do think, though, that you're in a bit of a rut." She lifted a shoulder. "You eat the same things, go the same places, talk to the same people."

Larkin sat up in her chair. "Really."

"I've actually been meaning to say something about it."

"And now is a good time?"

Kate joined in. "Maybe it is. Might it not be time to break out a little? Not a lot, just a little. Just a trip, or a date, or a new experience."

"A date? Did you slip that in there, too? Don't start on me about dating. I'm not ready."

"Why are you not ready?" Sukki sat immobile, staring her down. "What is it you're waiting for?"

Larkin thought, then started to talk. She didn't know if she had it in her anymore, the part of a woman that turns to a man with longing and intent, the reaching across yourself to touch another. She wondered if she was making herself feel this way out of loyalty to Pat, or if it was an emotional reaction to the grief she'd suffered. She knew there was more to this than missing her husband; this was death in her somewhere, it wasn't normal, and she wasn't sure if she should try to fix it or give herself over to that space and live in it.

Larkin took a shaky breath. Sukki reached over and touched her hand, and looked her in the face. "If you were a patient of yours..."

"Client, not patient."

"Ok, client. If you were a client of yours, what would you say?"

"It all depends on what was wanted." She took her hands, suddenly cold, and held them between her knees. "Do they want to change? Do they want to be less isolated? "

"Good question." Kate scooted her chair closer to Larkin, and put a hand on her back. "What do you, Larkin May, want for your life? Are you content living in the box you've built, as pretty as it is?"

Larkin looked at them. "It's true that I haven't been paying much attention."

"Larkin, no one is saying that your loss wasn't huge," Sukki said. "The question becomes to what level you want to recover. Do you want some color back in your life?"

"I think I do," Larkin said, "but I'm going to need a little help here."

"I vote for a trip. Go somewhere you've never been for at least two weeks, and you'll come back with color," Kate said.

"A trip would be good." Sukki nodded. "You used to love to travel, except for the flying thing. Can you get away?"

Bubba wandered over by Larkin's feet. She scooped him up and let him settle in, making himself even smaller to stay on her lap.

"Actually, this would be good timing. My current group is done in two weeks, and I haven't lined up another. I could take the next month off, if I chose, but that seems like a really long time."

"How about taking the month for something? You don't have to travel the whole time." Kate said. "OK, now, where? What attracts you? Do you want beach or culture?"

"How about Ireland?" Sukki asked in her thoughtful voice. Larkin turned to her. "How many times has Brynna asked you to come?"

"Brynna?" Kate asked.

"Mr. Carney's daughter," Larkin told her. "She comes to visit him every year, and every year in her Christmas card invites us to visit. She has a Bed and Breakfast in Athlone, on the Shannon River."

Sukki continued. "Think about this. You could go to Athlone and stay with Brynna. That way, you won't be completely by yourself, you'd have someone to show you the place, a local to get you in where you couldn't go if you were a tourist."

Larkin smiled at Kate. "Sukki has innate disdain for tourists." To Sukki she said, "You're right, though. I'd like to have a home base."

"Brilliant! Let's make reservations." Kate said.

"Not so fast. I need to talk to my boss and I need to call Brynna. Either one might end this."

Kate looked sternly at Larkin. "Don't you punk out. Do you promise you'll go?"

"I think I promise but I need to consider some things."

Kate looked at Sukki. "Will you keep her focused?"

"I will."

"Ok, then. My work here is done."

After taking Kate back to her hotel, Larkin took Bubba for a long walk. They wandered all over town, and ended up by a new restaurant with outdoor seating and a massive fire pit. A couple sat close in two of the chairs, each holding a glass of wine in their outer hand and each other's hand in the middle. They were sitting quietly watching the fire when the man leaned over and kissed the skin at the top of the woman's shoulder.

Just like Pat used to do.

Larkin turned and walked slowly home. It came to her that feeling safe was not the same as feeling joy. She wondered if it was time to make some changes; if it was time to stretch.

She woke in the night from a dream. As she came to the surface of her consciousness, the dream faded and by the time she was fully awake, the only thing she was sure of was that there had been music.

3.

The following afternoon, carrying groceries down the sidewalk, Larkin was surprised to see Mr. Carney out tending his roses. Usually, he did his gardening earlier, in the heat of the day. Larkin questioned him once, with his uncovered head turning red, why he didn't wait until the sun had passed a bit. He sat back on his heels and told her how cold it was in Ireland when he was a child, and said he was getting his share of the sun now.

He was a retired railway worker and had emigrated from Ireland in the 90's, when unemployment was high there and lower in the States. He worked for the same company for 18 years before retiring three years ago.

Larkin had never known his wife. She died fourteen years before, just a year after buying the town house. Sukki knew her the year she lived here and spoke of her as a whisper of a woman, slight and gentle, picking up James as a baby and murmuring to him in Irish, stroking him under the chin and passing a hand over his head.

"Oh, he has a lovely shaped head, doesn't he, like my own Garvin. Ah, he's a lovely gossoon, aren't you now?"

She died of a stroke at 53, Mr. Carney finding her when he got home from work. She was lying in the hall between the mailbox and the kitchen, a letter from her daughter and the electric bill in her hand, and a cup of tea gone cold on the table.

When he flew home to bury her in the town where they grew up, he said it was as if she had become a fairy or a ghost, and everywhere he turned, there floated a piece of her; her favorite old songs sung in the pubs and flowers she loved blooming out of season. He walked the streets where they'd romanced from a distance and finally kissed. He stood in front of the hotel where she worked while they were courting, tossing sandwiches out the window to him as he waited for her on his bicycle. He smelled her in the breezes, heard her voice as the river passed under the bridge, and saw her a dozen times, the back of her head turning toward him or her walk on another woman's frame. Even though they'd been gone for seven years, the town came to see her off, filling the church and trailing after the casket down the street.

When he came back to suburban Chicago, he planted roses and didn't travel for five years, his children coming to him until he could face Ireland once again.

Today, she called to him as she made her way up the sidewalk.

"Mr. Carney! Isn't it a lovely day?"

He looked up at her and straightened.

"Larkin."

Larkin loved the way he said her name. He made it sound as if there were a bar of music between the "r" and the "k."

"You're gardening now? Was there no sun earlier?"

"There was, of course. I've been waiting for you."

Larkin stopped.

"You've talked to Sukki?"

"In a way, I suppose. Mostly, Sukki talked to me."

Larkin stood, her bags hanging from her hands. "She hasn't wasted any time."

"Go in, now. Empty your parcels, and let the dog out to water my roses. Then, we'll have a chat."

Larkin unlocked her door, and stood aside to let Bubba run past her to Mr. Carney. As she turned to put her groceries away, she heard him talking to the dog, "Well, now, how have you been? I haven't seen you in ages. Yes, yes, shed a little tear for Ireland. Feeling better?"

Larkin found two cans of Harp in the refrigerator. She ran up the stairs and stuck her head out the door.

"Mr. Carney? Would you join me in a pint of Harp?"

"I wouldn't mind a drop."

She poured the cans into pint glasses and carried them up the stairs. She opened the door with her hip, slid out, and handed him his beer.

She took a sip of her own. "What has Sukki told you?"

Mr. Carney smiled. "All of it, I believe. It seems she was placed in a position of some responsibility to get you out of the country. Do you have a side of this I haven't yet heard?"

"Probably not. What do you think?"

"Larkin. It's not for me to say. What would be your reason for going?"

She sat on his porch, her beer between her feet. Mr. Carney continued to kneel in the dirt, a trowel in his hand and rose manure in a bag close by. Bubba lay down on the grass next to Larkin. She turned, put her cheek on her knee, and studied the roses. There was the creamy white Iceberg, blooming in clusters, and the Tropicana, flamboyant in its orange petals. The coral pink America climbed a trellis, a nod to the new country, and the tiny apricot-colored Jean Kenneally reminded him of the old. The pink and yellow Chicago Peace sat happily between the light orange Perdita shrub and the vibrant pink Marie Louise, and the Blue Girl, soft violet in color, touched petals with the pale flushed Penelope, scented and rich. Larkin's eyes played over them all, straying finally to the Saint Patrick, yellow and strong. She closed her eyes.

Mr. Carney, three years ago, had stripped that bush when Pat died and presented them to her the day of the funeral. She carried them to the gravesite and placed them on the dark grain of the casket, the only flowers allowed in the hole that swallowed her husband.

"Larkin?"

"Isn't it something how dogs always find the softest place to lay down? I think if there was a piece of paper on the floor, Bubba would lie on that as opposed to the tile."

"Larkin."

She turned her chin to her knee, facing him. "I'm not sure why I'm going. I think I have to start somewhere, and I hear from knowledgeable sources that Ireland is lovely this time of year."

"It is, at that. Perhaps that is enough for now, that you know you need to go. When would you be leaving, then?"

"I haven't called Brynna yet, but I could leave as early as next Friday."

"Friday week? I think that will be fine with her, yes, fine. I happened to ring her today, and she told me, purely by chance of course, that she's needing a little help at the B&B, working help, that is, and if I knew of someone that would care to come and spend a month or so, she would be pleased to offer her a place to stay and a small wage. I said I would certainly make a few inquiries. Isn't this nice, how it's all worked out."

Larkin shook her head, her chin still on her knee. "Mr. Carney, it's a shame you and Sukki aren't more of an age."

4.

Larkin spent the ten days until she left in a flurry. Kate emailed her a long list of things to do that Larkin would have missed, like changing her dental appointment and pre-paying her utilities; things she would have remembered on the plane. After all the calls were made, she took herself shopping to find a suitcase suitable for the trip.

Inside the mall, she became suddenly aware of herself. Her skin seemed to fit just right, and she was walking with a long stride that matched the day. She smiled as she headed up the stairs.

At the top of the stairs, a man was turning toward her, a cell phone in his hand. As she got closer, he looked her full in the face, ignoring his phone, and said something to her. When he spoke, he tipped his head a bit to the right and smiled, and Larkin knew that she had caught his eye. She smiled and kept walking. She didn't look back. It was enough.

After finding the perfect suitcase and fighting traffic to get home, she went through the closet to go over last-minute details with Sukki. She and the kids would be seeing to Bubba while Larkin was gone. Larkin had wanted to bring him with her, but Irish law stipulated no animals could enter the country without six month quarantine. In the course of conversation, Larkin related the story about the man on the ramp.

"Could it be you're starting to pay attention?" Sukki asked.

"I guess. I can't remember the last time I noticed a man for anything but poor driving."

"They'll be fighting over you soon."

"Don't get excited. Men don't naturally adore me the way they do you."

"Adore me? I wouldn't have called it that, but I know what you mean." Sukki smiled. "There are times I can charm them out of the trees. Any woman can, if she knows what she's got. And it's a confidence issue, not beauty or body or the way she's dressed." She grinned. "Give me a night with me in the right mood and inside of an hour and a half, some man will be thinking he's found me at last. The difference is men translate that into wanting sex and I want to preen in the admiration of it all and go home."

In the morning, the packing done, Larkin looked over her house. Things were orderly, anything perishable was gone, and the bills were paid. All that was left was to take a walk. She started up the stairs toward the door and heard the knock. She swung it open. Mr. Carney stood on her step, his arms filled with flowers.

"In case you might be thinking of going to the cemetery today, here are a few of the yellows for himself, there."

The Saint Patrick roses he held were almost in full bloom. In the other hand he held a variety of roses bound in paper, a cornucopia. Larkin lifted her eyes. She tried to speak, and cleared her throat.

"And those?"

"I would be very grateful if you would take these with you, and when the time seems right and the day is at its best, you could stand on the bridge in the middle of Athlone and let them drop in to the Shannon, let them float for their time in the water and let me again think of my dear wife, who loved her flowers and loved the river."

"Her flowers?"

"It was her name, Larkin. Her name was Rose."

5.

Even with its close proximity, Larkin didn't go often to the cemetery. She had no wish to pretend to visit Pat, no belief he could hear her if she spoke. She did, however, see to the care of the grave, pulling weeds and picking up stray litter.

Pat was buried next to a child, long dead, and every time she went, there were new toys at the grave: windmills and bears, seasonal decorations, and once a Frisbee. How did the mother decide what to get, walking the aisles at Toys-R-Us? Did she buy things appropriate to his age now or when he died?

Larkin looked at the grave. There were new Hot Wheels cars today, clean, and unmarked. She looked at the stone, did the math. The boy there would be eighteen now, too old for Hot Wheels. The mother must still see him as young, as the age he died. He was nine when he came here, and Larkin hoped the loss had not stopped her growth as it had her son's, frozen in time as a fourth-grader forever.

She passed the boy's site to Pat's. The stone here was plainer, more masculine. She liked the look of it still, stalwart and solid. She bent over, laid the flowers so they rested at the base of the stone, almost hiding the years of birth and death. She turned and walked to the bench that sat nearby. She leaned her head back and closed her eyes to the sun.

Occasionally since Pat's death, Larkin was surprised by something that would affect her strongly; something she would not have guessed would strike a chord in her.

A couple of weeks ago, she had been shopping and stopped for lunch in a tea shop she hadn't been to since before Pat died. While eating, she remembered being there with him, his size and manliness seeming out of place at the small table as he looked in astonishment at the modest, but very attractive, plate of food he was served. She told him, smiling, that the point was to not eat so much for lunch you didn't have room for the homemade apple cranberry pie. He ate all of his food, most of hers, and two pieces of pie.

That day, with her shopping bags on the chair he would have occupied, she was swamped with feeling and, barely holding herself together, got her meal put in a box, and escaped. She cried all the way home in the car, and then sat on her couch in the dark for hours. Nothing like that had happened since, but Larkin was aware it could.

Today, though, it was just pleasant memories; thoughts of what had been, not what would never be. After a time, she gathered herself up from the bench, stretched, and walked back to the grave. She read the words, brushed her fingers over the stone, and walked home.

Once in the house, she climbed the stairs to the bedroom and stood at the door. She walked over and put her hand on the surface of the bed.

"Larkin!" Sukki was calling.

"Upstairs."

Sukki walked in the bedroom. "Have you been here? I've been calling you from the kitchen."

"I just got home." She turned and looked at Sukki. "Did you know Mrs. Carney's name was Rose?"

Sukki smiled. "Was it really? I suppose I must have known that, but I never called her anything but Mrs. Carney. Explains a couple of things, doesn't it?"

"It does. Is it time to go?"

"Very close."

They walked down and through the closet to find Sukki's children lined up with their hands behind their backs. Sukki moved Larkin over in front of James, who grinned.

"I have a present for you. I know you hate to fly, so I got you something to read on the plane." From behind him, he produced a book, "Fight Your Fear of Flying," and offered it to her. Larkin laughed, took the book, and reached up to hug him.

"Take care of things while I'm gone. Keep an eye on your mother."

Emmy was next. "You'll need these," she announced, "in case they don't have them there." She handed Larkin a party-sized bag of peanut M&M's, both of their favorite candy.

Larkin gave her a hug, "I can't believe you're parting with these. Thank you."

There was Errol, looking serious. Larkin dropped to her knees in front of him.

"Errol."

He brought his hand around to the front.

"It's so you don't forget him."

In a frame there was a picture of Errol holding Bubba, taken when the two played out in the snow together the past winter. Errol was sitting on Larkin's stoop, holding the dog inside his coat to get him warm.

"I would never forget either of you, but I'll keep this where I can look at it every day." She held out her arms and Errol stepped into her.

"I'll miss you, Tee."

"I'll miss you, Errol." She looked up. "I will miss you all."

"It's time to go." Sukki looked down at Errol. "Do you want to get Tee's small suitcase? And you," she turned to James, "can get the big one."

They made their way to Sukki's car. Down the sidewalk, neighbors poked heads out of doors to wave and Bubba made the walk with Larkin holding the leash. At the curb, she scooped him up and put her face nose to nose with his. She put his head in the space between her chin and her collarbone, standing for a minute before depositing him back on the sidewalk. She handed the leash to Emmy and got in the car.

As Sukki drove her away, Larkin wiped her eyes.

"You'd think I was leaving for a year. What is the huge deal?" She mopped her face and sniffed.

"You tell me. Get it done now, though. I hate crying at the airport."

Standing in the line to check in, Larkin thought once again how much she disliked airports. There was not a more transient place in the world. There was one set of people waiting to fly and another set streaming out the door to look for a way home.

Even the light was terrible, the most elegant of women looking overdone and false and the rest looking like pallid refugees, surrounded by luggage and fast food.

After check-in, she and Sukki made their way to the International waiting area. There was a food court, a duty free shop, and a book store. The tables were long and mostly filled, but Sukki spotted two chairs free and pointed Larkin in that direction.

"Do you want something to eat?"

"I suppose I should."

Larkin dragged her carry-on to the table and fell in a chair. She looked at her watch. An hour until boarding, eight hours in the air, two hours to Athlone...only eleven hours until she felt some degree of normalcy. As this was an overnight flight, she could count on it being a wakeful one; she had never been able to sleep on a plane.

Sukki came back with a tray of food for them to share.

"Why do I only eat McDonald's at the airport? I wouldn't dream of it anywhere else," Larkin said.

"It's because the airport is the only place that McDonald's is the best choice. Hey, I've been meaning to ask you. What did Bunny say when you told her you were going to Ireland?"

"You'd have loved it. She decided somewhere in the conversation that it had been her idea. She gave me family names to look up and crystal patterns to find. She said I shouldn't come back without a nice Aran sweater, whatever that is, and sent me travel guides and brochures for places I can't pronounce."

"Perfect. And here's my guess: your mother has never been to Ireland."

"Never once."

With the food gone, Larkin glanced at her watch.

"It's time."

Sukki put a hand on Larkin's arm.

"I want to tell you a quick story."

"You don't tell quick stories."

"I'll cut to the chase. Do you remember my friend, Nell?"

"The one with M.S.?"

"That's the one."

"How is she doing?"

"As well as she can be, but some adjustments are harder than others. She was a runner, remember, so the loss of her hobby and her sense of control over her body is gone."

"That must be awful for her."

"It is. Running has always been her outlet, and now, when she needs it most, it's gone." Sukki shook her head, then continued. "A couple of weeks ago she stopped over, and she was just bubbling about a race she'd been in. She was animated and energetic, and she told me she'd started out and just did what she could, never running, but working herself as hard as possible without falling over. She laughed and said she'd slept for two days afterward, but that it was completely worth it because she'd found an entirely new perspective on her life."

"Which was?"

"She told me that before going that day she had lost all hope of her life being anything but gray. She was able to manage the disease, but without her running, she felt dull and slow. What that experience taught her was that there different ways to feel alive. She could see the course, feel the sun on her back, be one of the participants. She said it wouldn't have mattered if she had done it in a wheelchair. She told me there was color back in her life, that she could face the hard years ahead with hope. And then she cried." Sukki paused. "It's what I'm hoping for you, Larkin, that you find your color."

"I am so grateful to you," Larkin said. "For everything."

"Have a wonderful time and come back and tell me stories. Experience everything. Come back with color." She reached out and the women hugged. When they pulled away, Sukki wiped at the tears on her face.

Larkin gathered her bags and went through security. As she walked to the gate, she looked back to see Sukki waving through the glass partition separating them. She smiled and waved back until the glass became a wall and she was alone.

Shannon Plate

6.

When Larkin boarded the plane, she thought, as she did every time she forced herself to fly, that air travel was the most unnatural setting in which she could place herself.

She dug out her book, glasses, and a notebook and pen. After stowing her carry-on, she sat down and arranged her possessions around her in the seat like a shield. Larkin buckled her seat belt, clutched her armrests, and hoped no one was seated next to her. When the plane started away from the gate, she quickly moved her book and glasses to the seat next to her.

As the plane gathered speed on the runway, she fought the panic she felt with every take-off, her eyes closed and fighting off tears. In the working part of her mind, she wondered why she reacted this way. Every time she flew, she felt this same breakdown of reason.

Pat used to tell her it wasn't flying she hated.

"It's a control issue." he told her, flying toward Hawaii on their honeymoon, "You don't like to fly because you're not the pilot."

She looked sideways at him, clutching his hand and shaking.

"Can we talk about this later? Like, after we land?"

He looked past her out the window.

"Wow! Check out that wing! Do you think it's supposed to come apart and move like that?"

She stared at him. He kept it up.

"Did you hear that noise? I don't think that's a normal plane noise. Maybe something's wrong."

She considered changing seats.

"Larkin, I'm kidding. Come on, lean on my shoulder. I'll pat your head for you."

"Yeah, pat this, pal."

Today, Larkin was flying Aer Lingus, so the mandatory safety speeches were in Irish accents. She paid attention to them, as she was fairly sure they would be landing in the ocean and needing their flotation devices. She checked for the nearest exit ("Keeping in mind, it may be behind you...") and figured out how to "tub up" her yellow floatie.

After the late night dinner and later movie, the flight attendants moved in circles around the cabin, asking those in window seats to close their blinds so people could sleep. How anyone could sleep was beyond Larkin, but looking around, she saw a variety of ways people did just that. There was a woman laid out on her tray table, a pillow under her head and arms hanging off each side. A medium-sized man screwed himself into a small ball, his back to the window, and covered himself with his coat and two blankets. Children were splayed over their parents, who took whatever form of rest they could. One tiny old couple lifted the armrest between them and slept with the same pillow between their white heads.

Larkin eyed the empty seat next to her. It was worth a try. She arranged herself over the available space and lofted the blanket so it covered the back of her. She laid her head on the pillow and closed her eyes.

Larkin tried to regulate her breathing. She was beginning to feel some benefit from the quiet, a kind of rest if not sleep, when the fleshy man in front of her struggled his way out of his seat. He poked his wife, dozing next to him.

"Honey, you want a drink? I'm getting a beer."

A nearby tour group roused themselves. They called to each other from rows away - as if, Larkin thought, it wasn't the middle of the night and people all around them weren't trying to rest. She opened her eyes to slits and looked around. She looked disapprovingly at the group huddled around the drink area, who paid her not the slightest attention.

When the group dissipated, she got up and asked for a cup of coffee. Although instant, it was coffee of a sort, and welcome. She raised her shade a couple of inches and thought of the month ahead.

She knew a bit of what would happen. What she could count on was Brynna meeting her at the plane and taking her to Athlone. She would be working for Brynna, helping run the B&B from Tuesday through Sunday morning. She had Sunday afternoon and Monday off, unusual in the business, but Brynna thought she should see some of the country and so had hired a girl to come in and relieve her.

As the sun came up, the flight attendant handed her a sandwich of a white roll with a piece of ham and a thin slice of cheese, and offered coffee or tea.

Things in the plane livened up. The shades were raised, lighting the cabin with a pale Irish sunrise. They were less than an hour from landing, and the crew was picking up garbage, gathering headsets, and checking for seat belts.

Larkin went to the bathroom with a comb and her make-up bag. She did her best with her hair and put on a bit of blush, then brushed her teeth.

At her seat, she put her belongings back in her carry-on, and strapped herself in, pulling the belt tight. Landing was the only thing worse than take-off, and her fear grew with every foot lost in altitude. As the ground neared, her eyes never left the runway. She held her breath and waited for the massive thud that signaled the desperate fight to keep the plane under control as it screamed down the tarmac. She pictured the pilot in the cockpit holding the wheel with both hands, panicking and breathing hard, shouting in his headset, "I can't hold her! She's breaking up!"

Larkin shook her head. It wasn't the first time it had occurred to her that having degrees in psychology did not make one immune to a bit of psychosis.

The plane was slowing and making a turn toward the gate. The second it stopped, Larkin drew up shakily from her seat, got her bag from the overhead compartment, and was first in the aisle ready to leave. The flight attendants were all standing at the door looking, to Larkin, remarkably calm after their brush with a fiery death.

"Thank you for choosing Aer Lingus."

After getting through customs, Larkin stepped into the waiting area of Dublin Airport. In the middle of pockets of waiting people stood Brynna, waving and coming toward her. She reached out and hugged her.

"Ah, Larkin, here you are. And how was your flight?"

Larkin took a deep breath and smiled. "It was fine."

They rolled the bags to the car, and Larkin walked to the right side to get in.

Brynna laughed. "Well, would you be driving then?"

Larkin looked in the car to see the steering wheel where the glove compartment should be.

"Come around now, you'll get used to it."

Larkin put herself in the car and hooked the belt. Brynna turned in her seat and faced her.

"Now, how are you, really? Are you fully exhausted?"

Larkin shook her head. "Strangely enough, I don't feel all that tired even though I didn't sleep on the plane. I'm kind of achy, I guess, but I don't want to sleep."

"That's good. You should really try to stay awake today as long as you can. Then, you'll wake up tomorrow and feel almost normal. Now off we go. It's a ways to Athlone, but the scenery is beautiful, and I'll be talking your ear off all the way home. Now then, how's my father?"

The little car sputtered out of the garage and headed for Athlone. They drove through towns painted bright colors, past cottages both occupied and abandoned, and stopped at crossroads to look for directional signs.

"After being in America, the signs here will confuse you. We don't have numbers for the roads, or sometimes even names. There are signs with arrows pointing you toward various towns, and with those and a map, you can get almost anywhere." Brynna drove the car around some sheep.

"Do you get lost?" Larkin held the map, trying to get some bearing.

Brynna laughed. "Ah, sure, all the time, but, thank God, Ireland is a small country."

Brynna pointed out her favorite pub in Cloncurry, stopped in Innfield for loaves of brown bread, and complained about a relative in Clonard who still had a shawl borrowed two years ago. She talked of which towns were reputed to have strong links to the IRA, and which had the best cheese. As they drove through the wide streets of Moate, she explained how the town was designed to accommodate cattle.

When they reached the outskirts of Athlone, Brynna pointed.

"Now look around. As we come into town, try and get a feel for how it's laid out, so you always know how to get home if you're out walking."

Brynna got to a roundabout, where various streets snaked off the edges. She took the turn and got off at Church Street.

"Church Street will take you through the center of the town. If you can get to Church Street, you can get to the river, and you can get home."

Larkin looked over her shoulder at the shops and pubs they passed, at the towering churches, and the houses with their painted doorways opening to the street. "Look at the flowers!"

Every business, from the grocers to the pubs to the wine shop, had window boxes or containers overflowing with flowers. The colors of the blooms, combined with the bright painting of almost every building, made for a striking picture.

Traffic stopped in town, and Larkin saw a window filled with china and crystal.

"I'll have to stop there. My mother has an obscure crystal pattern she wants me to find."

"Connell's, yes, they're good for that."

The car worked its way over the bridge, and Larkin got her first view of the Shannon River. It was wider that she had thought, but calm. In the distance, Larkin saw men fishing from the shore, wearing waders and flipping lines far out in the murky water.

"Is fishing big here?"

"Ah, of course. It is a large part of the tourism trade; 'angling' it's called. The men come from everywhere, but mostly England. They can drive and then take a ferry. I see some of the same faces year after year. And now, here we are."

The car stopped at the side of large building a few blocks from the bridge. It sat tall between a pub and bookstore and faced a huge stone structure overlooking the river. The house was a straight three stories up with a beautiful front door - dark wood inlaid with stained glass and topped with a dome of curved iron.

"Let's get your bags from the boot."

Larkin struggled to get her larger bag out of the trunk and wrestled it to the sidewalk. Brynna brought the smaller bag, and unlocked the door. As it swung open, Brynna called in for her husband. He bustled to them, arms outstretched to Larkin.

"Ah, here you are. How are you, lovey? How was your travel? Here, let me take that." He took her bag and started up the stairs. "There's tea in the kitchen, ready to be poured. I'll get this to your room."

"Thank you, Des. It's gotten heavier every hour." Larkin turned to Brynna. "Your dad warned me. He said I should get a bag I could manage on my own."

"Well, you'll not have to manage it on your own while you're here. Come now, a cup of tea and some toast or a sandwich?"

Larkin was happy to be led, to be put in a chair and given food and hot drink. Here, it seemed perfectly natural to let Brynna make a sandwich with thick white bread, butter, tomato, and cheese, and pour tea.

While eating, Larkin sniffed the air.

"What is that smell? I noticed it on the way home and again in the house. It smells like incense."

Des joined them in the kitchen, humming as he poured a cup of tea for himself.

"'Tis the turf, Larkin. Turf is one of the ways we heat our homes here, the way we heat the water, and make electricity. It comes from the ground. We have a bog we harvest in the summer, and the turf dries there. We bring it home, and use it for fuel. It's hard work, but the way it's been done for centuries. We have oil heat we use now and again, but it's the turf that keeps the fires burning. Isn't it nice, that you like the smell. Even now in the summer, there gets a chill in the mornings and sometimes in the evenings, and a fire is always welcome."

Larkin finished her sandwich and sat back in her chair. "I bet. Now, Brynna, what will I do here? I've never done this kind of work before."

"Of course you haven't, but didn't I tell my dad when he rang that there's nothing complicated about it, just talking to people and changing beds and doing laundry. We'll not talk about it now. Tomorrow is soon enough. What would you like to do with the rest of the day? Do you want a rest?"

"I don't think so. I'd rather do what you said and stay up as long as I can. I want to shower and change, though."

"It's the air on those planes. I always get off feeling like I've spent the day in a mine, with no fresh air to be had. Let me show you your room. The easiest way to get there is the back stairs here from the kitchen. It's all the way up at the top of the house, I'm afraid."

The two started the walk up the narrow back stairs. At the highest point, the landing opened to a hallway leading to Larkin's room and two other doors, closed.

"This floor was servant's quarters in the old days."

Larkin stepped into her room and smiled. It was multi-leveled, with the bathroom right inside the door, and the bed three steps down. The ceiling sloped to the head of the bed, with dark beams showing between the white plaster. Walking past the bed on a red and blue runner, Larkin walked up the five steps to a loft area with a desk, a two-drawer dresser, and a bar to hang her clothes. There was a round window surrounded by brick over the desk, and soft chair next to a bigger window that looked over the street. The long wall facing the bed was ancient brick, hung with local art, and the floors were varnished honey-colored wood, the old scratches left in. In various nooks, there were items of interest – a small sculpture, or a pretty bowl. Larkin bent to smell hyacinth in a crystal pitcher on the dresser. She turned to Brynna, waiting by the door.

"How is it I get the best room in the house?"

"Ah, never mind. I'll leave you to it, then. Get settled and see what you might like to do. I can't go out with you now, I have to get things ready for tonight's guests, but you might want to take a walk and get some feel for the town."

Larkin unpacked, hanging clothing and folding socks, and put the picture of Errol and Bubba on the dresser. She put her toiletries in the bathroom, arranging them on a metal tray table. There were white towels there, clean and coarse. Larkin loved white. It seemed elegant to use white things; things that needed more care by virtue of their ease in being ruined.

She unpacked the flowers from Mr. Carney. She ran water in the sink and set them there, out of their paper, until she could get something to put them in. She didn't want to rush her appointment with the river. It was to be something special, a ceremony; she would wait until she was ready.

She showered the smell of the plane from her, and covered herself with lotion. Mr. Carney had told her the water was different here, and it would dry her skin to flakes if she didn't take care. Dressed, she went looking for Brynna.

"Look at you, fresh as a daisy. Feeling better?"

"Much. I think I'd like to take a walk. Where should I go?"

"Well, when you get outside, just keep going straight until you hit Church Street, then on over the river. There are shops and pubs to see, and you could wander around the Castle, if you like, that big stone circle you see from your window. Then later, we'll have a bite to eat and take you into town for a drink. Take something to put on. When the clouds come, it can get cool."

Larkin closed the door behind her and stood for a moment. I'm in Ireland, she thought. I need to pay attention. I'm about to see things I've never seen before.

She walked away from the house until she found Church Street. At Church Street, she wound around the main part of town, looking in windows, passing doorways of pubs, listening to bits of conversations from the people she passed on the street. It wasn't the words she heard as much as the rhythms and accent - the cadence unusual to Larkin's ear. People smiled when they caught her eye, and children ran around her legs to pass her on the bridge.

She walked all the way down one side of the street then crossed and walked back on the other. At the wine shop, she went in. There was no particular reason - she didn't intend to buy wine - but the front of shop was red and green with begonias and pansies trailing from its window boxes, and it felt homey.

The man behind the counter came toward her.

"You're all right, then?"

Larkin was startled.

"Yes, I'm fine, thank you."

"You're American?" Larkin nodded. "Would you be wanting wine today?"

"Maybe I should. Though I'm not sure what I should buy."

"Is it for yourself?"

"No, a gift. For the Egan's. Do you know them? Brynna and Des Egan?"

"Ah, of course I do. You'd be the friend of Brynna's dad, then. Just here yesterday or today?"

"Today. Just hours ago, really."

"And out walking by yourself already. A brave girl, you are. Well, now, a bottle of wine for the Egan's. They tend to like reds, nothing too full, Chianti...this one, perhaps." He plucked a bottle from a bin, took a cloth from his back pocket, wiped the bottle shiny, and presented it to her.

Larkin looked at the label and the price. She'd take his word, and if he was wrong, it wouldn't break her.

Back on the street with her purchase, Larkin became aware of fatigue. Her legs were tired to the point of shakiness and she stretched her shoulders back. She made her way to a bench outside a pub and as she dropped in it, she took stock.

She wanted to remember this, this state of her mind fighting her body, one vibrant and the other failing. Everything she saw was new, and it felt unfamiliar and a bit out of her control.

The only notion that got her off the bench was the overwhelming desire for coffee. She went to the nearest café. The waitress brought her a metal pot full of dark coffee with milk and sugar on the side, and slices of brown bread, dense and grainy.

Larkin sipped and sighed. She ate her bread with the beautiful yellow butter, alternating with sips of coffee. She stayed until she could brave the walk home, then paid her bill and left.

When she rounded the corner to the house, Brynna was opening the door.

"Thank heavens! We thought we'd lost you the first day."

Larkin offered up the bag. "I've brought you wine."

"Ah, you've been to see Garret. And what have you brought? Oh, a lovely wine. Look, Des. Larkin's brought us wine for your roast."

"You're a good girl, Larkin May."

After the meal of roasted beef dripping in gravy, potatoes, and parsnips, the three cleaned up the kitchen and set the dishwasher humming.

"Well, what do you think? Are you coming for a pint or are you done for?" Des lifted a bushy eyebrow at Larkin.

"No, let's go. Afterward, I'll come back and go into a coma."

They pulled on sweaters and set out on foot.

"There's no place you can't go on this side of the river, Larkin. Be careful on the other side, though, late at night. Best to be back in the neighborhood by closing time." Des pointed. "The river divides two counties, you see, Westmeath and Roscommon, and two provinces, Connaught and Leinster. Loyalties run strong for both. In the past it was patriotic issues. Now, it's football teams. There's always something to fight about."

They took her to Sean's, just around the curve from the house. It was long and narrow, a dark wood bar with mirrors across the back and fishing memorabilia hanging from the ceiling.

"Look at that mantle, at the carving on it. Where did that come from?"
Larkin stood in front of the fireplace, lit for the night chill, and touched the
deep crevices in the old wood.

"Sean says his old father won it playing cards, but I'm not sure I believe it."
Des called at a big man behind the bar. "Evening, Sean, a Guinness, a cider,
and what would you be having Larkin?"

"I don't know. What would you suggest?"

"Try a cider, why don't you. Another cider, Sean. It's fermented apple
cider, gentle going down. Don't drink too much of the stuff, though, or your
stomach will complain."

Pints in hand, they sat at a small round table on short stools. Larkin sipped
the cider, cold and brisk.

"Is there alcohol in this?"

Des nodded, foam on his lips. "About the same as beer, I believe. It's
popular in the summer."

The cider continued the process in Larkin started by fatigue. As she sat
chatting with Brynna and being introduced to people wandering by, she floated
somewhere in between alert consciousness and complete jet-lag. She wasn't
worried. These people would get her home and to bed. She could be a bit
adrift.

Brynna touched her hand. "This is Conn Nevin, Larkin. He's Des' sister's
brother-in-law. Conn, this is Larkin May, here from America to help me at the
house."

Larkin looked up at the man, broad and black-haired. He nodded to her.

"Good to meet you, Larkin. How long are you staying, now? Is it your
first visit to Ireland?" He pulled up a stool, and sat his pint on the little table.

"It is. Brynna's dad is my neighbor at home, and he encouraged me to
come."

"I hope you enjoy yourself. It's a lovely country, you'll find. There's a lot
to see, if Brynna there lets you out of the house."

"Go on! She's off every Sunday after breakfast till Tuesday morning, just
for that very reason. I'm hoping she'll do some traveling, see the coasts."

"Perhaps I could take you around one day. Show you the sights." Conn
stood, picked up his beer. "I'm in Athlone a day or two every week. I'll stop
by, see if you're free." He smiled at Larkin, nodded to Brynna and Des, and
rejoined his friends at the bar.

Brynna leaned in near Larkin. "Hard to pin down, that one. Don't take much of what he says to heart."

Larkin nodded. She would be surprised if he really came, but thought she'd be pleased if he did. She liked his voice, liked the tone of it, and the way he looked at her when he spoke. And, he smelled good.

Sukki would be delighted, Larkin thought, that she'd noticed.

Des was asking if she wanted another. She shook her head.

"I have to get to bed in the next ten minutes, or I will embarrass you by stretching out on the floor right here."

Brynna finished her cider, and put her arms in her sweater. "Let's be off. It's enough for one day. You've been a trouper."

They walked to the house, Larkin's arm tucked in Brynna's.

"What should I do in the morning?" Larkin asked her.

"If you're up, you can help a bit with breakfast in the morning, but if you want to sleep, go ahead. You'll start officially the next day, so if you need a full day to adjust, that's grand."

Standing in her bathroom, Larkin swayed. She noticed Mr. Carney's flowers were in a vase. She gave her face a cursory wash and used the toilet, the flush sounding all through the house. She stripped her clothes, got into a nightshirt, and pulled the bedspread down. The bed was fitted with white sheets, crisp and clean.

Larkin smiled. Here I am, she thought. She buried herself in the sweet-smelling sheets, brought her knees up to her chest, let out a breath, and slept.

7.

Larkin awoke early. She showered quickly and bounded down the stairs. Brynna was aproned and engaged in the morning cooking.

"Larkin! Up at the crack of dawn, you are. How did you sleep, ducky?"

"Like a log. I think it was the cider. Now, what do you want me to do?"

"Well, we've a full house today, so you can put out juice at the tables. Pour it in these glasses, about 3/4 full. There you are. Teresa will do the bread and take orders today, but watch her. It's what you'll be doing tomorrow."

Brynna turned back to the stove, cooking strips of meat on a griddle and slicing tomatoes on a board on the counter. The smell whet Larkin's appetite for whatever sat sizzling and spitting in the pan.

The guests began filing down from their rooms at eight, coming in twos or threes. Teresa greeted them, gave each table a basket of brown bread and white toast, coffee or tea, and got their orders for breakfast. Most asked for a "full fry." In the kitchen, Brynna wanted Larkin to watch what she did, watch how the plates were arranged, and learn the names of the different meats.

Larkin repeated Brynna's words to herself. "Rashers" were the strips cooking on the griddle. Like your bacon, Brynna told her, but leaner. "Black and white pudding" was round, one dark and the other light. The sausage was familiar, and a fried egg sat in the middle of the plate, with tomatoes on the side. Full, the plate looked to Larkin like enough to feed a family.

"One person can eat all of this?" Larkin asked.

"We want them to leave well-fed, not to feel they have to stop for lunch when they're traveling. I give them three rashers and three sausages - more than most B&B's, so they'll remember me next time they're in town."

Brynna traveled the length of the kitchen with sureness, missing the sofa and laundry baskets without looking down. She moved covered in food - two plates for guests on one arm and a platter of meat in the other hand.

Larkin bet she was a graceful dancer.

After the guest's breakfasts, Brynna sat a plate of food in front of her. It was a smaller version of the full fry, just one of each meat, an egg, brown bread, and sliced tomatoes.

"There you are, ducky. Eat up, now."

The rasher and sausage tasted just the way they smelled, but the black and white pudding gave Larkin pause.

"What is this, exactly?"

"Well, the white pudding is pork parts, spices, and oats, stuffed into entrails. In the black, they add congealed pig's blood. It's a favorite." Brynna smiled at her. "Don't feel you have to eat it. I'll save it for Des if you're not feeling adventuresome."

The upstairs work began. The beds were stripped and changed and the duvet covers removed to be washed. Bathrooms were scrubbed, the vacuum chased around, and whatever dust had accumulated in the past 24 hours was swiped away.

All the while, the dishwasher ran and the washer whined. Brynna went up and down the stairs, her head poking out from clouds of linen, and Larkin perfected hospital corners on the beds. Wet, the sheets were slung on the line outside, drying in the turf-blown air.

"You always have to be watching the sky," Brynna told Larkin, "for if it starts raining, it's out to the back to save the sheets. On altogether rainy days we dry them in the tumble dryer, but I'd rather have them outside. They smell better, and electricity is very expensive here. It eats up some of the profits to use the dryer more than we have to."

Larkin went back to the kitchen, emptied the dishwasher, and put in another load. Brynna followed with the last crumpled bunch of linens.

"Finally. When the house is full, the sheets threaten to take over. Now, there's shopping to be done. Do you want to go, or stay and deal with laundry?"

"What would you rather?"

"If it's all the same to you, why don't you shop and I'll stay. We'll trade off now and again, but I get in to a rhythm here, and it's hard to get started again if I quit." She pulled a chair from the table, and sat down with paper and a pencil. "Here's what we need and pick up things for yourself as well, some yogurt or cereal or whatever else you like. Here, take some shopping bags."

Larkin took the list and went where Brynna told her. She fumbled with what brands to buy, and had no clue what "'Roosters'" were, although she was guessing they weren't the obvious. The cashier led her to a host of potatoes, all different brands and sizes. There were tiny new potatoes, larger Golden Wonders, Aran-Banners, Kerpinks, and the elusive Roosters.

Larkin got a bag, added it to the pile, and sorted out the five and ten Euro notes to pay.

"Have everything you need, do you?' The cashier asked, putting it all in the bags and shoving them across the counter.

"All for today. Thanks for your help." Larkin muscled the bags down, and out the door. After the first block, she started to think of the trip as a good upper body workout, and after another two, she had to stop and rest. She got it all home, and dumped it on the floor of the kitchen.

As she unpacked the food, she wondered how many experiences she would have like this one. Being out of her depth in a grocery store was unusual, which made her feel two things: first, tomorrow she would know more than she had today. Second, it was reasonable not to know what a Rooster was. She had wanted something to take her by surprise; she just didn't expect it to be potatoes.

Brynna walked in and saw her putting the groceries away.

"Ah, you didn't carry those all home, did you? They would have delivered them right to the door. Did the girl not tell you?"

"She didn't, but it's OK. It was good exercise. Now, what's next?"

"You're finished for today. What time is it? Half two. That's about right. Some days may go a bit longer, but mid-afternoon is about the time you'll be done."

"What should I do with myself now?"

"You could see a bit more of the town or maybe go to the cinema."

Larkin nodded. "More walking, I think. I want to go back where I was. I don't remember what I saw, except for the wine store."

"We'll eat about seven. Then, if you like, there's music at Sean's tonight. Would you like to hear some Irish music?"

"Yes, I'd love to. Is there anything else I can pick up?"

"Not a thing. You go enjoy yourself, now."

Larkin stepped out the door into sunshine, pure and warm. She walked away from the house, then backtracked, went up the back stairs, and came down with Mr. Carney's roses.

Brynna looked up. "Are those from my father? For my mother?"

Larkin nodded.

"I thought they might be. Where are you going to put them?"

"In the river. He said I should do it when the day was at its best." Larkin stood, wondering if she should give the flowers to Brynna or invite her to come along.

"And it is. Look at that sun! You'll be wanting to go before it disappears. Give her my love, Larkin. Tell her I miss her every day of my life."

Larkin closed the door behind her and walked toward the bridge. She thought of Mr. Carney at home tending these roses as a monument to his wife. He had no grave to visit in town, no place to see something with her name on it, so he worked the garden and lived his good life.

When she got to the bridge, she walked to the middle and looked down over the rail. The river looked murky from this distance, brown peaty water, but it pulled smoothly along.

Larkin thought of the woman these roses honored, thought she must have been a woman worthy of celebration, to have those who loved her miss her so. She leaned over the water, with both hands holding the blooms, and closed her eyes, letting the breeze play her hair away from her neck and smelling the heat of the sun off the river. She thought of Mr. Carney and wanted to remember this, to be able to describe the day for him. She thought of his wife and the years they'd spent as a couple, the children they'd raised, and what they'd accomplished together.

She looked in front of her past the fishermen, past the town, to the curve that took the river from sight, and she wondered where it started. She turned her spine to the rail and saw as far as she could where it went. As she turned back she raised the bouquet, flung it out over the water, and watched the flowers drop. The water moved toward her from the south, lapped up the flowers, and flowed under the bridge and past the rest of the town. It went past the new condo high-rise and the old semi-detached houses that had been there a hundred years, past the white bridge and the green grass banks where children threw bread to the geese; past the world the Carneys had been born to.

Larkin crossed the street to watch the specks of color on the brown water float as lazily as a Sunday paper until they disappeared.

She thought she would like to become a woman for whom flowers might be grown.

That night at Sean's, Larkin's thoughts went back to the bridge. She sat, her shoulders touching the wall, and wondered whether she could be so cherished again, and if she could feel for a man what she wanted to feel from him.

There was music tonight. A group had taken over the small area next to the bar, and was well into the first set. There was a guitar player, a woman playing the violin, another man with a selection of whistles and a flute, and a woman with a round drum she held standing up on her thigh, one hand on the inside of the frame and other holding a mallet. They all took turns leading, and most sang as well.

"Black is the color of my true love's hair,
Her lips are like some roses fair
She's the sweetest smile and the gentlest hands,
I love the ground whereon she stands."

The music was haunting, Larkin thought, the words to the songs almost universally sad. Someone died, someone lost his only love, or the war came and took everything.

"I love my love and well she knows
I love the grass whereon she goes,

But I know the day it will never come
when she and I will be as one."

After the sad songs, they would break into a medley of instruments, and the
tone turned happy, people in the pub stamping the floor. It was her first
audience of Irish music, and she thought she could listen as long as they would
play.

A man loomed over Brynna.

"Brynna, have you any urge to row this year? Iona Rooney is pregnant
with her third, says she won't fit in the boat. We're short one for the women's
four."

"Row? Duncan, what could you be thinking? I haven't had my arse in a
boat for years."

"But you were fine then. Will you consider it?"

"I won't. But maybe Larkin here." Brynna turned. "Larkin rowed in
university, didn't you, Ducky?" Larkin nodded. "Like to have a go at it again?
It's great fun, and grand exercise. This is Duncan McKenna. He's in charge of
the rowing teams here for Sean. Duncan, this is Larkin May, our friend from
America."

Duncan squatted down next to Larkin.

"Larkin, is it? Nice to meet you, Larkin. You've rowed before? We'd love
to have you. We practice three nights a week and races are on Saturday
afternoons."

"I haven't crewed for years. I'd hate to mess up anyone else."

"Ah, you won't. We're in it for the fun and the work of it. Like to try?"

Larkin looked over at Brynna. "Can I be finished at the house in time on
Saturdays?"

Brynna nodded. "We'll see to it. And, I'll stand by the shore and watch you
fly by."

She turned to Duncan. "You're sure I won't be a fly in the ointment?"

Duncan looked at Larkin, then Brynna.

"A what?"

"A bother, a problem," Brynna told him, "more trouble than she's worth."

"No, Larkin, I'm sure you won't be..." he smiled at her, "...a fly in the
ointment. If you like, I could get you in a boat a few times before you get in
with the girls."

"I'd appreciate that very much."

They set a time to meet at the dock, and he drifted off.

Larkin turned to Brynna, surprised. "What did I just sign up for and why did I say yes?"

"Don't worry, you'll enjoy it. You'll get to know more people in town, spend some time away from the house. Something to fill your nights. And you said 'yes' because Duncan asked you." She leaned into Larkin. "He has beautiful eyes, your man there. I've never been able to say 'no' to him while looking him in the face. Good thing he's never asked for anything out of line. I don't know what I'd do."

8.

The days developed into a pattern. Larkin and Brynna worked well together, their voices chiming through the house, and Larkin discovered the secrets that kept the business successful. She learned Brynna laid the cooked rashers on top of the tomatoes in the oven, and the juice from the meat gave the tomatoes a wholly different flavor, as if they were grown in a smokehouse. She saw Brynna pick up guests at the train, make them tea when they returned from a long day shopping or fishing, or run a load of laundry for them if they were desperate for clean jeans. These were extras she provided, and the effort came from her naturally, as one who liked to take care of people, not one who had to. The house was always clean and warm, and the hot water flowed all day, a luxury Larkin took for granted but many Europeans did not have available.

"It's the cost of heating, Larkin. It's much more expensive than the States. People just can't afford it."

Larkin continued to do the shopping, becoming quickly proficient, but turned down offers for delivery. She figured any upper-body strength would come in handy with rowing days away.

Her fourth day, heavily laden, she heard a call from across the bridge.

"Larkin!"

Deirdre walked toward her on the other side of the bridge, surrounded by children and pushing a stroller. The women had met twice at Sean's and again in a rowing meeting, Deirdre the coxswain and captain of the team Larkin was joining. Always, there was a child nearby, hanging off her leg or asleep in her arms, a round head burrowed into her shoulder, and a little arm hanging down her back like a pale braid.

The first time Larkin saw Deirdre, she was drinking tea at Sean's with her toddler sitting on her shoulders eating bread. She stood with one hand cupping a little knee and deep in conversation, her dark hair liberally covered with crumbs and bits of butter.

Today, Deirdre had her three children and three more she watched while their mothers worked in Galway. Larkin snaked her way across the bridge to them.

"Do you need help with your parcels?" Deirdre reached a hand for one of the four hanging from Larkin's arms.

"That would be great. My Roosters are about killing me."

Deirdre took the potatoes, and scooted the child in the stroller over to make room. She found space for another bag, and fit it in on the other side.

"That better?"

Larkin took a deep breath, and tried to slow her heart.

"I think you saved my life."

They walked toward the house, chatting easily. At the front door, Larkin got her bags and voiced thanks. Deirdre flipped a hand to her and walked away in a moving wave of children.

As she unlocked the door to the B&B, it occurred to Larkin that not only did she have her potatoes straight, someone she knew had just walked her home, the girl in the store called her by name, and she recognized people she smiled at on the bridge as living in the neighborhood. It was curious to her that only four days had passed since her passport was stamped, and yet she felt so at home.

After the food had been squirreled away, she went up to her room. She sat at the desk in front of the window looking out over Athlone, and thought how her life had gotten smaller here. All her possessions were in this neat little room, and her job required sweat but not much thought.

She hadn't known, really, how tightly she had been stretched at home, that the strain of the past few years had brought her close to the end of her energy.

None of it was hard - it was just constant - and, besides sleeping and eating, she had done nothing to fill the reserves those activities required.

Larkin took out her phone and typed in a quick text to Sukki.

You are amazingly smart ☺

9.

Sunday dawned cloudy and cool. Larkin was used to feeling the chill in the mornings, and was learning that the start of the day foretold nothing about the rest of it. Sunny mornings could darken to rain by noon, and clouds were a near constant effect in the Irish sky.

The clouds here seemed different to Larkin. They had more personality, she thought, deeper colors and more depth. There were certainly more of them. At home, she noticed them at sunset, in the pinks and purples of the Midwest sky, but here she could be fascinated all day with the clouds; they seemed wild and brazen to her eye.

Sunday was a full house, and Des was helping Brynna in the kitchen. Larkin was working the dining room until Theresa came in to clean up and perform the upstairs work. Larkin was in the groove of serving and taking orders when the front door opened. Larkin turned to find Conn Nevin standing there, wet with mist. His eyes found her, and he watched as she served the plate she was holding and walked the length of the dining room to where he was taking off his coat.

"I was nearby, and thought I'd see if I could get Brynna to cook me breakfast."

Conn moved closer to her, then took a step past her toward the kitchen. As she poured tea, she could hear their voices, Conn's low, and Brynna and Des' animated.

Larkin walked through the kitchen door, and headed to the counter for more tea. Brynna called to her from the stove.

"Take this man out there, Larkin, and give him tea. He seems to think his flattery about my cooking will get him breakfast - as of course, it will."

Larkin filled her teapot and walked toward the door. Conn opened it for her, stepping aside to let her pass him. She caught a scent from him on her way by, a natural smell of clean man and turf-blown clothes.

Once he was seated with his tea and bread basket, she continued serving, chatting with the guests, clearing plates. She was conscious of him; alert that he was watching her.

Most of the guests had finished by the time Conn's plate was ready. When all the tables had cleared of people, he spoke to her on her way to the kitchen.

"Have you eaten?" At the shake of her head, he asked, "Come sit with me, then, can you?"

"I'll get something, and be back." Larkin smiled, then went to the kitchen and got a plate. She took a rasher, tomatoes, and brown bread, raising her eyes to find Brynna looking over at her, then calling to Des.

"Look at Larkin, there, pink in the cheeks! Is it Conn doing that to you?"

Larkin grinned at them, put her back to the door, and joined Conn at his table. They chatted about their weeks and the weather, and Conn reached for his tea.

"Now then, it's Sunday, and I was thinking you might have the afternoon to spend in some way." Conn added milk, stirred, and looked at her. "Would you like to come for a spin, see some sights, have dinner later, perhaps?"

Larkin nodded. "I would, but I'm not done with work for at least a half-hour."

"Then I will be forced to drink more tea." He smiled at her, his eyes dark over the steam from his cup.

"I'll be done as soon as I can." Larkin took her plate, pushed back her chair, and walked toward the kitchen, knowing his eyes followed her. She put her plate in the pile by the sink, opened the dishwasher, and started to fill it with the stack Des already rinsed. Brynna waited for a moment, then lost patience.

"Well? What's going on out there? Conn's never been so taken with my cooking before."

"We're going for a drive; we'll see some things, and then eat later. When I'm done, of course. Not trying to get out of my work."

Brynna shot a look at Des. "Listen to her, 'when she's done,' the girl who works harder than any two of us. You're done, you're done. Go, change your clothes and go on. Teresa will finish in here. Des, see if Conn needs tea, will you?"

Larkin smiled at Brynna and ran up the kitchen stairs. She tore off the clothes that smelled of morning cooking, and put on a moss-green tank, clean jeans, and a light-weight gray fleece jacket, short to the waist and soft. She went to the bathroom to fluff her hair, and add mascara to her eyes. She sprayed perfume on her neck and touched her wrists to it.

In the mirror, she saw Brynna standing in the doorway, her hands in the pockets of her apron.

"I'm feeling like I need to say something before you go, Larkin. I don't even know what, but there's something here to be said."

Larkin turned, touched her arm.

"It's all right. Don't worry."

Brynna took her hand. "Keep in mind, Conn's not a bachelor at 37 by getting involved easily. He's a bit wild. I don't want you hurt."

"It's a drive, maybe dinner. Nothing more, just a...date." Larkin stopped. "It's a date." She drew in a breath, and smiled. "That's all."

"All right, then. Have a wonderful time. Have him take you to The View. It's lovely there."

They walked back down the stairs to find Conn and Des waiting.

"Look at the two of them. What do you think they've been talking about?" Des smiled at Brynna, who waved an arm at him on her way by.

"Nothing that concerns you, I'm sure. It's back to work with us, or the sheets will never get hung. Have a good day, you two. Mind yourselves."

Conn and Larkin walked to the car. Larkin looked to the sky to see the sun trying to make its way through, the bunched-up clouds moving over the ground in no hurry.

"It looks like it may clear up, after all." Larkin opened her door and climbed in the little car. Cars felt small to her here, and low, as if she were sitting in a kayak.

"The thought here in Ireland is if you don't like the weather, wait a bit, and it will change." Conn started the car, put his hand on her seat to twist around and look behind him.

"That's exactly what's said about Chicago weather. Imagine that."

As they pulled out of the driveway, Larkin felt a flutter of fear, and took a sharp breath looking at the front door going past them. She wanted to make Conn stop and let her out, or stay in the neighborhood where she knew where she was. She looked out the window, clutched her hands in her lap, and tried to gather herself.

She wondered if she should explain. My husband died, she could say, and this is the first time I've been out with a man since. She could imagine the ensuing conversation. What happened? How long has it been? Then would come sympathy, then silence, and where was there to go from there? Would there be any place to go but home?

No. She would just be a woman he was interested in, that he had made special arrangements to see. He had remembered what Brynna told him about her, and he came at the first opportunity. Larkin's breathing steadied. She turned from the window and looked at Conn, driving with one hand on the wheel and one on the gearshift, eyes ahead, unaware of her dilemma.

"So, where are we going?"

They traveled miles, leaving Athlone and going south to Ballinasloe, where Conn pointed out picturesque cottages and meadows. They went east from there to Shannonbridge, and there sat with pints outside a pub called Killean's, talking of Conn's job traveling around the country doing building inspections, and Larkin's work at the clinic. Larkin took off her jacket to feel the sun, breaking out in goose bumps when the breeze blew, but feeling it worthwhile for the intermittent dry heat on her shoulders. Elbow on the table, her hand touching her collarbone, she lifted her face to Conn's and smiled, comfortable at last.

Conn laughed. "Don't be sitting there with those eyes looking at me. Finish your pint; we're not half done yet."

From Shannonbridge they drove north to Clonmacnoise, a monastery dating back to 492 AD, but by then, rain was pelting the windshield, and they didn't stop.

Conn was disappointed. "It's a great spot, very historical. Ah, well. Next time."

In Moate, they decided they'd worked up an appetite, so they stopped at The Grand Hotel to eat. Larkin had trout as pink as salmon, broiled with butter and flakes of spices. Crowding the plate were oven-roasted potatoes, salted and browned, and a huge stem of broccoli. Conn had a pile of beef, sliced in a pool of gravy, mashed potatoes, and carrots. Classic Irish fare, he told her. He picked up a hunk of brown bread, broke off a corner, and dipped it in his gravy, lifting it to her mouth.

"Taste."

She took the bread, a drop of gravy hitting her lip. Before she could lick it, Conn brushed his thumb across her mouth, wiping the gravy away. It was the first time he had touched her intentionally, and it stopped her. She felt a shift, and it must have showed on her face, for he stopped as well.

"What?"

She swallowed. "Good gravy."

His face cleared, and he laughed. "I'll buy a liter if you keep looking like that."

After dinner, they went northwest to Glasson, driving slowly in the dusk. On a long stretch of road, Conn reached over and took Larkin's hand, laying it palm down on his thigh while he drove, winding his fingers around hers. She took a breath, deep and quiet. She had completely forgotten this. This was the incredible sensitivity of touching someone new, someone unfamiliar. She was completely aware of what was under her hand: the roughness of his jeans, the muscles moving as he drove the car. He loosened his hand to move the gearshift, and she left hers where it lay, flat on the middle of his thigh, obvious.

He reached down and picked up her hand, kissed it, and put it back.

"It's been a lovely day, Larkin."

They stopped in Glasson, where there were roses. There was a profusion of them, growing in hedges, up the sides of buildings, in planters and from the ground, surrounding the businesses and all the homes.

"Brynna's dad would love this. Where did they all come from? It doesn't look like they just sprouted."

"No, it's taken years of work." Conn reached in his pocket, looked around, flipped open a pocketknife blade, and cut her a pink bloom from the front of a small building. "The people here decided they wanted something different from the usual planter boxes seen all over, so they voted on roses as the town flower. Everyone started to plant them, and this is how it ended up."

"I bet they wouldn't be real thrilled about the one I have in my hand here, would they?"

"Well, no need to go showing it off to the locals."

Larkin laughed, and put her nose to the flower. "What is this building?"

"This was built as a schoolhouse a hundred years ago. See the door there?"

There was a door in the front of the building, off-center to the right.

"Come with me." Conn reached out his hand. He led her to the back, pointing. "See that door? Just like the front, but slightly on the other side. The building was originally walled down the middle, sharing a fireplace for heat, but segregating the boys from the girls. They had to use separate doors and didn't see each other all day, except for a joker or two who would make faces through the fireplace."

"Did it keep the peace?"

"The nuns and priests who taught here thought it did."

"What is it used for now?"

"It was falling apart, so the town got together and raised some money to fix it up. See where the stone doesn't quite match there? And there? It was put back together on the outside and gutted on the inside. They left the fireplace, but took the wall down, and now it's used for community affairs: dances and concerts, or a speaker that would come and talk about some new sheep feed or a way to paint your walls. It gets used quite a bit."

"I'm glad they managed to keep it. I hate to see old buildings torn down."

Conn turned toward her, pulling her closer to him, but not so they touched anywhere but their hands, still clasped.

"Well, I'm out of things to show you unless we go further north, and then it might be hard to get back tonight. We could keep going, though, and stay somewhere. What do you think?"

Nicely put, Larkin thought.

"No, I want to get back. Brynna said we should go to The View, whatever that is. Is it on our way?"

"Ah, a fine idea. I had forgotten about The View. By all means, let's go."

They got back in the car, and pulled away from Glasson. On the way to The View, they drove back through Athlone, crossing the bridge and heading north out of town. Conn slowed, turned his head to her.

"Would you mind stopping at a pub for a bit? I don't often get here, and they pour a gorgeous pint of Guinness."

"Fine with me. Do they pour a gorgeous pint of cider as well?"

"Cider. Who started you on that? Must have been Brynna. It's nasty stuff, that is. Rot your stomach right out."

"Unlike what you drink, right?"

"Ah, you don't insult a man's Guinness, Larkin. We Irish are sensitive about our Guinness."

Larkin laughed, got out of the car, and followed him into a tiny pub. It was outfitted with tables made from black iron sewing machine bases, stools set around, and a bar the length of the small building.

They sat at the bar, Conn ordering and talking to the barman as he poured her cider and filled another glass to the brim with foamy black stout. He set it under the tap, and waited for it to settle. They watched the beer slowly separate to black below and foam above, a changing line in the glass.

Larkin leaned toward Conn.

"I think I understand now. It's not that Guinness is good, really, but by the time you finally get it, you'll drink anything."

The barman added to the glass and put it in front of Conn.

"There you have it, Larkin. The perfect pint of Guinness. And you'll see when I drink it that foam will be left all the way down the glass when I'm done. That's how you can tell the quality of the pint."

Conn took a long pull. When he finished, there was foam covering the empty inch of glass. He nodded to the barman.

"Cheers, Paddy. Before she goes back, I'll have her drinking what's good for her."

Larkin laughed. She was feeling good about the day. It felt like she'd expected a first date to be. There had been some silences in the car when Larkin searched her mind for something to say, but they'd laughed together and talked well. The bit of touching had been stirring, too, making her think things were waking up once again.

When they left the pub, Larkin was surprised to feel tipsy. She'd had all of three ciders, spaced out over the day, and had eaten besides.

"You're not used to it, is all," Conn told her, "And I'm driving, so there's no worry."

They headed for The View, Conn explaining it was a spot where the Hodsen River came to the land, making inlets and islands and swirling around the banks. The way the light moved over the water made it a popular place to visit, and the sunsets were usually spectacular.

"Too late for that, but it will still be something to see with the moon so big tonight."

After a short drive, they turned into a parking lot. They got out of the car, and walked to a curved stone wall facing out over the expanse of water and land, the glow from the moon touching the water and highlighting the clouds still present in the sky.

"It is beautiful." Larkin put her hands on the wall and leaned over to look down to the shoreline.

"Be careful." Conn reached, circled her waist with his arms, and pulled her back to rest against him. "In your condition, you could go right over."

Larkin leaned back and closed her eyes. They stood there, his chest solid behind her. She felt safe. He bent his head down and nuzzled her, kissed the space where her neck curved, pulled her jacket to the tip of her shoulder and kissed where the sun had warmed her earlier, running his hand down her arm to her fingertips.

"I've wanted to do that since Shannonbridge. Ah, you're so lovely, Larkin."

Larkin was still, barely breathing. She wanted to savor this; could have stayed there for hours just that way, the breeze brushing her face and the feel of Conn behind her.

Conn moved his feet.

"It's late. I should get you home."

When he stepped away from her, he kept her hand, led her to the car, and shut her in. They pulled out of the parking lot and headed for Athlone, her palm back on his thigh, his hand rubbing hers.

Once at the house, Conn asked to use a bathroom, but Larkin hesitated.

"Would you mind waiting?" she asked.

"No, of course not."

Larkin walked to the door, then turned and faced him.

"I had a wonderful time. Thank you so much."

Conn moved closer to her. She wasn't sure what she wanted now, but her neck still tingled with his kiss. He took two steps, reached around her, and raised her to her toes. She took a breath, lifted her face.

He pressed his mouth on hers, pushing his tongue past her lips, pushing her back to the wall behind. His mouth was hard and sharp, and she pulled away, stunned. He pulled her back to him, one hand behind her head, and forced her lips apart again. His hands started to move, one following the curve of her side brushing her breast, the other moving down her back, heading, she was sure, for other parts of her body she didn't want touched. She cringed, twisting in his grasp.

Conn was whispering to her, "Larkin, you're so lovely, you're perfect. I want you, Larkin, let's go to your room, let's finish the day."

He was walking her closer to the door. She tried to slip away from him, to disengage. He caught her wrist with one hand and her waist with the other, and in a move, brought her hand to his groin, covering himself, still whispering.

"Look what you're doing to me, Larkin. Come with me, now. You want this, I know it. You want me, and I want you."

She tore her hand away from him. She put both palms to his chest, and pushed him a step back.

He moved toward her again, his voice bending around her.

"Larkin, don't push me away. You know you want this, don't spoil the day for us, you're so lovely."

She stood glaring at him.

"Spoil the day? I think you've managed that for us both."

"Larkin, don't be like this."

"Time for you to go."

"Larkin, don't be a child."

"I am done talking."

She stood with her arms crossed over her chest, her shirt half pulled out of her jeans.

He stared at her, ire changing his face.

"Grow up, Larkin. What is it you think I came for? How did you think the night would end?" He looked her over and gave her a mean little smile. "Ah, it's too bad, Larkin. It would have been good for you."

"I think not."

He turned and walked to his car, pulling the door shut hard behind him.

Larkin jumped when the door closed. She got inside the house, sat down, and covered her face with her hands. She checked her watch. It was past midnight here, making it 6pm at home. She crept upstairs and pulled out her cell phone.

She stumbled over Sukki's number, trying twice before getting it right. It rang and rang, but finally, Sukki picked up.

"Hello?"

"Sukki. I'm so glad you're home."

"Larkin? What's wrong? Are you all right?"

Larkin bit her lip.

"I went on a date."

"A date. Well, what happened? Was it awful?"

"The date was fine, it was a really nice day, but he was crummy at the end, and now I've wasted it, I've wasted my first date and my first kiss on a guy who just wanted to get laid, it didn't have to be me, it could have been anyone, and I've wasted it." Larkin sat on the top step.

I will not cry, she thought. This man will not make me cry.

"Peachy guy. Reminds me why I quit dating."

"Great idea, I'll quit too. Can you quit after only one date?"

"Not if it's the only date in the last three years. You just need to choose better. What did Brynna think of this loser you went out with?"

"She didn't say much, just that he was a bachelor for a reason, and she didn't want me hurt."

"Are you? Are you hurt by this man?"

"No, I'm not hurt. I'm so disappointed, though. I just wanted a nice day, a nice guy, with maybe a kiss at the end."

"What was it that made you want to go out with him to start with?"

Larkin smiled into the phone. "He smelled good."

"OK, there must be more than one Irishman that smells good. Next time, make sure the guy understands this is casual, you're leaving in a month, not looking to get romantic, just spend a little time together."

"If there is a next time."

"There will be. Now, what did you learn here?"

Larkin tucked her hand under her knee. "Well, I'm not a pushover. There wasn't a doubt in my mind what to do; I was appalled at what he did, but I reacted well, I think."

"Good for you. Would you go out with him again if he apologized for his behavior?"

Larkin shook her head. "Absolutely not."

"Good girl. Larkin, did he stir your pots at all?"

"Did he what?"

"Did he stir your pots? Did you feel anything for him, before he turned bad?"

Larkin smiled.

"I did. It was nice, like I remembered it."

"I am happy to hear that. I remember looking at you sometimes when you were looking at Pat, and I knew you couldn't wait to get your hands on that man, you were just holding off long enough to get in the house."

"That's true, but I don't know if I'll ever feel that again. I think that was attached to him. But, things are definitely functioning in areas I had forgotten about."

"Good. Are you feeling better?"

"Much."

"Other than that, are you enjoying yourself?"

"Oh, very much. Brynna and Des are great, and Athlone is beautiful, even in the rain."

"Everything is fine here. Bubba misses you, but he's sleeping with Emmy, and that seems to be holding him."

"I miss you all. Give the kids my love, and give Bubba a liver biscuit."

"How about I give him some buttered popcorn instead?"

"No butter."

"Picky girl."

"You know, you would love it here. We'll have to come back sometime by ourselves."

"Do you think the country is really ready for the 'Sukki and Larkin Show?'"

"If any place can stand it, it's Ireland."

"I've always wanted to go someplace nuts enough that I blend right in."

When Larkin went to bed, she tried to put the day in its place. Sukki had helped with perspective, but it was still up to her to gauge if it was a good choice to have gone at all, or if she could have done something to avoid the unpleasant part at the end.

Larkin let her thoughts travel to different points of the day. She had certainly run the gamut, from nervous to charming to aroused to angry. She had been warm, cold, hungry, and satiated. She went from sober to tipsy to very sober. It was a whole life in a day. Thinking back, it was probably more emotion than she had felt in a month at home. It was what she had been hoping to find here.

Just not, she thought, all in one day.

It was good to know she still had it in her, the ability to be something more than medium, to be different than gray. She had tasted the food, really noticed the freshness of the fish and how the broccoli had a different character to it than the broccoli at home. She'd longed for the sun on her shoulders, and stood for some discomfort to get it. She got fully angry in a situation that deserved it. For the past three years, it was a stretch for Larkin to remember what mattered enough to get her outside center C. She'd certainly used all the keys on the piano today.

Falling asleep in her white sheets, Larkin was content. It had been a day worth having.

10.

In the morning, she walked into the kitchen to find Brynna sitting with the paper, having tea.

"I don't think I've ever seen you sit before noon," Larkin told her, pouring coffee for herself.

"We're a bit slow today, only four rooms filled last night, and they were all off early. Are you hungry? I have some nice black pudding." Brynna looked up from the paper and smiled.

"Nice try. I just don't think I'm a congealed-blood kind of girl. I'd be happy for a rasher, though. Any of those left?"

"Of course, but before you go home, you really must try the pudding, just to say you did."

"Well, I haven't felt the need to bungee-jump just to say I did, or get a tattoo. I think black pudding is in the same category."

Larkin sat, scooted her chair to the table, and added milk to her coffee. Brynna studied her.

"You're looking cheerful this morning. Am I to think you had a good day with Conn?"

Larkin sipped her coffee.

"It was a nice day. We drove all over, and had dinner in Moate at a hotel."

"The Grand, probably. That would be the best food, there."

"That was it. Then we went to Glasson and then The View. It was dark by then, but it was still beautiful. It must be stunning at sunset."

"It is, at that. Then he brought you home?"

"He did."

Larkin buttered her bread, and looked up. Brynna was looking back, twirling her cup in a circle. She looked away.

"And how did that go, at the end of the day?"

Larkin stopped eating and wiped her hands on her napkin.

"It certainly didn't end the way Conn would have liked it, but I feel just fine."

"Will you be seeing him again?"

"No, I won't. He wasn't ...nice. He's not for me."

Brynna smiled. "Like black pudding?"

"Like black pudding."

Brynna sighed. "It's a shame we have to come across the bad ones before finding the good ones."

"Good ones, like Des." Larkin smiled. Des, who hummed or sang his way through the house, helpful and charming to the guests, and to Larkin. It was clear that he adored his wife, and his courtesies and attentions to Brynna reminded Larkin of Pat. "I'm so glad I'm getting to know him better."

"I am a lucky woman there. I was close to mucking up my life forever!"

"Mucking it up how?"

"Before I met Des, I was engaged to a man, a boy really, from Mullingar. He was a wild one, drinking and carrying on, and my mother never liked him. She didn't say much about it, though, invited him to Sunday tea, but then just sat with her hands in her lap. She knew anything she said would just put me closer to him for the opposition, you know. Well, when it seemed like we were getting close to making wedding plans, she took me to Galway to do some shopping. We went for tea at a fancy place off Quay Street, Cooke's Wine Bar it was called, and sat at a pretty little table with a white tablecloth. We got a pot of tea, and the waitress handed us menus, but before we could open them, my mother reached over and put her hand on top of mine. She fixed me with a deadly stare and said to me, 'I'm going to say my piece, and then I'll never say a word again, I promise you.' She took a deep breath and spoke very slowly, like I'd turned deaf or stupid overnight. 'If you marry *that man*, you will cry bitter tears for the rest of your life.' Then she took her hand back, opened her menu, and said, 'I understand the fish is lovely here.'"

Larkin laughed. "That's perfect. What did you do?"

"As she promised, my mother never said another word about it, but from then on, whenever the man made a wrong move, her words appeared like this flashing billboard over his head. *Bitter Tears! Rest of my Life!* Poor man, he didn't last long after that, and he was shocked, I'll tell you, when I gave the ring back and sent him on his way."

"How long after that did you meet Des?"

"It was under a year, that I know. The first time he came to tea, my mother couldn't keep a smile off her face. And now we've been married, let's see, 24 years last July." Brynna sipped her tea, clinking her wedding ring on the side of the cup. Then she turned back to Larkin.

"So what will you do today? Your first full day off?"

"I don't have a clue. Any suggestions?"

"Talking of Galway makes me think you should go there, have a walk around and a bite to eat. The trains leave every hour from here, and the last one leaves Galway about half-eight, I think. I must have a schedule someplace."

"Is it all right for me to be there alone?"

"Of course. It's summer; there will be tourists everywhere, lots of people-watching for you to do, and shops galore to poke around in. Maybe you'll come across that crystal you're looking for."

While she was talking, Brynna was digging in a drawer for a train schedule.

"Look, if you get going now, you can be in Galway by 11:00, shop and eat and be home by 7:00 or so. What do you think?"

"Will I get lost?"

"The train station is right across from the main square, and the downtown area is around the corner. If you do get lost, just ask how to get to the station, but I don't think it will be necessary."

"All right, I'll go. Maybe I'll eat at Cooke's Wine Bar."

Brynna smiled. "The fish is lovely there."

It was a sunny day, so Larkin turned down Brynna's offer of a ride to the train station. As she turned the corner before the bridge to head to the west side of town, she glanced up to see Duncan McKenna headed toward her, his face intent on what looked like an opened blueprint. She wondered if he knew the street so well he didn't have to look, or whether he was in danger of just walking into traffic unaware.

When he got a few feet away she said his name. He looked up, smiled at her.

"Ah, Larkin. A lovely morning to you."

"What's on that blueprint that's so fascinating?"

"We're doing a room addition on the next block here, and the stairway is an awful mess. I'm off to argue with the architect. And where are you headed?"

"I'm taking the train to Galway, to wander around and have lunch."

"Well, you've picked a fine day for it. What's today, then? Monday? Are we still on for rowing practice tomorrow?"

"You bet. I need all the help I can get. Six at Sean's, right?"

"Yes, grand. If I'm a couple of minutes late, hang on. I'll be coming right from work."

"I'll be drinking cider, calming my nerves."

"No need to be nervous. It's like riding a bicycle. All right, then. Till tomorrow." He smiled again, the light from behind her making his eyes look bright in his face, as if they drew the sun to him by force.

Brynna was right, Larkin thought, about those eyes.

They started to walk on in their opposite directions, but Duncan paused a few steps further on the sidewalk, and turned back.

"Larkin!"

She turned, waited.

"Galway is lovely, but you must be a bit on the watch this time of year for pickpockets and such. Mind yourself, now."

Larkin smiled.

"I will."

The train left on time, and Larkin took a place next to the window. The train was designed so the seats faced each other with a table in between, and a man pushing a cart through the cars offered coffee, tea, or pastries. Larkin asked for tea and dug in her pocket for change.

She watched the land speed by. The train made stops in Drum, near Kitconnell, in Attymon, in Glennascaul. As the conductor trilled the names of the coming stations, Larkin repeated them softly, her face to the open window.

Coming into Galway reminded Larkin of taking the Metra train into Chicago, the fabric of the land changing to accommodate more people, more cars. There was less grass, taller buildings, and wider streets. As the train pushed around the turn to the station, Larkin stood and walked to the doorway, holding to a rail so she wasn't jerked off her feet.

Outside the terminal, she saw the square to her left. Circling it were stores selling Irish souvenirs and music, and an open air market with hawkers selling imitation designer handbags. She took a cursory walk around the square. In her traveling experience, the stores closest to a hugely public area were the ones she liked the least, and these seemed to be no exception. They carried Guinness t-shirts and little bibs with leprechauns. There were shot glasses and four-leaf-clover shaped ashtrays, cheap jewelry, and tiny tin whistles with directions for the beginner.

Following Brynna's directions, Larkin passed through the square to Quay Street. These roads were closed to traffic, the streets crammed with people of all nationalities. Walking in the crowd, Larkin thought she detected some German, bits of Italian, several groups of Japanese, and, now and again, a stray American. She passed restaurants and smelled hot oil and fried fish, warm bread, and then some Mediterranean scents of oregano and lemon. She was disappointed to see a McDonald's.

She saw "The Euro Store," which must be the equivalent of "The Dollar Store" in the States, and passed designer stores one can find in almost every corner of the world where credit cards are accepted.

As was usually the case, the farther she got from the main drag the more she enjoyed what she saw. The shops on the fringes had more interesting things in them, were more artistic and, she noted, pricier.

She walked to a store called Red Barn Interiors. Inside, she smiled. Nearly everything in the store was white. There were napkins and tablecloths, chenille bedspreads and eyelet dust ruffles. There were small pieces of furniture in softer whites and creams, painted lightly with pink flowers and leaves. On shelves sat milk glass vases and pitchers, and on a dining room table in the center of the room, a set of white dishes with a thin gold band of stars around the edge.

Here and there was a bit of color. Pillows tossed about were white with blue, white with ecru, white with mauve. A white bowl had lilac grapes painted in the bottom, and cotton towels had a strip of pink braid between the white toweling and an edging of heavy lace.

The whole place had a smell like freshly ironed linen.

She walked around the store, fingering the towels, eyeing the pillows for use in her room in Athlone. Finally she found what it was she didn't know she needed.

On one of the dressers sat a table runner, white with delicate multi-colored flowers embroidered at the edges. She lifted it in her hands, as light as gossamer, held it up to the light. It was so fine she could see through it, the fabric as delicate as a handkerchief. It was a perfect memento. She paid for the runner, the woman wrapping it in white tissue and easing it into a parchment bag with care.

She went on to other stores, looking at original watercolors depicting barren cottages, and sculptures made from thousand year-old wood found in the bogs. At a small shop off a side street, she was drawn to a scarf in silk, all blues and purples, sheening with a texture of mottled threads. She thought of Sukki the moment she saw it, and carried it to the checkout after having choked a bit over the price.

It's not a scarf, she thought, it's art.

As she paid, Larkin discovered the girl taking her money had made the scarf, and, on hearing it was a gift, offered to write Sukki's name in the corner. She watched as the girl worked Sukki's name into the swirls of the design.

With her bags, Larkin walked back toward the main street, looking for Cooke's Wine Bar. Reading the menu, she thought she needed something more continental than fish today, and ended up at an outdoor café, redolent with baked cheeses and the heat of fresh bread. She looked up at the sign, "Trattoria," then sat at a metal table, put her bags down beside her, and smiled. The street teemed with people, but she felt protected by the white fence bordering the tables.

A waiter in a white apron came to check on her. Larkin ordered baked brie with fruit and bread. He suggested a glass of wine. She smiled and told him to bring her whichever he thought would be best. Sipping her wine when it came, she knew the taste of that wine would forever remind her of this day.

Her food came, beautifully presented - the French bread sliced in italics in a red-napkined basket, and the brie oozing out toward the fruit that painted the plate the colors of summer. Almonds were crushed over the top of the brie, giving it a crunchy crust, and when she spread it on a piece of bread and took her first bite, she smiled.

When she finished, Larkin ordered coffee, and propped her feet up on the chair across the small table. She was happy to be exactly where she was. As that thought formed itself into words in her mind, she turned back to study it. Was it happiness she felt?

In retrospect, ever since the decision to come to Ireland had been made, Larkin had felt freshened. It seemed the decision itself was enough to shift her, and she was aware of a vitality she had thought lost.

It helped that it was beautiful here, and calm, giving her time to think and rest. What she had been learning was shocking. She was finding, after all this time, that she could be content without Pat. She had truly thought she would languish forever, but she had to admit, somewhat remorsefully, that she could be whole without him. It was a letting go of part of her, the sadness she'd felt for so long, and it was as if she'd had surgery to remove an extra finger, or excess weight. It was an improvement to be without the constant grief, but she would occasionally reach for it and be surprised not to find it there.

She would never be glad he was gone. She was certain sadness would still overtake her at times, but the texture of her sorrow had changed. It didn't torment in her anymore. Now, it occasionally came to visit, like a guest with smelly shoes; impossible to ignore, but with the knowledge that soon it would leave and she stop holding her breath.

What came to her then was that her future was no longer set. Her sorrow had made dating impossible, her lack of motivation kept her at her current job, and her inability to function at a higher level of energy had kept her tied to merely maintaining her current activities. She'd had nothing to give to new pursuits.

Now, though, she could feel parts of herself rejuvenating.

It must feel like this when someone gets blood, she thought, this sensation of potential, of a flooding new strength.

Larkin looked around her. She seemed projected into this lovely scene - the sun, the food, the colors, the perfect wine – and it all seemed such a gift. She was, all at once, so grateful for this time to choose her next steps.

I will not take this for granted, she promised.

She put her feet down, and gathered up her bag. The waiter came forward with the check. She glanced at it and left the correct amount, then added a tip.

"Need change, do you?"

"No, the rest is yours."

Larkin walked back toward the station, turning into shops, taking her time. She bought a necklace with a Claddagh and an Irish knot intertwined, a t-shirt for Errol, and soap that smelled like lime. She watched one girl braid buttons and beads into another's hair, her head resting on the other's thigh, tresses pulled out over her lap. Street musicians played on nearly every corner. An artist drew a picture in chalk on the sidewalk - a woman in a flowing intricate dress and a huge matching hat. It must have taken him hours, and Larkin wondered why the sidewalk was his chosen canvas, where a rain would certainly ruin all that work and stranger's feet smudged the corners of the frame he had drawn around it. She left him to it, and walked through the park.

She walked by a statue and touched a bronze arm on her way by, warmed by the sun and children's hands.

The train was much more crowded going home, but she found a seat next to a window. Rocking in time with the train, Larkin speculated about the future. In finding herself suddenly in a position to choose, she wondered what would interest her. It was a relief not to be bound, but she was a Midwestern girl, after all, and just because one had choices didn't mean one always had to exercise them. It was enough for now to be aware of possibilities.

Larkin smiled, leaned back in her seat, and daydreamed all the way home.

11.

Monday evening, she was waiting at Sean's when Duncan arrived. They walked out of the back door toward the dock. The two-seat boat sat in the water, rocking in the current. Duncan steadied the shell, and motioned her in it. She took off her shoes, climbed in, and sat where he pointed in the front seat. He climbed in behind her, reaching for the oars still sitting on the dock.

"We'll go fairly easy today. Let me know when you've had enough, and we'll come back in. Now, then, how much of this do you remember?"

Larkin sat perfectly still, not risking tipping the boat in any direction.

"I don't quite remember the boats being quite this tippy."

"Ah, in truth, I've made it a little harder for you there. The pair's boat is the hardest to row, but it's the best for me coaching you, without being in a separate boat all together. I didn't think you wanted to be in the boat alone on your first try back."

"You're right there." Larkin was holding on to the sides of the boat.

Duncan handed her an oar.

"Get that set in the oarlock, now.   Got it?   All right, are your feet comfortable, snug in the stretchers? Have them velcroed tight on you? Grand. Here we go."

He pushed the boat away from the dock, rowing to move them into the gentle current. At once, Larkin felt more at ease, and gave a few easy paddles to keep them off a collision course with the buoy next to the dock.

Once they were out in open water, Duncan pointed out the course they would follow.

"See the orange buoys there and farther down? That's our course, and it's supposed to be off limits for any other boats on the river. The water is plenty big for the fishing boats to be able to avoid us, but occasionally one will fly by and swamp a shell. Do you know what to do if you get full of water?"

"I think so, although it would be difficult to flip the boat over if I was out here on my own."

"For the time being, let's say you don't come out by yourself. Now, to row. How much do you want me to say? I know you've done this before."

"No, pretend I've never been near water. After you see me row, it won't be hard to imagine."

"Right, then. We'll start with the actual mechanics of rowing. If you remember, there are four parts to every full stroke. Can you turn around a bit and watch me? First there is the 'catch,' where the oar drops into the water, then the drive, where the oar pulls the boat through the water, then the finish, the lifting of the oar out of the water, and then, recovery, when the oar travels back to the starting position again."

As he spoke, Duncan demonstrated a stroke. Because Larkin wasn't rowing, the boat was traveling in a slow curve, pointing back toward the bridge.

"Why don't you try with me, Larkin?"

"I'm nervous. It's really been longer than I'll even say, and I crewed only my freshman year."

"Why did you stop?"

"I changed majors, and my new schedule didn't allow for 6 a.m. crew practice."

"6 a.m.! Did everyone practice at that time?"

"We did. You should have seen it. It would be freezing. No one would wear much on to the boat because we knew in minutes we'd be sweating, but putting the boat in cold water up to our knees was usually a heart-stopping experience."

"Keep talking, but start rowing. We're heading back toward the dock."

Larkin took her first stroke. The oar felt completely foreign in her hands, rough and out of her control. She grabbed the wood tightly, grunted, and pulled the oar through the water.

"A good start, Larkin, but you're using too much arm. Pull with your legs, that's it....even more. Better."

They rowed for a half a minute before Duncan spoke again.

"That was a good catch, but you're opening your back too soon. Use your legs on the drive almost all the way to the end. Yes, better. Eighty percent of the work will be done by your legs, fifteen percent by your back, and only five percent by your arms. The drive should be long, using your legs to power the boat. There, better."

Larkin rowed in silence. "How was that?"

"Better, but you're still forcing the catch. Let it fall in the water where it feels right. No, you're still deciding. Again. Again. There! Did you feel that?"

"I did, but I don't have any idea what happened."

"That is the essence of rowing. We can try to become technically proficient, but sometimes it just feels right. Ah, you'll be fine at this, Larkin. It will just take practice."

Larkin was breathing deeply, working hard.

"My novice coach told me there are no prodigies in rowing."

"She was right there, after all. The best rowers in the world are nearly 40. It's not something only for the young, like gymnastics or football. It's a sport you can do your whole life. At the inter-county championships, there is an over-70 category."

"You're kidding."

"I'm not. The same five men race in it every year. Not the same one wins, though. It's usually very close. How are you feeling?"

"Stupid."

"You shouldn't. You're doing very well for your first time out."

"I've forgotten the little I knew."

"Larkin, give yourself a few days. Are you always this impatient with yourself? Rest a bit, now."

Larkin stopped rowing, and at Duncan's instruction, laid her oar on top of the water to steady the boat.

"You think I'm impatient?"

"So far, only with yourself."

"I don't have a lot of time here. I need to be fairly proficient by next week."

"No one is expecting you to be perfect, Larkin."

"I certainly don't want to mess up the race for the rest of the team."

"I know, 'the fly in the ointment.' I'll come out with you as often as you like, and at the boathouse, there are several machines you can work out on to strengthen the muscles you'll need, and to tell you how hard you're working. It wouldn't hurt to run a bit, if you like to run. And, there's the tank."

"The tank?"

"It's a stationary boat suspended in a long pool of water. In there, you can work on your stroke in an environment that is as close as you can get to being on the water."

"How often can I do that?"

"Every day, if you like."

"I can do that."

"Good girl. Now, let's start again. Begin easily, Larkin, slowly, slowly, all right, put some power into it now, there you are, more legs, longer, longer, now back, then arms. Good. Legs, back, arms. Legs, back, arms."

They stayed out on the water for nearly two hours, Larkin trying to make her motions consistent, the oars sometimes flailing around in the water and occasionally several strokes in a row that felt just right. Then, something would change in her posture or handling, and the pattern was broken by poor strokes, the oar barely clearing the small waves, slapping the water and ruining the smoothness she tried so hard to master.

When they pulled back up to the dock, she was exhausted, her legs tight and her breath fast. Duncan took a long look at her standing on the dock, her shirt soaked and her face wet.

"You worked hard, Larkin. Maybe too hard for the first day. I should have gone easier on you, perhaps."

"There's no time to go easy on me."

"There's no sense in working you to death, either. I expected you to complain at some point, and I would have stopped."

"I complained silently."

"You're going to be sore tomorrow."

"I don't think I'll have to wait that long."

"Hmmm. All right, let's get the boat back in the house. When you're with the team, Deirdre will give very specific instructions to get the boat in and out of the water, but for now, just do what I say."

Larkin looked at the boat in the water.

"We could get help."

"We don't need help. Reach down and grab each side of the boat. Now, we're going to swing it up over our heads. Do you remember this?"

"Then it will go on our shoulders?"

"Exactly. Ready? Up."

The two heaved the boat up and over their heads, the water from an occasional splash raining down on them as they had the boat, straight armed, above them.

"Bring it down to your shoulder now, Larkin, there, good. Comfortable?"

"I have a boat on my shoulder. I don't think comfortable is an option." Larkin tried to shift the boat so it didn't feel like it was cutting into skin and sore muscle, but in the end gave up and gritted her teeth.

"Walk forward now, toward the boat house. I'll keep track of where we're going. Slow down, a little to the right, good, straight in now, way enough."

"'Way enough.' I'd forgotten all about 'way enough.' Does it still mean 'stop whatever it is you're doing?'"

"It does."

"Do you know where that phrase came from?"

"All right, lift the boat off your shoulder onto the slide, careful; keep it as low as you can so as not to hit the riggers on the shell above. Slide it in, slowly. Good. Done."

Larkin rubbed her shoulder.

"When I rowed before, I thought there must be a better way to get the boats in and out of the house."

"After a time, you won't even notice."

"Probably not. So, do you know where 'way enough' came from?"

"Ah, I don't, and I've never heard anyone explain it. It's just always been used."

As they talked, the two walked back to Sean's through the back garden where groups sat at small tables close to the water. Just inside the back door, Larkin made a motion at the Ladies.

"Give me a minute?"

Duncan nodded, stopping to wash his hands, and then he found seats and ordered drinks.

Larkin splashed her face and washed her hands, taking a wet paper towel to her neck, and tried to make sense of her hair. When she finished, she was cold. She hadn't noticed while rowing that it had gotten darker and windier, but the walk back from the boathouse and the water on her face had chilled her, and she gave a quick shiver.

Looking for Duncan, she was pleased to see him at a small table close to the fire. Sitting next to him, she saw a pot of tea at her place.

"Oh, perfect. I'm freezing all of a sudden."

"You were starting to look chilled when we got out of the water. It's easy to forget while you're rowing that it's cooler on the water, but it's important to warm up when you get out, isn't it."

"What a good coach you are." She poured the tea, added milk, and took a sip. "Lovely. Thank you."

"So what did you think, your first time out?"

"I need work."

"Besides that, Larkin, how did it feel? Did you like it, was it fun at all?

"I think today, I wasn't looking for fun. Today it was a job I need to learn. When I get more proficient, it will be fun."

"You must remember to be aware of things, Larkin. The water was beautiful in the light, and there were ducks that swam next to us for a time. I know you didn't notice them tonight, but in the future, you must look. It's not just for the rowing that you're out there. It's the feel of the water under you, and what you can see from the boat that you can't see from the dock."

"You're telling me to pay attention."

"I am."

"You and everyone else. What else should I watch for?"

"It's usually quiet. If you practice in the morning with the team, it's likely you'll be the only ones out there, and the quiet on the river is like quiet nowhere else."

"I get very pragmatic. Once I set my eyes on something, I tend not to see much else till it's done."

"Ah, but if you do that with rowing, you'll miss a good part of it. Rowing isn't just the body. It's the mind and the senses and the body. Not to get everything is missing the point."

"I will remember that." She paused. "Do you row?"

"I do, of course. I row in the men's eight."

"What seat?"

"The stroke - the seat face to face with the coxswain."

"What seat will you put me in?"

"Probably the three seat, right behind the stroke. You'll have the stroke to watch, and Deirdre won't be far away."

Larkin sipped her tea. Since she landed in Ireland, she had been careful to look for beauty, for feeling. Hanging the sheets, she looked at the clouds, smelled the clean cotton in her hands, and lifted her face to the breeze. She closed her eyes listening to music in the pubs, wanting it to get in her like a flu, breathing it deeply and letting it fill her head. She was doing some of the evening cooking for Brynna, and was finding her taste again, experimenting with spices, butter, and vinegar.

However, give me a job, she thought, give me a goal, and I miss the pretty stuff.

"How can I be paying attention to all this beauty if I'm concentrating on rowing? Deirdre won't like it if it costs me a stroke."

"Too true. Deirdre can get fairly rabid in her role. You'd never know looking at her how intense she can get in a boat."

"My cox as a novice was too mild. She wanted badly to be a part of the team, but didn't want to row, and didn't really want to have to goad us. She wouldn't raise her voice and as a result, we just kind of floundered around out there."

"The coxswain must be the authority figure in the boat. It's her job. They are responsible for not just the race, but the safety of the crew and keeping the shell in one piece. It's a huge obligation. Deirdre does it very well."

"I bet."

"When I talk about paying attention to your surroundings, I don't mean during a race. Racing is a different page entirely. During a race, you must focus on what the coxswain is saying, and do exactly what she tells you. If the

Titanic went in your path, you would be expected not to notice. That's the cox's job. Your job is to do what she says. Practices, though, can be lovely. You'll work hard, like you did today, but there will be more time for seeing and feeling."

"I'll be open to that."

"Good. Are you hungry?"

"Starving, now that you mention it."

"Let's get something to eat. Want to stay here, or go wandering?"

"Let's stay. I love the fire."

They ate what Sean suggested, talking easily during the meal, and the night darkened. When Larkin looked up, the sky was almost black.

"What time is it?" she asked. "I forget it stays light so late. It must be past ten."

"It is. Half-ten, actually."

"I've got to go. Half-five comes early."

She gathered her jacket around her, reached in her pocket for money. Duncan waved her away.

"You're all right, I've got it."

"No, I have it right here." She counted out a combination of bills and coins on the table.

"Do you want to go out on the water again tomorrow?"

"Absolutely. Same time?"

"Yes, or a few minutes past."

"Perfect. I'll see you then."

"I'll walk you home." Duncan was rising, reaching for his fleece.

"No need. I'm fine by myself."

"You're sure?"

She smiled. "Quite. I'll see you tomorrow."

"All right, Larkin. Mind yourself."

She walked home slowly, the sun still not completely gone. She took note of what parts of her body felt different, knew that the morning would find her aching. She liked being physical, but had not the motivation or vigor in the past years to push herself.

Rowing would push her.

She smiled, imagining the machines at the boathouse, getting back in the water with Duncan, following the instructions of the coxswain. She couldn't wait. She had loved feeling her heart pound and breaking a sweat. She didn't think of winning and losing, but of exerting herself, and it felt as foreign to her as the oar had felt in her hand a few hours ago.

It was time to be pushed.

12.

Working in the morning with Brynna, Larkin made an involuntary sound while lifting the mattress to tuck the sheet.

"What was that?" Brynna asked her. "You're not allowed to moan like that until you're my age."

"I'm just remembering how much fun it was to row." Larkin straightened and massaged her shoulder where the boat had rested.

"Ah, you'll get used to it in no time. Within a week, you'll be fit and ready, I'll lay wager."

"We'll see. I row again tonight with Duncan, and start regular practices with the team tomorrow."

"I can't wait to watch you race. I wish my Dad were here. He'd have some fun with this, I can tell you. He rowed on and off all the time I was a girl, depending on his schedule with the trains. I did it for years, but I was never very good. I'll have to get a picture of you on the water for him."

"I hope it will be a shot with me in the boat and not falling out."

"Oh, you rarely get a boat to tip over. Stop dead in the water, get out of line, catch a crab, yes, but rarely does one sink."

"Catching a crab. I'd forgotten that."

"It was my favorite trick. I'd get that stupid oar in at just the wrong angle, and the next thing I know, the handle is hitting me in the ribs and about taking my head off as it whizzes by."

"I caught some crabs as a novice, but we were never going fast enough for it to do much damage."

"Things happen. Mostly, they're taken with grace. For everyone's hard work, this isn't a professional league, and mistakes are made, aren't they."

When the work was finished, Larkin went to the boathouse. There were other people from the league there, and Nessa, the stroke in Larkin's boat and the only other member besides Deirdre she'd met, gave her a quick tour and some basic instructions for the various machines.

"I'll be in the tank for a while if you need anything," she told Larkin. "Don't do too much all at one time - you'll surely pay for it tomorrow."

Larkin picked the ergometer at the end of the line.

No need to make a spectacle of myself, she thought. I have no idea what I'm doing.

She took the straight bar of steel in her hands, positioned her feet in the stretchers and pulled. The cord attached to the bar gave resistance to her effort, and she used her legs to pull it toward her chest, trying to recreate the movement Duncan had approved of in the boat yesterday. In some ways, it felt the same, and after a time, she noted the same frustration of not being able to perform a good stroke two times in a row.

She settled into a rhythm, not sure if she was doing it right, but thinking that the exercise was a plus whether or not her form was good. Nessa came by and watched her for several strokes.

"I think you're opening your back too soon, Larkin. Try not using your arms for just another second at the end of the drive. Ah, grand. Feel the difference?"

At Larkin's look, she laughed. "For the first runs, you don't feel the difference, do you? It's just hit or miss most of the time."

Larkin let the bar snap back to the starting position, and leaned back to rest.

"I'm so new at this," she told Nessa. "I need all the advice I can get. I have a lot to learn before the first race."

"That will just be the start of it, you'll find. A race is so different from all the practice you'll do; it's hard to imagine if you've never been in one. It's the only sport in the world that starts and ends with a sprint, so it's several minutes straight of trying to get enough air in your lungs to power your body."

"I've run off and on for years, but even today, I'm sore from yesterday."

Nessa smiled. "It's going to get worse before it gets better. Deirdre will take you to an inch of the best you can ever do, and then demand a foot more. She's a tough one, Deirdre is. She's made me better than I ever thought possible."

Larkin spent another hour and a half in the boathouse. Late in the afternoon, she went home to shower and eat, and was early and waiting for Duncan.

Out in the boat, he called instructions to her with no small talk, correcting and commenting as needed until she was sweaty and tired all over again.

Finally, he stopped.

"It's enough for tonight."

"It certainly is." Larkin wiped her face with a towel.

"Did you go to the boathouse today?"

"For a couple of hours this afternoon. I tried everything, including the tank, but I think it's the ergometer that will eventually do me in."

"It's hard, true, but the measurements can be a real help in telling you where you need to improve."

"So far, I'm not worried about measurements. I just want to be able to stay on the thing for the full time it would take to row a race."

"The first race will not be pretty. The first of the season never is. Boats get out of their lanes, coxes call bad races, someone catches a crab. It all happens early on. It will be especially hard for your team, as you haven't raced together before."

"Just thinking about it makes me nervous."

"I know one man who still vomits before every race."

"You're kidding. He still rows?"

"Ah, he wouldn't not row, Larkin. He loves to row. It's the tension he can't stand."

They brought the boat to the dock, got out, and hefted it up over their heads and on to their shoulders. They walked the boat into the house, and placed it carefully on the carpet-covered rails.

"Come this way, Larkin." Duncan led her to a different section of the boathouse, and made a motion with his hand. "Here are the eights."

"Beautiful." Larkin walked down the middle of the long room between the shells, leveled on rails from the floor to a foot or two above her head. There were four on each side, each shiny white and clean, with a name painted on the stern.

"Juliana, Mrs. Kelly, Stephen P., Mr. Tully," she read. She called over her shoulder to Duncan. "Where do the names come from?"

"Most often, it's the name of rower who's died. A collection is taken up from the teams and his family to buy a new boat, and it's then named after him. Or a family involved in rowing might buy a boat for the town, and then they get to name it."

"That certainly seems fair for such an investment."

"Ah, it is, of course."

They walked from the boat house to Sean's, where Larkin had tea and Duncan, a Guinness. While they chatted, Deirdre pulled a stool to their table.

"Mind if I join in?"

Larkin scooted over to make room for her. "We've been talking rowing, but I've forgotten everything I ever knew. I'm going to need a lot of instruction."

"Ah, that's my job, Larkin." Deirdre took a pull of her beer. "I'll be telling you every stroke what to do. The most important thing you can learn at this point is what the commands mean. I'm not so sure it's done the same way here as in the States. From the time we first get ready to touch the boat in the house until the boat is put back on the rails and we all step away, everything you do will be at my call. All you have to do is follow instructions."

"In a different language."

"And I will push you, Larkin. I have to get every bit of effort out of you."

"Nessa mentioned that."

"Were you at the house today?"

"I was getting acquainted with the ergometer."

"Oh, and how did you like that?"

"It's a torture device, but everyone seems to think it will help."

"It will, at that. Watch your measurements to see your improvement. Did you spend time in the tank?"

"I did - about a half hour, I think. For some reason, the ergometer seemed to do more good."

"You'll need to do both, of course, but keep on the ergometer for the most part, if you're comfortable with it."

"I am, I think."

Deirdre nodded. "Tomorrow will be fun. Don't worry too much about it, Larkin. All novices make mistakes, they're expected to. This team is grand, all good girls. They'll help you in any way they can, and not just to win. They have good hearts, all of them." She looked Larkin up and down. "You're lighter than most rowers. Weight and strength are advantages in the boat. What you can't make up for in weight, try and make up in strength."

"I'll try."

"That's all I can ask of you, Larkin. It will be fun, you'll see. You've met Nessa before, but the rest of the team?"

Larkin shook her head.

"Nessa is the stroke, as you know. You'll be in the three seat, and there's Lara in the two, and Kerry in the one. Kerry has rowed the longest, since she was a girl, really. She could teach you loads about form. She's very good. Lara started only a couple of years ago, but she's doing very well, and Nessa and I rowed together at University."

She got up to leave, reaching down to the table for her beer. "They are a fine group. You'll like them."

"Are they patient?"

"They are, of course. They were novices once, too."

They arranged to meet at the boathouse the next evening. When she left, Larkin turned to Duncan.

"That's the quietest I've ever seen you."

"Deirdre knows all there is about rowing. She didn't tell you she and Nessa rowed a pair that nearly won the All Ireland finals. She's was brilliant, and since she hurt her back, she has made herself into a first-rate coxswain. It hurts her not to row, though. Watch her face when you're all in the boat. She'd much rather be rowing with you than shouting orders."

"What happened to her back?"

"I'm not sure. Something happened in childbirth with her second."

"Is she in pain all the time?"

"She is, yes. She won't take the drugs the doctors prescribe. She says they make her stupid, not fit to watch the children. She'd rather be uncomfortable, she says."

"Is there anything I can do to help? Without bothering her?"

Duncan thought. "She's not to lift the boats, or heft anything over 25 pounds or so. As the cox, she's not in that position much anyway, but on a rare occasion, she might get asked to help get another boat in or out of the water. She won't do it, but if you could offer to help, it would save her having to find someone else. The heavy work at home, her husband does."

"I'll keep an eye out."

"Now then, Larkin, are you nervous about tomorrow?"

"Sure. I don't have the experience they do, or the knowledge, and I could mess things up horribly."

"But I don't think you will. You're a hard worker, Larkin. If you work, the results will come. Conditioning is good, but it's time in the boat that will help most. I'm happy to go out anytime you have an hour or two in the evening." He walked to the bar, got a pen and a scrap of paper. "Here's my mobile number. I keep my phone with me at work. If you think you're wanting to get on the water, try to let me know by three or so, and I'll do whatever I can to be at Sean's by six. All right?"

"That would be great." She smiled at him. "I really appreciate your help, Duncan."

"Ah, it's a pleasure, Larkin." He looked her full in the face and smiled back.

Finishing her tea, she got up, put her coat over her shoulders, and said her good-byes.

"Shall I walk you home, Larkin?" Duncan asked. "I'm finished as well."

She turned back to him, and paused.

"Only if it's on your way. I can make it fine on my own."

"It wasn't that I thought you couldn't."

She nodded, watched as he rose and shrugged into his coat, and put his empty glass on the bar. They walked out the front door to the street, the air almost cold and mist rising off the Shannon. Larkin shivered, and put her arms through the sleeves of her fleece jacket.

"No wonder fleece is so popular here. It's perfect for Irish nights."

"You'd think it came from the sheep, for all of it in the stores. I still prefer the wool sweaters, but the fleece is easier to wash."

They walked a block in silence, Larkin's hands in her pockets and her mind blank. Turning the corner to Brynna's, the wind, buffeted by the tall buildings next to where they'd walked, hit them head on.

Larkin made a noise, and pulled her jacket closer. "Isn't it supposed to be summer?"

"The days can be warm, but the nights stay cool year round." He took her arm, moved her to the other side of him, more protected from the wind. "If you stay here, you won't feel it as much."

She walked quickly, hunched in her coat, a step off to the side and slightly behind him. She scurried to the door of the B&B.

"I don't mean to be rude, but I'm freezing."

"And you're tired besides. Go in, now. I'll see you tomorrow after practice."

"All right. Good night."

She opened the door and stepped in, waved, and closed the door behind her. She watched through the window as Duncan walked back down the brick path to the street. He looked back to the door, lifted a wave, then put his hands in his pockets and turned left to head home.

13.

In the morning after breakfast, Brynna sat Larkin down at the table with a huge plate of food.

"What is this?" Larkin asked. There were two perfect eggs, two rashers, a sausage, brown bread with orange marmalade, and tea.

"You can't be doing all this rowing on the tiny little bit you eat. You'll fall over flat, you will."

"I don't think I'm in any danger of wasting away. If I eat like this every day, I'll sink the boat."

"Nonsense. The more weight the better. Now, sit and eat."

Larkin pulled up a chair. "Where's yours?"

Brynna brought a plate from the stove, half as full as Larkin's. "Before you say a word, I'm not rowing, and I have plenty of weight, fat woman that I am."

"You're not fat." Larkin looked at Brynna. She wasn't fat, only solid; her arms and legs firm from work and her back strong from carrying the basket of wet sheets out every day.

"I'm fat enough. Now, how is it going, the rowing?" She forked a bit of egg, then scooped up more with her bread. "Do you like it?"

"I'm still trying to figure out what I'm doing. Tonight is the first night with the team, so it will be interesting to see how we work together. It might be fairly comical."

"Eat." Brynna waited until Larkin took a bite of food. "Good. Don't forget this is supposed to be fun, Larkin. I work you hard enough here."

"Oh, yes, you're a real slave driver." Larkin smiled at Brynna.

"All right, it's not so horrible, but there's a lot of it. I get tired of it sometimes, so I assume you do as well."

"Don't forget, I've only been doing it a week. You've been doing it 20 years. I haven't had time to get tired of it."

"I suppose. Just don't forget to enjoy yourself. What are you doing today?"

"If I ever finish this breakfast, I'll go to the boathouse and work out, then go to practice tonight. The first race is Saturday, so there's no time to waste."

"Do you need some time off? I could get Teresa to come an extra day."

"Thanks, but no. If I start taking days off, my boss might fire me, and then I'd be on the streets of Athlone, sitting on park benches like old Mr. Murphy. Don't start spoiling me, or I'll be good for nothing when I leave."

"Spoil you? Ah, I'd like to spoil you, Larkin May. It's about time someone did."

"What are you talking about now?"

"You're turning heads in town; don't tell me you don't know. Garret in the wine shop keeps asking how you are, and Bobby at the butcher wants to know how long you're staying, and do you like football? Any of the lot of them would be spoiling you if they could."

"I'll take your spoiling any day."

"Look at you, you finished your breakfast."

Larkin looked at her plate. "I did. Aren't you smart, putting that all in front of me?"

"Go on with you. I'll finish in here, and you start the sheets, all right, Ducky?" Brynna took their plates to the dishwasher and kept talking over her shoulder. "Take a good look at Bobby when you get meat today. Mind you, he's no Duncan McKenna, but he's not so bad for all that."

Larkin headed for the stairs, then stopped. That was certainly true. Bobby was no Duncan McKenna.

When it came time for practice at the boathouse, Larkin had worked herself into a panic and sorry she had ever taken this on.

"Slow down a bit, Larkin," Nessa had said. "You're not going to change that much in a single day. Don't overdo now, or tonight you'll have nothing left for the water."

It was good advice, Larkin thought. Now, in the water, after meeting the team, she wished she'd listened.

Deirdre was sitting in the cox seat, flipping through a manual. Larkin looked down the river. All the teams were out tonight for the start of the practice schedule, and Duncan and his team were just now putting their eight in the water.

Deirdre put on her headset and tested it. Larkin could hear her clearly from a speaker under the stroke seat. On windy days, the speaker would be the difference between hearing the cox and not.

"All right, girls, it's the start of a new season. We're all glad to be here, and we've all come to work, right? We have our rookie this year," Deirdre smiled at Larkin, "so we'll be going over some elementary things that will be good for us all to practice again."

Lara, sitting in the two-seat behind Larkin, reached forward and did something to her shirt.

"Your tag was out," she whispered. "It would drive me nutty to see that all practice."

Deirdre continued. "Tonight we'll work on starts and beginning strokes. Every race has a strategy, Larkin. It's the only sport known that begins and ends with a sprint, but you can't sprint for seven minutes. We start out with partial strokes, then sprint, then go steady, then sprint if we need to overtake, then steady, then sprint to finish. It's a bunch of sprints broken up by hard work."

Larkin gripped her oar, lying on top of the water with the rest, keeping the boat steady.

"Larkin, as I told you last night, we begin a race with several short strokes. After that, everything is done is groups of ten, by the cadence I set. Let's try a couple of starts."

Deirdre gave the "row" call, and they began, Larkin intent on Nessa's back to know when to begin and end. After the first five strokes, Deirdre stopped them with "way enough."

"All right, good start. Nessa, you're a bit fast on the stroke, Larkin, watch your back, you're opening up too soon. Lara, move your hands in on the oar about an inch. Kerry, you're fine for now, but watch your catch. Good. Let's do it again. All ready, row."

They worked the start again, Deirdre making corrections to them all. At one point, she had Larkin stop and watch Nessa's back for the time to open it; all the way toward the very end of the stroke, just before using her arms.

"Remember, Larkin, your arms aren't the ones doing the work here. Your back doesn't even do much. It's your legs, use the power in your legs, then a little of your back, and even less of your arms."

Larkin watched, saw the moment at which Nessa began use of her back, later than Larkin would have thought prudent, and the final bit of pull she did with her arms.

On the next five strokes, she earned Deirdre's praise.

"Larkin, much better. See how that feels? It's different, isn't it?"

Larkin nodded. She felt the change in her posture, in the force the boat traveled over the water.

"You have to remember," Deirdre continued, "that the point of rowing is not to move the water under the boat. It's to push the boat on top of the water. The oars don't move much once they're submerged. In theory, they're supposed to go in and stay where they are, moving the boat past them on top of the water. Do you understand the difference?"

Again, Larkin nodded. It wasn't moving the oars quickly that mattered, it was moving the boat. It was a different goal.

Deirdre kept them working for nearly two hours, back and forth on the course in the water marked by buoys. They passed all the other teams at one point or another. From his position in the stroke seat, Duncan called to Deirdre.

"How is your novice there doing?"

"The pity of it, Duncan McKenna, is that she rows just like you. It will take me weeks to break her of your poor habits," Deirdre called back.

"I wanted her to know it could be enjoyable before you kept her from having any fun at all."

"Ah, go on with you. In fact, we'll race you back to the house. Ready, girls, row. Full stretch now, for ten, nine, eight, seven, six..."

Larkin listened to Deirdre's voice and watched Nessa's back and thought she could do this all night; the movement of the boat, the sounds of the oars dipping in the water and dripping over the waves on the recovery, the grunts of her teammates as they strained to keep ahead of Duncan's boat. Deirdre called another ten, the last of the night, and exhorted them to give more; it was all over for today, might as well go home with nothing as opposed to keeping some for later. Work, work, back it in, and finally, way enough.

Larkin lifted her oars, gasping for breath. They were easing toward the docks, where someone from the house was there to bring them in close enough to get out without harming the shell. Duncan's boat came in behind them at the long dock. He was calling to Deirdre as he climbed out of his boat.

"And that's the only way you'll ever beat us, is to cheat. Next time, make it a fair start, and we'll see who has open water when it's done."

Deirdre laughed, and started to climb out of the boat. Larkin's eyes were on her as she stopped suddenly, one foot in and one out, a flash of pain across her face. Duncan was there in an instant.

"Easy, now."

"Easy, my arse." She took his hand, pulled herself the rest of the way up. She stood for a second, reached her arms above her head, and stretched. She nodded to Duncan, then turned back to the women in the boat.

"Untie."

The girls reached down to release the Velcro from the foot stretchers.

"One foot up and back, other up and out."

Larkin watched Nessa's every move, and got safely on the dock with the others.

"Two and four, oars."

Nessa and Lara took the four oars to the boathouse and put them away. They returned at a trot.

"Hands on."

All four reached down and grabbed each side of the boat.

"Waists, ready, up."

They brought the boat waist high, level, their upper bodies leaning over the boat.

"Heads, ready, up."

They swung it over their heads, the extra water the boat accumulated splashing down on them.

"Shoulders, ready, down."

Larkin winced as the boat came down on the sore spot on her shoulder.

"Walk it in."

Deirdre took hold of the stern to guide it, giving instructions until they were in the boathouse and the boat was safely on its slide.

"Good job, girls. A fine first practice. Same time on Friday and everyone try and get some time in on the machines. All right? Who's to Sean's?"

They all went, going in the back door and making their way to the bar. Larkin and Deirdre ordered tea, and Nessa and Kerry each had a beer. They got a table by the wall and sat on their stools.

Nessa took a sip of her beer and sighed.

"Ah, I've been waiting for that."

"And, don't you always," Kerry said. "'Tis the only reason you row, is the beer afterwards."

"It's not true. The beer is for strength. I have to row hard enough to make up for what you're not doing in the stern."

Kerry laughed, and Deirdre looked up from a paper she'd gotten from Sean at the bar along with her tea.

"All right, our first race is Saturday. The first of the season is always a bit nerve-wracking, but we'll do our best. I'll get the schedule to you all by next week, but it looks as if we race every Saturday and a couple of Fridays as well." She turned to Larkin. "How long are you here, Larkin?"

"My ticket is for July 29th."

Deirdre looked back at her paper. "You'll be here for most of it, then, but you'll miss the championship by a week." She looked up. "I'll have to keep an eye out for a substitute. But you'll get the lion's share - six races in all, and ten or more practices."

"I would understand completely if you wanted to substitute me earlier. I can't imagine it would be good to change team members the week before the biggest race of the season."

"No, we'll keep you until you leave, Larkin. We can get extra practices with a new girl if we need them. Probably, it will end up being someone we know, someone from another team who doesn't make the finals, so we won't be starting from scratch."

Kerry, seated on Larkin's right, nudged her. "Ask her why she's so sure we'll be in the finals, Larkin. She seems certain, doesn't she, talking about a championship weeks away to which only twelve teams get invited."

Larkin looked to Deirdre and raised her eyebrows.

Deirdre smiled.

"My team has never not made it into the finals. Not in the six years I've been coxing here, not in the years I rowed at University, and after that, when I rowed for Sean. Never."

"No pressure there, Larkin." Kerry said.

Larkin looked at Deirdre. "I would hate to ruin your record after all this time."

"You won't," Deirdre told her.

"What she means," Kerry said, "is that she won't let you. Get ready to work, Larkin." She raised her glass. "Here's to the season. May we all live through it!"

The team laughed and raised their glasses, and resolved to make their coxswain proud.

14.

Practice went well Friday and Saturday dawned clear and cool. Larkin knew it was no indication of good weather by race time, but was still a relief to have the sun shine as she served breakfast and changed sheets.

At noon, Brynna shooed her out.

"Des and I will finish. Change your clothes and go find the team. No sense running in at the last minute."

With Brynna's words, Larkin stopped, dumped the load of sheets she was carrying on the laundry room floor, and wiped a hand across her forehead.

"What could I have been thinking? Is it too late to sneak out of the country?"

Brynna laughed, leaning into the washer to empty it for the next load. "You'll be fine, Larkin. It's only pre-race jitters you're feeling now. You'll either feel better around the team, or you'll want to be sick. Either way, you'll be better off there. We'll be at the finish line, Des and I, cheering our heads off. Do you want breakfast before you go?"

Larkin made a face.

"You must eat something. Take some brown bread with you." Brynna reached for a hunk of bread, cut slices, and slathered them with butter. She wrapped them in a piece of foil, and handed them to Larkin. "There. Now, be off."

Larkin ran upstairs and changed, putting on shorts and her team shirt, covering it with a two-piece running suit for warmth until it was time to row. She came back down the stairs two at a time. She burst into the kitchen.

"Have you got your bread?" Brynna called from the laundry room.

Larkin made a noise, turned and ran back up the stairs to her room, grabbed the package and ran back down. In the kitchen, Brynna waited, reaching out to hug her before she ran out the back door.

"Good luck, Ducky. If it will help, think of my dad. He'd be so proud of you."

Larkin stopped. Brynna was right, he would be proud. He had always taken quiet satisfaction in her accomplishments, she and Sukki both, and it sweetened the few things she'd found to feel good about these past years since Pat died.

In that moment, standing in his daughter's kitchen, Larkin had a piercing desire to see him, to have him here for her first race. Brynna put a hand on her arm, smiled and nodded.

"Ah, you can call him tomorrow; tell him how it all went. It will be the next best thing."

Larkin stood a moment longer. Suddenly, she felt far from home, unprotected. What if she caught a crab, messed up the timing, or opened her back too soon? Not only would they lose, but the rest of the season was at risk, along with Deirdre's record and the respect of the other women in her boat.

She shook her head and turned to the door. The only small comfort was that no matter what happened, in a few hours, it would be over.

The boathouse buzzed. Nessa waved Larkin over to the team, sequestered in a corner near the ergometers.

Deirdre turned, her eyes gleaming. "And how are you feeling, Larkin? Excited for your first race?"

"Nauseous."

"It will pass."

Nessa laughed. "And, if it doesn't, don't be losing your breakfast on me."

Deirdre turned back to the group, all business. "All right, girls, get stretched. I'll sign us in and get lane assignments."

She walked towards the registration table, not stopping for calls of her name, or waves to other teams. Larkin watched her go, saw the straight line of her back and the determined set of her steps. Lara nodded to Larkin.

"She gets even more...." she searched for a word, "...Deirdre-like on race days. She'll be this way until the boat is back in the house when we're finished. Don't expect much in the way of chat."

Larkin turned to the registration table, watched Deirdre gather the papers she needed and make her way back to the team. She looked stronger to Larkin, and although she knew it wasn't true, Larkin would have said that said Deirdre had grown taller since yesterday.

Looking around, Larkin saw other teams; saw looks of determination, of expectation, and several that she thought might mirror her own.

Duncan sat on the floor with his eight, stretching, circled around their coxswain, who gave them last-minute instructions. The cox looked small in the midst of the rowers, chosen for his slight build as well as his skills. Duncan lifted his eyebrows at her, smiled, and then turned his attention back to the team.

Larkin's team finished stretching and sat in front of Deirdre as she outlined the race strategy. They had been over it in practice, but it was comforting for Larkin to hear it again, to be able to picture the race in her mind, and hear Deirdre's voice calling the cadence.

"All right, girls," Deirdre said. "Time to warm up."

They got the boat from the sliders and walked it toward the dock, waiting in line until they could lift the boat from their shoulders over their heads, then down to the water.

Kerry and Larkin held the boat while Lara and Nessa ran back to the house to get the oars. The oars were handed around and secured in the oarlocks.

Deirdre called out, "One foot in," and all four women put their right feet in the boat. "Sit in," Deirdre finished, and they climbed in and sat, strapping their feet in the stretchers and making sure the bolts on the oarlocks were secure.

Deirdre climbed into the coxswain seat in the stern of the boat and plugged in her equipment. The "Cox-Box" was a combination sound system, timer, and stroke rate counter. During practices, it kept track of different sets of exercises and compared the cadences and times. During a race, the coxswain was constantly aware of the stroke-rate of the boat, and how much time was elapsing - all information she would pass on to the team.

As the team shoved the boat away from the dock, Larkin's nausea, nearly calmed during stretching, made itself known once again. She swallowed hard, took a slow deep breath, and focused her eyes on Nessa's broad back.

Deirdre took them through some quick, light strokes to set the balance and timing of the boat, calling corrections to hand placement or back position, and then some strokes at full pressure. They did a short sprint, and Larkin listened to the boat hiss as it cut through the water.

Deirdre checked her watch.

"Way enough. All right, time to head for the starting line. Let me say a couple of things first. I've been watching the other boats, and it seems we're right about in the middle of the pack by size and weight. Size and weight don't always make a boat, but it's a good start. What it doesn't take into account is heart, and I'm sure we have more heart than any of them. This is our first race together as a team. We'll remember it for a long time, so let's do it well, let's do it with all the heart we've got. Are we ready to do that? Kerry?"

"Ready."

"Lara?"

"I'm ready."

"Larkin?"

"Ready," Larkin choked out.

"Nessa?"

"Ready."

Deirdre leaned forward and looked them over, narrowed her eyes, and bellowed at them, a booming burst of emotion that made Larkin's arms tingle and made a thin line of determination form on her lips.

"Do not forget," she blasted, "I want your best! Let's get to the starting line. Ready, row."

They made their way around other boats to the line. There were a total of six women's fours racing. On the dock, the man in charge of holding the stern of their boat tried to keep them aligned. Larkin flexed her shoulders and shivered. She had stripped down to rowing gear before climbing in the boat, and was getting chilled in the wind.

"Is there time yet to puke?" she murmured to Nessa.

"Ah, Larkin," she said, barely moving her head, "you should have done it before you left home."

Finally, the boats were aligned and the starter began polling the lanes. Deirdre had told Larkin the starter's commands would be in French, starting with asking if each team was ready, and then starting the race.

Deirdre's team was in lane 4. When the starter polled them ("Lane four, prets?"), Deirdre looked at them as she answered, her hands on the rudder lines and looking more determined than Larkin had ever seen her.

"Ready!"

Larkin's stomach twisted as the last team announced themselves ready.

The starter hesitated a moment, then called out the start.

"Etes vous prets? Partez!" (Are you ready? Leave!)

Deirdre's voice came over the speakers immediately, hard and strong.

"Row. 3/4, 3/4, full slide, give me ten full, and one, two, three, go deeper Larkin, four, five, hands up Kerry, six, seven, eight, nine, ten. Good, another ten; one, two, come on, girls, three, four, go after it, five, six, let's get 'em, seven, eight...."

Larkin watched Nessa's back pull, watched the muscles in her shoulders flex with each stroke of the oar. She timed herself with the movement of Nessa's body, the slide in the seat, the last pull with her arms.

After the race, Larkin would think back and find it strange that she couldn't remember the feel of the oar in her hand, or smell the water a few feet from her face. All there was to the world was the sight of Nessa's back filling her vision, and Deirdre's voice filling her head.

The pain was there, too. It didn't set in until the second minute of the seven-minute race, but it came quickly, the burning in her chest, the clenching in her thighs and calves. Every sport had pain. It was what differentiated sport from hobby.

Deirdre had them hard and steady for twenty strokes, and then upped the ante.

"Here's where we are girls. Four seats ahead on lane one, dead even on two, two seats behind on three, open water on five, and six has open water on us. Unacceptable! Let's catch them with a power ten in two, one, two, now!" Her voice raised in intensity. "One, move up on them! Two, go for every stroke! Three, we're closing the gap, four, harder! Five, a meter away, six, a half meter, seven, we've got their stern! Eight, give me more! Nine, push from your legs, ten, we've got their coxswain!"

Larkin held her eyes on the blue of Nessa's shirt, grunting with every stroke, her chest filling and emptying in cadence with the movement of the oar.

Deirdre called out, "Good, now ten more, let's walk up on them. In two, one, two, now. One! Stay with it, girls, two, we're walking, three, got their one seat, four, they're pulling away, five, get it back, six, got it, seven, good job, good job, eight, don't let them get away, nine, pull! Ten, back to the coxswain."

She knew she couldn't ask for another power 10 yet, so she kept them steady for another ten, encouraging them, letting them bear up for the next sprint.

In the midst of it, Larkin remembered what Deirdre told her the other night at Sean's.

"It's constant, Larkin. There's no slowing down, only speeding up. You'll give all you have and then I'll call for more. It's not like walking and running, it's more like running and running faster."

In the race, her voice calm, but stern, she let them know the positions of the other boats.

"All right, we've got five seats on one, two seats on two, one seat back on three, still open water on five and just keeping the cox on six. We can do better than this. Give me a hard ten in two; let's move on lane three, one, two, now! One, push! Two, that's it! Three, we're moving on them, four, we're even - pull ahead! Five, a half seat up, six a full seat, seven, walk on them! Eight, two seats up, nine, back it in, ten, steady at two seats up!"

How much longer? Larkin thought. Her lungs burned. Every breath was painful, and her legs and back stretched to capacity.

Deirdre called, "Steady ten at 34. OK, here's where we are. We're up two on lane three, six has moved on us, so it's them we have to catch. We'll take a power ten in two..."

No way, Larkin thought, panicked. There's no power left.

"...you can do this, you have more in you, one, two, all right! One, you're 3/4 done, girls, two, push off your legs, three, we've moving on six, four, back it up, five, c'mon, more! Six..."

Larkin narrowed her focus. With every pull of her oar, she counted with Deirdre, not counting the strokes passing, but counting how many left. With each stroke, she pushed her legs, pulled her back, and brought the oar to her sternum, every stroke closer to being done, to finishing this punishment wrought by water and resistance and commitment. With her eyes trained on the growing sweat stain spreading over Nessa's back, she clenched her teeth and worked, Deirdre's voice her compass and each stroke one closer to the finish line where she could finally stop.

Never again, she thought. She gave her head one shake. After this race, I'm done. They have plenty of time to find someone else.

"Good job, girls. We're up one seat on six. Go ten at 34. Keep your head straight, Larkin."

Bite my oar, Larkin shot back silently.

Deirdre talked through the ten, reporting their position, estimating how many strokes left to the end of the race, egging them on.

"Only 35 strokes to the line, make sure there's nothing left when we're done, nothing at all, nothing to get you out of the boat. What do you want? Where do you want to finish? We can still beat them all, we're down one seat on three and dead even with six. Time to go, time to work, the time is now. I want a ten in two, one, two, now! One, work it, girls, two, again! three, work those legs, four, no hang at the catch, five, we're moving on three, six, closer, seven, I've got their coxswain, eight, get me by her, nine, walk them up! Ten, we're up a half, give me another five, one, keep going, two, six is making a move, three, back this sucker in, four, two more for the pain, five, make it go!"

Larkin strained against the oar, against the water. Sweat ran down her face into her eyes and she blinked hard, the salt stinging.

Great, she thought. Something else that hurts.

"All right, girls, twenty more. Take it up to 35 for five and let's finish this big. We're up one on three, and on six's arse. Give me what you've been keeping back, in two, one, two. One, make this worth it! Two, we're moving! Three, finish big! Four, push off hard! Five, give me more! Six, up two on three! Seven, six is pulling away! Eight, chase them down! Nine, here we come! Ten, closing in! Another five, one! This is it, girls, two, pulling away from three! Three, even with six! Four, they're moving! Five, finish hard!" They crossed the finish line, inches behind the six boat. "And paddle. Good job, girls, good job."

The four women lifted their oars and laid them flat on top of the water, leaning over in the boat, unable to speak. The boat drifted in the lane along with the others, all the women trying to regain their breath. Soon, congratulatory calls passed from boat to boat, Deirdre's team getting their share for their close second place.

"Thought you had us at the end there, Deirdre," the coxswain of the six boat shouted over.

"Not this race, but watch for us next time." Deirdre smiled and raised a hand to her opponent. "Good race. Congratulations!"

"You rode us hard. Nice job on the second."

Larkin felt a hand on her back. She turned to Lara.

"Good race, Larkin."

"And you. Good race, Kerry."

"And you, Larkin."

Larkin turned back to Nessa.

"Good race, Nessa. I'm certainly glad to have you to watch."

Nessa turned from Deirdre's congratulations to Larkin's. "And 'good race' to you as well. A fine job for a novice. Actually, a fine job for anyone."

"Thanks." Larkin stretched her back, suddenly tired to the bone.

Deirdre called instructions.

"Let's get the boat back to the house."

She directed them to the dock, waiting in line for their turn. They got the boat up and out of the water without incident, walked it into the boathouse, and put it carefully on the slides.

When the boat was in its final position, Deirdre stood in front of them, hands on her hips, her clipboard and cox-box at her feet.

"Our first race as a team. Well? What did you think?"

Nessa spoke first. "We did very well. I didn't think it would go so smoothly," she turned to Larkin, "not only because of you being new, Larkin, but because the first race is often fairly ugly."

Deirdre turned to Lara and Kerry. "And you? What did you think?"

"It went well," Lara agreed. "Better than I had hoped."

Kerry nodded. "I thought we had them. It was only by half a seat we lost first."

Deirdre looked at Larkin. "And our novice? What did you think?"

Larkin looked back at her. "I think you made me work harder than I ever have before."

"Did you like it?"

"Not every minute. Somewhere in the middle, I had really nasty thoughts about you."

"But now that's it's over? What do you think now?"

Larkin thought.

"I'm pretty mad we didn't win."

When they got back to the river, they received their second place medals, the hometown crowd cheering their near win. The team shook hands with the first-place winners, and then wandered to the bank to watch the other team throw their coxswain in the river, her arms flailing and making a sizable splash.

"Do they always do that?" Larkin asked Nessa.

"Ah, of course. With every win, the cox goes in."

"When was the last time Deirdre got wet?"

"It was last season, about in the middle." Nessa winked at Larkin. "I think she'll be washing river water from her knickers more often this year."

"It was only the first race."

"I have good instinct for this. Wait and see."

"If you say so."

"I say so. You just keep working the ergometer."

They watched the next race, already in full swing. The boat from Athlone was beaten from the start, so the end was anticlimactic, but Deirdre's team stood together and received congratulations from passers-by as the race progressed.

Duncan was in the crowd by the dock further down the bank, and catching Larkin's eye, smiled and pumped his fist up in the air.

"Thanks," she called at him.

He pantomimed, "See you later?"

She nodded, pointed. "At Sean's, after."

He turned back with his team to get their boat in the water. His race was after the next, and they were out to practice a bit before it started.

She watched the next race, the men's four, which quickly became a fight for win between the Athlone team and the team from Mullingar.

"No hang at the catch," she murmured. "Come on, push."

The noise of the crowd built to a roar as the Athlone team inched ahead in the last 200 meters and won by a full two seats at the line. Larkin looked at the crowd, then turned to Deirdre.

"Were all these people here when we raced?" she asked.

"Sure, of course. There's always a fair number at the end. Why?"

"If you had asked me, I would have guessed no one was here."

"Larkin, there was a crowd cheering, yelling themselves silly when we finished. Duncan was there, don't you remember seeing him?"

"I don't."

"You do get focused, don't you?"

"I guess. Either that, or I didn't have enough oxygen to use my ears."

"Ah, go on. You loved it."

"Not at the moment. I love it now, though."

Deirdre laughed. "Larkin, there are some things you love to do, and some things you love having done."

"Nicely put," Larkin said.   "Like housecleaning or balancing your checkbook."

"Or using the ergometer."

Larkin stopped.

"Actually," she said, "I kind of like the ergometer."

Deirdre shook head. "You're mad."

They turned their attention to the last race, the men's eight. Duncan's team sat in lane four, the same lane Deirdre's team rowed. A wind had popped up, and the boats were having a difficult time getting aligned. For a full five minutes, the boats wagged back and forth in the water, causing two false starts and necessitating re-alignment each time.

Finally, the boat's bows sat straight, and the starter clipped through the polling of the teams. Then,

"Etes vous prets? Partez!"

The boats surged in the water, taking short strokes to get started and then longer strokes to gain distance. Deirdre and Larkin walked the path toward the finish line, far ahead of the boats, but still able to see the entire race.

At 500 meters, there were four boats fighting for first when the six-seat in Duncan's boat caught a crab. The handle of the oar flew toward the man's head, making him lay almost in the lap of the oarsman behind him to avoid being hit. He struggled with it, taking precious seconds to get the oar back under control. The rest of the team slowed for a moment at the coxswain's command, then dug in hard when the offending oar was back in place.

"Ah, bad luck," Deirdre said, making a face. "They're out of it, now."

Larkin watched as they worked to get back in decent position, but the other teams had used their misfortune well, putting meters of open water between them. At the end, they had managed to pass two of the remaining five boats, but came in a disappointing fourth.

"Bad luck," Deirdre repeated. "Ah, well, first race of the season. You never know what will happen."

They started toward Sean's. The rest of the team had beaten them, but saved stools at a table, and had drinks waiting.

"And how did the men's eight finish?" Nessa wanted to know.

"Caught a crab at 500 meters and finished fourth."

"Too bad," Nessa said. "I bet it was the six-seat."

Larkin took the stool next to Nessa. "It was. How did you know?"

"I told you, Larkin; I have an instinct for this. He'll be nothing but trouble all season, mark my words."

The pub was packed, and as people passed the table, they tossed words of congratulations to the team. Brynna and Des stopped by, effusive in their praise. Music started from a trio in the corner, and Larkin leaned back against the wall.

After his race, Duncan came to Sean's. He strode over to Deirdre, reached down and gave her a hug, then congratulated every other member of the team. When he got to Larkin, he looked at her a long moment, smiling.

"And you were nervous about being a, what was that? A fly in the ointment?"

Larkin smiled back. "It was a lucky day for rookies."

He turned back to Deirdre. "And what did you think of this one here, this beginner, hadn't been in a boat for fifteen years?"

Deirdre bumped shoulders with Larkin. "Ah, I don't mind her."

Duncan pulled up a stool next to Larkin, motioning Sean for another pint for them both. The cider was going down well, Larkin's mouth dry, and the cider sweet.

Duncan nodded to her. "Cheers."

Larkin smiled. "And to you. Thanks. Sorry about your race."

"Ah, it's the first of the season. We've some time to get it right. Deirdre says you're doing beautifully, working hard. Liking it, are you?"

She nodded. "Very much. And the girls are wonderful. I wouldn't be nearly this far if not for their patience with me."

"Good." He seemed preoccupied, took a drink of his Guinness, and turned back to her. "Larkin, can I ask you a question?"

She nodded.

"Are you married?"

She paused, then shook her head. "No, I'm not."

"Larkin, I've been wondering if perhaps you'd like to have dinner sometime, go to Tullamore, there's a nice place there, they do good food and lovely music."

Larkin's hand stopped on her glass. She looked at him, took a breath, started to say something, and stopped.

He saw her discomfort. "If you'd rather not, it's fine, Larkin."

"No, it's not that, I'd like to go. It's just that I want to be up front. I'm only here another few weeks."

"Let's call it a friendly dinner. We are friends, aren't we?" He smiled at her, trying to put her back at ease.

"Of course. I just don't want any confusion."

"Consider it understood."

A beat passed. In a small voice, she ventured further.

"I was, once. Married."

Duncan's voice was gentle. "It happens like that, sometimes."

"No, it wasn't that. We didn't divorce. He died."

Duncan turned his whole body to face her on his stool. He reached out, took one of her hands.

"Ah, Larkin, I'm very sorry. I didn't know. When did it happen?"

She looked at his hand on hers, then back up to him. "It's been three years now."

"And how are you managing?"

"Much better lately. The trip has done a lot to move the process along."

"Ah, good." He took his hand away, put it on his thigh.

She hesitated. "I haven't...dated much since he died, just once really, and it didn't go well. I'm a bit of a coward about it."

"No need to be a coward with me, Larkin. I'll follow whatever rules you have, no worries. If you enjoy dinner, we could go and see some things, get you out in the country a bit, but just in a friendly way."

Larkin smiled at him. "That would be lovely. I'd like that very much."

"When for dinner, then? Do you practice tomorrow?"

"No, Deirdre's giving us the night off. I'm free." She raised her eyebrows at him and smiled.

"Well, then, how about I pick you up at half six? We'll drive to Tullamore, eat, and listen to some music."

Larkin nodded. "I'll be ready."

15.

They went to Tullamore, as Duncan suggested. They ate well, each with a glass of excellent wine, and drove home the way of Clonmacnoise. It was too late to stop, but he promised her a visit the next day he could take off work. In Shannonbridge, they stopped at Killean's for music, sitting at a small table near the band. After the wine, Larkin didn't want more to drink, so she had a cup of tea, and Duncan had a Guinness.

Throughout the evening, Larkin had watched him for signs. She waited to see if he would reach for her hand as they walked to the car, if he sidled up too close to her at the table, or pressed in next to her at the bar. He did nothing to startle her. On the way home, she hoped he wouldn't grope her at Brynna's door, hoped he wouldn't make her say "no" to him.

At Brynna's, he walked her to the door.

"I had a lovely time, Duncan. Thank you." She backed a step away from him.

"As did I. Would you like to do it again?"

She stopped. "I would. Where would we go?"

"Larkin, there's much you haven't seen. We could go east to Mullingar or west to Ballinasloe. Or Dublin. Have you seen Dublin yet?"

"No, only the airport when I got in."

"Ah, you must go for the sights. I wouldn't live in Dublin, myself, but I like knowing it's there, with good music every night and the doors."

"The doors?"

"Dublin is famous for its doors. If you take the bus all around the city, they point out all the interesting doors, painted nicely, or with unusual windows or shapes. Perhaps, we'll take a day and see Dublin?"

"Perhaps. A lot will depend on how your work is going, won't it?"

"Of course, but I sometimes can get the lads started and then take a day. Every now and then."

"I'd love to see the doors of Dublin."

Duncan paused. "There is another thing I've wanted to talk to you about, Larkin. You know the rowing season doesn't end until the beginning of August. If I'm not mistaken, you're scheduled to leave before that."

"My return ticket is for July 29th."

"I'm wondering if you can stretch that another week. Deirdre asked me to talk you into being here for the Inter-County Championships. They run on August 4th. What do you think?"

"Another full week? I could call the clinic and see when my new group starts. I asked them not to begin it until I'd been home for 10 days or so. I want to be completely done with jet lag when I go back to work."

"You'd still have four days or so, won't you? Could that be enough?"

"It could be if I made it enough. I was giving myself more leeway than I really needed. I'll call and see when the group starts, and go from there."

"Ah, good. Deirdre will be pleased, I'm sure."

"Why didn't she just ask me herself?"

"I don't know, exactly."

Deirdre has seen those eyes, too, Larkin thought.

"You tell Deirdre I'll try."

Larkin got her keys out of her pocket. She turned to face Duncan. "Thank you again. I had a great time."

"Me, too." He reached out his hand to her. She reached over and squeezed his for a quick moment.

"See you tomorrow, then?"

She nodded. "Tomorrow."

The following night on the boat, Deirdre seemed out of focus, and distressed. She called wrong instructions, fussed about small things, then came close to tears when she made a mistake. Larkin watched her, wondering if her back was bothering her more than usual, but her professional antennae was saying it was something in Deirdre's head, not her back.

After practice, they went to Sean's. Deirdre went directly to the bar and ordered a Smithwicks. Larkin took the seat next to her and ordered a cranberry juice. Deirdre's face was pinched and angry. She took a long draft of her beer, but made a face and put it down.

Larkin reached over, touched her hand. "Hey. Are you all right?"

"What? Ah, yes, of course, I'm fine, fine, never been better."

"Sure you are. What's going on? I'm worried about you."

"No need to worry about me, Larkin, nothing you can do. Nothing anyone can do, is there? Isn't it my own fault I married the biggest eejit in Westmeath?" She took another drink of her beer, and then put it down hard on the bar.

"What happened?"

"Nothing out of the ordinary. He just has to be in charge, as always, has to have everything his own way, what I want doesn't matter in the least. It's an old story, Larkin, ancient, in fact."

"So, not the first time this has come up."

"Hardly! What's happening now is he still will not put my name on the deed to the house. He says it was his money that bought it, and why should I be upset, of course I know he'll will it to me when he dies, so what am I worried about?"

"Him telling you not to be upset clearly isn't working."

"Please! We've lived there together for fifteen years, it's my sweat in the walls as well as his, it's not like I've done nothing. I haven't brought in much money with the children still small, only the little I get caring for Maureen's and Margaret's babies, but I clean that house and cook the food, and the man always has clean shorts, doesn't he? But, no, that's not enough, if I'm not bringing in as much money as him, I don't deserve my name on that piece of paper."

"You've put time and effort in the house, so it's yours, too. Have you told him all that?"

"Why should I tell him? It's not like the man doesn't know how I feel about it. It's a battle been going on for years, comes up every time we need something to fight about."

"What brought it up this time?"

"This time it started when the man went out for bread at two in the afternoon, and didn't he get home at half-seven, smelling more like the pub than a bakery, I'll tell you that."

"That sounds frustrating."

"I was yelling at him as he was dragging his arse in the door, with dinner ruined and him looking like he got run over by a lorry. I had a lovely roast, oven-browned potatoes, carrots, everything."

"Then the house issue came up."

"Ah, Larkin, it just became a part of it all, what with the rest of the yelling and him tripping over his own feet. At some point, the man said, 'and I suppose you're going to bring up that nonsense about your name on the deed again?', so I did, gave him a piece of my mind about it, the lunacy of it, that only his name is there. That's when he stopped listening to me altogether; just waved his hands around in the air, sat on the sofa, put his feet on the coffee table I'd just dusted. Ah, the nerve of him, it boils my blood to think of it." She picked up her beer again, took a swig, and turned back to Larkin.

"I am right, don't you think, Larkin? It should be my name on there as well. Just like on the marriage certificate, that mistake of a piece of paper."

Larkin looked at her, in such a state. Deirdre was a tolerant soul, patient with children and adults alike, kind in her ways. It wasn't just the deed issue that was bothering her; it went deeper, further into the marriage. This was lack of respect Deirdre was feeling, lack of consideration in a situation where she felt she'd earned and deserved a say.

"Deirdre, what would happen if he put your name on the deed?"

"What would happen? Nothing, I suppose, until the man drops over dead, which could be soon if I have my way."

"What you're saying is that in reality, your name on the deed doesn't make a real difference until he dies. What would happen if your name wasn't on the deed when he dies?"

"Em, let's see. If the house was willed to me, it would be the same. If not, I'd have nothing."

"And, it's a possibility he won't will you the house."

"Ah, no, Larkin. He'll will me the house. But that's not the point!"

"What is the point?"

"It's the manner of it; that he won't, that he doesn't feel he should. That's what makes me so screaming mad."

"You feel disrespected."

Duncan had walked into Sean's, gotten a beer and was heading for the pair of women, smiling. He came into Larkin's sights before Deirdre's, and Larkin waved her hand at him, warning him off. He went off to the other end of the bar, sat, and watched them.

"Of course! The man doesn't even think of my side, doesn't even think of how I would feel about it. He just does what he likes without a single thought."

"That's what you thought about him disappearing for hours and letting dinner go cold, too."

"It is, of course. I cooked for him. The kids, as well, but they don't care what they eat, they'll eat a rock if I put it in front of them, but this was a roast, his favorite, and I know just how he likes it. So, again, he didn't give a thought as to how I would feel when he went off to the pub, he just went because it was what he wanted. The man just wants a woman to come home to; he doesn't want to have to consider me."

"You've told him this."

"Told him? Larkin, why should I have to tell him? It's plain as day. He should know."

"You don't usually speak of him as inconsiderate."

"No, he's kind, usually, will go out of his way to help people, he's good to the kids. He takes good care of his mother, and of mine, too. You've met him, Larkin."

Larkin had met him. He was a big man, huge next to Deirdre. He treated her well in public, sat with her at Sean's, and was always there to cheer her on at races. He seemed to adore her.

"And, for the most part, how does he treat you?"

"For the most part? Fine, I suppose. He's never raised a hand to me, or the kids. He'll go shop with me, carry the heavy things, doesn't spend all our money at the pub. He can be funny, as well, slagging me till I laugh, and he'll take it from me, too. And, as you can see, he's a fine looking man." Here she stopped and smiled, the first Larkin had seen all day.   "I still think he's gorgeous, and we've been together now for 17 years."

"So, do you think it's possible he doesn't understand how you feel about this because you've never explained it to him the way you just explained it to me?"

"But how could he not know, Larkin?   How could he not already understand? It's a simple thing."

"You're a teacher - it may be time for you to teach him."

Deirdre stared at Larkin. "Do you really think so? Do you think it would make any difference at all?"

"You know him and I don't. What do you think?"

"It's possible, I suppose, that I haven't been clear. All right, I'll try it." She finished her beer in a swallow and got down off the stool. "I'll do it now, while it's all still fresh in my mind." She stopped, looked at Larkin. "And how did you know what to say to me when I've been stumbling over this for years?"

Larkin smiled. "This is what I do. I talk to people, try to help them make sense out of something that's causing pain in their lives. If they want to change, sometimes I can help walk them through it."

"Well, you've done a fine job here today, Larkin, and I thank you."

"It was my pleasure."

Deirdre walked toward the door, calling good-byes as she left.   Larkin stayed where she was, and Duncan walked over from where he'd been watching.

He put his beer on the bar. "And what was all that about?"

Larkin shrugged. "Just a chat."

"Looked like more than that to me. Whatever were you two on about?"

"Nothing that concerns you."

"Will you not tell me?"

Larkin shook her head. "No, I surely won't."

"And, why not?"

"It's not mine to tell. If you want to know, ask Deirdre. If she chooses to tell you, she can."

"It must have been something about her man, then.   That's when you women get shrewd."

"That is a possibility, I suppose."

"Not going to give me anything, are you?"

She smiled again. "No."

"Well, you must be dry from all your secret talk. Would you care for a cider?"

"All right."

Larkin sat and listened to Duncan talk about the house he was working on, a smile playing on her face. She had loved feeling like she was using her skills again, even for a few minutes.

Her mind went back to the group work she did in the clinic, to the first meetings with new group members. Black eyes and casts were common in these first weeks. Others were bruised under their clothes in places Larkin couldn't see, but knew were there by how the women sat in their chairs, or the faces they made involuntarily when they shifted. The hardest were the women with no discernible injuries, the ones battered in their emotions but not in their bodies. It was easier to point at a broken arm and get infuriated with abuse visible to the world.

When Larkin started treating abused women, she would go home exhausted, her emotions taking a beating from what she was witnessing in the lives of the women she counseled. She understood her place in the mix, to be empathetic but not cry with them, although she still sometimes at home cried for them.

Years ago, she went home shaken and asked Pat what it could be that made a man think it the correct choice to beat his wife. She knew the psychological nature of men who battered, but she wondered out loud, looking at Pat, what it would take, if there was some line she would someday cross that would turn him to her with violence. He went to her and held her, let her cry over the bruised lives of the women she was trying to help. He told her again that he loved her, that he admired what she did, that he was so sorry for the women in the group and what had happened to them all at hands of the men who professed to love them, even while breaking their bones.

Nothing had ever made her more aware of Pat's goodness than her chosen work. It was not always clear if she was of help, but she remembered a lecture from a favorite professor in graduate school.

"Words are never wasted," he told them. "Words can be stored up and used later, when a client has the strength or the will or a better reason to change. It is a process, a journey, and it can take a lifetime."

She looked up to see Duncan smiling at her. "Where have you been?"

She smiled, and reached for her cider. "I heard every word you said."

16.

The days divided themselves easily. Larkin worked with Brynna in the B&B, learning more about the intricacies of running the business. This was a full-time, long-standing tradition of cordiality, and Brynna could have written the book on it. Her sense of hospitality was ingrained, but still she looked for new ways to serve and surprise her guests.

There was the day she came home with a huge bag of the cookies Larkin liked best.

"If I eat these, I won't fit in the boat," Larkin told her.

"They're not all for you. I'm keeping them for other Americans that stay. I don't think they like the cookies I put in their rooms. More often than not, they come back uneaten, don't they."

"Just because I like these doesn't mean all Americans will."

"I know, but there is something you like better about them. You don't care much for the others, either."

Thinking about it, Larkin told her, "These taste a bit like a Girl Scout cookie I ate as a kid - Thin Mints, I think they were called."

"There, you see? I'm trying these out on the next Americans."

Rowing practices took up several evenings a week, the team improving steadily. Larkin got to the boathouse most afternoons to work out for an hour or two, and was rewarded with added strength and the respect of her teammates. The next race found them in second again, pitted against a very strong team, and Deirdre's eyes had narrowed with anticipation for the season.

The bulk of the rest of Larkin's time was spent with Duncan. He took his job as "tour guide" seriously, putting her in the car at least twice a week and running her to a different town for dinner and music. He pointed out interesting buildings along the way and once insisted on stopping to have tea in a castle, revamped into a high-end hotel.

It was beautiful, dark and elegant, with high ceilings and red velvet curtains, and Larkin felt very under-dressed.

"Ah, Larkin, you're fine, no worries," he told her. "I told them you're a foreigner."

She rolled her eyes, and then looked over his jeans and pullover shirt. "How are you explaining yourself?"

"I don't have to dress up. I live here."

It was leaving the castle on the way to dinner in Kildare that they came up behind an accident scene, red lights flashing, and an ambulance at the side of the road. Two cars sat crushed into each other, the metal twisted and torn, and Larkin made a noise as the ambulance pulled away, its siren screaming.

"I hope they're all right," she said, turning to look as the ambulance picked up speed. As she turned back to face the front of the car, she found herself near tears, and twisting her head back to the window, hoped Duncan hadn't noticed. Duncan drove past the scene without talking, gave her time to compose herself, and waited till she turned back to the front of the car before trying to talk to her. He spoke of the night, how glad he was for no rain, how much prettier the sunset would be without the clouds hiding it. Larkin nodded and made appropriate noises, and by the time they arrived in Kildare, she was calm.

"Larkin," Duncan said.

She looked at him over the menu.

"What's good here? I can't decide between the trout and the smoked salmon."

"Larkin, what has upset you? Was it the accident?"

Larkin carefully folded her menu and put it next to her plate.

"Yes, it was the accident. I'm sorry."

"There's no need to be sorry, Larkin, but I'm wondering what happened."

Looking down, Larkin folded her napkin into smaller and smaller triangles, the stiff fabric finally refusing to fold again. She let it go, and it expanded in her hands like a flower.

"It's a long story."

"We have all night."

"It's a sad story."

"I can hear sad stories."

She looked at him, and nodded.

"All right, but I suppose we should order first. The waiter will get crabby if we don't."

"I don't care about the waiter. Are you even hungry?"

She shook her head. "Not at all."

Duncan took his napkin from his lap. "How about this? Let's go into the bar and find a table. I'm happy with a sandwich, and we won't have to stand for the waiter staring at us if we take a long time."

"Yes. Perfect." Larkin put her napkin on the table and walked toward the bar, letting Duncan deal with the waiter. She found a small round table in a dark corner. Duncan came after her, carrying her tea and his beer.

"Good. Now, are you sure you don't want anything to eat? Not even a toasted cheese?"

"That sounds good, actually."

"Grand. I'll order and be right back."

He waited at the bar until the sandwiches were ready, had a short conversation with the bartender, and returned.

"There. And I've told the bartender not to bother with us, that we'd come to the bar if we needed anything."

He sat on his stool, arranged her plate in front of her, and waited.

Larkin bit her lips together and took a breath.

"You remember I told you my husband died."

"Of course."

"This is the story of how he died. Are you sure you want to hear it?"

"Quite sure, Larkin. If you are ready to tell it."

"This is as ready as I'm ever going to get."

17.

When she thought back on it, it had begun as a completely normal day. There was no sense of drama in the air, no portent of danger or change. The alarm sounded at 6:30 and Larkin went to the kitchen to make coffee while Pat showered.

Pat got to the kitchen dressed and ready in khakis and a short-sleeved shirt.

"I've got a breakfast meeting, so I'll just do coffee," he said.

Larkin reached out and fixed his collar on his way by.

"What?" Pat asked her.

"Your collar was twisted. Good thing you have me, or you'd have gone around all day with a twisted collar and people would have pointed at you and whispered, 'Oh my goodness, did you see that otherwise very handsome man with the horribly twisted collar? We couldn't possibly buy expensive construction hardware from him!'"

"You're right, Larkin. You probably saved my business today. Imagine what else might have happened. I mean, other drivers could lose control of their cars while looking over at my collar. Trains would stop in the middle of town. Planes might even land right on Northwest Highway, everyone pointing at my collar. So really, you've saved Western civilization as we know it by your selfless act."

"And what do I get for it? No such thing as a free civilization."

Pat reached down and kissed her lightly.

"Enough?"

"For the saving of civilization? I don't think so."

He bent down, reached his hand behind her head, and ran his fingers up into her hair. He brought his mouth to hers, and kissed her again. When he pulled away, he looked in her eyes and smiled.

"I am grateful you saved civilization, Larkin."

She smiled back, and wished his meeting were not quite so early or important.

"My pleasure."

Pat moved to the counter and got coffee.

"What time do you want dinner?" she asked him.

"I should be home by seven at the latest."

"So dinner at 7:05? You'll be crazy hungry by then."

After Pat left for his meeting, Larkin spent an hour straightening the house, threw in a load of laundry, and showered. She drove to work and got to the clinic twenty minutes before her first group began.

She looked over the files of the women in her first group. They were battered women in various stages of transition - some living in shelters, some with family, and two still living with the men bruising them at regular intervals. They were coming together as a group, and Larkin was pleased with their progress.

She moved to the group room, set the chairs as she liked, and started coffee. She turned on instrumental music, sat in a chair and waited.

The women straggled in, talking softly at first, the decibel level rising as more arrived. Larkin got them seated, turned off the music, and began the session. They always started by going around the circle, individually talking about what had happened since the group met the week before.

Between the second and third woman, there was a knock and the door to the room opened. Larkin turned in surprise. There were to be no interruptions to the group outside of an emergency. The receptionist motioned to Larkin, and looking past her, Larkin saw Sukki standing by the door of her office.

Larkin stood, staring. She excused herself, walked to the door, and closed it firmly behind her. She walked to Sukki, her thoughts racing. Which child? Did James break an arm wrestling? Did Emmy fall off a trampoline? Was it Errol; oh no, was it Errol hurt or broken or stolen by his father?

Larkin stood in front of Sukki waiting to be told, her mind racing to what she could do, where she could drive, what phone calls she could make - anything, she would do anything.

Sukki's face was tight. She reached out, took Larkin's upper arms, and held them.

"There's been an accident. We need to go to the hospital. The police are going to take us right now. Where is your purse?"

Larkin stared at her, swallowed. "Which one?"

"Which what? Where's your purse?"

"Which child? Is it Errol?"

Sukki shook her head.

"Larkin, it's not the kids. It's Pat."

Larkin's eyes opened wide.

"Pat."

"Yes, he had a flat tire on the way to work and while he was fixing it, a car full of kids came up over the hill and hit him. It is very serious, and we need to go to the hospital now."

Larkin turned to the receptionist. She made a motion toward the door where her group sat waiting for her return. The receptionist nodded, her eyes wet.

"I'll take care of it. Sandy can sit in. Go!"

Sukki took Larkin's arm, found her purse, and led her out the door toward the squad car. Two officers waited for them in the car, parked in the handicapped spaces in front of the clinic.

Sukki and Larkin each opened a back door and got in. Larkin turned to her.

"How did you find out?"

"When the police came to get you, you weren't home so they knocked on my door to see if I might know where you were. I came with them to get you, and let Mr. Carney know what was happening in case anyone else came looking for you." She rubbed Larkin's hand, unresponsive and cold.

"Is it bad? Like, really bad?" Larkin looked at Sukki, her eyebrows together. Somehow, she couldn't imagine it being serious. How could something change so much in two hours?

Sukki's hand stopped moving. She squeezed Larkin's and she looked in her eyes as directly as she could on the narrow seat.

"Larkin, they say it is very, very bad." She paused. "The police don't come looking for you unless it is really serious."

Larkin stared at Sukki.

"No."

"It's not over, Larkin, he's still alive now, he's in surgery, they took him in right from emergency, but it's drastic and his injuries are substantial."

Larkin closed her eyes and tears coursed down her face to her chin.

"The doctors are doing everything they can, but I talked to the ER nurse on the phone, and she said his chest wound is very bad and what they're most concerned about."

Larkin closed her mouth and kept it closed to keep herself from vomiting. She breathed through her nose, leaning with the turns of the car, until they reached the hospital. The squad came to a stop, the officers hopping out to help her from the car as she opened the door. Their faces held sympathy and they said something to her that she didn't catch as she thanked them, and ran for the doors to the ER.

They went to the first available woman behind a desk, who was checking in a couple with a baby wrapped in a yellow towel.

Sukki interrupted. "Excuse me. We're looking for Pat May. He was brought in and we think he's in surgery now. Who can we talk to for information?"

The woman looked up, irritated.

"Try surgery waiting." She pointed. "Take that hallway to the right and see the woman at the desk."

Larkin was turning before she finished, leaving Sukki to thank her, to apologize to the couple for the intrusion. She walked fast, and when Sukki caught up to her, she took her arm. They hurried, ending up at a desk manned by a volunteer with a name tag.

Sukki got her attention away from the TV in the corner of the room.

"Excuse me, Margaret, we're looking for someone who can tell us something about Pat May?"

She smiled at them and touched her hair, a whipped mass of white curls. She looked at a computer screen and shook her head.

"I have no record of a Pat May. Was it outpatient surgery, perhaps? That would be down the main hallway to the north end of the building."

"No, it wasn't outpatient surgery. It was emergency surgery. He was in an accident." Sukki's voice was getting steely. Larkin laid a hand on her wrist and spoke.

"It's my husband; he was taken into surgery from ER. Who would have information on that?"

"Oh, emergency. That's a different screen." She tapped at the keyboard. "Here he is, he went in at 9:30, and as far as I know, he's still in there. As soon as he's finished, a doctor will come out and talk to you. If you like, I can call and find out how long they think it might be."

"We would appreciate that." Larkin kept hold of Sukki's wrist.

The woman reached for the phone, fumbling with a card listing the different departments of the hospital. She found a number and punched it in, asked questions, listened, and hung up. She reached her old hand over to pat Larkin's. Her voice lowered.

"They say he's still in surgery and probably will be for a couple more hours yet. If you like, you could go for coffee in the snack shop. I would come get you if there was anything to hear." Her mouth closed, her pink lips mashed together. "I'm so sorry for your trouble."

Larkin slid her hand out from under Margaret's.

"Thank you. We'll just stay here. We'll be," she looked around and pointed to a row of empty chairs facing away from the TV, "right there if anyone calls."

Larkin and Sukki went to the blue chairs and sat facing the desk. Once there, Larkin turned to her.

"Okay, tell me again what you know."

Sukki started. "It happened on Pat's way to work, although it was later than he'd normally be going."

"He had a breakfast meeting with a vendor."

"That makes sense. He got a flat, they think, from glass at the corner of Colfax and Quentin. There had been an accident and there was still some glass on the road. He pulled over to change the flat and got out the jack. He got the old tire off and was leaned over the trunk getting the spare when a car full of kids ditching school came up over the hill on Route 14. They were weaving back and forth across the road, and didn't see him until they were right on top of him. Pat turned at the noise, and the driver tried to miss him, but hit him as he was holding the tire up to his chest. Then the other car veered off the road into a tree. When they found them, the kids were sprawled out all over the place with cuts on their heads from hitting the windshield and smashing into each other, and Pat was barely breathing, lying on the tire with a huge bruise on his chest and his legs broken."

"Were the kids drinking?"

"No, they were just idiots."

"How are they?"

"They'll be fine. A few of them got stitches, the police said, but they've all been released to their parents. They're in huge trouble, but what's that?"

Larkin looked out of the window to the day. It was still sunny, still warm. It was still the day she woke up to this morning. She looked back to Sukki.

"Should I call Pat's dad? Or my parents?"

Sukki considered it and shook her head.

"Why not wait till he's out of surgery? You'll have more information then, and can answer more questions."

"OK. I meant to ask you in the car, how did you get the ER nurse to talk to you? I'm surprised they would give you any information."

Sukki's eyes wandered over Larkin's head.

"I said I was you."

"Ah. Well, I'm glad you did. Just imagine having to count on Margaret," she lifted her head in the receptionist's direction, "for information."

Larkin looked around the room. There were people sitting around, in singles or pairs. Some had come prepared, reading books brought from home, having snacks from Ziploc bags and bottled water. Others read the dog-eared magazines common to all public waiting areas. The rest watched TV, the light flickering over glazed eyes.

Sukki fidgeted.

"What now?"

Larkin looked at her. Waiting was not Sukki's forte.

"I'll stay here. Why don't you get coffee or something? Or, see if there's more information. I would really like to know everything."

Sukki rose quickly.

"I'll be back."

As Larkin tried to calm herself, she knew that this day would forever change her. No matter what happened, whether Pat lived or - her mind shied away from the word - died, her life would be different in ways she couldn't even imagine.

The phone on the desk rang, and everyone in the room turned toward the sound. Margaret called out a name, and a woman gathered her belongings and went to receive instructions. The rest of the room let out their breath.

Larkin played with the strap of her purse, hooking it, unhooking it, hooking it. She laid her purse to the side and clasped her hands in her lap.

When legs appeared in front of her she looked up. Sukki was standing there with a man in a blue uniform. When Larkin looked into his face, he gave her a sympathetic smile and said how sorry he was.

"Thank you." Larkin looked at Sukki with question.

"This is Dave Wericki, Larkin. He's an old friend of mine, and a paramedic in town. He was there this morning with Pat."

Larkin motioned to the seat next to her.

"Please."

Dave sat on the edge of the chair.

"I can only stay a minute, but Sukki wanted me to tell you about the accident scene. I don't know if it will help you, but I'll tell you what I can, if you want."

Larkin nodded, and swallowed. The phone rang and she turned, Margaret calling out a name. A couple made their way to the desk, then disappeared down a hallway.

He started. "The call came in a little before nine. Somebody on a cell phone witnessed the accident, and reported it. When I got there in the ambulance, the police were already on the scene. We were just thirty seconds or so behind them, so it couldn't have been five minutes from the time it actually happened. We saw all the people lying around, and ordered more ambulances." He stopped. "Are you all right with this?"

Larkin nodded.

"Well, we did triage - that's finding out who's hurt and how much - and it was evident right away that your husband's injuries were the most severe. By then there were seven firemen there, and a bunch of police. Some of the firemen were checking the vehicles for safety issues - leaking gas or the brake off - and the rest of us were seeing to the people. The other ambulances arrived, and the kids were sitting in those, getting bandaged for the ride to the hospital. They'll have a lot of stitches between them, and a couple of concussions, but not much more.

Then, we gathered around the paramedics that were seeing to your husband, and all together, so we didn't aggravate his injuries, turned him over onto a backboard. He was unresponsive at that point."

"He didn't talk at all?"

"No, ma'am. He wasn't conscious. His breathing wasn't great, and his pulse was thready. We got him into the ambulance, and started to cut his clothes off. We were assessing things, getting more information. We took his blood pressure..."

Larkin interrupted. "How was it?"

"It was very low, 50 over 0. We hung two bags of ringers..."

"Ringers?"

"An IV fluid to help stabilize the body. When the guy cutting his clothes got to his shirt, he said to me, 'Look at this.' It was a bruise from the tire, I imagine, since we found him lying next to it. He must have been holding it when he was hit. His legs had compound fractures as well, and his face got all scraped up when he went down, but it was the bruise we were most concerned about. It spread over most his chest and abdominal region. We were guessing pneumothorax with some broken ribs, so we looked for a tracheal shift and muffled heart tones."

Dave was looking at Larkin when he spoke. She nodded and made sounds, never looking away.

"We hooked him up to a cardiac monitor, started the IV, and got on the phone to the hospital."

"What happened at the hospital?"

"We rolled him into ER, and the four of us transferred him to the ER cot. We gave our reports to the team there, and the doc was calling orders to the different departments, for respiratory therapy, for blood work, and several x-rays. They had it under control when we left. I was here for another call, and found Sukki trying to badger the ER receptionist for information." He smiled at Sukki. "I recognized the name, and here we are." He shrugged. "That's really all I know."

Larkin nodded again and shook his hand. He stood, hesitating.

"It's not procedure to tell you as much as I have, but Sukki said it would help you." He nodded at her. "I hope he's all right."

"Thank you so much for what you did for him this morning, and your time now."

Dave left and Sukki sat in the chair next to Larkin.

"Leave it to you," Larkin said. "I'm surprised you didn't run into the doctor at the coffee shop."

"The coffee shop! I forgot about the coffee. I'll get it now."

The phone rang on the desk. Larkin felt a tingling in her fingers.

"Wait."

Margaret waved to Larkin. She stood, got her balance, and walked to the desk.

"It's the doctor," Margaret said.

"Mrs. May? This is Dr. Hensfield. Your husband is out of surgery. He'll go into intensive care from recovery. I'll meet you in the Intensive Care waiting room in about 15 minutes to discuss your husband's injuries. All right?"

"All right."

The doctor hung up. Larkin handed the phone back toward Margaret, but let it go before it reached her. It clattered to the desk, all of them fumbling for it. The people in the waiting room looked up, then turned back to their books.

"I'm sorry," Larkin said to Margaret.

Sukki searched Larkin's face.

"What?"

"He's alive. The doctor didn't say much, but he said he would be transferred to Intensive Care, so that means he's alive!"

Sukki covered her mouth and reached for Larkin. They hugged, smiling, then turned to Margaret, and got directions to Intensive Care.

The Intensive Care waiting was heavy with anxiety. People there sat smaller, shrunken with worry or dread, their eyes blank. It was a room of pain.

There was a middle-aged couple, holding hands. Both of their faces were blotched and pale. The woman held a handful of wadded-up Kleenex and she worked it in her hand, squeezing it like a rubber ball. Her husband gave off involuntary shivers that transferred to her through his touch. A child, Larkin wondered, or a parent?

A woman sat alone, clutching rosary beads in her lap and staring blankly toward the far wall. Her eyes were huge and rimmed in red. She had the look of a person who hadn't had a good night's sleep in months.

There was a man, hunched over his knees. A woman sat next to him, patting his shoulder, whispering.

It was probably his mother sitting with him, Larkin thought. They had the same high forehead and the wave to their black hair.

A teenager sat alone, glued to the small TV attached high on a wall. The sound was off, and she used the remote to change channels constantly, never more than a second or two on each.

There was a small table with a telephone. A chair sat on each side, both empty.

Larkin's attention turned toward a man standing in the doorway. He was dressed in green scrubs covered by a white lab coat. Brown moccasins stuck out from under his scrub pants.

"Mrs. May?" He looked to Larkin and Sukki, from one to the other.

Larkin paused, then rose quickly.

"Yes."

Sukki rose as well, both walking toward the door to stand in the hallway. Larkin faced the doctor, and waited.

He put out his hand. "I'm Dr. Hensfield."

She reached forward and shook his hand firmly.

"I was the thoracic specialist on call when your husband was brought in this morning."

Larkin nodded.

"Would you come with me? There is a private room where we can talk."

He led them to a room around the corner. It had a small round table and several chairs. He sat across from them and crossed his legs.

"As you have heard, your husband's injuries were extensive. He had several broken ribs on his left side, and his spleen was literally in pieces. The ribs caused some bleeding in his chest cavity, and the ER doctor put in a chest tube to drain that blood. He had a hemothorax as well, and a concussion, with some peripheral bruising around his head. His blood pressure was very low when he came in, but we've been able to raise it. He received six units of blood in surgery. He has compound fractures of the long bones in both legs."

Sukki put a hand on Larkin's back. Larkin crossed her arms over her chest, grasping near her shoulders with each hand.

"But he is alive." Larkin spoke firmly.

"He is." Dr. Hensfield shook his head. "However, it was difficult surgery, intricate and touchy. He came out of it well, but he's not out of danger. They haven't set his legs yet, but will as soon as the orthopedic specialist is confident he's stable."

"I would like to see him."

"Please be prepared. He's hooked up to a respirator. The surgery has him bandaged up to his chest, and there is a tent over his legs until they're set. His face is quite scratched up from the tree falling on him, and his color is not good. He is very swollen and hooked up to several monitors."

"I want to see him."

"I wasn't trying to talk you out of it, Mrs. May. I'll go with you in case you have any questions." He turned to Sukki. "Are you family? I'm sorry, but only family is allowed."

"She's my sister." Larkin said firmly.

"I'm her sister." Sukki nodded.

The doctor looked from one to the other, from Larkin's tall frame to Sukki's short one, and from Sukki's light eyes to Larkin's dark. He smiled briefly.

"Of course."

The Intensive Care unit was round, with the nurses in the middle watching the screens that measured the vital signs of every patient. The rooms where the patients lay were fronted in glass.

They followed the doctor to the room. Because of the tent covering his legs, Larkin could see nothing of Pat until fully in the room. Dr. Hensfield led her to one side of the bed, Sukki staying on the other.

As she came around the obstruction of the tent, Larkin took a deep breath. She saw a bit of his hair first, matted and sweaty, and then his face, the tube coming from his mouth and the left side swollen and scratched. His eyes were closed, dirt caked under the bottom lashes, and a new bruise was forming on his right cheek.

Her eyes moved down. Part of his chest was covered in gauze, but the bruise the paramedic described was evident above the bandage. She watched his chest for his breath and saw it move slowly up and down. The tent covered him from his pelvic bones down, but Larkin could see where the bruise stopped, the discoloration ending below his navel.

She was glad she couldn't see his legs.

It looked as if his arms were the only things not damaged. They lay at his sides, inert but recognizable. She walked closer to the bed and touched his hand lightly. She smoothed the hair on his wrist, brushing it the way it was supposed to lie, smoothing it toward the inside of his arm, toward his pulse.

Sukki came around next to her and put an arm around her waist. Larkin turned to the doctor.

"Doctor. Are chances good he'll be all right?"

The doctor thought a moment, choosing his words carefully.

"His chances are good, but the extent of his injuries will necessitate weeks, maybe months, of care. From the hospital, he would probably go to a rehabilitation program. Between the recovery of his internal injuries and the compound fractures of his legs, complete recovery is a very long way off."

"But it is a good possibility that he will completely recover?"

"It is a possibility, yes. There will be several hurdles to get over before we speak in those terms, however. He is not yet breathing on his own. We will be watching him closely over the next 12 hours. His spleen is not functioning at all at this point and that will cause grave difficulties if it doesn't kick in. Pneumonia is a danger as well."

"When do you think he will be out of danger of dying?"

"At least 48 hours, depending on what happens in the areas I've mentioned. He'll be in Intensive Care for at least that long, perhaps longer if things don't go well. Again, it's very difficult to say. I can't guarantee anything."

Larkin touched him and felt the warmth of his skin, the silkiness of the hair under her fingers. She clasped him just below his elbow.

"So, after all this, he still might die." Her voice was steady, but tears ran silently down her face, dropping from her chin as if she didn't know they were falling. Sukki reached to the bedside table, pulled two Kleenex from the box, and handed them to her.

"It is still possible, Mrs. May. His injuries are very extensive. He is strong and seems otherwise healthy. That will help."

Larkin turned back to Pat. "What can I do for him?"

"It's quite possible that he can hear you. Talk to him."

"What else? Should we give blood?"

"Yes, give blood. Even if your type isn't the same, it will go under his name." He turned to Sukki. "They probably won't take yours. I can't imagine you weigh 110."

Sukki smiled. "Close enough, and with a roll of quarters in my pocket, it will work."

"Mrs. May, if you have any questions, please have the nurses page me. I'll be here all day. If I can't get back to you right away, you'll know I'm in surgery, but I will answer as soon as I possibly can." He held his hand out to shake Larkin's, then nodded to Sukki and left the room.

Larkin turned back to Pat, reached over, and laid the flat of her hand on his forehead, feeling him for heat. She looked closely at the scratches covering the right half of his face and checked for dirt. She took the Kleenex in her hand and dabbed it to a scratch still seeping. She talked to him.

She told him what had happened, in case he was confused about where he was, told him she'd be right there, and that she loved him. She told him about his injuries. She said he looked a bit beaten up, but not as bad as he did after camping trips. She told him again that she loved him. Throughout her discourse, tears ran down her face, but her voice was even.

"Larkin?"

Larkin turned to Sukki.

"It's probably time to call the parents. Do you want me to do it?"

Larkin bit her bottom lip. Tempting.

"No, I better do it. Will you stay here?"

"Of course."

Larkin leaned forward to kiss Pat's forehead, listening to the respirator hiss. She could smell the plastic of the tubing going down his throat and the tape holding it to his mouth. She felt a gag coming on, took a breath to combat it, and stayed at his head until it was over. She straightened and got her purse.

"I'll be back."

Opening the door, she walked to the nurse's station. She stood there, waiting for one of the nurses to finish writing. The blond in front of her looked up and rose to her feet.

"Mrs. May? I'm Diana. I'll be taking care of Mr. May today."

"Thank you. I have a couple of questions. First, do you have regulations about how long I can stay with my husband?"

Diana shook her head. "No, you can stay as long as you like. Actually, the chair in there opens up completely, so you can sleep here if you care to. Family is allowed at any time."

"Great. How much information can I get about his condition? I have some medical background, so I'd like as much as I can get."

"We're monitoring his every move, so just ask if you have any questions about what's happening with his breathing or blood pressure. Other than that, it will be between you and the doctor. If you need anything, please let me know. We have drinks and snacks, nothing too exciting, but something if you get hungry."

Larkin nodded. "Thank you. I have some calls to make and then I'll be back."

Larkin walked out to the waiting room. It was empty. She would have found a different place had it still been crowded, but now sat in one of the chairs and pulled out her cell phone. She called Pat's father in Wyoming, alone since his wife's death several years ago. She explained what was happening. His voice lowered, but stayed strong.

"Well, honey, do you think I should get on a plane? Are they saying he might not make it?"

"Vern, they're not saying anything definite. The surgery went well, but he is still in danger."

"Then I'm coming."

"Let me know what time and I can send someone to get you from the airport."

"No, I'll get myself there. You don't need another thing to think about. What hospital is he in? I'll come straight from the airport to the hospital, then go to your place after."

"Ok. I'll be here."

"Have you called your parents yet?"

"They're next."

"Now, darlin', brace yourself. No offense to your mother, but she can get a bit dramatic and I imagine it's the last thing you need. How are you? Holding up?"

"I'm trying, Vern."

"I'll see you later on today, depending on when I get a flight."

"OK. Just come straight to Intensive Care. Family can come and go anytime."

"All right. I'll see you later. Keep your chin up."

Larkin smiled as she hung up. One of the reasons she'd been so sure about marrying Pat was his father.

Then she sighed, closed her eyes for a moment, and dialed her mother.

18.

On the way back to Pat's room, Larkin looked in the rooms she passed. There were several other patients: an older man, a younger woman, a child. A family gathered around the bed of a grandparent, Larkin couldn't tell what sex, and in one room, two men sat -- one on each side of a woman probably their mother, playing cards on the blanket.

Larkin opened the door to the Pat's room. Sukki turned from the bed, held up a finger, and finished telling a joke. When the punch line had been delivered, Larkin joined her at the bed.

"Pat loves my jokes."

"No, Pat stands for your jokes. If he can hear us, he's trying to make a face."

"Did you make your calls?"

"Yes. I called Vern, who's probably getting on a plane about now, if he can, and then I called my parents, and then work."

"How did Bunny react?"

"I don't know. I asked to speak to my father and told him. I didn't think I could quite take her histrionics at the moment. They'll probably come by within a couple of hours."

"What did you tell them at work?"

"I told them that I would need a leave of absence."

"For how long?"

"I didn't say. It depends on what care he needs. I can do most of it at home, I think. I have a medical background; I can do most things a visiting nurse would do."

"Medical background? What kind?"

"I was a nurse's aide all through high school. I was actually in nursing school when I changed my major to psychology, but I bet I can still change dressings and empty bedpans."

"I'll keep that in mind."

"For what?"

"For when I'm old and gray."

"Don't hold your breath." She looked at Pat. "Oh, Sukki. My poor man. He is going to hate this. He detests having a cold, much less what he's going to have to go through in the next few months."

"He'll be fine. He'll be mad to start with, and then he'll buckle down and do whatever it takes. You know he will. It's the kind of guy he is."

Larkin bent over Pat's chest. She watched it rise, took a breath with him, and squeezed his hand.

Larkin's parents arrived, Bunny sweeping into the room. After seeing the extent of Pat's injuries, she had to be led from the unit, weeping, Larkin and Sukki trading looks as she disappeared.

Hours later, Vern came, suitcase in hand. He reached out to hold Larkin for a moment, then turned to his only child lying naked and helpless, hooked up to machines and beeping with every forced breath.

Larkin pulled a chair to the side of the bed for him. She stood behind him, her hands on his shoulders. She heard his breath catch and felt him try to control himself, his shoulders clenched. He put his hand on Pat's arm, as she had done. His big fingers circled Pat's wrist, the fingertips lying on the vein underneath, beating a pulse.

Sukki excused herself and Larkin pulled another chair next to Vern's and sat close. She explained what she knew about Pat's condition, and Vern nodded, his face in a shape she hadn't seen since Pat's mother's funeral. Tears leaked out the corners of his eyes, getting lost in the wrinkles running down his cheeks. He stayed until the doctor came to check on Pat and asked good questions. After he left, he told Larkin you could see on their faces what they thought. He said he knew when his Daisy was dying by the doctor's faces. They got to looking far away when they were about to lose a patient, he told her, when they knew one was going.

He didn't see that on this doctor, he said, so he thought he'd go to the house and unpack. Sukki reappeared and offered to take Vern home. Someone from work had dropped off Larkin's car.

"Do you want something to eat before we go?"

Larkin shook her head. "If I get hungry, the nurse said she's got stuff here."

"Like what?"

"I don't know. Probably those little containers full of applesauce or pudding or ice cream. Hospital snacks."

Sukki made a face. "I'll make you a sandwich or something and bring it when we come back."

Larkin stopped her on her way out. She held Sukki's hands, her eyes welling.

"I can't ever thank you. I can't imagine how this would have been..."

Sukki smiled, and put one hand on Larkin's face.

"It's what a sister does."

19.

Hours passed, a day, then two. People came and went, family coming into Pat's room and the rest staying in the waiting room, comforting each other and waiting for news. Larkin left Pat only to go to the bathroom.

At noon on the second day, his eyes opened. Larkin leaned over, stroking his forehead, saying his name. He blinked hard, opened them again, trying to find her in his rising consciousness. Larkin turned to Sukki.

"Can you get the nurse?"

Diana came quickly, got out a tiny flashlight and flicked it in Pat's eyes, then smiled at Larkin.

"About time. All right, I'll call the doctor. Sit tight."

Larkin smiled back then leaned over to kiss Pat's forehead.

"Quite the nap you had. Do you remember anything?"

Pat shook his head slightly and grimaced.

"Don't move anything. Who knows what hurts on you, about everything's broken. I'll tell you, but before that, have I mentioned lately that I love you? I've been saying it for a couple of days, but somehow I don't think you've heard it. Well, hear it now. I love you, husband, and I've missed you terribly these last 48 hours."

She told him of the accident, how long he'd been here, and who had come. His eyes widened at mention of his father, and Larkin sent Sukki to get him. She put her hand in his, squeezing it. He gave a little pressure back and her face collapsed. She bent down to his neck, buried her face in the pillow that sat under him, and wept. All the while, the pressure on her hand continued, tiny squeezes; comfort from her husband just returned from a world she couldn't reach.

She sat up and wiped her face.

"Oh, boy, am I glad you're back. How do you feel?"

His eyebrows raised, his eyes roaming the room.

"You're lucky you're here. It was a bit touch-and-go for a while." She smiled. He tried to smile back, the tape on his mouth moving.

The door opened. Vern walked to the bed and stood over his son.

"Look at you," he whispered. He reached out his hand, Larkin guiding it to Pat's, Pat giving it a minute squeeze.

"Oh," Vern breathed, "Son, I've been waiting for that."

Over the next hours, the room quietly buzzed with visitors. Pat slept off and on, waking always to Larkin and his father plus one or two more. Doctors came and went, checking numbers, listening to his chest and mumbling to each other.

"We're going to keep him here one more day. There's a sound in there we're not happy about."

At five in the afternoon, Larkin was eating applesauce with one eye on Pat, who had been sleeping off and on. Vern sat in a chair, his head leaning against the far wall, dozing. Pat's eyes opened and widened, then turned to Larkin. Larkin rose quickly and went to the bed.

"What is it, honey? Are you uncomfortable?"

He looked up at her and stretched his fingers out on the sheet. She laced hers through his, her eyebrows knitting, and pushed the nurse's button attached to the bed.

"What is it, Pat? Are you feeling pain?"

Vern awoke and rose.

The P.M. nurse came in the room. Larkin spoke to her, never taking her eyes off Pat.

"I don't know what he's trying to tell me, but I think something's wrong."

The nurse leaned over Pat and checked his eyes. She asked him questions, and he answered by raising his eyebrows. She looked back to Larkin.

"I'll page the doctor. I don't know what it is either, but something's changed."

Vern had come to the other side of the bed, and rested his hand on Pat's forearm. Pat's eyes turned to his father for a long look, then blinked hard and turned back to Larkin. His eyes began to close, and he forced them open. He started to drop off again, but Larkin said his name and he came back. His eyes opened once more, fully, looking straight at his wife, and then slowly closed. For reasons she didn't understand, Larkin started to cry.

"Pat? Honey, wake up."

At her words, buzzers went off at the nurse's station. Larkin turned her head and looked out to see the nurses heading for them, for Pat, rolling equipment, opening the door. She bent down, whispered in his ear, and felt a hand gently moving her aside.

"Mrs. May, would you wait outside, please? Mr. May?"

The door closed behind them, and the curtain was drawn. Dr. Hensfield rushed in; more people moved by her, more equipment came. There was noise and talking, the doctor's voice constant in the midst of it all.

In twenty minutes they came out to tell her he was gone, it was over, they did what they could, but he didn't respond. Patrick Wilson May had died.

It was most likely a fatty embolus, the doctor said, a result of the fractures in his legs. Larkin looked out the window and closed her eyes. It's Thursday, she thought, a sunny day in late spring. She opened them, shook her head, and tried to breath. It's Thursday, a beautiful June day, and my husband is dead.

Sukki had gone home before them. When they got out of the car in front of the townhomes, the neighbors were out, standing in groups. As Larkin and Vern moved up the stairs, Sukki started toward them. The rest of the neighbors followed. Sukki moved faster, running, and when the group got to Larkin and Vern, they surrounded them; laying hands on their arms and backs, and saying words no one remembered later, a jumble of attempted comfort. Sukki held out her arms to Larkin, crying, and said her name. Larkin raised her face, her eyes empty and dry, and stumbled. Sukki caught her and eased her to her knees. The neighbors bent down around her, shielding her, and there on the sidewalk Larkin put her face in her hands and her forehead to her knees and wept as a person does who has lost that which made life grand.

20.

After the night in Kildare, Larkin felt lighter. She hadn't told the story of Pat's death in that detail to anyone, and doing it now seemed right. Duncan responded just as she would have hoped; he listened well and never took his eyes off her face. The ride home was companionable, not awkward, and seeing him since then convinced her it had made their relationship better, not awkward.

On the Monday following the third race, she walked in the dark to the boathouse. The previous Saturday's race had been the most difficult to date, Deirdre's team trailing in at fourth. The team had rowed well, but lacked the final strength to finish hard, and had been passed by two other teams in the final fifty meters.

Deirdre was adamant.

"This is something we can fix. I know you're all busy, but we have to get more time on the machines, more miles run. And, we need another practice next week."

Polling the team, it was finally decided an early morning practice was possible on Monday.

Larkin hadn't been out at this time before, being busy serving breakfast until at least nine, but now, before 6:00, the streets carried the feeling of the night but also the promise of the coming day.

Larkin stopped for a moment and took a sip of coffee from the cup Brynna had put in her hand on the way out. The air was cool, but there was no wind yet, and no rain. The sky was cloudy and the moon already gone. It wouldn't be long before the sun came up.

She made her way to the boathouse, and got there just as Deirdre pulled up in her car.

"Good morning, Larkin. What a good day to be out on the water."

"It is, isn't it? I'm looking forward to it. I haven't rowed in the morning since college."

"Ah, it's a fine way to start the day. It will be all downhill after this."

Deirdre went off to find her cox-box and a clipboard. Larkin dropped her bag and stepped back outside to finish her coffee. Lara arrived on a bicycle, rolled it into the building, and slumped against the wall.

"This is too freaking early to be here," she said, her eyes closed. "What is the woman thinking?"

"She's thinking we need all the practice we can get." Nessa said, walking in behind her. "Especially you, lazy one. You think because you're in the bow, I don't know?"

Lara stuck her foot out as she passed, but Nessa side-stepped it and put her bag down next to Larkin's.

Kerry rushed in.

"Am I late?"

"No," Deirdre told her, coming back to the group from the office. "You're right on time. Let's get moving. We have only an hour and a half."

At the dock, Lara swore under her breath.

"What was that coming from you?" Nessa called back.

"The water is a bit frigid at this time of the morning. I don't suppose you even feel it, cold-blooded as you are."

"Of course I feel it; I'm just not prone to complain about it."

"Enough," Deirdre said. "Let's get the boat in the water. Heads, ready up."

The women pushed the boat up and over their heads and got it safely in the river, Kerry and Larkin running back for oars. Soon, they were free of the dock and alone on the river.

Larkin looked around. As they went under the bridge, she looked left and could see the very beginnings of light, not the sun yet, but threads of air that looked less dark. It was quiet; the only sound was the oars cranking as they dug in, and the *shwoosh* the boat made as it ran over the top of the water.

Deirdre's instructions matched the mood of the river, calm and subdued. There was none of the fierceness of race day, only attention to detail and finding improvement, and Larkin found it easy to work hard and still pay attention, noticing the smell in the air and the blooming of the day.

At one point, Deirdre called a "way enough." The women stopped rowing, breathing hard, and laid their paddles flat on the water to steady the boat. Deirdre had them turn slightly to the left, and there, across the flat land that made up the town barracks, the sun rose for them. The sky went from purple to dark blue to dark gold to yellow. It happened in the space of a few minutes, and the five of them sat and watched, suspended in the water, and quiet. When it was bright, Lara turned back in her seat with a sigh.

"That was worth it," she said.

The week progressed; the B&B full most days, and workouts and practices taking most nights. Only once was Duncan able to get Larkin away for dinner, the rest given over in precedence to Saturday's race. Deirdre wanted this one; she wanted the win. The team from Ballinasloe had beaten them badly the previous year, and the pit-bull tenacity that made Deirdre so good in the coxswain's seat was in full force. She was working them in details she'd documented in practices since the beginning of the season, and Larkin could feel the team coming closer, their strokes matching and steady. She was aware of the difference in her own performance and the fact that it wasn't nearly as obvious she was a novice.

Saturday dawned soggy and windy, the rain falling when Larkin awoke and still coming down at race time. Gathering in the boathouse, Deirdre's face kept any of them from mentioning the fact that wind and rain made any race more difficult.

Once in the boat practicing, the women fell into their learned rhythms, evidence of the past week's practices noticeable. When she stopped them to talk before the race, Deirdre was stern, her face hard and her words simple.

"It's no secret I want this one. I want to wipe them up, the ones that hit us so hard last year. I want open water on them, and nothing else will do." She looked down the boat. "Are you with me or not?"

The women nodded.

"Not enough," Deirdre said. "Not by far. Unless you want this as badly as I do, it won't happen. Remember last year? Not only did they beat us, they made sport of it later, not good sport, but nasty sport, calling names and maligning the team. They had no call to do that, no call to throw shite around. I won't have it. This year, they will know we've been there when it's over. I want open water. Are you with me, girls?"

This time as she scanned the boat, the team's faces matched her own.

At the start, aligning took even more time than usual, the brisk wind keeping the boats moving. Finally, they were released, "Etes vous prets? Partez!"

Deirdre took them immediately into power strokes, changing the order of her commands from previous races, but she'd warned them; she'd told them to bring absolutely all they had for this one, that she'd be taking it all and more.

OK, Larkin thought, here we go.

As the boat skated over the water through the wind and the rain, Deirdre was bent further over than usual. Larkin had concern for her back, but in the midst of the race, there was nowhere for that concern to go.

Larkin concentrated, let Deirdre's words carry her; let her body follow every direction Deirdre pointed without reservation. When Deirdre told them they were halfway through, Larkin was surprised, thinking she could go all day like this - the oar in, pulling the boat over the water, lifting it out.

With 500 meters to go, Deirdre's tone changed.

"Here's where we are. We're up on everyone but the ones we need to beat. They've got a seat on us, and it's time to move. Push it, girls, push it to win. Give me a power ten in two, one, two, now! One, pull, Nessa! Two, give me more, Larkin! Three, burn it, Lara! Four, now, Kerry, now! Five, we're making our move, six, here they are, seven, coxswain to coxswain, eight, they're staying with us, nine, pull! Ten, pull harder!"

She muscled them through another power ten, gaining two seats, the boat they were chasing surprised at their movement, and hating the words they heard Deirdre shouting at her team.

"Steady at 34, get ready, we're moving on them, we're going to walk straight up, I want open water!"

Larkin clenched her teeth, took a breath, lifted the oar, and waited the fraction for Deirdre to belt out the command.

"One! Do it now! Two, I've got their one seat! Three, jump off your legs! Four, you've got more than that! Five, they're staying with us, six, hunt them down! Seven, get it now! Eight, I want their bow ball. Nine, give me their bow ball! Ten, ten more and we're done!"

Ten more, Larkin thought. Ten.

"One, it's our chance! Two, I want open water! Three, I've got their bow ball! Four, I want open water! Five, pull with your legs! Six, do it right now! Seven, give me what you saved!"

In the time it took to hear Deirdre's words, Larkin searched her body and found an atom's more energy, a tiny particle she hadn't used, hadn't even known was there, and she willed it to her legs for the final strokes, for the final chance.

"Eight, yes! Nine, I have open water! Ten, open water, you did it!" They crossed the finish line. "And paddle."

They stopped, laid their oars on the water, and gasped, Deirdre's arms above her head, pumping her fists in the air, her face a silent yell of triumph. She brought her hands down and threw her arms out to the team.

"You did it, and you did it big!" She looked over at the team they were chasing, and gave Nessa's leg a slap, grinning. "Look at them. They don't know what's happened."

They looked at the second-place team, bent over their legs, still trying to heave air in their tired lungs. Kerry's voice floated over the water from the back of the boat.

"I'll bet they'll think again before farting with us."

Deirdre nodded to her team. "Indeed they will."

They had crossed the line in first, which made accepting their medals on the dock even sweeter. When they'd walked off the dock, Nessa stepped aside to let Deirdre pass and waited until the others had caught up to her. With quick murmured instructions to the rest of the team, they hurried up behind Deirdre and cleanly surrounded her.

"All right, then, is it going to be hard or easy?" Nessa stood directly in front of her, barring her way.

"Not today. It's raining, and the water is probably freezing." Deirdre was inching away, eyeing the boathouse. The unwritten rule stated if the coxswain made it to the boathouse after the race, she wouldn't get thrown in.

"You worked us to death out there and it's time for your reward," Nessa said.

Deirdre stopped moving. "You're right, at that. It seems the least I can do after you all rowed your hearts out. Just let me put my box down." She moved toward the boathouse, taking off her headset.

Nessa watched her for a moment, then ran up next to her.

"Nice try. You've done this before, if I remember correctly, spoken so nicely and then claimed refuge in the boathouse." She looked around and called a woman passing near them. "Lena! Here, would you hold this for Deirdre? No, not long, just long enough to get some river water in her knickers."

Nessa turned Deirdre back towards the dock, hustling her along. Larkin caught up to Lara and ventured, "Lara? About Deirdre..."

Lara smiled but kept walking. "Is it her back you're worried about, Larkin? Ah, don't be concerned. Nessa's the one's been through it all with her, she knows what to do not to hurt her."

They got to the dock, Deirdre still looking for a way out, when Nessa scooped her up in her arms, walked to the end of the dock, and hurled her in.

Larkin turned to Lara. "That was being careful?"

"It was, of course. If Nessa had put her in head first, we'd have to fish her out. This way doesn't bother her at all. Watch."

The onlookers hooted as Deirdre swam back to the dock, wiping water from her face and pushing her hair back. When she got close to the edge, Nessa and Kerry reached over, each grabbed an arm, and they hauled her out of the river, dripping and laughing.

"Good," Nessa said. "Now I can go have a beer."

"I'll buy," Deirdre told her. "If Sean will take wet money, that is."

"He'll take it any way it comes," Nessa said.

As they headed towards Sean's, Larkin called that she'd be in after the next race. Duncan's team was headed for the start, and she would watch.

"Bring him luck, then." Deirdre called back. "Make sure he sees you at the finish."

Larkin walked the path along the riverside that led from the starting line to the finish line, a worn trail muddied by the rain. She wanted to be close enough to the start to see it, and be able to walk fast enough to see the end as well. She ended up at about the halfway mark, her hand shading her eyes from the rain, the wind hurling it at her face.

She shivered. She felt the cold now, the wind biting and the rain relentless.

She heard the starter let the boats go and turned to watch. The teams came out strong, oars lashing the water. It was a clean start, so she watched them row for a minute, coming closer to where she stood, then walked further along the path until she was twenty yards from the finish line.

As the boats got closer, she checked their positions, hard to gauge from further away, and saw Duncan's team in third, gaining on second, and the team from Mullingar almost a full boat length ahead in first. It looked as if Mullingar wouldn't be giving up their lead, so the competition lay between second and third.

As they got closer, her eyes were on Duncan. She watched him strain with the oar, his back and shoulders flexing, his slide in the seat even and rhythmic. As the teams came even with her and passed, she watched his arms as they brought the oar to his sternum, his wrists, straight and lean, the tendons riding under the skin.

Duncan's boat beat the other fighting for second by a bow ball, the Athlone team giving a yell at the finish. Larkin watched as they docked the boat, lifting it over their heads with ease, the rainwater from the bottom of the boat washing over them again, and walked it into the house. She followed at a distance.

When the boat was put away, she approached Duncan. He was pulling off his wet and sweaty shirt, dropping it on the floor, toweling himself off, then reaching for a dry t-shirt from his bag.

He turned when she said his name.

"Ah, Larkin, out there in the rain, were you? Are you about freezing?"

"I started out cold but that exciting finish warmed me right up," she told him.

"A mere second. Nothing to your first." He smiled at her.

"Such a good fight. You worked hard."

"We did, at that. We could have won, but Ned, here," he nodded at their coxswain, "didn't want to take a swim."

"Deirdre wasn't too happy about it either."

"I bet not."

They left his team there and walked to Sean's, where Deirdre's team had saved them seats. They took off their coats, got a drink, and settled in, the warmth from the fireplace welcome, and happy in each other's company.

Later, on her way back from the bathroom, Larkin was aware she'd had entirely too much to drink. Her body was listing, like she had a bad foot, and she had to concentrate on getting back to her seat. She furrowed her brow and pointed herself, ending up very close to where she needed to be. She held on to the stool next to hers, shuffled over, and hoisted herself up.

It was the strangest thing. She knew, obviously, that she'd been drinking. She had felt the effects of the first couple of ciders. Then, people were buying rounds, lining glasses up on the bar and toasting the win. She'd bought a round and drank what was in front of her. She felt the changes, the slowing down of her movements, wanting to say something but not getting it out in time. The conversation swirled around her, too fast to keep up with and too complicated to track. At this point, she was sitting with her back to the bar, holding her glass, and tipping slightly, like she was listening for clues.

Duncan moved in front of her. He peered in her glassy-eyed face and smiled at her.

"Had enough, have you? Would you like to be getting home?"

Larkin nodded, putting her nearly full pint back on the bar. She reached for her jacket, and tried to put it on. Duncan took it from her, shook it out, held it behind her, and guided one arm in, then the other. She made a move for the front door, staring a straight line at it, but Duncan turned her, and led her through the pub to the back door and out by the river.

"Let's stand a minute, clear your head a bit, all right?"

She nodded, holding on to the rail, looking out over the water to the Leinster side of town. She stared at the waves, rolling and undulating, flapping up the side of the wall. She moved back from the rail, looked at Duncan with big eyes, and did a fast walk back into Sean's.

When she came out, she looked better, though pale.

"I'm sorry."

"Don't be. You wouldn't be the first to lose a night's drinking in the pub where you got it. Are you feeling better?"

"Better, but stupid. Did I make a fool of myself in there?"

"My guess is no one even knew you were fluthered. Now, how about we take a walk around; see how you do on your feet."

He stepped away and put his hand in the pocket of his coat. She reached out, put her arm through his, and hung on. The walked, their steps slow and matched, and the moon bright off the water.

They wandered the town, stopping for coffee at Bonne Bouche, and shared an order of fries as they walked Church Street. They talked of Duncan's childhood in Athlone, with the town half the size it was now, and when at Christmas, all the shopkeepers gave their good customers a Christmas box, filled with some of what they'd bought all year. Duncan told her there was always flour and butter and oats and potatoes, and in the bottom, enough individual pieces of chocolate so every member of the family could have their own.

His father, he told her, didn't like chocolate, and would split his into six pieces, one for his mother, and one for each child. His mother always got the biggest.

Larkin yawned, big enough to make Duncan laugh.

"Boring you, am I?"

"All of a sudden, I'm exhausted. What time is it, anyway?"

"It's half-two. You've a reason to be tired. Let's get you home."

They walked the silent streets to the house. When they got to the door, she turned to him.

"Duncan, thank you so much. I don't know what would have happened if you hadn't gotten me out of there. I'd probably be passed out on a back table by now."

"Which could have caused an international incident. I was only looking out for the good of Ireland."

She laughed, reached out her hand, and touched his arm.

"I really am grateful."

"It was a small thing, Larkin. Not nearly what I'd like to do for you."

She stood before him, her hand resting on his wrist. She felt it under his sweater, lean and strong, and her mind saw him rowing, his arms straining against the water, and spray casting out from the oars. She looked up at him and tried to be playful.

"Oh, really, and what is it you would like to do for me?"

Duncan saw her shiver and reached for her jacket, pulling it closed in the front, then let his hands rest lightly on her shoulders.

"Whatever you might want, Larkin. What would you like? If you could have anything, what would it be?"

"Anything I want? Let's see...I'd like no hangover tomorrow. Can you see to that?"

"Of course I can. My old mother gave me a wonderful remedy. Let me see what Brynna has in the kitchen."

They stepped into the dark house. Larkin pointed out the cupboards he might need, then ran upstairs quietly and brushed her teeth.

When she got back to the kitchen, Duncan was mixing something lethal-looking in a tall glass. When he finished, he stirred it and brought it over to the kitchen table where Larkin sat in the dark.

"There," he whispered, "now drink it down all in one shot."

"Are you kidding?" she said, "There's a quart of liquid here."

"All at once, Larkin. Down the hatch, now."

Larkin lifted the glass to her mouth and drank as much as she could in three gulps. She stopped, gasping, and stared at Duncan.

She whispered across the table at him.

"Are you trying to kill me?"

"Larkin, you must finish it all. Pretend it's cider."

"Oh, aren't you funny."

She tipped her head back again, and managed to finish what was in the glass. She made a face.

"Now I need coffee. Would you like a cup, or tea, perhaps?"

"Coffee would be lovely."

Duncan sat back and watched her move around the kitchen, starting the pot and reaching for cups above the sink. Their talking was all in whispers as Brynna and Des' room lay just beyond the kitchen shut off only by a door.

Larkin brought the coffee back to the table with milk and sugar. When she had blown the steam away and sipped, she made a sighing sound, and stretched her legs out under the table.

"Better now?"

"Much. Tomorrow morning will be the test, but I feel better already."

Duncan put down his cup. "All right, Larkin, now what else would you like? You get another wish."

"Why?"

"Why, what?"

"Why do I get wishes from you?"

Duncan looked at her, then lowered his eyes. When he raised them again, they were bright on her and as beautiful, she thought, as any she'd been privileged to see.

"Consider it a gift, Larkin. I'm sure you have a birthday sometime and I'm just as sure I've missed it, so call this your birthday present."

Larkin studied him. They had spent a lot of time together these past weeks. She liked his manner, his thoughtfulness. She was impressed with the way he performed his job and with the respect he received from the men with whom he worked. In his dealings with her, he had been beyond reproach. He had been forever sensitive to her wants and she had been pleasantly surprised at what he had been able to figure out about her. Even tonight, he had rescued her, let her be sick, walked her for hours, and was now sitting here drinking coffee at three in the morning when he had to be at work at eight.

He had never made an untoward move; never an inappropriate touch. His attitude had been, from the beginning, to have her enjoy her time in Ireland and he had gone out of his way to see to it.

This was a different side to him. At once, a different thought presented itself, and she spoke without really thinking.

"Duncan, what happened in your marriage?"

He frowned at the turn in subject.

"Where did that come from?"

"Just sitting here, I can't imagine you not being able to work things out, whatever happened. What was it that you couldn't fix? Or is it too personal?"

He shifted in his seat.

"No, it's not too personal. There was nothing to fix, Larkin. She didn't want me really, she just wanted to marry. I was very young as well, and didn't know until we were a few years into it that she had all she wanted - the children, a home. But not to be a wife. She didn't care about that part. When it became clear, I added a little apartment off the back of the house so I could be there for the kids. It would have made things very hard for them had I gotten another place; difficult for her to take care of the one we had. I was in no hurry to find someone else, and neither was she."

"How did that work out?"

"It's worked out as well as it could have, I suppose, and Nora and I are friendly, for all that. We divorced when it became legal, and I built another house a few blocks away, but for those years my children benefitted from me being there and I was able to take care of things."

"What will happen when the children are grown? Will you get the house, or will Nora?"

"She can have it, her and the kids. I've built another."

Larkin reached across the table for his hand. He looked up, surprised at her touch.

"You are an honorable man, Duncan McKenna."

Duncan moved his shoulders. "It's been for me as well, Larkin. I've wanted to be close to my children."

"You know, we're not so different here. We've both lost."

"You more, I think."

"I don't know. At least I had some closure. You still see every day what you can't have."

"But Larkin, that wouldn't be what I'd want anymore. Not for many years, now."

"What do you think you want, then, do you know?"

Duncan smiled and shook his head. "Another thing I can't have, most likely."

"Like what?"

Duncan paused.

"You, Larkin."

Larkin stopped, her hand stilled.

"Me?"

"You." He looked her in the face and got her full attention. "I love you, Larkin."

Larkin stared at him. The words came easily from him, not as if they were a new thought, but something that felt natural to him.

"Remember that first race? I knew then, watching you out there working yourself about to death. At the finish line, I wanted to lift you out of the boat and carry you off somewhere, so I could find out everything there was to know about you, every word you thought, every hair on your head."

He turned his hand up and laced his fingers with hers.

"Then, when I asked you to dinner, you told me you didn't want involvement and I thought I could be content with just being friends, just for the month you were here."

"That's what you've been."

"Because that's what you wanted."

"And the wishes?"

"You leave in a week. I want you to have whatever I can give before you go away."

Larkin stared at him.

"You love me?"

"I do, yes."

"That's what the wishes are about? Because you love me?"

"Yes. For you, and to give me something to hold onto after you leave."

Larkin nodded. She knew exactly what he meant.

She wished she could tell him she loved him back.

"Duncan. If I were in a position to love anyone, I would be honored to love you, but I'm not. Can you understand that? It's just been recently that I can go through days not thinking of Pat with every breath. I'm much better but I'm still not ready to love anyone, even you."

"I know, and it's all right. It doesn't stop me from loving you."

"It's not fair."

"Remember when I said I was in no hurry to find someone? Now that I've found you, I'm still in no hurry. And, if something changes, it would certainly be worth the wait."

The feelings that had built up over the weeks welled in Larkin. She could see them separately, she could categorize them - the respect she felt for this man, the growing feelings she'd called "friendship," the way she'd pushed the thought of going home to the back of her mind this past week. She'd found herself watching him walk, admiring how he moved. She touched him in passing, would brush his hand when she could. During the past couple of weeks, the days she hadn't see him held little shine.

Thinking back to watching him row, she thought he quite definitely stirred her pots.

Larkin wasn't ready to call it love but she certainly felt more than she had put a name to.

She knew, too, what her wish was, and that it would be difficult. She leaned forward across the table, still holding his hands.

"Duncan, I have a wish."

"Anything, Larkin."

"Can I be selfish?"

"It won't be."

"Then I know what I want. I want you to rub my back, to touch me like you've known me forever. Do you know what I mean? Not sexually, I don't want that, but I would just love your hands on me."

Duncan smiled, his eyes gentle.

"Larkin, I would love to touch you in any way you'd like."

"Duncan, I'm serious about not wanting sex. I'm not leading you on."

"I didn't think you were. I promise you I won't take advantage."

"Are you sure, Duncan? It would be bad for us if you tried."

"You can trust me, Larkin."

She looked at him, her eyes serious, then nodded.

"I believe you."

Duncan stood. "Let's go up."

They moved to the stairs, her hand trailing back to his, softly treading up toward the top of the house. He stopped outside her room, and turned to her.

"Do you want to change?"

Larkin thought, nodded.

"All right. Let me know when you're ready for me to come in."

Larkin went in and closed the door behind her. She dug to find a long night-shirt and quickly changed into it. She walked back to the door and opened it.

Duncan came in and closed the door after him. Turning to her, he saw her shiver, and reached out to take her hand.

"Are you cold?"

"I don't know. I don't seem to have any control over this, no matter what it is."

"Come here for a minute."

He opened his arms to her. She hesitated, then walked into them, reaching up to put her arms around his neck and feeling his circle her, holding her up.

Larkin laid her head in the nape of his neck, feeling the soft of his sweater on her cheek, and was aware how careful he'd made his stance; not to make the embrace too personal for her, not to intrude. She took a deep breath of him. He smelled of turf, work, and a scent particular only to him. He held her for a time, rocking, until her shivering died away and she stepped back.

"Better?"

"Yes."

She stood in the middle of the room, unsure. He smiled at her.

"Lie down, Larkin."

She turned, went to the bed, and lay on her stomach with her face toward Duncan. He skimmed off his sweater but left on his t-shirt and squatted down next to her. He smoothed the hair from her face and got level with her eyes.

"This is your wish, Larkin, so if anything isn't the way you want it, let me know and I'll stop. All right?"

She nodded into the blanket and took a deep breath.

"Move over a bit."

She scooted over to the middle of the bed. Duncan stretched himself out next to her, not touching, but close. She watched the path his eyes took as he reached a hand to her face, smoothing her cheek, touching her nose, brushing her hair behind her ears.

He whispered to her while his hand moved.

"You fascinate me, Larkin, everything about you intrigues me."

His hand dipped into her hair, lifting it from her neck, and running it through his fingers.

"Talking to you is like opening a present, there's so much in there, so much I want to know."

He moved his hand to her back. She stiffened for a quick second and he lifted it.

"Larkin?"

"It's ok."

His hand opened on her and stilled, letting her get used to him as if she were a skittish kitten. He moved it in small circles at her shoulders, getting wider as he moved down her spine. She made a sound, more breath than voice. He got up on his knees next to her.

He started at her right shoulder, kneading the sore muscles in the side of her neck and up the back to her hair, and working down to each arm to each finger, then back up and over to the left side, his hands working a rhythm. He moved down the middle of her back, one hand on each side of her spine, using his thumbs to dig into the muscles there. He splayed his hands over her back, rubbing where he found soft tissue, and brushing lightly over bone. He got to her waist and worked his way back up. When he got back to her shoulders, he bent toward her ear to whisper.

"Ah, look at you, Larkin, you're beautiful. The moon is shining on you here," he touched the middle of her back, "and here," he ran a hand over her hair, "and it's making you shine, like you're a part of it, part of the sky."

He moved himself over to the other side of her, and she turned her head so she could see some part of him, his leg bent at the knee or the sight of his hand on her arm. She reached out and put her hand near him.

"It got to where I almost couldn't work. I was making mistakes and not paying attention to what the lads were telling me, and they laughed at me, wanted to know where my head was, and all I could see in my head was you, walking home from the store or in the boat with the rain on your hair. Everywhere I went, there you were, until I couldn't ignore any more what I was feeling for you, until I knew for certain I loved you."

Larkin moved under his hands, tiny motions.

"I knew you would leave, knew it would be harder for me than before you came, having you so far away, but I let myself love you anyway, you were already so deep in me."

Larkin lay under his hands. It was perfect, how he touched her, his hands moving on her as if she was familiar ground. She relaxed in it, drowsed in it, let herself loosen to a point she hadn't reached for longer than she could recall. Minutes passed as he talked to her softly, phrases not connected to each other, and his hands never stopped moving; rubbing, smoothing, and brushing her skin like he was trying to memorize her. His movements twined with his words, surrounding her, filling the room.

Duncan slowed.

"Are you falling asleep?"

"Not if I can help it." Her voice was muffled.

"Why don't you get up and do whatever you need to do so when you do drop off you won't wake in the morning unhappy?"

"That would mean I'd have to get up."

"It's true."

"It would be better though, I suppose."

"It's up to you."

Larkin sighed, rolled to the edge of the bed, and stood. She headed for the bathroom.

When she came back to the bedroom, Duncan stood, flipping the duvet back, and motioned for her to get in.

"Snuggle up, now."

Larkin climbed in and turned to face him. He sat on the edge of the bed and reached out to comb her hair out over the pillow with his fingers.

"Duncan."

"Yes?"

"How do you know how to touch me? How did you know what I wanted?"

"I've watched you. I can tell when you're sore from the rowing, or from work. I can feel which muscles are tight in you and what happens when I rub this one," he touched her neck, "or that," his hand went back to her spine, "and how you react to it." His hand ran up her back slowly, lightly. "If I know, it's because I want to know."

"I love how you touched me. It was exactly what I wanted, exactly my wish."

"I'm glad. Don't walk around thinking how selfless it was, though. I've wanted to touch you for weeks and never thought I'd get the opportunity. It's a fine memory I'll have."

Larkin paused, trying to frame a question.

"Duncan?"

"Yes, love."

"Would it be asking entirely too much of you to lie here with me for a few minutes?"

Duncan looked down at her.

"What are you asking, Larkin?"

"Just for more, I think. I don't want to be done."

"Would you like it if I stayed until you're asleep?"

"Would you?"

Duncan turned and twisted his body so he was laid out next to her on top of the duvet. She reached for his hand and brought it under her cheek. He kept his body away from hers, but put his other hand to her face, then ran it back over her hair, smoothing it from her shoulder.

"You are lovely, Larkin."

She smiled, her eyes drooping.

"Thank you so much for this, Duncan. I can't imagine anything more perfect."

"Again, it was my pleasure."

She paused, her eyes closed and smiled.

"I don't suppose you could sing me a lullaby?"

"Ah, you're getting into next year's wishes now."

His hand still moved over her face, from her forehead around her ears, through her hair, and back again. She sighed.

"What a wonderful touch you have."

"Go to sleep, if you like. I'll be here."

She burrowed further in the bed, keeping his hand between her cheek and the pillow, her eyes closed and her breath coming more evenly. She stirred once.

"Good night, Duncan."

"Good night, love."

21.

It was her waking thought that Duncan was still there next to her, but her eyes opened to an empty pillow. Larkin hoped he'd at least gotten a couple of hours sleep before he had to go to work. The thought of him up at dawn made her check the clock. It was already ten. He'd been at work a good two hours before she even woke up.

Larkin lay back down, flat. The words Duncan said made her different. She'd heard those words from people in many different settings. She had, at turns, taken them for granted and wished for them in the dark. They had been used to manipulate her, to adore her, and she heard them once from a client who held a knife to his own wrist.

Duncan's words were not to take anything from her, or as an admission of helplessness. It was knowledge in himself he shared. It was a choice to love her and he had decided, despite obvious obstacles, to do just that.

Larkin swung her legs out of bed. She padded to the bathroom and turned on the shower. She thought with amazement that she felt just fine, with not a trace of a hangover.

Downstairs, the kitchen was in its natural state of morning activity. Brynna turned from the meat and waved at Larkin with a spatula.

"Now, look who's awake! Could it be a rowing hero, right here in my own kitchen?"

"Hero? Did I get promoted overnight?"

"Lots of things can happen overnight, can't they?" Brynna winked and turned back to her cooking.

"Brynna! What would you mean by that?"

"Well, I had to ask myself, what were these two coffee cups in my sink when I got up, and what was the door closing at four o'clock this morning?"

"Not what you're thinking. Listen to you! Your father would be shocked."

"Ah, well, I was hoping something was brewing with you and Duncan. He's a fine man, that one, you couldn't do much better."

Larkin smiled and got a cup of coffee.

"Actually, I thought I'd take him some lunch today. Maybe he needs a little break."

"A lovely thought. What do you want to eat?"

"I don't know. It's a brand new idea."

"Let's see. Perhaps sandwiches with ham and that cheese he likes, what is it? And crisps and fruit, and apple tart, and tea."

"Of course."

"Of course. And a tablecloth to lay on the grass, and napkins and an umbrella, just in case."

"A picnic. Perfect. A person might think you provided hospitality for a living."

"Go in the pantry, on the top shelf, do you see it? A big basket? Get that down, that's a duck, now go outside, and knock the dust off it."

Larkin did what she was told, brought the basket back in and watched Brynna assemble a picnic as effortlessly as she made a bed.

"There is a small issue here," Larkin said. "I haven't asked him yet."

"Something tells me he'd have a hard time refusing you anything."

Larkin raised her eyebrows at Brynna.

"How is it that you haven't said a word about Duncan before, but seem to have such strong opinions on the subject now?"

"I was leaving you two to work things out. I didn't have to worry about Duncan like I did Conn. I knew Duncan would be good to you. The more it went on, though, the more I saw him falling for you. Poor man, I didn't want him left with nothing when you went home, not after what he's put up with all these years. Then you opened up a bit, and I thought it would all be all right, that you were feeling more for him than just a friend, just a man to show you about the place. Is that right? Are you feeling something for him?"

"Brynna, it's not that easy. We live in different countries."

"Not at the moment, you don't, and I didn't ask what you were going to do about it; I just asked what the two of you felt."

"Duncan seems sure of his feelings." Larkin played with a fork on the counter. "Mine aren't so....definite."

"But something's there?"

"Oh, yes, something is definitely there. I'm just not willing to call it what Duncan's calling it."

"Duncan is a patient man, that one." Brynna folded napkins, placed them in the basket, then laid a tablecloth over across the top. "If you need time to work it out, he'll give it to you. I've known him for thirty years or more, and your man there is a cut above, let me tell you. Even after the trouble with Nora was plain, he didn't cat around, although there were several women that would have been pleased to take his mind off his troubles. I've kept half an eye on him, knowing him so long, and there's not a better man around. Sound, he is."

Larkin finished her coffee, rinsed her cup, and walked over to look at the finished basket.

"That's beautiful, thank you." She turned to face Brynna. "Here's my question. Why me? He knows I leave in a week. He's always known. Why get tied up with someone who lives an ocean away?"

"Now, who would you be asking that question of? Duncan or yourself? Because it sounds to me like you're trying to talk yourself out of him before giving it a try."

Larkin shook her head. "It would be difficult, don't you think? Long distance phone calls and emails, texting, and an occasional visit?"

"Listen to you. And what's to keep you from staying here or Duncan going there? You must think a little broader, Larkin. Look at this man, decide what you feel about him and at the end of the day, the rest will settle itself. That's my opinion and for free, too."

Larkin stepped out of the house and walked three streets over to where Duncan was still working on the house with the problem stairway. Once there, she listened for voices at the open front door, but hearing none, walked around the back to the kitchen door. There, she heard Duncan and a man talking, heard the whine of a saw and smelled new cut wood.

She stepped into the kitchen. Duncan looked up from a piece of wood, a carpenter's pencil in his hand. A beat passed as he looked at her.

"Hi," Larkin said.

He smiled. The other man looked at Duncan, then at Larkin. He grinned at Duncan, took his tape measure, and disappeared into another room, whistling.

"You're on my mind so much I almost didn't recognize you in person," Duncan said.

Larkin smiled up at him.

"You rescued me last night so I thought I'd return the favor. If you need a reason other than Brynna's picnic, you could probably sneak in a nap."

"Brilliant. Give me a minute."

Larkin waited in the kitchen and they walked to the front of the house. She asked about the work; when they'd be finished and if he was happy with it. He told her stories of dry rot and uneven corners, of pipes that went on to nowhere and an electrical system that dated back to the war days of 1921.

She told him of Sukki and the door between the houses, her only construction tale, and he said he'd have to meet this woman, and that mitering was probably overrated.

They walked through town, over the bridge and further down Church Street. At Friary Lane, they turned right and headed down the hilly street toward an inlet of water off the river. There was a small beach there with seagulls to beg whatever they decided not to eat.

As they passed the Catholic Church on the left, Larkin slowed. There were flowers trailing from huge containers at the door and more billowing from boxes hanging on the fence. She turned in and stood in the middle of the courtyard. Duncan followed her, carrying the basket, and looked at her with question.

"This is my favorite church," she told him.

"Really, and what made you pick this one, with the many Athlone has to offer?"

"One Sunday morning after breakfast, I walked all over town and visited every church I could find. I'm not Catholic, but I went in and sat in the back for a few minutes in each one. They were all beautiful, but this one felt different in some way. I go to services at the Protestant church, but I visit this one often."

They walked into the vestibule and stood in the main aisle way leading to the altar.

"What do you believe?" she asked Duncan.

"I believe in God. I have no doubts there. He had a son that came and was sacrificed for the sins of the world. Some of the rest is confusing, the words and the rites. Remember, Larkin, religion in Ireland is fraught with problems. There's a terrible mixture of God and wars, God and politics, God and fear."

Larkin shook her head. "How do you get past all of that to decide what you believe?"

"It was harder as a child, Larkin, but as an adult, it's a choice. You have to find God in it somewhere, but He's worth it, for all that."

They turned back to the street and made their way down the hill to the river. They chose an area near trees, in case of rain, and spread the tablecloth.

While they ate, there was a current between them and Larkin wondered what to do with the feelings she had that were gathering as quickly as the clouds overhead.

"Duncan."

"Yes?"

"Is it all right if we talk about...what we talked about last night?"

"Of course."

"I'm wondering...why, I guess. I leave in a week, and who knows when we'd see each other again. Why put yourself in that position?"

Duncan finished his orange and wiped his hands on a napkin. He stretched out on his back and looked at the sky for a long moment, then turned his head to look at Larkin.

"Larkin, it's been a long time since I've felt what I'm feeling for you. I had almost forgotten what that spark was like, how it turned me around." He rolled up on his side to face her. "I've been alone in that way for years and to suddenly have these feelings again surprised me. I'm happy to be feeling what I do for you, no matter what happens. I'm glad to know I can."

"So you don't really care what happens after this?"

"Ah, I never said that. I would love to be with you, to see how far this could go. You haven't given any indication that's a possibility."

Larkin folded and unfolded the napkin in her lap, her eyes on her fingers. Duncan reached over and tapped her knee.

"Would you think out loud, Larkin?"

"Well, I guess I'm saying there's the possibility of a possibility. You need to understand how careful I've been since Pat died. My life has been very structured. I've wanted it that way."

"And what do you want now?"

"I'd like to try things out without giving up too much control, though it doesn't seem fair."

"One person is usually giving more than the other at any given time. In good relationships, it trades off."

"I suppose. It doesn't seem right to ask you to be first."

"Larkin, why did you come to Ireland?"

She smiled. "I was bullied. My two best friends needled me into doing something different and Ireland was the best choice."

"And what have you gained here?"

"It's been wonderful. I've been able to think about what my life could be what I want to do with the rest of it."

"Have you decided?"

"I haven't answered all the questions, but things have come back to me I didn't even know were gone. Like, I can really taste food again," she said, "and I see things now, feel things I missed for a long time. A year ago, I wouldn't have noticed that breeze on my face, felt the grass, or seen how beautiful the water is. Of course, a year ago, I wouldn't have been here with you."

Duncan smiled.

"So, I haven't really made plans but I am, as my friend Sukki says, getting some color back in my life."

"Has it been a long enough stay? Do you think there is more to learn?"

"There might be, but I need to go home. They're expecting me back at work in ten days, and I miss my dog and my house and my friends. This has been very important for me, maybe even lifesaving, but it's time to go, it's time to take my eyes off myself."

"You're here, how many more days, six? What would you like for those six days?"

"I would like to get to know you better, to talk more about important things with you."

"Larkin, do you care for me?"

She nodded. "I do. I just don't know how much I can give. I don't know if it will work, not because of a lack of feeling for you, but because of a lack of ability in me."

"How about this? I can leave Dinny to work at the house. How much longer are you working for Brynna?"

"Teresa comes full-time on Wednesday morning. Brynna wanted me to have free time at the end of the trip and I need to be here on Saturday for the last race."

"And you fly home on..."

"Sunday."

"What do you think of this? Let's take a few days to see more of the country. We could spend some time together, see how that goes. You could kick my tires a bit; take me for a test drive."

"Where would we go?"

"We could go west, see some of County Clare. There's a little town called Doolin on the coast. We could see the Cliffs of Moher; spend a day on the islands."

"What islands?"

"The Aran islands, out from the coast of Clare."

"Do they make sweaters there?"

"Of course, the finest."

"An Aran sweater. My mother will be so happy."

"We could leave on Wednesday morning and return Friday night or Saturday morning, whichever you like."

"Perfect." Her face changed. "Duncan, I need to say this now."

"Yes?"

"Even if things go well with us, I don't want intimacy."

"I expected you might feel that way."

"I can't do that, and then leave. It's a big deal to me, not something I take casually."

"I want nothing from you you're not ready to give."

Larkin looked off to the side then, with a face Duncan couldn't read. Her voice dropped a notch.

"I have to tell you though, ever since last night when you held me, I have very much wanted to kiss you. Actually, it started long before then, but especially at that moment, I wanted your kiss."

Duncan smiled, shifting himself up to sitting, and reached for her hand.

"Did you, now? And do you still feel that way?"

She nodded, bringing his hand up to rest on the curve of her neck.

"It would be all right, it works into all your conditions?"

She nodded again.

"Larkin, I would love to kiss you, provided you understand it's not something I do at all casually."

Larkin laughed, then looked down. Duncan moved both hands to her face and lifted it. She looked up at him and was struck again by his eyes.

"I love you, Larkin."

He bent his head forward to meet her, hesitated, and touched her lips to his, a breeze of a kiss. He pulled back a moment, then returned to her, fitting his lips to hers with his hands cupped half in her hair, his thumbs laying on her cheekbones. When he drew away, Larkin's hand reached for him. He brought it out of the air and she used it to pull him close to her again. A beat passed while she looked at him and then put her free hand at the back of his neck and reached herself up, bringing his mouth to hers, making certain it was what she thought; that the feel of him was as good as she'd ever imagined it to be.

After, they each sat back and looked at each other.

Larkin let out a breath. "You kiss me like you touched me, like you've known me forever."

Duncan shook his head. "I can't explain it, Larkin, you just feel natural to me. There's none of it planned."

"It was wonderful."

"There's plenty more of it." He smiled at her, then got to his knees. "Now, as much as I hate to ask, what time is it gotten to be?"

Larkin checked her watch. "It's half-one."

"Listen to you, talking like a paddy."

They packed up the basket, throwing bits of bread and apple to the birds, and walked back up the steep hill to Church Street. Larkin slowed down near the top, and Duncan reached his hand behind him to help her up the last few feet. She continued holding it after they were on even ground and Duncan looked at her.

"I'm feeling very brave," she told him.

They walked back to the house, making plans for the trip until Larkin stopped dead in her tracks.

"What about practice? I can't miss practice before the last race. Deirdre would kill me."

"You'll practice tonight, as usual, and tomorrow. You'd only miss one night on the water, and you could most likely get some time on Friday night or Saturday before the race."

"I'll call her and see if it's OK." They got to the front door of the house and stood for a minute facing each other.

"Going to Sean's tonight?"

"I could be convinced."

Duncan leaned forward to kiss her lightly. "Can I come by and get you around eight?"

"Come by and get me?"

"We're more official now."

"I like this already."

He took her hand again, lightly.

"You made me very happy today," he told her.

She smiled, turned away to put the key in the lock, then grinned over her shoulder at him and walked in the house.

22.

The night before leaving on the trip, Larkin dreamed of Pat. After he died, she'd had nightmares, violent dreams of tires screeching and trees falling, the crash of metal on metal. The dreams always ended with Pat being crushed between cars, always with his eyes on her as blood flowed from his chest, all the rest of his body covered in the branches of a tree. In the beginning, she would wake from the dreams crying and shaking but as they progressed she taught herself to wake up when they got close to impact. When she learned to control her reaction the nightmares lessened and then stopped altogether.

Later, when she dreamt of him, he would be in misty places and they would walk together, but never touch. She would reach for him and he would step away in perfect proportion to how far she reached. Some dreams were sensual, waking her with a desire she couldn't satisfy, and her breath would come short and labored, her body in turmoil.

After a time, all the dreams stopped. She missed them.

On this night, she dreamed in vibrant color. Pat was there, strong like he'd been, leaning on a tree and explaining something to her. She tried to get closer to him, told him she couldn't hear what he was saying. He put out his hand for her to stop and raised his voice to call to her.

"No, stay there, stay in front of me! It's dangerous here. Stay where I can see you. I'll watch for you from here."

Then he went back to speaking in a normal tone of voice, and again she couldn't hear what he said. He was animated, using his arms to gesture and point, but she didn't understand, and could only hear single words now and again.

"Don't....anywhere....again....home..."

She strained to hear him, tried to read his lips.

"What? I can't hear you!"

He took a step toward her and she took one toward him, but the distance between them didn't change. She ran a few steps but knew it was useless, knew she wouldn't get any closer than this.

"Talk louder!"

He raised his voice but a wind came, rocking the tree, making the branches rub against each other, the noise high and penetrating. He kept trying.

"Never... only...heart..."

And finally,

"Anyone....Duncan."

When he spoke Duncan's name, Pat motioned for her to stay put, stay where she was, don't move, don't move.

Larkin woke in a sweat. She tried to go back to sleep to finish the dream, to find out all of what Pat was trying to tell her. She lay there, her eyes closed, breathing too quickly. When she gave up, she got out of bed and looked at the clock. Four in the morning.

The dream disorganized her. It wasn't the content, but the vividness, the detail. She could see Pat so clearly, could see the scar that was part of his eyebrow from a toboggan incident as a child, the little patch of hair in the back of his head that grew darker than the rest. She saw his wedding ring.

She looked over and saw her bag packed for the trip. She looked away and pulled on jeans, a sweatshirt, and shoes. She walked down the stairs and eased out of the back door, stepping into the night. She was the only person still wandering around, the pubs closing hours ago. She was glad for the deserted streets.

Larkin walked by the Castle and around the block to Sean's. It was dark, but she bet there were a few people still inside who'd talked the barman into letting them stay.

Once last week, she'd been awakened by a group passing under her window. They stopped in front of the house to stand in a circle and talk, interrupting each other, their voices rising to the window where Larkin sat and watched them. Seeing them made her lonely for Sukki, lonely for people who knew her well. She had seen the group earlier at Sean's, clustered around each other, buying rounds of beer. Brynna had leaned over to her, told her they were Army men, off soon to a six-month peacekeeping mission in Gaza.

The group was breaking up, talking in each other's ears. Then, together they looked up at where Larkin sat like Rapunzel in her window and each raised a hand to her in parting. She laughed, caught watching them, and waved back.

Tonight, Larkin made her way to the bridge, stood in the middle and looked out toward Clonmacnoise. She still hadn't made it there, but she knew it was there up around the bend in the river.

A car stopped behind her on the bridge. She turned, anxious all at once about being out so late alone.

"All right there, miss?" It was a member of the Garda Siochana, the Irish police force.

"I'm fine, thanks."

The Guard opened the car door, stepped out, and joined her on the bridge. He looked at her and took a whiff of the air near her.

"And what might you be doing out so late, here on the bridge?"

"Just taking a walk. I couldn't sleep."

"And have you had a little bit to drink, then?"

"I had a cider at about ten o'clock, but that's all. Why?"

"It's become something common for people to have a bit too much to drink and then to fling themselves off the bridge."

"Not me. I have a terrible fear of heights."

"Ah, good. I wish more did. Would you like a lift home?"

"No, thanks. I'm going to walk some more."

"Are you an American, then?"

"Yes."

"Are you sure you know your way around? It can get confusing on the Leinster side."

Larkin smiled. "As long as I can get to Church Street, I can get home."

"All right then. Mind yourself, now."

Larkin walked to the other side of the bridge as the Guard got back in his car and drove by. She waved and then was alone.

She walked Church Street past Heaton's, past Bonne Bouche, then down the hill toward the mall. She turned right, walked through the parking lot of the new condos up around to the secondary school, then past the Strand and up the hill past the Friary back to Church Street. Her steps were the only sound she heard aside from an occasional passing car or the shabby dog that ran alongside her for a long block, hoping, no doubt, for food.

Just like that, she thought. In the space of one lousy dream.

He was back. The dream brought Pat back to her with stunning clarity. She had only one small picture up at home and she hadn't brought it with her but now he filled her mind. Larkin stopped at a bench and sat. She bent at the waist, her face crumpling and her grief as harsh in her as it was in the first days after his death. She shook her head, tears flowing, and tried to breathe. After he died, she kept him in her head for as long as she could, including him in all of her decisions and clutching at the things still connecting them. Tonight, all she wanted in the world was her husband, to feel his presence, whether in person or just back in her head. She would take whatever she could get.

Larkin pressed her forehead to her knees. One word would do it; one word would bring him back.

That word was *no.*

No to change, *no* to Duncan, *no* to color.

She tried to bring Duncan up in her mind, tried to picture him. He wouldn't come; she couldn't remember his touch or his kiss. She thought of going to his house and banging on his door. She thought if she could see his face for just a minute, maybe she would be saved.

As quickly as that thought came to her, she discarded it. This was not a pick between Pat and Duncan. This was in her, a decision to make.

Larkin cried in her hands, bent over on a bench in the middle of Ireland in the dead of night. She cried for her husband and for the miserable hand she had been dealt, cried for the nights missing him and lonely meals without him, and cried for the babies without his face.

She cried, too, because she knew she couldn't do it. She couldn't live half a life again. She remembered sleepwalking through days and weeks. She had worked herself out of it, lifting her head when she walked, and talking when she didn't want to. It wasn't until recently that she'd felt alive on most levels and not until Ireland that she'd laughed easily, or attempted anything new. It wasn't until Duncan that she'd looked in a man's face to see herself loved.

For all her longing for Pat, she couldn't go back. He would have to stay dead.

She sat up and wiped her face on her sleeve. She got up and headed for the house, the sun starting its slow climb around the clouds, following her home.

23.

She let herself in the kitchen as Brynna was making the fire. She looked at Larkin, tired and red-eyed.

"Holy Mary, look at you! Whatever happened?" She hurried to Larkin and stood in front of her, holding her arms. "Are you all right? What were you doing out?"

"I couldn't sleep."

"Ah, I think there's a bit more to it than that, isn't there?"

"Oh, Brynna." Larkin sat down at the table.

"I think you need a cup of coffee, would you like that, Ducky?"

Larkin nodded.

"All right, you just sit; I'll have it to you in a quick minute." Brynna started the pot, and in a minute, placed a cup of coffee and a cup of tea on the table, pulled out the chair across from Larkin and sat.

"Now, what has happened? Did you and Duncan battle?"

"Oh, no. Nothing like that. I had a dream about Pat and it got me all worked up."

"Worked up, how?"

"I got mad all over again about his death. It's was so difficult to build a life without him, and now that I'm succeeding a bit, it all came back in a rush."

"I think I understand. When Mammy died, I was in bits. For months, I would listen to music she loved that would make me cry. I would read letters she had written me, wear her jewelry, and buy her favorite chocolate, even though I can't eat it."

"I did that. I used to buy Pat's shaving cream. I had nine or ten of them stacked up until Sukki's son started to shave, then I gave it all to him."

"Exactly. I remember one day I put on a CD that was a favorite of hers, and I sat and waited to cry but I didn't. I just sat there like a lump. When it was over, I felt awful. I felt guilty, like I had abandoned her. That wasn't it, of course. I was healing; I was going on with things."

"Going on."

"Of course. It doesn't mean I don't miss her. Every day I think of things I'd like to tell her, or questions to ask her. I send a prayer up that God will let her know I love her and I'm thinking of her."

"This just hit me out of nowhere. One dream and I was right back where I started."

"It was probably the trip that brought it on. This is a big thing, a real start to you and Duncan. Maybe you had to get by this before you left."

"But am I 'by' it? Is it going to happen again, even while I'm gone? Poor Duncan."

"Poor Duncan, my arse. He loves you, Larkin, and I'm sure he's more than willing to put up with whatever necessary for you. And, you'll have to put up with something from him before it's over, won't you. You're neither of you perfect." She reached over and took Larkin's hand. "Are you packed?"

Larkin nodded. "Almost."

"Why not go up and shower. Are you two wanting breakfast before you leave?"

"We didn't talk about that."

"Well, if your man gets here before you're done, I'll feed him if he likes. Take your time, now, and collect yourself." Brynna reached over and smoothed Larkin's hair back from her forehead.

"I must look awful."

"Even at your worst, Ducky, you're not too bad. Go on. I'll look after Duncan."

Larkin dragged herself to her feet and made her way up the stairs.

In the shower, she cried again. She ached from exhaustion and felt overwhelmed and shaky.

She dressed. Looking in the mirror, she thought she looked just as someone should look that had been crying for hours. It was tempting to crawl back in bed. Larkin sighed, put a cold washcloth on her eyes for a few minutes, and tried to make something of herself.

She put cover-up beneath her eyes, swollen as they were, and eye shadow over her lids. She layered on mascara and used two colors of blush. She tried different hair styles, pulling it back, which seemed to make her face stick out, and letting it down to hide it as much as possible. Looking in the mirror, she shook her head.

Great, she thought, now he won't even recognize me.

She reached for a washcloth and scrubbed her face. She put cream on once again, a bit of blush and a light coating of mascara. After brushing her hair, she clipped it up behind her and left it.

Standing at the top of the stairs, bag in hand, she stopped. One hand on the bannister, she thought again of Pat. It might never be again, the depth of love she felt for him, but the only way to find out was to let him go. She asked that she be free to live; to remember him always, but not be held captive there.

She got to the kitchen, took a breath, and opened the door. All eyes turned to her - Brynna's, concerned, Des', cheerful, and Duncan's, happy, then changing as he saw the paleness of her face, the puffiness of her eyes.

"Larkin, are you all right?"

In a step he was next to her, taking her bag and putting it down, a hand to her face.

She smiled up at him and laid her hand over his on her cheek.

"I'm fine." She turned to Brynna. "Did he eat?"

"Not a bite. Said he was waiting for you."

She turned back to Duncan. "Do you want something? I probably won't eat for a couple of hours, so if you're hungry, you might something now."

"I had a bit before I left home. I can wait."

"All right, then. Let's go."

Larkin walked to Brynna and gave her a quick hug then stepped over to Des and gave him a peck.

"Have a good time, now," he said. "Mind yourselves."

Brynna walked them to the door, opened it to a sunny morning, and took a deep breath of air.

"Ah, it's a lovely day for your trip. Go on, then."

Duncan, carrying Larkin's bag, held the door open for her as she stepped by him to the sidewalk. They walked to the car, opened the trunk, put her bag in next to his. As Larkin walked to the side of the car, she waved once to Brynna, still standing by the door, tears in her eyes.

I'm fine, Larkin mouthed to her, nodding.

Duncan started the car and they backed up and pulled away.

24.

They headed northwest from Athlone toward Ballinasloe, the little car winding through bright towns along the way, passing stone walls on each side of the road covered in ivy. Larkin looked out the window while Duncan drove, not wanting to talk about what happened and put a pall on the trip.

She would spare him the confusing details.

Duncan was quiet as well, pointing things out along the drive that he thought might intrigue her but mostly leaving her to herself. They stopped in Loughrea for something to eat, Larkin finally hungry. They found a pub and got seated. They looked over the menu, Duncan having bacon and cabbage, and Larkin deciding on smoked salmon on buttered brown bread.

Larkin shook her napkin out and smiled at Duncan.

"It's funny. Since I've been in Ireland I don't think about eating until I'm really hungry. Here, it just happens, all of a sudden, boom, I'm hungry and then I eat."

"Why is that, do you think?"

"I don't know. I think at home my time is more structured. Get up, work out, eat. Go to work, do some reports, eat. Go home, get the mail, stick something in the microwave, eat."

"Stick something in the microwave? Larkin. Don't you cook properly for yourself?"

"I used to," she waved her hand, "before, but now I can't be bothered."

"Ah, but you must. Eating well is important."

"Well, what do you eat? Do you cook?"

"Of course. I enjoy cooking. The kids eat with me several nights a week, with Nora working evenings, and we cook together."

"It's more fun when it's not just for you."

"Well, we'll have to cook together some night."

After they ate, they paid and got to their feet. When they got to the door of the pub, Duncan held it open for Larkin to pass in front of him. As she walked by, he brushed his hand over her back. She turned to him and smiled. The light touch brought her back to the day. She reached out, ran her hand down his arm, and grasped his wrist gently.

"Thank you, Duncan."

They walked back to the car. Duncan looked sideways at Larkin. She stopped.

"What?"

He took a breath. "I was wondering if you're all right. If you're better than you were this morning. I was wondering what had happened, if you wanted to talk about it."

She stood at the door of the car.

"I'm all right, Duncan. As far as what happened, please know it had nothing to do with you. Is that enough for now?"

"Larkin, I'm not trying to pry, but I am concerned."

"You are a good man. Let's go to Doolin."

Her mood lifted the further they traveled from Athlone, but Duncan had something more to say.

"Larkin."

She smiled. "You sound very serious."

"I want to tell you that whatever is it that's bothering you, now or whenever, I want to know. Not telling me out of a need for your privacy is fine, but don't not tell me to protect me. I don't need to be protected."

"I will certainly keep that in mind."

"I mean it, Larkin."

"I know you do and I thank you for it." She clearly wanting the subject dropped. She looked at him, could see frustration in his profile, and knew she hadn't given him what he'd wanted.

"Duncan, could we please just let it go for now? I'm fine. Really."

He glanced at her. He nodded and reached for her hand.

"Let's follow the coast past Ballyvaughan and then we'll see water all the way to Doolin."

"You're in charge."

"It's longer this way, more complicated," Duncan told her, "but it's worth it."

25.

When they got to Doolin, Larkin was charmed. It was a tiny town; B&B's dotting the streets, a few specialty music shops, and three pubs.

"Do we have reservations?" Larkin asked.

"We do, indeed. We're booked at Brannock's."

They wound their way around and pulled up to the side of the B&B, and were met at the car by a one-eyed dog.

Larkin bent down.

"Look at you, now. Hello, would you like a quick pet?" She had her hand out for him to sniff, but he never got close enough for her to touch.

They went to the front door of the cheerful house, passing a garden filled with flowers. Duncan rang the bell. A smiling woman opened it for them, and motioned them in.

"Hello, are you all right? I'm Mrs. Brannock. Are you booked?"

Duncan nodded. "We have two singles under McKenna."

"Two rooms? Are you sure?" She checked her book. "My mother had you down for one room with two beds."

Duncan shook his head. "No, it was to be two rooms. Have you two available?"

"Ah, I don't, no. You could check around in town, though. I'm sure someone will have something for you."

Larkin turned to Duncan. "No, it's all right."

Duncan looked at her, then turned back to Mrs. Brannock and nodded. "That's fine, then."

She walked to a dresser in the hall and picked up a key. "It's straight down there, the second on the right, Number 2. There you are, do you need help?"

"No, we're all right. Thank a million."

Larkin followed Duncan down the hall past a conservatory filled with potted flowers. Their room was unlocked, the door ajar. They stepped in and looked around.

There were two twin beds, separated by a table. There was a huge window overlooking what Duncan would point out as the back of the Cliffs of Moher. A door led off the other end of the room to the bathroom, and a wardrobe stood facing the beds. It was done in shades of peach, with thick duvets and a pretty chair in the corner with a lamp for reading.

Larkin turned to Duncan, smiled. "It's lovely."

"Are you sure this is all right, Larkin? We can check another place if you're not comfortable."

"No, I'm really fine here."

"Only if you're certain."

"I'm certain." She sat in the chair in the corner and watched him deal with the luggage. He hadn't let her carry anything once they got inside and she'd let him manage it. When he'd gotten it settled, she smiled. "All right, where to? The cliffs right away, or somewhere else?"

Duncan smiled. "It's good to see you're feeling better."

"I am feeling better. Get me out and blow the stink off me."

Duncan laughed. "What in the world might that mean?"

"It means to get some fresh air. A phrase used by my paternal grandmother."

"Ah, the things I'm learning from you, Larkin."

They went back to the car with a camera, a bottle of water, and a map.

"Like this will do us any good," Larkin said, looking over the map.

"It's true; it's not always easy to get around in Ireland." Duncan was backing out of the B&B onto a gravel road.

They drove through Doolin, noting where they wanted to stop later - Larkin voting for the Magnetic Music Shop, just so she could find out what it meant, and Duncan pointing out the sweater shop across the street.

"Didn't you mention an Aran jumper?"

"Don't you think it would be cheating to buy it here instead of on the island?"

"The sweaters are made all over Ireland, not just on the islands."

"Where do the designs come from?"

"The idea was that each fisherman would wear a different design, particular only to his family. Then, if a body was found it could be identified by the design on the sweater."

"Oh, lovely."

"It was a very dangerous occupation, Larkin."

"Maybe I'll get a nice piece of crystal instead."

They pulled into the parking lot at the Cliffs of Moher. There were buses lined up on one side of the parking lot, and cars and bicycles on the other.

Larkin tied a jacket around her waist and turned to the Cliffs.

A whipping wind blew at her, pushing her hair up around her face in a whirl.

"Wow! Quite the breeze!" She turned to Duncan, in the process of pulling on a sweater.

"Indeed. It's always like that here, Larkin. That is the Atlantic Ocean, after all."

"The Atlantic Ocean? My Atlantic Ocean?"

"We share it, I believe. The saying goes, 'next parish, New York'."

Larkin turned on the stairs to get her first glance at the Cliffs, monolithic and prehistoric. She faced them, amazed.

"Come up higher. It's even better." Duncan reached for her hand and they finished the walk to the round tower, going up the spiral staircase to get an unobstructed view. He stood behind her and put his arms around her, linking his hands with hers.

She stopped and sighed. Closing her eyes, she leaned back into him, feeling the warmth given off by his body and felt the muscles tighten in his arms. He reached down kiss the side of her neck and buried his nose in her hair.

"You are beautiful," he whispered.

"And you are kind. I don't know when I've ever looked worse."

"There was that practice, remember, when the boat went over and there you were, standing in the muck at the edge of the river. You looked much worse then."

"Thank you for that." Larkin turned her head to look at him. "Be informative, would you? How tall are the cliffs?"

"They're about 750 feet high, I believe."

There was a sheer drop from the green grass at the lip of the cliff to the rocks and waves below. A cave cut into the face and birds swirled in the air currents created by the water smashing into the rocks. They floated in circles, tiny patches of white against the dark of the rock.

"What a great place to be a bird," she said.

"You'd have to pay attention, though," Duncan told her. "One wrong move and the wind would dash you right into a stone wall."

"So this is like graduate school for birds?"

"I would think so. Only the best get to live here, the strongest."

Larkin looked at the base of the cliffs where the waves crashed against the rocks.

She shivered. "Do people ever get hurt here?"

"Ah, yes. Probably once a year, someone gets too close to the edge and loses their footing. It's usually something that can be avoided."

"How would they get close enough to fall?"

"There are paths," he disengaged his hand and pointed, "up there that go the length of the cliffs, around the side where you can't see. Although they're far from the edge and there's a wall you would have to climb over, occasionally someone thinks it would be a good idea to hang off the side of the cliff for a really great picture."

"Can we walk the paths if we behave ourselves?"

"Of course. Do you want to go now?"

They wound their way around the spiral staircase back down to the gift shop and out the door towards the paths. When they got to the grass, she turned to him.

"Were you ready to go?"

"Go where?"

"Go to the paths. It occurs to me that most of the things we do are at my wish. I'm getting pretty spoiled here."

"It is my pleasure to spoil you, Larkin."

"I want you to know I don't expect it."

"I just want you to enjoy yourself."

"But I want you to enjoy yourself as well. I don't need to be spoiled all the time."

They walked up the side of the cliffs, following the path and staying far from the edge. The wind was cold and biting but the sun shone and Larkin lifted her face to it.

"Why is it I never feel really cold if the sun is shining? At home, it gets to below zero, but if the sun is out, I'm all right."

"It really gets that cold in Chicago? I can't imagine it."

"Layering is everything. In the winter, people die from getting stuck somewhere in their cars and freezing, or falling into snowdrifts where they can't get out. We get ice on the streets and ten foot snow drifts."

"Do you like the cold?"

"Not at all. I'm cold from November to May. It's the thrill of my life when the tulips come out and I can be comfortable for a while."

They walked for a half an hour, the path running ahead of them as far as they could see.

Larkin stopped, turned to look over the expanse of ocean in front of them, then looked back the way they'd come.

"We've covered some distance here." She smiled at him. "Are you ready to go back?"

"Are you?"

"No, this one's up to you."

"What do you think? Want to see more?"

"I think I'll go along with you."

"But this is your trip, Larkin. I can come back anytime."

"When were you here last?"

"It's been ten years or so."

"So you can come anytime, but you don't."

"That's true enough, I suppose."

"So, what do you want to do?"

Duncan smiled at her insistence, then considered. "I could go a bit more."

After they left the Cliffs, they spent the afternoon driving the area, stopping in towns to walk the streets or have tea. Larkin felt the last of the darkness in her drift away. Duncan told her about Lisdoonvarna, the town that hosted a matchmaking ceremony every year. It was their claim to fame and the festivities got bigger every year, people coming from all the counties to take part. Larkin was amazed.

"They come here and someone they've never met pairs them up with someone else they've never met and they get married?"

Duncan shook his head. "I don't know how many actually marry. I think many more just...meet."

Larkin nodded. "I get it. It's a big singles bar for a week."

"I'd say that's fairly accurate."

She looked at the side of the road. "What are those pretty purple flowers?"

"They grow wild all over the country. I don't know what they're called."

"I love purple flowers. They're the ones I always favor, whether I'm planting or looking at someone else's garden."

Duncan pointed up to the hills in the distance. "Before we go home, I'll find you some heather. Not only is it purple, it smells like heaven. If we were close enough, you'd be able to see it like a blanket on the mountains. We'll get you some to take with you."

"I don't know about taking it home. The U.S. Department of Agriculture takes a dim view of bringing in plants from other countries. I think that's how we got the Asian Long-horned beetle."

"Ah, quite right. A country has to be careful. Do you know we have no rabies here? It's why domesticated animals have to go through such an extensive quarantine when they come."

"I wanted to bring Bubba, but he would have been in quarantine longer than my stay, so it was silly."

"Bubba?"

"My dog. He's a toy poodle, and he's stolen my heart entirely."

"My competition, then?"

"No sense competing with Bubba. You can only lose. Did you notice that picture on my dresser at Brynna's?"

"When I was in your room, I can't say I noticed anything but you."

Larkin smiled. "There is a picture of him with Sukki's youngest, who is, big secret, my favorite of Sukki's children."

"It's strange to think of your life there, a whole life I know nothing about; your job and your friends, your home. I'm used to you here, knowing where you are and what you might be doing. When you go home, I'll be wondering all the time."

"No need to wonder. We'll keep in touch. Do you email and text?"

"I do."

"Then, thanks to technology, you won't have to wonder. And we can call on the weekends, when it's cheapest."

"What a practical woman you are."

"Very practical. Nearly boring, if fact."

Duncan looked over at her, and reached for her hand. "There is still a lot I don't know about you yet, Larkin, but I'm quite certain you're not boring."

26.

Doolin was famous for traditional Irish music, so when night came, they walked to the closest of the three pubs. They were more peckish than hungry, so each had a toasted cheese sandwich at the bar before the music started.

Duncan took a walk around the pub to see where the music would be, finding two vacant seats in a good spot to watch. He waved to Larkin and they sat at the end of a table for six, the other four chairs occupied. They smiled at the people already seated. At the table in the corner, five musicians were setting up: two guitars, a fiddle, an accordion, and one man with an assortment of whistles.

Duncan leaned over to her. "These are local people, Larkin, who have been playing and singing since childhood. In the country, it was the only diversion and everyone in the family played something."

"Was it like that in your family as well?"

"It was, indeed. Music is a huge part of the culture here. My mother taught me to play the accordion when I was very young. She didn't teach me in the sense of showing me, but she'd have me take it down off the wall while she washed up after supper, and she'd sing and have me pick out the tune."

Larkin stared at him. "You play the accordion?"

"Of course, and the guitar and the piano."

"Why have I never seen you play?"

"I don't know. I play now and again at a session at the Castle Inn, near Sean's. I suppose you've never been there on a Sunday."

"I'll be there next Sunday, you can bet on that."

"Next Sunday you're on a plane for home, Larkin."

I'm not ready, she thought. I won't be ready.

She leaned into Duncan's shoulder. He looked down at her and smiled, and she knew that he wasn't ready either.

Walking back from the pub, Larkin lifted her face to the falling mist. The stars were plentiful in the black sky with the sliver of a yellow moon.

"The sky is so black here," she whispered.

"'Tis how it should be, Larkin. In the cities, there are so many lights; the sky gets no rest from them. Here, it's just the cliffs and the stars and the sea," he stopped and turned her to him, "and you."

She reached for him, stretching up to put her arms around him. All evening, she'd wanted to feel the length of him touching her, to rest with her head in the curve of his neck. He held her, his arms crossing over her back and his face in her hair, rocking. They stood for minutes, his hand tracing the curve of her waist, her lips lying on his neck. One of her hands ran down his arm to his elbow and back to his shoulder. He moved to kiss her, his hands moving to her face, to stroke her cheek and lift her swirling hair away from her mouth.

She opened her eyes to watch as he bent to her. He hesitated, and she put a hand to his neck, brought him the last inches, and pressed herself to him. She felt the rough of his sweater under her fingers and laid them flat on his shoulders, his arms, to feel them tighten on her as his mouth touched hers.

Duncan made a low noise, and desire bloomed in her, the night suddenly urgent and real, and in a short space between their lips, Larkin spoke words, single words of want she wouldn't remember later. Duncan answered her with his hands, running them down her back, bringing her hand to his mouth, finding the spot on her neck with his lips that made her shiver. He held her up, whispering words she couldn't hear, words of love and want and hope.

She knew she could swoon and he would catch her. She knew he would do whatever she asked of him, as much or as little, and the knowledge made her bold.

She put her face to the air and smelled it, felt the mist and the night and was, in that space, elemental. She was not a random woman, but in that moment could have faced this man, taken his hand, climbed up the side of the cliffs to the top and had him there, as remote a place as the first night of earth.

He felt the shift in her. He pulled away, looked in her face and saw it there - her want, her openness. He stopped, his hands stilled on her back and he let her experience what she felt without expecting anything from it. He whispered again.

"What a woman you are. Look at you; I can feel that, such a powerful woman you are, Larkin."

She whispered back, exhilarated, "It's you, Duncan, this is you I'm feeling."

He smiled, shook his head, and pressed his hand to the small of her back, a thrill running the length of her, murmured in her hair. "No, Larkin, it's right there, in you. And I love it, I love knowing it's there."

"It's been waiting."

He put his arms all around her, lifting her up the few inches to make her face even to his. His eyes were huge on her, reflecting the moon. She remembered the day she went to Galway, when she saw the sun in them.

This man, she thought, with the light of the sky in his eyes.

He whispered to her. "Tonight, it is enough to know it's there."

"How long?"

"How long, what?"

"How long will you wait for me?"

"Long enough for you to come to me."

He put her down and took her hand. They found their B&B and tiptoed past the other rooms. When they got to their door Duncan unlocked it and opened it for her.

"You go. I'll wait until you're finished."

She changed quickly, pulling on a white nightshirt, then washed her face and scrubbed her teeth. She climbed into her bed and waited.

He knocked and opened the door a couple of inches.

"All right?"

"Come in, I'm done."

He came in, closed the door quietly, and looked over at her, snuggled in.

"Look at you. Comfy, are you?"

"I certainly am."

He went in the bathroom and closed the door. She heard the water run, heard the splash in the toilet and the water run again. He came out, took off his sweater, and turned to her.

"Larkin, I sleep in my jocks. Will that make you uncomfortable?"

"Of course not. What else would you sleep in?"

He turned his back to her, took off his shirt, and slipped out of his pants.

"Nice butt."

He laughed and then slipped into his bed. He faced her, propped up by his elbow.

"How was the day? Did you enjoy yourself?"

She nodded. "Very much. The cliffs were breathtaking. What will we do tomorrow?"

"Depending on the weather, we may try for the islands. If it's raining, though, probably not. The islands are remote, really, and the fun is climbing the hills. If it's raining, we'd end up in a pub for the day, with a wet trip back on the boat."

"So if it's raining, what will we do?"

"We could drive the area more around here, have lunch, and try and find that jumper you keep talking about. At night there will be more music."

"Wonderful. Either day sounds great. I officially don't care if it rains or not."

"That's a good attitude for Ireland."

"I suppose it is, isn't it."

"Do you know how Irish you're sounding? Not an accent, but your phrasing is getting more and more like a Paddy."

"No big surprise, really, since I'm around you Irish people all the time."

Duncan reached for the clock.

"When should we get up?"

"What time is it now?"

"It's half-twelve."

"How about half-eight, although I'll probably be up earlier."

He set the clock and put it back. There was a pause, Larkin deciding whether to get up and kiss him goodnight. In the end, she stayed where she was.

"Thank you for the day, Duncan. It was lovely."

"It was my pleasure."

"Goodnight."

"Goodnight, love."

She turned on her back, the duvet to her collarbone, smiled at the ceiling and slept.

In the black of the Irish night, Larkin awoke. She turned on her side to see Duncan asleep, a pillow encircled by his arms in front of him. His hair had gotten curlier in the heat of the night. She hesitated a moment then slid out of her bed, quietly moving next to him and sat on the floor level with his face. She got close enough to feel his warmth and watch his body move with his breath.

How would it be, she thought, to lie in bed with a man again, to wake up together, have breakfast, be married? She knew it would have to be marriage. She was, as a friend told her in high school, "the marrying kind."

Could she be married to this man? Could she come home to him and be happy when he came home to her, impatient for his presence? Could she cook for him and be appreciative when he cooked for her? Would they argue about silly things, about budgets or laundry or some horrible shirt he insisted on wearing?

Would she forever want to touch him as she did now?

She lifted her hand and very gently laid it on the thickest part of his sleeping arm, near his shoulder. He didn't stir. She felt the heat coming from it and felt his strength. She flushed with the thought of what it would feel like to be where his pillow lay, encircled by those arms. She leaned over to smell his skin. She put her cheek on him, felt the rise and fall of his breath, and watched as his eyes opened to her.

"Larkin?" His voice was low and quiet in the dark room.

She smiled at him, but left her face pressed to his arm.

"Is it time to get up?"

"No, it's the middle of the night."

"Why are you awake?"

"I don't know. I woke up and looked around and there you were. I'm just visiting."

"Visit all you like." He smiled at her, sleepy-eyed. "What a lovely thing, to wake up and have you in front of me."

"Duncan, what do you really think of all this? Do you think it is a good thing?"

"I think it is a wonderful thing."

"Do you think you'll ever marry again?"

Duncan's eyes opened wider, and his smile grew. "Are you proposing?"

"Not this minute. Just supposing you met someone and things became," she smiled back at him, "wonderful, do you think you'd want to get married again?"

"Well, I've given that some thought, as of late, and I've found marriage to be a consideration."

"If I lived here, or you lived in America, would we date?"

"For a while."

"What does that mean?"

"It means I think we'd know fairly soon which way the grass was growing. I love you, Larkin. We wouldn't be starting from scratch."

"But I don't live here and you don't live there."

"True, but the world is a small place, thanks to phones and computers and planes."

"Where does that leave us?"

"It makes communication easy and travel possible."

Larkin moved her cheek on his arm. She lay silent for a bit, then smiled.

"I love your skin. It's so smooth, and it smells like nothing I've ever smelled before."

"There's lots more of it." He reached his arm out to her and cupped his hand on her shoulder. "Larkin, you're freezing!"

"I suppose I am."

"Come closer. Here, wrap this around you." He dragged the duvet off himself and tried to cover her with it.

"No, stay there, no sense in you being cold as well."

He moved over in the bed and lifted up the duvet. "There's room here to warm up. I'll be good, I promise."

She hesitated, then crawled in with him, the duvet making a cave as he lifted it over her. Duncan kept his distance. He didn't speak and didn't touch her. When she turned to face him in the bed, he made no move toward her, but let her determine the distance between them.

"Better?" he asked her.

"Very cozy in here, I must say. I didn't know how cold I was until now."

There was silence then, not entirely comfortable, as Larkin tried to be easy with where she was. "My feet must be freezing."

"They are. Put them here," he put her feet on his calf, "and I'll warm them." He put his other leg on top, sandwiching them.

"All right," she said. "You've officially proven yourself."

Larkin stirred. "How far can I push you?"

"How much can I stand, do you mean? I can stand a lot from you."

"Could I kiss you, now, here?"

"I've been waiting."

Larkin moved in close to his face.

"Do you know you have the most beautiful eyes I have ever seen? I don't know if I've ever told you that."

She moved closer to him, leaving a space between them. She put a hand to his face, felt the stubble of his beard and touched her cheek to his, scuffing her face.

"I'll shave in the morning," he murmured.

She put her hands on either side of his neck, kneading the muscles that ran down into his shoulders and then slowly pulled him to her, her arms winding around his neck. His hands found her back, and they drew together carefully.

They kissed as if kissing was all there was, just as pleasure unto itself.

Duncan pulled away. "Perfect," he whispered to her.

She nodded, then brought his mouth back to hers and smiled, feeling his mouth follow the same path. When they finished, she turned her back to his chest, pulled his arm over her, and slept without dreaming.

27.

The pelting rain woke Larkin before the alarm. It was windy, making the water sound like hail against the windows. She eased away from Duncan and out of bed and looked at the clock. It was still before seven so she crept to the bathroom, then back to her own bed. She lay there, the duvet pulled over her, and watched Duncan sleep. He was flat on his back, the duvet pulled down to his chest, and his hair pasted to his head. He was snoring quietly.

She stayed there until he woke, before the alarm. He turned to his side, still asleep, shivered, and covered himself to the shoulder. His eyes opened, then closed again, then opened fully to find her looking at him.

"Good morning." His voice was gravelly.

"A good morning to you. How did you sleep?"

"I had a lovely dream." He smiled at her. "What time is it?"

"Half-seven."

"Early birds, we are. Ready to be up, or do you want to sleep more?"

"No, I'm up"

He lifted himself up on an elbow and looked out the window.

"Unless something changes, it looks like a driving day."

"A shopping day."

"Ah, I did promise you that, didn't I. Can't go home without your jumper."

"Are you still sleepy?"

"I could stay a bit more."

"How about I get showered, and then wake you?"

"Grand. Take your time."

She got out of bed and turned off the alarm. As she walked by him to the shower, she reached out to touch his bare shoulder on her way by. When she was finished, she woke him, then waited in the conservatory for him get ready. He came out, smelling fresh.

"Breakfast, then?"

There were three other people in the dining room already eating. They looked up as Duncan and Larkin took their seats.

"Good morning," the woman said.

Larkin turned at her accent.

"Where are you from?"

The woman smiled. "Florida. You?"

"Near Chicago."

"We're nearly neighbors."

Larkin laughed. Anyone with an American accent became a quick neighbor in a foreign country.

After breakfast, they headed for Kilconnel where they shopped for the ideal sweater. They finally found an oatmeal cotton and linen pullover, soft to the touch and not too bulky. When she tried it on, Duncan approved.

"I think you might just be saying nice things so I don't spend any more time looking."

"Ah, Larkin don't be silly. It's only been a hundred or so you've tried."

She bought the sweater and they walked the streets looking for a promising pub. They stopped at The Fiddlers, more because Larkin liked the look of the place than any knowledge of food. It was stone with blue shutters and a red door, with violins outlined in gold on the windows. Even better, the flowers in the containers outside were all purple. They had traditional Irish fare, the beef tender, and Larkin's salmon flaky and dotted with butter and dill.

After lunch, they spent the rest of the day driving the region, passing the Burren, a rocky stretch of land miles wide and covering the countryside and dropping in at stores Larkin felt were worth the stop. Later, they had apple tart with cream and tea. When it got toward eight, they headed back to Doolin for music.

Tonight, they picked one of the other two pubs in town.

"How do you know there will be music?" Larkin asked.

"It's Doolin, Larkin. I don't suppose on any night but Christmas there wouldn't be music."

They were early enough to get good seats with direct view of the band. Larkin wasn't hungry, but Duncan ordered a bowl of soup and some brown bread. When it came, Larkin reached over and broke off a corner of the bread.

"I thought you weren't hungry," Duncan said to her.

"I'm not."

"Do you want more? I can get you some."

"No thanks."

"I'll order you some."

"I don't want any, thanks."

"What would you like to drink? A cider or a beer?"

"Nothing right this minute. In a bit."

He walked to the bar, got himself a Heineken, walked back to the table, setting it next to the soup. Before he sat down, Larkin reached over and took a sip.

"Larkin. Would you like a pint of your own?"

"No, I really don't. I just wanted a sip of yours. I'm sorry, I should have asked. Is it all right that I had a sip of your beer?"

"Of course, Larkin, you're welcome to anything, but if you'd like one, I'd be happy to get it for you."

"No, I'm fine."

Duncan sat, ate his soup, and buttered his bread. After putting down his knife, he tore off a bit of his buttered bread, offered it to her. She opened her mouth, and he popped it in, smiling.

"Would you like some more?"

Larkin finished chewing and swallowed. "Nope. It's just fun having an occasional bite of yours. Mind if I have another sip of your beer?"

"By all means, Larkin, help yourself."

The band was setting up. When Duncan finished his beer he got up to get two more, stopping to talk to the guitar player on his way to the bar. He returned, a pint in each hand.

"How did you know I wanted one?" Larkin asked him, smiling.

"A lucky guess. Now, Larkin, I talked to the guitar player, and he has said you can sit in with the band if you like."

"Sit in with them? What would I do?"

"Nothing. I just you might like to have the feel of a session. What do you think?"

"I'd love to, if you're sure I won't be in the way."

"You won't." Duncan looked over at the band and caught the eye of the guitar player. He made a motion for Larkin to come, get a seat. She looked at Duncan.

"Go on, you'll enjoy it," he told her.

"You'll be all right by yourself?"

"I'll be watching you. Go on, now."

She moved over to the corner with the band. The guitar player pointed to an empty seat between a selection of whistles laid out on the table and the wall.

"Have a seat there, next to Eamon," he told her.

She settled herself in, her back to the corner, and looked over at Duncan. He smiled at her and nodded.

The whistle player came in, hurrying, and took his seat. It was the same player from last night. He turned to her.

"Now, what have we here?"

"I'm just watching."

"Ah, you're American. Didn't I see you last night at O'Connell's?"

"You did. You were there, as well."

"I was, of course. Thought you were a lovely girl."

"Did you, now?"

"I did."

"Well, thank you. You're too kind."

"Ah, it's the truth, it is." He studied her. "Then again," he said, "maybe I have terrible taste." He looked at her, straight faced, and she burst out laughing. He grinned.

"Maybe you do," she told him.

"But I don't think so. No, I believe my taste is beyond reproach."

He grinned again and picked up a thin rod, trilling notes faster than she would have believed possible.

He turned his attention to the guitar player. The band launched into a reel and Larkin settled back into the corner, listening and watching.

From her vantage point, she could see the band and watch the people in the pub. Some hit their heels on the wooden floor in time and some just sat. Some talked all the way through the music. She hoped they weren't Americans. The Irish took their music seriously, she had found, and didn't take kindly to talk while they were playing. She had heard more than one band admonish the crowd with "If you're wanting to talk, go someplace we're not playing."

After a selection of reels, the guitar player slowed things down.

"Here's a Scottish song for you," he said into the microphone. "It's called Caledonia."

Eamon chose a different whistle, and leaned over to Larkin.

"This is a love song to Scotland. Liam, there, has a soft spot for Scotland, I've no idea why."

For this song, the guitar player started alone, playing, and then singing. He sounded nostalgic, Larkin thought, and listening to words, she understood. The song spoke of longing, of the harkening a place could create in one's heart, and Larkin wondered if that is how she would end up feeling about Ireland.

Eamon joined at this point, whistle poised, and he and the fiddle player eased in on the chorus. This was one of the haunting songs Larkin knew she would remember, one that would come to her in her random thoughts of her time in Ireland. She closed her eyes and tried to commit it all to memory - the song, and how she was feeling hearing it.

For the rest of the set, she sat sipping her beer and watching. The music was varied, traditional with a sprinkling of current songs, an occasional U2 selection, and once, a John Denver song with the verses sung in the wrong order.

When the set finished, the whistle player turned to her, sweat on his forehead.

"There, now. And what did you think?"

"It was...wondrous," she said to him.

"Wondrous? Well, now, that's a first. I don't remember anyone calling us 'wondrous' before."

"It must be my lucky night." She looked over at Duncan. "Will you save my seat? I'll be back."

She slid out of the booth, got her beer, and walked to where Duncan sat talking to the people at his table. There was a couple from France, honeymooning, but with the look of a couple long married. She found after talking that they'd been together ten years and engaged nine, so marriage held fewer surprises for them than most. At the other end of the table sat a mother and daughter from Canada.

Larkin liked the look of them, their faces so similar but for time, and listened to stories of where they'd been in the country. She wanted to know how they ended up together in Ireland for three weeks.

"It was our husbands," the daughter explained. "They gave us this trip to Ireland for my 30th birthday and my mother's 60th."

"Slainte!" The mother said. "Isn't it a wonderful night to be in Ireland!"

Before the third set, Duncan encouraged her to get her seat back next to the whistle player.

"It may be your only chance," he told her. "But tell the whistle player to mind himself."

"Nothing I can't handle," Larkin told him.

She walked back to the corner with the band. When they started again to play, she settled in, her beer forgotten and warm in front of her.

In the middle of the set, the guitar player played a few notes, and Eamon raised his head. He turned to Larkin.

"Ah, you're in for a treat now." He motioned for silence at the tables near the band, who spread the word until the place was nearly quiet. When only a few voices were left, the guitar player began.

Larkin's spine tingled as his fingers traveled the strings. She didn't know the song, but it was beautiful, the notes shining, each a seamless path to the next. It was clear even to Larkin's ear that he played it brilliantly. Mesmerized, she knew she'd never remember this song with no words to peg it by, but would recognize it anywhere and trace it back to Doolin, to this night.

His fingers moving, the guitar player lowered his head until it rested on the curve of his instrument, turning his face so his cheek lay on the shiny wood. He closed his eyes.

Watching him, Larkin felt her eyes fill and she brought her hand up to hide her mouth. She didn't know why she was so moved, but hoped there was something in her life she did as well as this man played this song.

When the final note died away, the pub erupted in cheers, and Larkin looked around. She looked at the guitar player as he turned to Eamon, setting up for the next song. He smiled at her and gave her a single nod.

Larkin put a finger up to her eye and wiped the tear that sat in its corner. She looked around the pub. She had to remember everything; she would need this when she was home.

There were times in life that were small pockets of joy, not earth-shaking or elaborate – and it was a gift. She recognized the night for what it was and would treasure it.

When the set ended and the lights were turned up, she stood, stretching.

"Thank you," Larkin said to Eamon. "It has been a complete pleasure."

"Ah, but the truth of it is, the pleasure has been all mine." He grinned at her, with all the charm he had to offer. "I don't suppose there would be any chance of seeing you again tomorrow night? I'm not playing, but we could find more music in town."

"A lovely offer, but no thank you. We leave town tomorrow."

"So you're traveling with your man, there?" He lifted his chin at Duncan.

"I am. We have one more day before we go back to Athlone."

"A lucky man, to have you to himself for another day."

"To have me doesn't mean he's lucky," Larkin said, smiling, "it means he's patient."

"I'm sure he hopes his patience will last forever." Eamon said, and turned to go. "Safe journey," he said, over his shoulder.

Larkin worked her way around the crowd to Duncan and the others at the table. Duncan moved over, making room for her. She set what was left of her beer on the table and looked at the mother and daughter.

"What did you think?" She asked them. "You have much more basis for comparison than I do."

"It was the best so far," the daughter said. "Of course, we've said that about every place we've been. Maybe it's all wonderful."

They got up to go, the daughter slowing her walk to fit her mother's. Larkin felt a stab, resolving once again to try to form some bridge with Bunny when she got home. She looked at Duncan, sitting comfortably slouched down on the bench, one arm resting on the back. She reached up, took his hand, and brought his arm to rest on her shoulder, only now realizing she'd missed him. He smiled at her.

"Are you ready to head home?"

She nodded and took a last sip of her beer. When they got to the door, Larkin looked back once more.

They walked back to the B&B, hands together, matching their steps.

Larkin leaned her head to rest on his arm. "How often is it like that? Perfect, I mean, where everything just works. Maybe it was just me?"

"No, it was a grand night for me as well. Sometimes, listening to the music alone brings me closer to it. Sitting there tonight, watching you, listening to the band - it gave me a new perspective, one I'd never had in the past."

They finished the walk in silence, gravel crunching under their feet.

In the room, Larkin took the first turn in the bathroom then crawled in her bed, still amazed by the night. When Duncan came out, he walked to her bed to kiss her goodnight.

"Still thinking about it?" he asked her, his voice low. She nodded. "Don't think it all the way through. Leave some of it as wonder."

He bent down to kiss her, lightly, then turned to his bed.

"One more," she whispered.

He came back to her, squatted down next to her, and smiled.

"All right, but only one." He kissed her again and she smiled as he walked to his bed.

"Always leave them wanting more, is that your theory?" Larkin whispered.

"I'm new at this. Is it working?"

"You bet."

28.

Friday dawned bright, the air washed by showers in the night. The flowers in the garden outside the breakfast room shone with droplets, and the windows were open to a scented breeze.

Although they sat together for breakfast, Larkin had awoken alone. When she had turned over to look at Duncan, his bed was rumpled and empty. She pushed herself up on an elbow, listening for activity in the bathroom, but heard nothing.

She got up and quickly showered. In the room, she packed the few things she'd brought, her attention trained to the door.

When he came in, she raised her eyebrows at him.

"Out so early?"

He raised his arm, a bag dangling in his fingers. "I was out of blades. Had to run to the next town to get them."

"I must have been sleeping hard. I never heard you go."

"It was seven or so." He looked at the bed. "All packed?"

"You left at seven? It's eight now. What took you?"

"I told you. I had to go to the next town."

Larkin shook her head. "Duncan, I'm a trained observer of human behavior and I spend my life discerning inconsistencies in conversation. In my professional opinion, you're lying like a rag rug."

"How suspicious of you, Larkin."

"Nope. You're fibbing, telling a tall one, yanking my chain."

"Larkin, I don't know what to say to you."

"It's true, though, isn't it?"

"Well, I suppose in the strictest sense I haven't told you the complete truth. I didn't lie, exactly, but it's possible I didn't share the entire purpose of my trip."

"Mr. McKenna, please tell the court why it is that you can't share the entire purpose of your trip."

"It would ruin the surprise."

"A surprise?"

"Yes, Larkin. It will already not be as much a surprise since you made me tell you there is a surprise, but it can still be somewhat a surprise if I don't tell you what the surprise actually is."

"A surprise."

"Are you done questioning me now?"

"I suppose."

Duncan showered and dressed, Larkin waiting in the conservatory. When he came in, she put down the book she was reading and stood to greet him.

"Wow, you look great. Clean-shaven, smelling good, nicely dressed. What a lucky woman I am to be having breakfast with such a man as you."

"I'm not telling you."

"You have a mean streak, do you know that?"

Over breakfast, they discussed plans. They were to be back in Athlone by late afternoon but had hours to meander before getting there.

Duncan buttered brown bread, breaking off a piece for Larkin.

"We could go south to Ennis and Limerick, then around to Nenagh and back north to Athlone." Duncan looked thoughtful. "Have you seen any of those towns?

"No, but remember, there are a lot more towns in this country I haven't seen than those I have."

"As well, we could go north to Westport and Castlebar, but that's a bit more driving. We might have a hard time getting back to practice and getting a good night's sleep before the race."

"I will sleep well because I have a clear conscience. I haven't kept secrets from anyone, so I'm able to sleep like a baby."

Duncan put down his fork. "I, on the other hand, will be up the whole of the night, tossing and turning, my conscience as heavy as a case of tinned beans."

"Tinned beans? Are they very heavy?"

"Dreadfully heavy, Larkin."

"As long as I know you'll be suffering, I'll go anywhere you like today."

"All right, we're off to Ennis and Limerick."

They finished breakfast, and Duncan paid Mrs. Brannock for the room. They stowed their luggage and set off, heading south from Doolin, the sun on their left and the scent of the sea leaving them at Kilshanny.

29

It's today, Larkin thought, as she woke. The race.

She swung her legs over the edge of the bed and kneaded her thighs. She was sore, but not hurting. Perfect.

When she and Duncan got back to Athlone last night, they'd gone to the boathouse for a couple of hours. The rest of Larkin's team was there, as well. They circled themselves in a corner of the boathouse, working the ergometers and listening as Deirdre outlined the strategy for the race.

"It's the last," she told them, "so make it good." Turning to Larkin, she pointed. "This is the one you'll go home with, the one you'll remember."

Larkin looked up from fixing her feet in the stretchers of the ergometer. "I'll remember them all."

"This race will be the one. Take my word for it."

Larkin shrugged, smiled. She looked over at Duncan, working in the tank with his eight. From where she sat, she could see his long back moving. She watched until his arms came to his midsection and flexed, then turned back to her machine.

Her team left early enough for a good sleep. Duncan walked Larkin home and at Brynna's door, she turned to him for a kiss and a hug.

He kissed her, then leaned down and lifted her up to be even with his eyes.

"Are you nervous about tomorrow?' he asked her.

"Of course, but I'm nervous before every race. I don't actually throw up, but there hasn't been one when I haven't been nauseous."

"It will be different tomorrow. There will be more people, more boats. They come from all over the country. There will be heats to see who rows in the finals, so it will be a longer day than usual, but we start by nine, so it should be all over by five or so."

"It's a workday. Nine to five. I can do that." Larkin thought, then asked, "Are you nervous?"

"Funny enough, I still get nervous, even after all these years. My stomach still flutters and my palms still sweat."

"Just like the first time you saw me?"

"Just like that."

"A good sign, don't you think?"

"Very good." He put her down. "Get a good sleep, now, and don't worry. It will be fun - and even if it's not, by five tomorrow, it will be over."

"It will be my last full day in Ireland."

"It's true. Will you come for supper after the races? I've wanted to cook for you."

"I'd love to. Will you have the energy after the day?"

"Ah, of course, Larkin. For you? On your last night in Ireland? Nothing could keep me from it."

"All right, then. I'll be expecting great things."

"Careful, now, what you expect. Go on, now."

Larkin reached up to give him another quick kiss and held his face in her hands. "Duncan, thank you so much for Doolin."

"You're welcome, Larkin. I'm happy you liked it."

"I think it's possible you could have taken me to Cicero and I would have liked it."

"Cicero?"

"A town near Chicago not known for its tourist appeal."

"Not as pretty as Doolin?"

"Not even close."

"No cliffs?"

"Nary a hill."

"I don't think you would have liked Cicero as well," he told her.

"See you in the morning."

"Good night, love."

Morning found Larkin anxious; ready to get started and ready to be finished. Her nerves were twanging, and now and again, she took a full, deep breath, just to remind herself she could.

Brynna was busy at the stove when Larkin burst in the kitchen.

"There you are, Ducky! I was just going to send Teresa up to find you. Are you wanting to eat before you go?"

Larkin made a face. "I don't think I can."

"Ah, but you won't make it the day unless you do. Here," she turned from the stove to the counter, deftly made a sandwich of rashers, tomato, and egg, wrapped it in a paper towel and handed it to her. "Take it with you, Larkin. You'll be wanting something in a while, maybe."

"Thanks. I'll take it just in case."

"Now, we'll be there to cheer you on before you start. Teresa's going to stay here for the afternoon, aren't you, lovey?"

Teresa nodded. "No offense, Larkin, but I've seen more rowing than I care to."

Brynna turned back to the stove, and Des came in from the dining room with an empty teapot in his hand.

""Good luck, Ducky!" Des called.

"I'll look for you guys at the start."

"And we'll look for you at the finish."

Larkin pushed out the door and looked up. It was cloudy but not dark. As she started to walk, the door opened behind her and Brynna stepped out on the porch, a towel over her shoulder, her hand reaching in her apron pocket.

"Larkin, I almost forgot." Her hand came out with a box. "I thought you might like a good-luck charm, something to have on during the race."

Larkin took it, the paper covering on the box worn, but impressive. Pinned in the box was a small medal, round and ornate with Celtic designs around the edge and a red medallion in the middle.

"It was my father's, from the Army. He did some brave thing, he would never tell us what, but he got this because of it and gave it to me when they went to America. I wondered if you'd like to wear it today."

Larkin looked up at her and smiled.

"You are very good to me," she said. "I was thinking of your dad yesterday, missing him. This is perfect." Larkin reached over and hugged Brynna quickly, her face brushing the rough of the towel.

"Well, I've said before, he'd be proud of you, Larkin. I know you've emailed him and I've kept in touch by phone, but he'd love to be here today. He told me to mind the details, that he would want a full telling."

"Between the two of us, he'll get it."

"Go on, now. Don't want to be late."

Larkin took the medal from the box and carefully attached it to her tank top, under her sweatshirt. She handed the box back to Brynna and smiled.

"I feel braver."

"Are you sick to your stomach?"

"Not yet."

"Maybe this will keep you from it. Now, go on." Brynna waved a hand, urging her away. "We'll see you later, when you win."

As she walked, Larkin took notice of the clouds - full and rounded, gray and yellow, moving across the sky slowly, but without vicious intent. The sun would burst through intermittently, but the clouds would overpower it again, the light appearing and disappearing on the sidewalk as Larkin walked toward the boathouse.

The boathouse was bedlam, with 72 individual teams from eight different counties wandering around and warming up. Most of the County Westmeath teams were from Athlone, and Larkin exchanged greetings with them as she searched for Deirdre, finding her with Nessa and Kerry in a corner, huddling.

Nessa moved over to make a space for Larkin. Deirdre looked up from her clipboard.

"Good, just one to go, and that's the one who's always ten minutes late for everything."

"I heard that," Lara said, dropping to the floor next to Kerry, "and it's not true. I would have been here right on time, but I couldn't find you in this mess."

"It is a bit of a circus, isn't it?" Deirdre looked at the mass of rowers, in various states of dress and undress, one man lifting weights in nothing but a Speedo. "Would you look at that bollux over there?"

"That's probably why Lara was late," Nessa said.

Deirdre shook her head. "Here's the lineup. First will be the heats for the men's and women's pairs, then the fours, then the eights. There are two heats for each event, a total of twelve boats entered in each category. The top six

will go to the finals. Our first heat is at 10:30, and the final is at 2:30." She
glared at them. "We will be in the final."

Larkin touched the medal through her sweatshirt.

"We'll go out to practice around 9:45 just to warm up. Looking at the
teams in our heat, we won't need to go all-out to end in the top three. These
are mostly teams we've seen before, with the exception of the four from Mayo,
whom we've never come up against. We'll stay well in place, but try to save
something for the finals. All right? Take the next hour to relax. Get in the
tank for a few minutes if you like, but no more than that. If we're not ready by
now, we won't be."

The team split up, Larkin going outside by the dock. She was grateful the
championships were in Athlone the year she was competing. Things were
familiar here.

The clouds were still competing with the sun, making a changing painting
on the waving water. There was a breeze but no stiff wind, and Larkin was
glad. A wind changed the tenor of a race, the only leveling factor being it
blew on them all.

Duncan came up behind her and put his hands on her shoulders. As he
touched her, she reached up past his hand to touch his face.

"Good thing it's me," he said to her, bending down to kiss her cheek.

"I'd know that touch anywhere."

"The water's lovely with the sun on it, isn't it?"

Larkin nodded and turned to him. "When is your first heat?"

"We go at noon. Yours?"

"10:30. I'm glad we don't have to wait till noon. I'd be in a straightjacket by
then."

"I'll probably be hungry. Just the thing. I'll be hungry, but too nervous to
eat."

"Can you eat now?" She reached in her pocket. "Here. Brynna made me a
sandwich I'm sure I won't eat."

"Really? I didn't eat this morning, not knowing when we'd be going out,
and I thought if there was time, I'd grab something at Sean's."

"Comparing Sean's cooking with Brynna's is no contest."

"What about you? You'll be hungry later and will have nothing."

"If I'm hungry later, I'll run home and get something."

"If you're sure..."

"I'm sure. Eat."

She stood with him while he ate until it was time to practice. Duncan kissed her lightly.

"Best of luck, Larkin. I'll be watching."

"I have a good-luck charm. Want to see?"

"Of course."

She took off her sweatshirt and showed him the medal pinned to her white shirt.

"I remember that," he said. "No one ever got the story out of him, and the Army kept it under wraps, as well. It must have been something big, though, because they don't give these out easily."

"I am feeling very brave."

"As you should."

"Good luck to you. I'll be waiting for you."

"I'll think of that."

She found the team in the same corner, having commandeered the small section of floor they occupied this morning.

When they were ready to go, Deirdre lifted a hand.

"One more thing. It's going to be even harder to get the boat in and out of the house with all these people. Mind the boat."

They ran drills in the water at half-pressure, then killed time until the last pair's heat was finished. They made their way to the starting line, Deirdre checking their assigned lane, then sat, their aligner holding the stern easily in the smoothly moving water.

As the other boats lined up, Larkin was surprised to feel little nervousness and no nausea. She glanced down at the medal.

The boats aligned, the race began. True to Deirdre's predictions, they were far ahead of three of the boats, dead even with one of the teams remaining, the other a half-boat ahead. She kept them steady at a competitive pace and the race ran smoothly. They finished second, barely edging out the third-place team, and Deirdre was pleased.

"Good, girls. Perfect, in fact. Second in the heat will get us good placement, and you've saved some for the finals, I can tell by looking at you."

Larkin nodded. Although she was breathing hard and had certainly broken a sweat, she felt as if she'd gone for an easy mile run, not a pounding race.

They got the boat back in the house and Deirdre gathered the team around her in their corner.

"All right, now, go watch some heats, eat if you like, and meet back here at 1:15."

Larkin and Nessa got out in time to watch the next women's four's heat. There was one team they watched whose form was excellent, and by the end of the race Larkin was nodding, her eyes following them as they came across the line in first.

Nessa spoke first.

"It's them," she said. "It's them we'll have to beat."

They watched as the team made their way to the dock, smoothly got the boat out of the water, and headed it back to their truck and trailer. Larkin and Nessa followed to see who they were, and saw the "Kilkenny Rowing Team" insignia on the side of the truck.

The men's eights heats were lining up. Duncan was rowing in the first heat. As the aligner got ahold of their stern, he looked up as Larkin was passing on the shore and she caught his eye. He lifted his eyebrows, then turned his attention back to the boat.

Watching the race, Larkin wondered if she was finally getting used to this, to the excitement and the noise, the people yelling from the shore. She felt no concern Duncan's team wouldn't qualify, and watched with a certain detachment as they won the heat, beating the pack by a full half-boat length. The team took the win with nothing more than a quick slap on the back of the man in front of them.

When the team had stored the boat, she asked Duncan about his reaction.

"It's not the race, after all. It's only the heat. No one is going full-out. The test will be the final."

"Is that it? I wondered why I wasn't nauseous."

"It's my guess that if you've been sick to your stomach with every other race, you will be with this one. Although," he said, touching the medal on her shirt lightly, "you didn't have this."

"We'll see."

"How much time do you have until you have to meet the team?"

Larkin checked her watch. "About forty minutes."

"Would you like tea?"

"Maybe. I'm actually getting hungry. Maybe tea and bread."

"We'll be safe with that. Sean buys his bread."

They took a small table in the pub, getting tea for them both and brown bread with butter for Larkin. She ate two small pieces and waved away more.

"If nausea is coming, no sense giving it more company."

"Save up your hunger for supper. I will feed you well."

"Decided what we're eating yet?"

"I had a few ideas during the race."

"Keep your mind in the boat. I don't want you losing because of me."

"The next one, I'll pay more attention, I promise."

They finished their tea and walked back to the boathouse. Before Larkin left to find the team, Duncan hugged her, hard.

"Do your best, Larkin."

"There's nothing left to save it for."

"It will be enough."

"Will you be at the finish?"

"I will."

"I will look for you." She took a deep breath. "I'm feeling nauseous. Must be close to race time."

"Don't forget the medal."

She found the team in their corner. Kerry was pacing, her face pale. Lara sat bent over with her feet out straight in front of her, her nose touching her knees. Nessa lay flat on her back, bringing one leg, then the other, bent to her chest. Deirdre was reading off of her clipboard and looked up when Larkin approached.

"Good, you're here. Everybody stretch."

When they were all prone, Deirdre sat down in the middle of them.

"We're early, so let's take a few minutes to review the teams in the final."

She started down the list, reciting every team's won/loss record, how they did in last year's championships, the name of their coxswain, and her record. The last team on the list was Kilkenny.

"It's this one that's our challenge, girls. They have a slightly better record than ours, but haven't rowed against teams as tough. They have a very steady pace, smooth action, and seem to be able to give as many power pieces as their coxswain calls."

Larkin nodded. "We saw them win their heat. It looked almost effortless."

"The good thing is they're in the lane next to us. I can keep a very close eye on them. Their coxswain's name is Colleen O'Sheedy. I rowed against her in university and she is very tough, very good."

Nessa spoke from the floor.

"I knew her, too. She's not as good as you."

"She is our biggest threat. The rest we can beat, I think. We've beaten better teams before, haven't we." She stood, gathered her gear and her clipboard. "Let's get out on the water."

They took off their sweats walked to the boat. Deirdre stopped and looked at them.

"This is it, girls. This is the end of it, the only race left. Treat it like you're never going to row again and this is your only chance to win."

The team nodded, Larkin closing her eyes for a short second.

"We have everything we need. We've worked hard. We've won before. We know what it takes. Most of all, we have each other. Be the best you are individually and as a team, and no one can stop us. Not Kilkenny, not anyone."

She looked at them all in turn.

"We can do this. Let's go," Deirdre said. "Let's win."

She had them line up next to the boat. "From this moment on, we are in the race. Ready, hands on."

The four put their hands on the boat.

"Feel the boat. You know what it can do. You know what you can do in it. Shoulder, up."

They lifted the boat to their shoulders.

"Walk it out."

They started the walk to the dock, stopping twice for people and obstructions. Deirdre kept her hand on the stern and got them safely to the dock.

If she rowed for years, Larkin didn't think she'd ever get used to the weight of the boat on the tender skin between her neck and shoulder.

"Heads, ready, up."

They lifted the boat over their heads.

"Toward the water, roll."

They eased it down, waist high.

"Set it in, ready, in. One and three, oars."

Larkin and Kerry steadied the boat while Nessa and Lara ran for oars. When the oars were secure in the oarlocks and the seats free from the cords that held them in place, Deirdre called, "One foot in, sit in." The four took their places in the boat, getting their feet in the stretchers, and checking their oarlocks and seats for loose nuts and screws. Deirdre got settled in her seat, and counted down her team.

"Seat one, ready?"

"Ready."

"Seat two, ready"

Here we go, Larkin thought. "Ready."

"Seat three, ready?"

"Ready."

"Seat four, ready?"

"Ready."

"Ready to shove, shove."

Larkin reached out and pushed hard against the rough wood of the dock. The boat floated away, far enough to free the oars, and they rowed slowly to an empty space in the river to warm up.

Unusual for her, Deirdre kept up a running commentary while they ran drills. The team sat quiet, letting her talk, the words keeping cadence with the slap of the oars and their breathing.

When the drills were finished, Deirdre had them hold steady. She checked her watch and her clipboard.

"You are my team," she began. "I know I don't really get to claim you, and it's your hard work, not mine, that got us this far, but it's how I think of you, how I'll always think of you. This year has been different. We've come together, unusual with a new member, but that just says how well Larkin fit in. We all thank you for your hard work, Larkin. You were a bit thrust on us to start, but I think I speak for us all when I say there's no one we'd rather have in your seat."

Larkin felt Lara's hand briefly on her shoulder. Nessa leaned back toward her with a "you're all right, Larkin," and Kerry made an affirming noise from the bow.

Deirdre went on. "We have our best team ever in the championships we have every chance of winning. Today will be a memory you will keep forever. It is in you to win. We are all born to this water, even you, Larkin. It is

natural to us, like breathing, and all we have to do today is what comes
naturally. We will know what to do. I will give direction, but, inside, we will
all know."

Deirdre checked her watch.

"It's time. Nothing more to be said, except maybe to remind you again that
you were born for this, born for this win. I don't know why I feel so strongly
about it, but I do. Let's go."

They rowed to the starting line, Larkin's mind searching for something just
out of her grasp. Deirdre's words had triggered a memory, but she couldn't pin
it down.

In the lane, trying to get aligned, she checked how she felt. She was a little
nauseous, but not alarmingly so; nervous in a way that would help, not hinder.
Raising her eyes, she was able to pick Duncan, Brynna, and Des out of the
crowd. In that moment, she desperately missed Sukki and Mr. Carney.

Looking to her right in lane four, she saw Kilkenny in their boat and ready.
Larkin heard the starter polling the teams, Deirdre calling "Ready" from their
spot in lane three. She sat halfway up on the slide, every muscle ready,
waiting for the words that would set them off.

"Etes vous prets?"

They tensed.

"Partez!"

Within the first minute she knew it was not going to be like the last race.
Then, she had been in a zone, a propulsion of athleticism, with almost no
knowledge of what it took to get there.

Not today.

Today, she felt it all; the almost immediate hardness of her breath, the
burning in her thighs, her constricted calves. As she pulled the oar toward her
midsection, she watched Nessa's back tighten, and felt the boat respond to the
final pull to the sternum. The boat almost jumped in the water, and Larkin
realized they were going harder than usual, maybe too hard.

Deirdre's voice was firm. "All right, keep it steady. We're two down on
Kilkenny. Let's get even, I want a power ten in two, one, two, and ONE, go
hard now, TWO, let 'em know we're here, THREE, getting closer now, FOUR,
moving up a bit, ..."

By the end of the ten, they were still one seat down on Kilkenny, who took
a ten at the same time. Deirdre kept talking.

"They took a ten, but we still gained a seat. Good work, girls, good. Breathe well in this twenty; we'll be taking another ten to get that next seat. We're now two up on one, still even with two, one back on Kilkenny, two up on five and one up on six. Let's get that seat from Kilkenny. One, dig in now!" She counted them down to the end of the ten, and gave them good news. "I'm coxswain to coxswain, good job! We'll go another ten in two, one, and ONE, keep it up! TWO, more power! THREE..."

Another ten, so soon? Larkin thought wildly. I won't have enough to last.

She dug in her oar and heard the *shwoosh* as the boat slid across the top of the water. Another stroke, *shwoosh,* another, *shwoosh.*

That's it, Larkin thought. I'll listen for that sound. Every sound is closer to being done.

When they reached the halfway mark, Deirdre dialed them up a notch.

"All right, half to go. Start using what you've been saving, girls, because in another few minutes, you won't need it. We're up on one, two, and five, even with six, and Kilkenny took back the seat we gained. Not acceptable! Give me a ten in two, one...and ONE, get it in there! TWO, no hang on the catch!" Deirdre continued the count, the team following her direction from the speakers under their seats.

Another power ten left Larkin panting hard, her lungs burning. It came to her then, what she had tried to remember at the start, some obscure quotation from a book she'd read in college and her mind clamped on it, her lips silently mouthing the words in time as she rowed, her breath heaving.

'It was then I saw, as one does who looks for magic, that she moved through the tide in a roar, her arms making foam of the waves and the sea fanning past, as if she were to water, borne.'

That's us, Larkin thought. We are waterborne, and strong.

She gritted her teeth and put her eyes back to Nessa's bunched shoulders, timing her strokes with hers, trusting in all of them, ready for the last draining push that would end the race, end the season, and end their time as a team.

Larkin tried to force air into her lungs, her body working against itself, each motion causing more pain, but each stroke closer to not having to stroke any longer.

Deirdre's voice changed, got steely. She had them steady at a higher cadence than usual, but necessary to keep them close to Kilkenny.

"Here's where we let them know who we are. We're up on everyone but Kilkenny, they're up one seat, one fecking seat, and we're going to catch them, we are going to hunt them down. Listen to me, now, clear your minds, and do what I say. We've got 25 strokes left in this race, and we are going to hunt...them...down. Bring it up from your toes, girls, everything you've got and everything you've ever had because we need it now." She paused, then, in as intense a command as Larkin had ever heard, shouted at them. "I want your best ten in two, and ONE! Give me what you've got. TWO! Push like you never have before. THREE! No hang at the catch. FOUR! Back it in, now. FIVE! I want your heart! SIX! We're moving on them! SEVEN! I'm past their stern! EIGHT, we're keeping steady. NINE! Keep moving! TEN! Walk it up!"

Larkin thought, the first ten, only fifteen more and I can breathe. I can do that.

"Ten more now, ONE! This is it, girls! TWO! We're moving! THREE! Almost even. FOUR! Harder! FIVE! I'm coxswain to coxswain! SIX, keep gong! SEVEN, get me past her! EIGHT, still even! NINE, inching past! TEN, only five strokes to go!"

Deirdre took a deep breath. "Last five! ONE! You were born for this!"

I am to water, borne

"TWO! Do it for Ireland!"

For Ireland, yes

"THREE! Do it for each other!"

For these good women

"FOUR! Do it for who loves you!"

Sukki, Duncan, Mr. Carney...Pat.

"FIVE! Do it for yourselves!"

For what I can be

They crossed the line and Deirdre threw her arms in the air and screamed.

"Yes! That's it! You did it, girls!" Her voice broke. "You did it!"

Larkin laid her oar across her lap, drew two full breaths, and cried.

30.

On the walk to Duncan's house, Larkin stopped at the corner before the turn and looked up. Although it was nearly eight, the sky was still bright, and the clouds were a moving silhouette.

Tomorrow I leave, she thought, and this sky will no longer be mine.

As unreal as it seemed when she was making her plans to come, it seemed very real to be leaving.

Her thoughts went back to the race. They received their medals on the dock, their arms around each other. It was nearly reverently that they carried Deirdre to the water and threw her in, then joined her in the peaty water of the Shannon, circling her like baby seals. At Sean's, they were greeted as the champions they were, and had drinks and congratulations until they were woozy with both. The five sat together, touching each other often, not wanting the team to end, not wanting to forget.

I never will, Larkin thought. As long as I breathe, I will never forget.

Duncan joined them after his race, coming in a close second. He hugged them all, then left to go cook. Larkin's team stayed at Sean's until Larkin was almost late, the team gathering in a circle to hug and congratulate each other one last time.

Still damp from her shower, she got to Duncan's house just on time. As she got to the door, she smelled cooking even before it opened. Duncan answered her knock and motioned her in. His hands were covered in flour and he had a smudge of it on his sweater.

"Welcome, Larkin. I'd hug you but you'd end up white."

"A kiss will do," she told him.

He kissed her quickly and she handed him the bottle of wine she'd brought.

"Ah, Larkin, very thoughtful of you. And what have you brought? A lovely French red, very nice. Did you get this from Garret? I hope he didn't soak you too badly."

"Not too. We don't have to drink this one now, if there's something you'd rather have. Save it for another time."

"Well, I have a white chilling as well. What would you prefer?"

"You're the chef. What would work best with that incredible smell?"

"I think, Larkin, that the red would work very well." He walked with her to the kitchen and brought down glasses from a built-in cabinet that took up an entire wall. Rummaging for a corkscrew, he called to her over his shoulder. "How are you feeling after the win? Calmed down yet?'

"Not really. You only get so many days like this one"

"Good girl. It was quite a day, at that."

He opened the wine and poured them each a glass. She was glad he'd chosen the red, if for no other reason than the way it looked in the glass. She took the glass he offered her.

"Cheers, then," he said, taking a sip. "Ah, lovely. You have good taste, Larkin."

"Well, Garret has good taste."

She looked around at Duncan's home. Although she'd been here before, it had only been for quick stops to pick up something forgotten, or to use the bathroom. Tonight, it was bathed in candlelight and there was muted music playing.

"What are you making?" Larkin asked him. "It smells heavenly."

"It's butternut squash which I will soon be putting into pasta, covering with sauce and feeding you."

"Squash. I wouldn't have guessed that." She lifted her nose and inhaled. It was a heady, almost sweet smell, rich and opaque. It made her think of autumn.

She sipped the wine, felt the warmth of it flow into her and could feel it travel the length of her body in a swoop, a byproduct of not eating most of the day.

"What can I do to help?" she asked.

"Not a thing." He was working at the island, mixing something into a lump. "Make yourself comfortable."

"Can I look around?"

"Of course."

Picking up her glass, she explored.

The living room was large and square, a terracotta tiled hearth on one wall and a couch and two chairs making a U shape around it. The chairs were a dark, simple pattern, framed in wood and wide for comfort. The couch looked inviting, the cushions deep green with a fleck of blue. The floor was wood with an area rug the same color as the fleck in the couch, and very close, Larkin saw, to the color of the darkening light outside. The tables were wood and straight, almost Frank Lloyd Wright in design, and were stained a shade or two lighter than the floor.

"Did you make the tables in here?" Larkin called to Duncan.

"I did, yes. Actually, I made all the wood pieces in the house. The table in here was my first. Not very well done, I'll admit, but I have an attachment to it, just the same."

Larkin walked to the dining room table and sat in one of the chairs. The table was thick and worn, with nicks and gouges, and a lovely, lustrous finish.

"Has this been refinished recently?"

"It was a year or so ago, I guess. I do it every few years. So much gets done on that table, it gets beaten up badly, but I sand it down and put a new coat of finish on it, and it's ready to go again."

"When did you make it?"

"Look on the corner. See my initials? And the year?"

"You made this table 24 years ago? When you were 14?"

"My father helped, but mostly he watched me and corrected my mistakes before I made them. He wouldn't lay a finger on the wood so I could say I made it myself."

Larkin ran her hand over the table, smooth and warm, and thought of Duncan as a boy.

"What a nice memory for the two of you."

"It is. He still mentions it now and again."

Larkin walked down the length of the hallway. There were four doors, one to the bathroom, one to an office, and the other two, bedrooms.

The office was neat and spare - a desk with a computer, a table covered with blueprints, and several filing cabinets on the far wall. The window was uncovered and looked out over the back yard, dark now, but from its direction, Larkin knew it faced east. She could imagine Duncan here with his morning tea, making the day's plans and checking email from vendors and customers.

The larger of the two bedrooms was Duncan's, with a shirt tossed on a chair, and his wallet and keys on the dresser. Larkin stopped at the doorway, but from there could see things that she had come to acquaint with this man.

Her eyes drifted from the books on his nightstand, most of which he'd shared with her, to a huge map of the world framed and hanging above his bed. She smelled him, his cologne in the air, and, when she got close enough, his own scent in the jacket hanging on the door. The duvet on the big bed was navy blue with a thin white stripe, and the dresser and wardrobe stained to match the headboard. It was masculine, but still with an eye for detail: a curved iron lamp on the dresser, and beautiful crown molding running across the top of the wall.

The other bedroom was small and simple, a guest room, she thought. It reminded her of her room at Brynna's - only the necessities, but add flowers and it became somewhere anyone could feel at home.

She drifted back to the living room, humming, then into the kitchen to see what Duncan was doing.

He had a big square of dough rolled out on a floured board in the middle of the island. When he was happy with the thickness, he put the rolling pin aside and took the squash out of the oven. Larkin sat on a stool to watch.

"How did you cook the squash?"

"I cut it in half, dotted it with butter, then sprinkled it with brown sugar."

"Yum."

Duncan smiled. "It cooked for 45 minutes or so, until it was soft, and then I turned off the heat and let it sit and cool a bit."

"Now what will happen? When do we get to eat it?"

"Hungry, are you? We won't eat it for a bit, yet."

"Keep telling me what you're doing so I can stop thinking about how hungry I am."

"Here, have some bread. I can't have you sitting there starving in front of me." He pulled a loaf of French bread from the counter behind him and reached for a cutting board. He cut it in thick slices and went back to the counter for a square of butter on a white dish. He gave her a small plate and a knife.

"Will that hold you until your dinner is ready?"

"How embarrassing, but, yes, it will. Want some?"

"Sure, of course." Larkin put a piece of bread in his mouth while he scooped the squash out of the rind, mashing it in a wooden bowl with a touch of paprika. The smell of squash and sweetened butter wafted over to Larkin.

"What is the dough for, again?"

"It's pasta. I'm putting the squash in it."

Larkin stopped, the bread halfway to her mouth. "Really?"

"Ravioli, actually. Butternut squash ravioli with walnut cream sauce."

"When you said you were cooking dinner, I wasn't expecting cuisine."

"Because men can't cook? Rather sexist of you, Larkin."

"All right, I stand corrected. But 'walnut cream sauce?'"

"My children and I like to cook."

"Is this the first time you've tried this recipe?"

"Ah, no. I couldn't take a chance on a new recipe with you coming. It had to be something tried and true."

As he talked, Duncan was dropping dollops of the squash mixture on the pasta, spacing it regularly. When the pasta was liberally dotted, he took a short knife and cut rectangles, each with squash covering half. He lifted the plain end and covered the squash, folding it over and crimping the edges with a fork. When he was finished, 24 squares sat on the board, of uniform size and edging.

"Nice crimping," Larkin told him. "Now what?"

"Now we will eat salad and bread, and perhaps have another glass of this excellent wine."

He reached in the refrigerator and brought out a large bowl, half-filled with various greens. In it, he dribbled olive oil and spices soaked in vinegar. He tossed the leaves in the bowl, adding a grinding of pepper.

"Do you like your salad milder or a bit biting?"

"I really like vinegar, so go nuts if you like. What kind of vinegar is that?"

"It's a balsamic. Very nice."

He put an extra slosh in the bowl, tossed the greens once again, and served them onto white plates. From the refrigerator, he brought out a container, and put a Greek olive in the middle of each pile.

"Only one, for taste."

He pulled a stool near hers at the island, and brought her a plate of salad and the bottle of wine. He refreshed her glass and his own and pulled the bread and butter nearer.

Larkin lifted her glass. "To you, the mighty chef. I place myself in your hands."

"Ah, no, Larkin. To you, to today's win, to your stay here. May you have enjoyed Ireland."

He touched her glass. As she took a sip of her wine, she closed her eyes. Once again, the thought of leaving had shocked her. When she opened her eyes, she took a deep breath and smiled into his face.

"If I don't eat, this wine will do me in."

"By all means, eat."

She took a bite of the salad, the lettuces fresh and smooth, a blend of green flavors, and the dressing a complement, not a covering, to the taste of the leaves.

"Perfect," she told him. "What is that spice I taste that I can't place?"

"Ah, perhaps the mint. It adds freshness."

"That vinegar is wonderful. I'll have to get some before I go."

"I'll send you some, Larkin. I get it in Moate."

They ate the salad and bread, talking about the race. Later, Larkin would wonder why they talked so quietly.

When they'd finished, Duncan cleared the plates and went to a large pot with water on the stove, hot but not boiling. He turned the heat on high underneath it.

He put four tablespoons of butter in a smaller saucepan, and turned a low heat under it, waiting for it to melt. When it was liquid, he whisked in flour, and when the flour and butter were blended, added a cup and a half of cream. When it was bubbling, he reached for a bottle of Marsala wine and poured a bit in, whisking it, and then dropped in a handful of chopped walnuts. He turned the heat down and came back to take a sip of his wine.

Larkin could smell the difference he was making in the sauce with every added ingredient. The butter and flour had a rich smell to it, the roux white and creamy. The wine added sweetness and the walnuts brought forth an earthy, brown smell. Slowly, the scent of the sauce overpowered that of the squash, and as it took on the hue of the walnuts, Larkin saw the sauce change to a color she'd never seen before.

She knew, then, this would be an evening she would remember for having satisfied all her senses at once. She still had the ping of the vinegar on her tongue, softened with wine. The room was lovely with candlelight and if she spoke to him, Duncan's voice would reach across the air to her, mingling with the music from the living room and the sound of the pelting rain on the windows. She knew that before the night ended, chances were quite good she would have this man's hand in hers and feel his kiss. She knew, in fact, she could have it now. She looked at Duncan, carefully placing the ravioli in the now-boiling water. She had thought of him in the dark of her room, wondered at things she hadn't thought of since Pat died, imagined the feel of him next to her and where her hands might fit on his body. She let her eyes sweep him head to foot.

Duncan turned from the pot. He stopped.

"What are you thinking about?"

"Why?

"You have the strangest look on your face."

"Strange, how?"

"Just a look I've never seen before."

"I have a lot of looks you haven't seen," she told him.

"You won't tell me?"

"Not this minute."

"But sometime?"

She smiled at him. "Perhaps," she told him.

When the pasta was done, he carefully poured it over a colander in the sink. From the colander, it went into a shallow white bowl. Duncan got the saucepan from the stove, stirred it once again, and poured the creamy brown sauce over the top of the ravioli. Gently, so as not to break the pasta open, he lifted the ravioli up through the sauce until they were bathed in it, fragrant and hot. He reached up in the cabinet and got two smaller pottery bowls, white with a carved leaf design on their rims, and spooned pasta into them, setting them on the table with napkins and forks.

"Please," he said to Larkin, holding out a chair for her. "And bring the wine."

She sat down and put her napkin in her lap. She liked the feel of it, stiff cotton with a texture.

Duncan sat across from her. She looked over the candle at him.

"You're so far away," she said.

"I can fix that." He pushed his bowl halfway across the table to where she could slide it in front of the chair next to her.

"Better?"

She nodded.

"May I eat what I've been smelling all night?"

"Be my guest."

She cut into her first piece of pasta and took time to admire the orange of the squash sitting in nutty brown sauce in the vanilla white bowl.

"You made pretty food, Duncan. Did you do that on purpose?"

"I did, of course. Just for you."

She put it in her mouth and smiled. It tasted even better than it smelled, rich and satisfying. The walnuts took the edge off the sweetness of the squash, and the sauce blended the flavors together until they were all one taste, unlike anything she'd ever had in her mouth before.

Some food was miraculous, she thought. You cook up a random selection of ingredients, and they changed to something completely unlike their beginnings.

"This is really wonderful. I wouldn't ever have guessed it would taste like this." She speared another ravioli. "Will you write the recipe for me so I can make it for Sukki? She'll be incredibly impressed."

"You watched me do it. It's not so hard." Duncan started to eat. "I'd like to know who thought it up. I don't know that I ever would have looked at a squash and pasta and put them together."

"Maybe it's all she had in her kitchen. She was making do, I bet, and came up with something people perform on cooking shows, when really, she just didn't want to go to the store again."

They ate until they were full, slowly and with pleasure. They talked about inconsequential things, the candle on the table sputtering as it melted. When they'd finished, they carried the dishes to the sink.

Duncan put the dishes in the dishwasher. He turned it on, the machine humming off key, then took her hand and led her to the couch. She kicked off her shoes and sat down, arranging herself in one corner, her wine glass held in both hands. He bent down over the fireplace and touched a match to kindling under the fire, already laid.

"Comfy?" he asked her. "How about dessert?"

She shook her head. "I'm full."

"Just as well," he said. "I have only butter cookies to offer you."

"Homemade butter cookies?"

"Homemade by the lady down the street that owns the bakery."

"Split one with me?"

"Would you like coffee as well?"

"I would love coffee. That would be perfect." She watched as he walked back to the kitchen. She said to his back, "I'm feeling very pampered."

"Ah, good. That was the point."

She let her head rest on the high back of the couch. The room was warm with the smell of the turf burning in the fireplace. She had been fed well. Coffee and half a cookie were on their way, brought by a man who professed to love her. She was still in Ireland, and so far, hadn't done anything that would preclude her from coming back.

Duncan returned, two cups of coffee and a large cookie on a tray. The prerequisite pitcher with milk and a sugar bowl sat on the tray alongside, even though Duncan knew well the two of them only took milk. He always offered sugar, no matter how many times she reminded him she didn't need it.

"It's a habit," he once told her. "In old days, sugar was very dear, but you always saved some to offer a guest, out of respect."

"No need to respect me that much," she'd said. "I still don't take sugar."

She took the milk and poured some into her cup, whitening the scalding coffee.

"In Ireland," she told him, "one uses milk in their coffee or tea as self-defense. It's so unbelievably hot, you'd hurt yourself drinking it."

"The coffee is an afterthought," he answered back. "Tea is the drink here. Coffee is just a nod to you foreigners."

Larkin laughed. Duncan broke off half of the cookie for her, put it on a small plate, and handed it over. She balanced it on her thigh and took a bite of the creamy cookie.

"With the quality of the butter in Ireland, it's no wonder that this is the best butter cookie I've ever had."

"Is the butter so different?"

"It is, of course. It's richer here, more butterfat or something, and that makes it yellower, even creamier than at home. I'm going to take pounds with me."

"And what else are you taking home? What treasures have you found?"

She thought. "I've gotten gifts for people, some hard-to-find crystal my mother sent me looking for, a piece or two of jewelry, and some things I've picked up as I've needed them, a fleece jacket and some clothes."

"That's all, then?"

"Well, there's a rowing medal I added to the pile just today. And, of course, memories. Lots of them."

"Which ones are important?"

Larkin smiled, put her plate on the floor next to her, and leaned back. "Things have happened to me here that I never want to forget. Ireland changed me and I have to make sure I don't relapse once I get home."

Duncan was sitting at the other end of the couch. Now, he shifted a bit closer, took her feet in his lap, and rubbed them through her socks. She made a sound of contentment, closed her eyes, and kept talking.

"Then, of course, there's you. You've found something in me I thought was gone forever. After Pat died, I closed that part of me down and it's behaved itself, until now." She opened her eyes, meeting his down the length of the couch. "Until you."

"And what do you think about that, Larkin?"

"I don't know what to think. I wasn't planning on this. It never occurred to me that it would happen."

"That what would happen?"

She paused. "What do you want me to say?"

He smiled. "Larkin, we haven't talked since Doolin. We said after we got home, we'd talk about what to do next. You're leaving tomorrow."

"What did you think about Doolin?"

"I knew what I felt for you before we went, but having that time to ourselves made it concrete for me. I have no doubts about how I feel. I don't have the slightest idea how you feel."

"Am I so hard to read? Some of it must be obvious to you."

"Some, yes, but I would like to hear you think about it."

"That's reasonable. The first thing that comes to me is that we have a lot of fun together. I've missed that so much."

"I like that part of us, as well."

"But I enjoy the everyday things we do, too. I like going to the hardware store with you, and grocery shopping. I have the urge to buy you shirts and do your laundry."

"That's a good sign."

"But is it 'us?' Or is it only that I've been without that kind of relationship for so long?"

"What do you think?"

"I don't know. It's not what you want to hear, I'm sure, but that's the truth of it."

"The truth is what I want, Larkin."

"At the end of the day, do I love you? I can't say. But, do I care for you, am I drawn to you? Absolutely," she nodded, "to a point that surprises me."

Duncan paused. "Larkin, have you considered not going?"

"Not going? You mean, not going tomorrow?"

"I mean, staying."

"Staying forever?"

"I don't know about forever, but for a time. You seem to like it here. Why couldn't you live her for a while, see how things go with us, get a job, make a life? Do you know the chiropractor in town? She's from the States, from Georgia, I think. She came and liked it, and ended up moving here. She seems very happy, her business is good, and she has friends, a car, and a home. You could do that."

Larkin stared at him. "I can't just move here."

"Why not?"

"Because I have my life somewhere else. I already have a job and a house and friends. It's just not here."

"But it could be, Larkin. You would be made very welcome if you stayed. Brynna would be thrilled. Do you know how much she's taken to you? You could work there until you found something in your field, until you found a place to live. Or, you would be welcome to stay here with me," he caught her face, "in the guest room for as long as you liked."

She looked at the fire. Stay in Ireland. Or, more likely, go home tomorrow, pack up her house and rent it, box up some things and come back. She could build a private practice or work within the social system. There would be licensing issues, but chances are they could be overcome. She wouldn't stay here with Duncan, but she could rent a small place to live, and look for something to buy, something with a view of the river, perhaps over by the Friary Church. Maybe that house she'd seen with the green door, if it was still for sale.

It was true that she loved it here. She loved the country, the feel of it, the history of oppression broken by the revolution that freed them. The war being within the lifespan of parents or grandparents made it real for people she'd talked to, and made their telling of the stories real to her. She'd been to cemeteries and seen the stones for boys and men, dying in the war years between 1916 and 1921. It was still close to them, still fresh.

It certainly didn't hurt that it was beautiful here, the flowers and the painted buildings, the clouds and even the rain lovely for the effect it had on the roses, grown as big as her hand.

If there was any drawback to the culture, it seemed when something bad happened, it was accepted as inevitable, even if, to Larkin's trained eye, it could have been avoided. "It's just the day that's in it," she often heard.

Staying would give her and Duncan time. She wanted to know how Duncan was in the course of a year, not a week.

"Larkin, what do you think?"

She turned to him, his hands still rubbing the soreness from her feet.

"It might be a possibility."

"Ah, Larkin, it would be wonderful if you were here. I can imagine nothing better."

"I'm thinking about it. It's..." she searched for the right word, "intriguing."

He got up, moving her feet from his lap and went to the end of the couch where she sat. He squatted next to her, took her hand to his, palm to palm, lacing their fingers.

"Just imagine, Larkin, being able to see each other every day, able to touch every day."

He ran his free hand into her hair, spreading it across the back of the couch. There, he smoothed it, stroking it on the fabric, his eyes on his hand moving on her hair. He looked back to her.

"To be able to come and find you, to have you still in the same town. Larkin, it's exactly what I would want. Is it what you want?"

"It is a new thought. I need to give it time."

"Is there anything I can say to help you decide?"

"Having you this close is nearly cheating. While you're touching me, it gets hard to remember my name."

He smiled, leaned in, and kissed her.

"And now?" he asked.

"Now, I'm thinking I was born here and I'm finally home."

In a motion, Duncan stretched out next to her on the couch, brought her to him, and kissed her again, taking his time, making certain she understood there was no question in him, no dilemma.

As she felt herself respond, Larkin marveled again at the feelings she'd thought dead.

She pulled away from Duncan and looked in his eyes then put a hand on the side of her own face like she was checking for fever.

She whispered to him, "There's much to this I haven't done since..." she paused, "...for years. I haven't shared my life with anyone for a long time. You'd be taking a chance."

"It's an easy chance to take, Larkin. There's so much to you, so much I want to learn. Stay in Ireland, give us the time."

They lay there, close, the fire burning and the rain plinking down in the dark beyond the windows. The music had stopped, and the air was still.

I could do it, Larkin thought. I could lie here with this man and not get up.

She thought of it then, all of it, of lying there with her skin against him, folding herself around him here in this night where there was nothing to stop them from being together. She felt him press against her, felt his need for her, heard him breathe her name. She took her hand from her face and curved it around his neck. She pulled his face back to hers and pressed herself into him. He made a sound and moved his hands on her back, rubbing from her neck to her waist, the pressure changing where they touched.

"I love you, Larkin." He spoke against her lips, his arms tightening around her.

Her hands stilled. He felt the shift in her, loosened his arms from around her, and waited. She felt his arms move. When he pulled back, she shivered at the cool air that rushed in between them, knowing it to be her doing, and took a handful of his sweater to keep herself warm, to keep him from going. She looked into his face.

"I would give a great deal to be able to say that back to you, but I can't."

"It's all right."

"It's not all right for me. I can't be with you without knowing. I can't move here on the assumption that I will someday love you, because that would be my real reason for coming, to see if we would become...what we each are looking for."

"Don't you think you might find out better if you were here? Wouldn't it be easier if we lived in the same country?"

"It would, no doubt. But I have a real life at home. I have work to do and people that depend on me. Think of how it would feel for you to move there, and under what basis you would consider it. Because, you'll notice, we're not talking about you moving to the States."

"No, but we could, if you like. I wouldn't put it out of the question."

"It would be a ways off, though, wouldn't it? You'd have to come, see if you liked it, see if you could make a living there. I need to do the same. As much as I enjoyed working with Brynna, the B&B is not how I'll want to make my living. As well, I have family to consider, and friends. I am not without roots."

Duncan was silent, tracing his hand from her shoulder to her fingers, slack on her thigh. He picked up her hand and brought it to his lips.

"Larkin, you must do what you feel is right. I would love for you to stay. I've said that. The offer remains, for whenever you might want to return."

"How long will you wait?"

He smiled. "You've asked that before."

"Really, though, how long? What should we do when I leave tomorrow?"

"It is up to you. I've traveled internationally and it's difficult to get back into a schedule, so we can pick up when you're ready." He shifted on the couch. "Now, tomorrow, can I take you to the airport?"

A fleeting thought came that it would have been nice had he not given up so quickly.

"I don't like airport goodbyes. I think I'm going to take the train to Dublin and get the shuttle."

"Larkin. I would feel completely inhospitable if you took yourself to the airport."

"I think it will be best. If you like, you can take me to the train, but the rule is a quick hug and a kiss."

"I'll do my best. When is your flight?"

"Half-three."

"Two hours in to Dublin, another half-hour to the airport, and they like you there two hours ahead for international flights. You'll be needing to get the train at half-ten."

Larkin shifted on the couch. Duncan moved away from her as she swung her legs around and sat up. She reached for her coffee, long cold. She didn't want to drink it; she just wanted something to hold on to.

"Would you like another cup?"

She turned to him, instantly annoyed.

"No, I don't want another cup."

"What was that for? Are you angry with me?"

"No, of course not."

"Larkin, you certainly seem angry."

"I'm not."

"Then what are you?"

"I'm not sure."

She paused for a long moment, her thumb rubbing the handle of the coffee cup, following the inside of the curve to the top of the cup and back to the bottom.

"I'm thinking that it doesn't seem to bother you that I'm not staying."

"Larkin, you explained why you wouldn't stay. Would you have me tie you to the chair?"

"At least I'm disappointed I can't stay. It doesn't seem to bother you a bit."

"Larkin, I didn't think there was even a small chance you would stay. Until tonight, I don't think you'd ever considered it, had you? I thought by putting the idea out, there might be a chance you'd come back in the future. It's not that I don't care if you stay. I'm trying to pave the way for you to return."

Larkin was watching him as he talked, felt his hands covering her feet to keep them warm as he sat in front of her on the floor.

"I know you can't leave your life this minute, Larkin. I was hoping to open the door so you'd think about it."

"Well, you have," she told him.

"Good," he said to her. "Now, would you like another coffee?"

"No, but thank you." She moved her feet in his hands. "After not feeling much for a long time, it's odd to feel things so strongly. It's not always good."

"Even unpleasant, Larkin, it's better to feel something than nothing."

"That may be the take-away of my trip. I haven't enjoyed everything I've felt but I have enjoyed feeling."

"I have enjoyed watching you."

She tilted her head. "You think you know me."

"You haven't kept yourself from me. I'm learning."

"You've made a fine start." Larkin looked around her. "I should probably go before I lose my resolve to go."

"I'll take you home."

"Let's walk."

"It's raining, Larkin."

"We won't melt."

Coat on, Larkin waited in the living room for Duncan. She made a slow turn, taking it all in again – the dining room, kitchen, and living room, then her eyes turning the corner to the bedrooms that lay beyond.

Duncan came from the bedroom with a large black umbrella.

"All right, we're off."

They set out, Duncan with the umbrella in one hand and her hand in the other. They walked slowly, taking the long way back, stopping at the doorway of Sean's. Sean hailed them from behind the bar to let him buy her last pint in the country. They sat at the bar, Larkin sipping a cider and Duncan, a Guinness. Larkin smiled.

"This was my first Irish pub. It was the first night I got here, and I was so tired I thought I might fall asleep on the table. I'd never had a cider before, never heard Irish music, never met you. It's a fitting way to end my stay."

"It is, at that."

They were quiet then, and when they'd finished, waved away the offer of another, and moved to the door.

Outside, the rain had stopped. They walked up to the bridge and looked at the water, then turned toward Brynna's. Larkin broke the silence.

"I know there will be days when I miss this all so badly."

"That will cause you some pain."

Larkin wiped her eyes, took a breath. "I love it here. I'm just not sure what to do about it."

"Whatever you decide will be what you'll do."

"I think you just called me stubborn, but I'm not sure."

"You are stubborn, Larkin, but I mean it as a compliment. You will decide what you want and get it. Look at the rowing. You hadn't rowed for fifteen years and now have a medal for a Tournament First."

"I should give half to you and the other half to Deirdre. Without the two of you, I never would have come back to it like I did."

"It was you doing the work, Larkin. Give yourself some credit."

They stopped at Brynna's door. The house was dark and felt huge and warm next to them.

Larkin turned to Duncan. He opened his arms to her and she stepped into them, reaching up to encircle his neck. She laid her cheek on his sweater, feeling the rough yarn on her face, and took a deep breath of him, then another.

"That's what I want to take home with me. I could find you in the dark, Duncan."

Duncan smiled and ran a hand over her back. "What a lovely thought."

"No matter what happens when I leave, I will always be grateful for what we've had."

"This is sounding like a goodbye."

"No, that's not how I mean it. I want you to know how much you have meant to me. You have been a good part of the growth I've done here."

"Then I'll have my say, as well. It is my deep hope that you come back, Larkin. I want very much to have the time to truly know each other, to see if we are as well-suited as it seems."

"Perhaps in the future."

"Don't wait until you forget me, Larkin."

"I won't forget you. I'd have to forget all of Ireland. I just don't know what to do about you."

"You have asked me how long I would wait. Let's start with Christmas. If you're finished with me, I'll stop waiting. If not, we'll come up with another date."

"That seems fair. I do better with a deadline."

"All right. You're getting cold, Larkin. I'll see you in the morning." He bent down and kissed her lightly, put his chin on top of her head and sighed. He pulled away from her, and reached around to open the door.

"I could probably stay out here and kiss for hours."

"But unfortunately, Larkin, I cannot. There is only so much I can take. One more is my limit."

She pulled him to her, kissed him, and gave him a swift hug.

He retrieved the umbrella from where he'd leaned it against the house and walked the path back to the street. At the street he turned, as she hoped, and she ran out to him.

"One more?"

He dropped the umbrella on the grass and grabbed her, bringing her up to his eye level, her feet off the ground.

"Don't you forget, Larkin," he said, his voice a fierce whisper. "Don't forget any of it."

He kissed her long and hard, her arms around his neck and their bodies pressed together. When they finished, her heart was pounding and she took a deep breath.

"You've made me breathless," she said to him.

"You've made me miss you more," he said, "but it was worth it."

He walked away in the light of the streetlamps, Larkin watching him until he turned the corner at Pierce Street. Turning back to the house, she noticed the umbrella lying in the grass at her feet. She picked it up brought it inside, knowing she'd give it back to him in the morning, but finding comfort in having it here in the house on her last night in Ireland.

31.

Larkin found her seat on the plane and sat down, her tote bag dropping at her feet. She looked out the window, knowing there was no one watching her leave and wondered if she'd made a mistake in not letting Duncan come to see her off.

A flight attendant leaned over her.

"Have your seat belt on, do you?"

Larkin looked up. She wondered if she would now forever listen for an Irish accent, if her head would always turn.

"No, but I'll do it now."

"Brilliant."

Larkin fastened her belt and turned back to the window. She heard American voices near her and felt a body sit in the seat next to her. She turned to see a man reach for his seatbelt and fasten it. He looked at her once, nodded, and ignored her for the rest of the trip.

After dinner and the movie, Larkin excused herself and got out of her window seat to go to the bathroom and take a walk up and down the plane. She tried to make sense of missing both where she left and where she was going.

She was glad to be going home - home to Bubba, home to Sukki and the kids, home to Mr. Carney, her job, and her house. She had missed them all. Along with that, she had sometimes found herself missing her things. She occasionally wished for a certain book, a little box she kept on her dresser for her jewelry, or a particular scarf.

The trip home felt to her like the trip there. She wasn't sure what awaited her. One thing was certain. The trip had been a resounding success.

She was changed.

Thinking on it further, Larkin decided she wasn't different, but more of herself than when she left. She was more determined and in better shape. She felt lighter, without burdens, and had more regard for her thoughts. She was attentive to things, to people, and able to engage in her environment. All of this would make for changes at home. She would reconsider her job. She would read more. She would cook more, work out more. She would discuss things of importance.

She had much to miss. She had come to love Brynna and Des and had made other friends. She knew parts of Athlone better than where she lived, having walked so much. She had thought of how to describe it to Sukki, who would badger her for details.

She would miss the smell. The scent of Ireland was the air there, and had settled in her hair, on her skin. All of her clothing still held it and she wondered how long it would last.

There was Duncan. Larkin smiled. She could still feel him, his hands on her arms and his breath near her face. She closed her eyes and had no trouble conjuring up his face, his words, and the vow he'd made to wait. She was so grateful for him. Equally fascinating was that he thought her a worthy recipient of what he had held to himself for years.

This morning, he had followed her rules going to the train. After tearful goodbyes to Brynna and Des and old Mr. Murphy waving from the Castle, they rounded the corner toward the train station with Larkin still waving out the window, tears on her face.

Duncan gave her time. He reached over and put his hand on hers, running his thumb over her fingers.

She turned to him. "It was just like this when I left home. I was crying about leaving everyone there. Now, here I am in bits about leaving everyone here."

"There's always a price to pay, isn't there. You can't come and stay as long as you did without caring about people, for all your talk about staying separate."

"I suppose."

"You'll miss them. It's worth a tear."

"I'll miss you. That will be the hardest."

"I'll take that as encouragement, Larkin. Now, then, here we are."

They got out of the car and went around to the trunk to get the luggage. In addition to Larkin's original bag, she had purchased a tote to carry the crystal and other breakables on the plane.

Duncan eyed the pile. "Are you sure you can manage this all yourself?"

"There are always porters to help, and I'll get a cart at the airport."

They walked over the gravel of the parking lot and Duncan put her suitcase on the train while she got her ticket. She found a seat by the window and put her luggage nearby.

She stood next to him, not knowing how to say good-bye. In the end, the porter called "All aboard!" and Duncan moved to her for a quick hug and quicker kiss.

"I'll talk to you in a couple of days, Larkin. Safe travels and God Bless."

He smiled into her face, turned and walked off the train. He stood next to her window until the train started to move. She waved to Duncan, one movement of her hand, as the tears ran down her face again. The train picked up speed as they moved further down the track, then rounded a bend to the right where, even with her face pressed to the window, she lost sight of him altogether.

On the plane, Larkin felt her throat tighten. She would miss all of it but it was Duncan who was enmeshed with most of her experiences

They'd promised each other time. It would be an adventure, a possible future, too far away to contemplate at the moment, but tantalizing. For now, it was enough to have this awakening; to be able to feel enough to want to reach for him.

All of it - the change, the growth, Duncan - it all came down to one thing. She knew what it was, knew what it cost her, and knew it was the right time.

She took a breath, and thought the words for the first time.

She was free.

32.

Getting off the plane at O'Hare, Larkin wondered if the flight had been easier or if it was the timing that had her feeling so much better than the flight over. This flight traveled through the day, not the night, leaving Dublin at 3:00 in the afternoon Irish time and arriving in at 5:30 Chicago time, putting Larkin at about 11:30 p.m. on her clock. She waited for her bags, negotiated customs, and walked toward the exit.

As she got to the clearing past the security area, something ran into her legs, knocking her off balance. She bent down.

"Errol! How are you? I've missed you so much!"

Errol hugged her, talking in her ear, too excited to put words together so phrases fell from him in clumps.

"Tee! We waited...Bubba knows, I think...your flowers are big...real long time...I missed you!"

He hung on her neck, his arms caught up in her purse strap. Larkin looked over him to Sukki waiting her turn. Larkin disengaged, took a step, and wrapped up Sukki in a tight hug.

Sukki laughed. "Finally. I've been waiting since you left for you to come home." She looked Larkin over. "So, how was it?"

Larkin laughed. "Want it all right now?"

"Give me the one sentence wrap-up."

"It was great."

They made their way to the car. Larkin stopped and looked up. The sun felt good, warm and strong, but the clouds were disappointing.

The ride home fascinated Larkin by what caught her attention after five weeks.

"Wow. When did that go up?"

"What?"

"That building. Funny-looking, right?"

Sukki was amused. "It was funny-looking before you left. Does it all really seem that different to you?"

Larkin nodded, her eyes still wandering.

"It does. Nothing is perfectly familiar." She turned to face Sukki. "Not even you. You look shorter and your eyes look different than I remember them."

"My eyes? How?"

"Lighter, I think. If I had described you, I would have made your eyes darker."

"Did you forget what I looked like, too?" Errol reached forward to tap Larkin on the shoulder from the back seat.

Larkin turned half around. "How could I? I looked at your picture every day, you and Bubba. You're taller than when I left, though. Did you know that?"

Sukki turned onto their street, pulling in around the back to her garage. They wrestled the luggage out of the trunk and opened the door to the laundry room.

Emmy and James came running at the opening of the door. With them came Bubba, tearing through the house at the sound of Larkin's voice, skidding on the tile of the laundry room floor in front of her. Larkin swooped him up.

"Bubba! I missed you so much!"

He settled in on her shoulder and panted.

"The flowers, Tee, you have to see them." Emmy grabbed Larkin's hand, dragging her through the closet to Larkin's side. She ran to the kitchen table and threw her arm out to the side in a "ta da" gesture.

On the table sat a vase bursting with flowers, all purple. There was iris, lilac, statice, a tiny splattering of lobelia, three perfect lavender roses, and hyacinth. A plastic holder held a small card. Larkin put Bubba down, walked to the table and bent to smell them. She came up smiling and looked at Sukki.

"Gorgeous. Where did you find them all?"

"Love to take the credit, but they're not from us. And, you'll notice, I didn't even peek at the card, although I am very, very curious and would really appreciate it if you opened it."

Larkin got the card and put her finger under the flap of the heavy ivory envelope. She read the card and smiled.

Sukki walked to the table, sniffed the flowers, and turned to Larkin.

"I take it you have stories to tell?"

When Sukki and the kids had gone home, Larkin took her bags upstairs. She was too tired to unpack but she rolled them into her room to deal with tomorrow. She changed into shorts and a t-shirt and went down to the kitchen for water. She would have to do a mammoth shop tomorrow. There wasn't an edible thing in the house, but she thought she had left a bottle of water in the fridge. Opening it, she found skim milk, raspberries, strawberries, smoked Gouda and good bread, a pound of her favorite coffee and, as a special treat, rice pudding.

Not for the first time, Larkin knew she couldn't buy a better neighbor than Sukki.

She got a spoon, a bowl, and the raspberries and pudding. She spooned pudding out of the plastic tub and sprinkled it with the fruit. She ate it slowly, looking at the card propped up on the flowers in front of her.

Larkin,
I'm ordering these from Doolin to
arrive when you do. Although not
the same ones we saw together, I
hope they will remind you of our time
here.
Love,
Duncan

Larkin finished her pudding and rinsed her dishes. She walked around her house, picking up objects and holding them before putting them back. She walked up the stairs to the living room, opened the china cabinet, and touched a piece of her collection of cut glass. It all sparkled in the light and there was no dust on the shelves. The cleaning service had done its job. She ran her fingers over the sharp cuts of a vase, withdrew her hand, and closed the door.

She went to the front window and stood in the shadow of the curtains, looking out to the west. The sun was drooping, but not enough yet to bring sunset colors to the sky.

Mr. Carney's roses were blooming and beautiful. She would go tomorrow and talk with him.

Downstairs, she turned on the computer. She sat in the desk chair, swiveled around, and looked at the pictures on the walls. She had done this room in a Tuscan style, with bright prints and friezes. She had never been to Italy, but liked the look of it. It seemed now contrived to her, borrowed.

She swiveled back to the computer. She had new messages.

"Not tonight." Larkin left the room and went upstairs to the bathroom. It seemed huge to her after her tiny bathroom at Brynna's. She wondered why bathrooms were so big here, what need there was for all that space.

She stood in the door to her room. The bed was smooth and perfect, pillows propped up against the metal headboard. Her eyes traveled the room to the chair in the corner, too antique to be sat in, but beautiful nonetheless. Her dresser stood on the far wall, perfume tray on top next to a basket of scarves. Pat's dresser was on the other side of the room, but she had long ago filled it with out-of-season clothes. An antique bachelor's dresser served as her bedside table, and there was an old pot-bellied stove on the far side of the bed, the top just big enough for a book or a glass of water.

She'd designed it to her taste. The house was filled with individual pieces of furniture and accessories, all with stories of how they were found, or what nightmares they were to refinish. It was her home.

She hoped it would feel that way again soon.

33.

Sukki waited until ten the next morning to come over and found Larkin doing laundry.

"I didn't want to wake you." Sukki watched Larkin shovel a load from the washer to the dryer.

"Are you kidding? I was in bed by 8:15 last night, up at 4:30, wondering what the heck to do. I didn't bring dirty laundry home with me, so I'm washing all the sheets and towels that haven't been used here." She straightened and smiled at Sukki. "Thanks for the treats in the fridge. The pudding was perfect last night. Want coffee?"

"Sure."

They moved to the kitchen. Sukki poured herself a cup, then sat at the table.

"I can't tell you how much better the coffee is here," Larkin said. "Most of it in Ireland is instant. I got used to it after a while but brewed coffee is so much better."

"No one has a coffee pot?"

"Not like ours. The most anyone would have is the European kind, an infuser. Do you know those?"

"I don't like them."

"Me neither."

Sukki patted the chair next to her.

"I know you can't tell me all at once what happened but give me a couple of crumbs here."

"Like the flowers."

"Not only that. I want it all, but it's my guess I'll get the details in bits and pieces."

"That's probably true. I can give you pictures of experiences. The big stuff, the changing in me; that will take longer to process and I can't explain it to you until I understand it myself."

"I'm in no rush for anything except who sent the flowers."

"Remember when I called and said there was a man who was going to show me around, but it was just casual?"

"Mm hmm."

"I may have spoken a bit too soon on that."

Sukki hitched herself up to the table, put her feet on the chair across from her, and waited.

34.

After a week, Larkin felt almost normal. She stopped feeling jet-lagged and got used to not hearing an Irish accent. She handed out the gifts she'd brought and called her mother with the news of the crystal she'd found. Sukki loved the scarf.

"Look at the colors! And, no, you can't borrow it. It would look better on you, and then I'd be forced to let you wear it."

"Can't happen. This one's got your name on it." Larkin showed her the fine black lines spelling out her name in the corner. She described the girl who made it, told her about Galway and the throng of people there, the meal she'd had.

"That was the best brie, the best wine."

"Sounds like it was a perfect day, no matter what you ate."

"Probably, but it was all one big experience: the day, the food, the cute waiter. I got past some stuff there. That was the day I knew I would be all right, that I could be happy."

"This is how you'll tell me about what really happened in Ireland. The important stuff doesn't come out in the first spin."

"You might be right."

"Of course I am. What's happening with Duncan? Have you talked to him?"

"No, but we've been emailing."

"Do you miss him?"

Larkin nodded. "I do, of course."

"That sounded so Irish, the way you said that."

Larkin laughed. "No doubt. About Duncan, though, I do really miss him. During the last couple of weeks I was there we saw each other daily. On the trip, we were together for a full three days."

Sukki fidgeted. "Larkin, on the trip..."

"What?"

"You know what. Don't make me ask."

"No, Sukki, I didn't have sex with him. We shared a room, but there was no sex."

"Did you want to?"

"You're very nosy, has anyone ever mentioned that to you?"

"I'm interested."

"Well, then, yes, I wanted to very much."

"But you didn't."

"It wasn't right. I had no idea where this would go and we had no commitment."

"That attitude would have kept me out of my second marriage."

"But then there would be no Errol, and the world would not be as good."

Sukki looked over at Larkin, leaning against the counter.

"What is it with you and Errol? You two have been close since the day I brought him home. I have, on occasion, been a tiny bit jealous of how he feels about you."

Larkin looked up, something passing over her face in a wave. "Errol and I bonded."

"You are two peas, no doubt about that. But why the look? You'll probably still have children."

"I'm 35 now and unless I marry tomorrow, which seems unlikely, time is running short."

"Have you and Duncan talked about children?"

"Sukki, Duncan and I are nowhere near talking about children. Right now I'm looking at the whole thing as a kind of practice. I'm having trouble seeing it work long-term."

"When did that happen?"

"I've been thinking about it for a few days and I wonder if it's just too much to take on."

Sukki's voice changed.

"Larkin, sit a minute."

"Why?"

"Sit. I'm going to tell you a story." She waited for Larkin, then looked her in the eye and began. "Remember when Emmy was around four, when I started reading all those books about what to do with a strong-willed child?"

"Ah, yes. That was your brush with insanity, those early years with Emmy."

"One day, we were sitting on her bedroom floor, nose to nose. She was crying, upset because I wanted her to do something unreasonable, like getting dressed or brushing her teeth. I was trying to make her understand consequences. I was telling her that either she did what I was asking her to do or she would lose her Barbies for two days. At that time, Barbies were everything to her. I sat there trying to make sure she understood. Then the light bulb went on over her head, and she got it. Now, she's really sobbing, like her little heart is breaking. I said, 'Honey, what's wrong?' She looked up at me, tears pouring down her face and said, 'I'm really gonna miss my Barbies.'"

Larkin burst out laughing. "Did she really?"

"Oh, yes."

"And your point?"

"That's you. You're not even willing to try. If you've got your hands on a good man, you'd better keep a decent grip. There just aren't that many left."

"Easy for you to say; you're not the one messed up in this."

"Easy?" Sukki sat up straight. "That would be the only easy part of my life, wouldn't it. Take a look, Larkin. I will never have the choices you have. I'm still paying for the ones I've already made. Don't get me wrong, I love my children and I am reasonably happy being on my own, but don't you think I would dance for a taste of what you and Pat had, or what it sounds like you and Duncan could have? I wish it were my choice to make. I would not be running from it, I assure you."

Sukki got up, splashed her coffee into the sink, and shoved the cup across the counter toward the dishwasher. She turned to face Larkin.

"You live in different countries? Work out travel plans. He has children? Read up on how to be a good stepmother." She gripped the counter. "This might be the bonanza here and you're piddling around with details."

She glared at Larkin, then moved off toward the closet to go home. Larkin took a step toward her.

"Sukki."

"What?"

"I didn't know. You make it look so effortless, like you wouldn't want it any other way."

Sukki turned back. "What would you have me do, whine? My job for the next several years is to raise my children well. The rest of it, like self-actualization or a new relationship? That will have to wait. So here's the deal. Figure out what you want. Do you love this man or not? If you do, then get to it. If not, tell him so he doesn't waste more flowers."

"Sukki."

"Do you love him?"

"I think I could. Maybe I do."

"Not good enough. Do you love the man or not?"

"Are you so sure I know?"

"Of course you do. If you don't love him, tell him so he can go find someone who does."

Larkin cringed. "I have to think."

"You do that. Give a thought to what you might be passing up, not how much trouble it might be to make it work." Her voice changed and she shook her head. "What happened to Pat just happened, but if you give this up without a fight, it will be a bad choice, and one you'll have to live with like I've had to live with mine."

Larkin smiled.

"What would I do without my nosy, pushy friend?"

They hugged, and Sukki walked the length of the family room before turning back, her hand on the closet door.

"Larkin, the envy I have for you, for what you might have with Duncan... it's not the prettiest part of me, but it's there, and I know it. Find out what's in you. Do you have it in you to love this man?"

"I don't know. If nothing else, I need to decide enough to tell him something."

"Good girl. I'll see you later. Glass of wine after the kids go down?"

"Love to. Or cider. I found some at the grocery store today. Probably not just the same, but cider nonetheless."

After Sukki left, Larkin went back to the kitchen, washed up the coffee cups, and stood looking out the window.

She was orderly by nature and knew this matter of the heart was going to have to be a process, not an impulse.

"My heart," she thought, "with so little practice lately."

She knew she'd have to dissect it and hold it up to the light, to find her feelings as well as be willing to feel them. After feeling nothing for so long, it was a pleasure to have love to consider.

She walked to the living room, put her iPod on the deck, and found good cleaning music. She set the volume high enough to hear it upstairs and walked up to her room. Inside, she opened the bi-fold doors of her closet, and stood in front of them with her hands on her hips. Her closet was long overdue for clearing out and it seemed a suitable project to undertake while sorting out her thoughts. She would look over each item and either put it back neatly or dump it in the bag for Sukki's yearly garage sale.

Even if I don't get a lifetime of happiness, Larkin thought, I do end up with a clean closet.

She focused on her subject matter. In turning toward Duncan even in thought, she felt herself soften.

Not so fast, she chided. This is thinking, not feeling.

She relegated herself to basics. Who was this man, what did she know about him?

She thought about her trip, how he had become the point at which Ireland really came alive. Ireland and Duncan were inseparable. She wondered if that was part of what she saw in him.

The first section of the closet held summer clothing. She went through it all, piece by piece, laying empty hangers on the bed and dropping outcasts in the bag. She arranged what was left in the closet from sleeveless to short-sleeved to long-sleeved.

Larkin had wondered since returning from Ireland if meeting Duncan had been a prelude to meeting someone here; if now that she was open to it, she might stumble into someone on the same continent.

She stopped for a moment, running through a list of single men she knew. Her contact with men had been limited, but there were still some options - lawyers with whom she worked on behalf of the women she counseled, her investment guy, or the smelly man who cleaned out the gutters at the town homes.

Slim pickins'.

Even the more presentable of the bunch stirred nothing in her. She went back to Duncan. She smiled and felt her stomach dance.

She could envision Duncan in her house. She could imagine him standing in the doorway, could see his face as she found his eyes, and watch it change as he found hers. She knew the power of his touch and even now, the thought of his hands on her back could change her breathing.

She knew then that it was him, it was Duncan, not just the first man she had cared about since Pat died. This wasn't practice and it wasn't geographical. It wasn't just a man, it was this man. She closed her eyes, a worn tank top in her hands.

She could see him perfectly, turning to find her - walking up the sidewalk at the B&B, in the doorway at Sean's. Larkin grew impatient on the days she was to meet him, watching the clock, hurrying her work, Brynna calling to her to slow down, she couldn't keep up.

She went to the next section of the closet, winter clothes. She fingered the wools, the heavy woven fabrics, the turtlenecks. They felt foreign to her, weighty.

Her thoughts went back to Duncan. How did one manage a transatlantic relationship? How often did you call, or visit?

She could probably get there a couple of times a year. She had no idea of Duncan's availability, what kind of time his work would allow him for travel. They would certainly email and Skype. They could talk every day, could share parts of their lives almost real-time. It might feel like coming home to someone.

She thought of things to ask him. She worked quickly to finish the closet, shifting hangers and straightening shelves. When she finished, she looked over her work and closed the doors. At the bed, she bagged the garage sale items, stuffed the pieces bound for garbage in another bag before she could change her mind, and laid the few better things aside for charity. When it was all neat, she walked to the living room and sat down.

It was time to decide. Intellectually, philosophically, logistically - it could work. It wouldn't be easy but it might be well worth it.

Now it's time for feelings, she decided. Practicality has been served. What do I feel?

She thought of him, thought of his words, his touch, the care he had shown concerning his children. She thought of her growing admiration for his work ethic, his character, and how he dealt with poor drivers. He was a patient man and he smiled easily. He made her laugh and laughed when she was funny.

His appearance delighted her. He was fit but didn't preen. Even though his eyes took most of her attention, she liked the rest of his face too, and she fit perfectly in the space next to him with his arm on her shoulder.

He was a man of overall quality.

She let herself get excited. All she needed to know was there and she felt the blessing of her head as well as her heart.

She smiled then, all by herself; grinned at what she knew was coming.

"Look at that," she thought, "I'm in love."

35

An hour later, she pulled the filled bags through the closet to Sukki's. Sukki looked up as Larkin pushed the door open with one bag, dragging two more. Sukki raised her eyebrows.

"And this is..."

"I cleaned out my closet." Larkin heaved the bags in the direction of the garage door then walked to the table and fell into a chair.

"That's all for the garage sale? You must have been fierce."

"Even my favorite threadbare flannel went to the rag bag, that last stop before the hamper in the sky."

Sukki looked expectantly at Larkin. "So?"

"So what?"

"So, what do you think? You haven't cleaned out your closet since you had to decide on a car and you didn't get rid of nearly as much. What did you decide?"

Larkin grinned at her. "Maybe I'll just keep you hanging awhile."

"That would be cruel."

"Too true. I decided Duncan was too wonderful to pass up and that we could probably make it work. At the very least, it was worth good try."

"Do you love him?"

"I do. I love him."

Sukki put a hand under her chin and studied Larkin's face.

"Congratulations. Have you told Duncan?"

"I thought he should be first. I called him before I came here."

"And his reaction?"

"He was..." Larkin paused, smiled, "enthusiastic."

"When is he coming to visit? I need to meet this guy."

"He's talking about after the first of the year or sooner if he can finish this job quickly. You can look him over then."

"You should see your face. You are actually aglow."

"I'm going to ride it as far as I can. It's been a long time."

"I am happy for you, Larkin. In fact, I'm so happy for you I'll take you out for dessert."

"Really? Where?"

"You're the one in love."

"How about Macaroni Grill? That chocolate cake with the hot fudge on it and scoops of whipped cream?"

"It's yours."

"I'm starving. With all this falling in love, I forgot to eat."

"Maybe I should buy you lunch."

"Nope. Just the cake. Lunch is too trivial."

"You shall have it."

"Sukki?"

"Larkin?"

"I want cake now."

Sukki laughed. "Can you wait long enough to get there?"

"OK, but I'll drive."

On the way home, fat with cake and coffee, Larkin turned to Sukki slouching in the passenger's seat.

"It's not like all I have to think about is Duncan. I have other things to manage."

"Of course you do." Sukki worked her way up to a sitting position. "But this will work its way into your life on different levels."

"What do you mean?"

"Nothing is compartmentalized. You don't only think about work at work, and you won't only think about Duncan when you're talking to him. You're in love, Larkin. It won't stay structured for all your trying."

"This will be a change."

"More than you can imagine, is my guess. Among other things, it's fun."

"So for a while, I just get to have fun."

"Absolutely."

"It would be more fun if he was here."

"You don't get everything."

"But if it works out, I might."

"It wouldn't surprise me."

"Will you come and visit me if I move to Ireland?"

"After the kids are gone, I'll move, too. Keep an eye out for adjoining closets."

36.

There were times Larkin made herself wait until after dinner to check the computer for messages, but most days she flipped it on the minute she came home. She spent time every night writing to Duncan, the dog in her lap and the words coming easily. They decided on a date Duncan would visit. He would arrive November 3rd and stay for a week.

With their lengthening emails, Larkin learned more about Duncan. There was time to read and ponder, to answer with deliberation instead of reaction.

Once, he asked her why she named a seven-pound dog "Bubba."

It's for his self-esteem, she wrote. It was either that or "Killer."

For Larkin this was the perfect way to get to know Duncan. It was like sticking her toe in. Even if it was the deep end she was testing, it was still just her toe.

On a Friday at the beginning of October, Larkin stopped on her way home to pick up a pizza. It had been a grueling week. A new group had begun, and the first few meetings were always full of sharp edges and tears, the women hunched over in their chairs. The stories were heartbreaking.

The range of abuse in this group was staggering. A certain amount of skin-thickening was necessary to do her job, but the things these men had done to the women now in her care were so appalling she could barely keep her composure. It would be a difficult seven weeks, but Larkin had seen it work before: slack-faced women finding resources from places they had forgotten they had.

She walked up the sidewalk toward her door. Sukki's opened, and Larkin watched as her arm snaked out toward the mailbox. She held the doorframe in her left hand, leaning out. Her left foot stayed in the house, her right leg stretching out behind her to hold the door open. Her right arm strained toward the brick wall with the mailbox, lifting the lid and squishing the mail together to bring it all out. At the peak of her reach, Sukki's body was a "T," one leg on the ground and her back and leg parallel to the porch. Only Sukki could make getting the mail a dance.

Larkin called to her.

"Why you don't just step outside?"

"My feet would get cold. I hate it when my feet get cold."

"Slippers?"

"The only thing I hate more than cold feet is slippers." Sukki looked at Larkin.

"What's up? You look beat."

"I am. Here's my evening - this pizza, big enough for you guys too, and Pride and Prejudice. Care to join me? I'll be the one on the couch."

"You're on your own tonight. I have the Potluck for the gymnastics team and the boys are going to different friends overnight."

Larkin dumped the pizza and the movie on the counter, took off her jacket, and reached for a cider. It wasn't as good cider in Ireland, but it would do. She let Bubba out and fed him.

Larkin eyed the pizza on the counter, turned the oven on warm, and shoved it in. She flipped the computer on and checked her inbox.

No mail.

She made a face. What didn't work? She exited the program, waited a minute, and tried again.

Still no mail.

Larkin sat back in her chair. In the six weeks she had been home, Duncan had never missed emailing her, nor she him. He would have told her if he would be out of touch today.

Wouldn't he?

"What's happening," she said aloud.

She left the computer on, walked to the kitchen, and took the pizza out of the oven. She got the movie, went back to the family room started it. She got a plate of pizza and stared at the TV through the credits. Putting her plate aside, she walked to the computer and made sure if an email came in, she could hear the noise.

She got a second cider from the fridge and settled in to watch the movie. She checked her watch. It was 8:00 here which made it two in the morning in Ireland. Too late to call. Larkin made a noise of discontent in her throat and put her plate aside. She turned off the TV and sat in the dark.

There were dozens of possible reasons he didn't email. It was Friday night. He could have gone to Sean's, had one too many Guinnesses, gone home, and went to bed. He could be in the middle of a session somewhere with a borrowed guitar and a crowd. His computer may have crashed.

He could have changed his mind.

Maybe one of his kids needed a ride somewhere far away.

Maybe he forgot.

He didn't forget. He never has. It must have been important. The man is nothing if not reliable, so there had to be a good reason.

Another woman would be a good reason.

It's not another woman. Maybe he had some small, insignificant injury at work that needed a stitch and he is sitting at the hospital.

Maybe it's more than a stitch.

No. Someone would call.

Who would think to call?

That's probably not even the reason. He's fine.

Maybe.

"He's fine." Larkin spoke sternly to the empty room.

She took a sip of cider but it had gone warm and tasted sour. She set it on the table and went through the closet looking for Sukki.

Sukki's house was empty. Larkin left a note on the kitchen table for her to stop over before she went to bed. She went home, checked the computer, turned the movie back on, and stared at it until it was over.

She jumped up and walked the house looking for something to occupy her mind until Sukki got home. She picked up books, and put them down. In the hall closet was a basket of small sewing projects: an open seam on a nightgown, loose buttons, the hem down on a pair of shorts. Larkin sat down at her sewing machine and fixed them all, changing thread colors and snipping ends.

Back in the family room, she fell onto the couch.

This is the tradeoff, she thought. I don't get to know where he is. I don't get to know why.

She exhaled a rush of air.

She pulled a lap blanket off the back of the couch, and put a pillow at one end. She lay down, tucked her feet under Bubba, and stared into the night.

37.

Sukki opened the closet door carefully. The couch was rumpled, the blanket hanging off the end.

Larkin was in the kitchen making coffee in her bare feet, her jeans loose and her shirt a mass of wrinkles.

"What's up? I got your note." Sukki leaned on the counter next to Larkin.

"Where were you last night?"

"I told you – the potluck. We got back late and I came over, but you were asleep."

"Pretty late for a potluck."

"It was."

"Hmm."

"Well, what's up? What happened?"

"Nothing."

"Larkin, what are you mad about?"

"Not a thing. I don't care what time you get home. It does seem a little late for Emmy to be out, though."

Sukki stood up straight. "Larkin, what is going on?"

Larkin turned the coffee on.

"Nothing."

"Nothing, my ass. Might as well tell me since I'm not leaving until you do."

Larkin got cups from the cabinet and set out spoons and milk. She turned to Sukki.

"Duncan didn't email and I'm worried. I came over to see you and you weren't home. I woke up this morning and still there was no email, and you hadn't been here. Worrying makes me crabby."

"I understand being concerned about Duncan but don't worry about me."

"I was already in a state. You were an addendum."

"What's the rest of the story?"

"I already said. Duncan didn't email me yesterday. He's never once missed."

"And you don't have any idea why?"

"I have lots of ideas."

"But none of them good, I bet. Have you tried to call him?"

"As soon as I got up. No answer at either number, home or cell."

"Did you leave a message?"

"I asked him to call no matter what time."

"Are you planning to spend the rest of the day staring at the phone?"

"Both of them."

"Don't do it. Go out, do something. You'll be a basket case if you stay here. Go shopping."

"Only you feel better when you shop."

"Ice cream?"

"I'm a psychotherapist, Sukki. Those are not healthy coping mechanisms."

"Maybe not, but they work."

"Not for me. I'll go grocery shopping, though. You know, psychologically healthy people don't ever get to this point. Their emotions stay within reasonable limits."

"Clearly, that ship has sailed. Larkin, it's probably nothing. I can't think of a good excuse either, but I bet he's got one."

"He'd better."

Saturday passed slowly. Larkin did her chores, scrubbing instead of wiping and rolling up the carpets to dust the hardwood floors underneath. She shopped for food, replaced the filters in the furnace, and weeded her patch of garden. She called Duncan's number four more times.

In the middle of the day, she stopped working, a rag in her hand, and threw it back down on the table she had just dusted. She stalked to the kitchen and opened cabinets and the refrigerator. She had a bite of cheese out of her dusty hands, a handful of cereal, a grape. She buttered a piece of bread, laid a thin coating of crunchy peanut butter on that, and ate it standing up at the counter. She got an orange, peeled it over the sink, and ate it.

When she finished, she washed her hands. She walked out on the deck, sat on the swing, and rocked herself with one foot on the ground.

38.

By Sunday morning, she was numb. Nothing had come from Duncan. In the afternoon, she went to a movie at the mall to stay out of the house as long as she could.

There were kiosks she passed on the way back to her car. Larkin stopped at one, her eye caught by beautiful lettering in a frame. It was a framed poem by Mary Brent Whiteside.

She read the poem again, then took it off its hanger and handed it to the cashier.

"Is this a gift?" The cashier reached for a bag.

"No, it's not." Larkin paid, took the bag, and thanked her.

At home, she slid the frame from the bag. It ended up on the wall next to the computer. She read it again and nodded.

"That's it."

"Who once has known heights and depths shall not again
Know peace.
Not as the calm heart knows low ivied walls, a garden close,
The old enchantment of a rose.
And tho' he tread the humble ways of men
He shall not speak the common tongue again.

Who has known heights shall bear forever more
An incommunicable thing that hurts the heart, as if a wing
Beat at the portal, challenging;
And yet, lured by the gleam his vision wore,
Who once trodden stars seeks peace no more."

39.

Monday was meetings, groups, and individual sessions for three new clients. Larkin came home tired. Coming through the garage door, Larkin heard the phone ringing. She dumped her purse and briefcase on the laundry room floor and ran for the kitchen.

"Hello?" She was breathless.

"Larkin?"

"Duncan! Where in the world have you been?"

"I'm so sorry, Larkin. I can't imagine what you thought when I didn't call back. Let me tell you where I was."

"Please do."

"I told you I was in the Army for a few years, didn't I? Well, a couple of times per year, I have to go and serve for the weekend. Usually, we go on Saturday and Sunday for eight hours, just like a normal workday. They have us do work around the base or climb the occasional mountain, but this time they surprised us and took us for the whole weekend and made us set up a full camp."

"You're kidding."

"Oh, no. Believe me, it was a surprise to us all. There were 50 of us and the Army had called the families to let them know we'd be gone but didn't let us bring our mobiles, and even if we had, they wouldn't have worked all the way out there. I didn't get back until very late on Sunday night and by that time, it was too late to call."

"If in fact, I had been sleeping."

"Ah, Larkin, I'm sorry."

"It's obviously not your fault. Of all the reasons I came up with for you not emailing, camping out wasn't one of them."

"I would have called if I had even known it was a possibility. Do you forgive me?"

"Of course. I have to admit it was a very long weekend."

"I'm sure it was. What reasons did you think up for me not calling?"

"You don't even want to know."

"I was wondering what I would think if the situation were reversed."

Larkin made herself say them out loud.

"Things like you had changed your mind about me, or that some woman there had caught your attention."

"Larkin, nothing could be more wrong."

"I feel silly, Duncan, but I want something. I don't even really know what."

"You want reassurance, Larkin."

"I suppose. I didn't want to think those things - I didn't want even to wonder."

"If you don't know what I'm thinking or how I feel, check with yourself. If anything drastic changes, we'll know, but for now, we're thinking with the same head."

"I found a wonderful poem while you were gone."

"Will you mail it to me? For someday when I can't find you?"

"Of course."

"It's only another three weeks or so till I'm there. I can't wait to get off the plane and see you standing there."

"That's so inconvenient. I thought you could just take a cab."

"I'll grab you and give you a big kiss."

"I suppose if you're planning on kissing, I'll have to come to the airport. Can't have you kissing the cabby."

"Plan on the kissing part, Larkin."

"Twenty-three days."

"Yes. I hope it goes quickly."

"Quicker than this weekend, anyway."

"Ah, I deserved that. I'll need to make it up to you."

"You need to go to bed. It's late."

"I will now that we've talked."

"It is wonderful to hear your voice.'

"Yours, too. Would you send me an email so I have something to wake up to?"

"I will, of course. Sleep well."

"I'll dream happy."

Larkin let Sukki know Duncan was all right, then sat at the computer. She first copied the words of the poem. She told him that the weekend had proven to her in many ways how much she did care and though she would not like it repeated, she had learned from it. Then she said the kissing part was all right with her, too.

40.

In the night, Larkin dreamed of Athlone. She saw the town laid out before her, smelled the river, and walked streets she hadn't even seen when she was there. She bought the candy bars she liked and had a long conversation with Mr. Murphy. She passed a bartender from Sean's on the street and helped Brynna hang heavy, wet sheets on the line. When she woke, the images were all still there at the edge of her and for a minute she closed her eyes, knowing that when she raised herself up they would be gone.

It had been like this when she first got home. She had a foot in each country, not completely at home here but in no position to go back.

She wandered to the kitchen in the cool light and made coffee. She stood still, looking out at the sunrise. In these minutes it wasn't Duncan pulling her, it was Ireland, and if she could have, she would have walked out the door and gotten the first flight back.

Larkin was well-acquainted with want. She had lived these years in the perpetual disappointment of having to do without. It was there when she slept and when she woke. This was different. This was something she could have, but chose not to take.

Without her roots here, she wouldn't have the resources or the support to leave, but having them also meant she voluntarily give up some absolute freedoms.

She got her coffee, went to the computer, and turned it on. Her eyes went left to the poem.

Who has once known heights and depths shall not again
Know peace.

This would be the un-peaceful part. This would be the part when nothing home had to offer would stand up to a cider at Sean's and a Cadbury Whisp-A-Bite.

She double clicked to email. Duncan's sat at the top.

Larkin,

I read your mail when I got up, even before I made tea. Not only are you thinking with my head, you're thinking with my heart.

I have to go to work, but will write when I get home. I just wanted you to know you are a part of every thought.

Love,

Duncan

Larkin opened a new mail to him.

D,

Please tell me about what Athlone was like today. Tell me about the weather. Are people wearing jackets? Did the wind blow hard enough to make the river rough? Was there fog coming in off the Shannon? I so miss being there. I want to walk across the bridge, go to that little Mediterranean place for dinner, and smell the air with the spices and the turf together.

I wonder if you might feel this way after you come here. Maybe you'll wake up in Ireland one day wanting to see the sunset from my deck or eat Chicago-style pizza. Do you think we'll ever be in the right place?

Love,

L.

Later, she received an answer.

Larkin,

The right place will be the one we're in together. We can learn to live with each other's view of the sky.

Duncan

P.S. It was cloudy today but the clouds were beautiful, yellow tinted and full, just like you like them. Athlone misses you, too.

The week passed. Work was exhausting but very satisfying for Larkin, the new group she was working with responding well to therapy and each other. On Thursday after work, she stopped at the store to stock up for a weekend with the kids while Sukki took a graphics class downtown.

Larkin took her job as "Tee" seriously. She put dedicated thought into the time she spent with them, especially when she had them to herself.

Sukki had quizzed her.

"What are you cooking this time? Maybe don't spoil them quite as much, OK? It took me days to get them back to normal."

"I didn't spoil them. We were just active."

"They'll probably all have homework to do, so get that out of the way first."

"Then I get to spoil them."

"They're still talking about when you let them make play-dough and throw it up into the ceiling fan."

"That got out of hand, I agree."

Larkin decided on homemade pizza for Friday night, blueberry pancakes and fajitas for Saturday, and going to the local breakfast place on Sunday morning. At the store, she gathered fresh ground flour and yeast, sauce, vegetables, pepperoni, and pineapple for the pizza, and huge round blueberries for the pancakes. She went to the deli for fresh mozzarella and a hunk of Parmesan, and found real maple syrup. She got flank steak and vegetables for the fajitas, along with avocados and sour cream, and found tortillas still warm in the bags.

On Friday, she left work early to get home before Sukki needed to leave. After she left, Larkin had the kids get their homework, then herded them into her kitchen and sat them at the table.

"Things are going to be a little different this time, you guys. You're older now, and probably you don't want to do the same things we've done before."

"We could do the play-dough thing again." James grinned at her.

"No possible way. Here's my plan. Aside from doing your homework, which you'll do as soon as we finish this conversation, the weekend is up to you. I have meal stuff planned, but after that, it will be up to you three to decide what to do when, where you'll sleep, when we'll stay home or go out."

James started. "So, we get to tell you what we're doing?"

Larkin nodded. "The catch is that you all have to agree. Which probably means no one will get to do all that they want, but it also means things will be even."

Errol nodded. "This is a good idea, Tee."

"You three are now equal leaders and you have to come to unanimous decisions. I am your advisor, but aside from body piercing or skydiving, as long as you agree, it's probably going to be all right with me."

The kids exchanged glances.

"This will be cool." Emmy was already planning.

Larkin held up a hand. "Why don't you get your books and get started so the hard part will be over."

"I need to be on the computer for English." James stood up and made a move to go through the closet.

"I need the computer, too. Let me go first. Mine won't take as long as yours." Emmy stood as well.

"And what about you?" Larkin reached an arm out to Errol, who walked to her and put his arm across her shoulders.

"Nope. I just have math."

Larkin nodded. "Why doesn't one of you use my computer? I'll make the pizza dough while you're doing homework and we'll all be finished around the same time."

Emmy looked thoughtful.

"I wonder if we should ask Mr. Carney to eat with us."

Larkin nodded. "Why don't you check with your fellow Presidents and get back to me with your decision?"

The kids walked to the family room and sat in a circle on the floor. After a short discussion, they ran back to the kitchen.

"We have voted 'yes' on asking Mr. Carney to dinner. Errol is going to go ask. He should come about six-thirty?" James asked.

Errol put on his shoes.

"I'll be right back."

He ran up the stairs, calling for Bubba, and let the door slam behind him. He returned quickly and was back in the family room.

"He said he'd love to come and what should he bring."

Larkin shook her head. "Tell him he doesn't need to bring anything."

Errol ran back up the stairs and out the door. In another minute he was back.

"He says do you want some dessert. He has a recipe for... flan?"

"Tell him if he'd like to make flan, I would be very grateful."

Errol headed for the stairs, then turned back.

"Does anyone have anything else to say to Mr. Carney?"

Larkin smiled. "This should be your last trip."

By 5:30, everyone's homework was done and they divided up the chores. Emmy set the table. James cut up vegetables, placing each into a separate bowl, and arranging them by color. Errol grated the cheese.

Larkin spoke up.

"What are you all planning to do after dinner?"

The kids stopped a moment and looked at each other.

"Ideas?" James asked.

"We could watch a movie." Emmy suggested.

Errol spoke up. "We could play cards or a game."

James turned to Emmy. "I think a game would be good. We must have a game Mr. Carney knows how to play."

Emmy nodded. "Or, we could teach him."

"Tee, what games do you have? Or should we get some from home?"

"No, I've got a ton here. I taught him to play cribbage one night and he whipped me. He's a quick study. "

At 6:30, the doorbell rang. Emmy ran up to get it and led Mr. Carney down the stairs to the kitchen. He had a plate of individual circles of flan and a vase with tiny purple flowers for Larkin. They were no bigger than lily of the valley, but intricate and detailed with yellow centers and black stamens.

"Oh, they're beautiful! What are they?"

"They're something I'm experimenting with inside the house. Yours are the first that have made their way out of the pot."

"They remind me of the heather. Thank you." She leaned forward to peck his cheek.

Emmy led him to the counter. There were five rounds of dough on individual plates, each with initials carved into the outer crust. She pointed to his.

"This is your own personal pizza and you get to put whatever you want on it. First you put the sauce on it and then there's all this stuff to choose from. After that you put the cheese and the spices on top and we cook them all."

They each designed their pizzas. Emmy's was only cheese, with a bit of spice on top. Errol did his in sections, one quarter with pepperoni, one with green peppers, one with tomatoes, and the last plain cheese. James piled it all on, the end result looking volcanic - high in the middle with cheese dribbling down the sides.

"And what do you prefer?" Mr. Carney surveyed Larkin's crust, still empty.

"I like lots of sauce, then pineapple and tomatoes, a little broccoli for conscience and just a handful of cheese. On top goes oregano and a few hot pepper flakes, and, there you have it." She flourished her finished crust. "Oven ready. Now, for you?"

Mr. Carney spooned sauce on his crust, then carefully placed a few slices of pepperoni around the edge. He looked at Emmy.

"What else do you think I'll be needing here, lovey?"

"Some red peppers, I think. You like those. And some tomatoes. They're not as good as yours. Tee likes the pineapple. Maybe that's an adult thing. There, now cheese and then spices."

The pizzas went into a hot oven, timer set. Everyone got something to drink, Larkin and Mr. Carney sharing a cider. He sighed and looked resigned when she offered it to him.

Larkin waved her hand at him.

"Oh, what is it with men and cider?"

"It's not a man's drink, Larkin. Hard on your stomach, you know. I'll manage it this once though, for you."

"Thanks so much."

"Just to be polite."

Larkin laughed and reached for potholders to get the pizzas out of the oven. While they ate, the discussion went to what to play after dinner.

"Don't forget, we have to vote." Errol said.

Mr. Carney looked at Larkin. "Vote?"

"The kids are presidents of our little country this weekend, of which you are a current guest. They have to come to a unanimous decision on what they'll do before we do it."

"Was I voted on?"

"Of course."

"And it was unanimous?"

"It had to be to invite you."

"Then I am especially pleased." Mr. Carney turned his careful smile around the table.

After the table was cleared, a vote was taken. The winner was Monopoly.

"Have you ever played?" James asked Mr. Carney.

"No, you'll have to teach me. And go easy on me, I'm only a beginner, aren't I."

"If I had a nickel…," Larkin murmured.

The game began. Two hours in it, Mr. Carney was stripping Larkin of her last dollar, foreclosing on her one remaining utility and giving her a benign smile.

"I am sorry, really, just following the rules."

Larkin frowned. "Do they have pirates in Ireland?"

"Everyone visited Ireland at one time or another." He turned back to the game. "Now, who just landed on my Park Place with the two hotels? James? Ah, it's too bad for you, isn't it. Well, perhaps I could purchase something of yours, there."

Larkin got up and made coffee. She got the flan from the refrigerator and divided it onto small plates. She thought it would take Mr. Carney another twenty minutes to clean out the remaining players, so she put them back in the fridge, walked to the computer and pulled up her email.

Duncan,

Do you know how to play Monopoly? Would you take everything I owned if we played?

Sitting around the table with Sukki's kids and Brynna's dad, I wished you were here to play with us. Maybe you would have lent me some money to stay in the game.

L.

After Mr. Carney won, they ate the flan, Larkin and Mr. Carney having coffee with theirs.

Larkin sighed. "Wonderful flan. Thank you so much. I don't make it very often because it's such a pain, but I love it."

"The very least I could do."

At 10:30, Mr. Carney rose to go.

"I thank you all. Larkin, do you think you might walk me home?"

She pulled a sweatshirt over her shoulders, opened the front door, and followed Mr. Carney home. They walked to his door, and he opened it in front of him, motioning her in.

"Come in, Larkin. There's something I'd like you to see."

Larkin walked behind him into the front hall, and at his beckoning, to the bedroom. She had never seen the upstairs of his home. She wasn't surprised to find it neat, but she was surprised to see it nicely decorated, with new-looking linens and decorator pillows on the bed. She was glad.

"What a lovely room."

"Thank you. My good wife did it up not long before she died and I've kept it up since. Here, Larkin. This is what I wanted you to see."

He handed her a picture. In the frame stood Mr. and Mrs. Carney. They were young, and Mr. Carney wore a uniform, the jacket boxy on his small frame and a beret on his head.

"When was this taken?"

"Let's see. It must have been 1947. I was in the Army, as you can see, and for three years we didn't see each other except on leave twice a year. They sent me all over the world then, to India and Israel and to the North."

Larkin looked up.

"I've been thinking of you and your man, there. It might be some time before you two are together more than a week at a time, so I thought it might be an good for you to know that even after three full years away, the love we felt was as strong as if we'd lived next door."

Larkin looked down at the picture. They were smiling at the camera, his arm on her shoulder, hers twined around his waist.

"How did you manage?"

"The same ways you are, I suppose. We called when we could, but mostly we wrote, talking about simple things, what happened in the course of a day, the weather. I still have them all."

"And when you came home?"

"We got married, straight away. And we never spent more than two nights in a row apart again."

"And when she..."

"When she died? Ah, you've been through it, Larkin. You know."

"But I wonder if the pain was multiplied by the number of years."

"I don't know, Larkin. I think if you love, you love, and if it's lost, it hurts. It was awful when she died, but I had to do something with myself, so I planted roses and lived the best I could. She wouldn't have liked it if I'd given up."

"You never dated."

"Larkin, I was much older."

"Older, but not forgotten. Look at all those ladies from the Senior Center that drop off cakes and food to you. You could be dancing several nights a week if you liked."

"I don't need the food, but it would hurt their feelings if I turned it away. Larkin, I'm not looking to marry again. I had my marriage. I had my children and lived with the woman I loved for a good long time. It was enough. Now, if I hadn't had that full life with her, I might be looking over the ladies with the cakes."

"What are you telling me?"

"I just wanted you to see it can work, even if you're apart for a time."

Larkin looked back at the picture, then walked the two steps to the table to see the rest of them. There were early shots of the couple, then with one baby, then two, then more. There were Christmas pictures, Easter dresses with white gloves, Brynna's brother in a sports uniform, Brynna dancing, babies in prams. Then, there were pictures of the couple aging here in this house, still close together in every shot, still touching. Larkin turned to Mr. Carney.

"How do you feel now? About her being gone?"

"I think of her every day, Larkin, every single day. But I made a life for myself. Someday I'll be with her again. The Bible says there's no marriage in heaven, but we will find each other, I'm certain of it."

"Until then?"

"Until then, I grow roses; I visit with my friends," he touched her forearm lightly, "I live a good life. And, I wait."

"And what do you see for me?"

"You know what I think of you, lovey, and I've known Duncan McKenna since he was a gossoon. Whatever happens, it will be right. You are reasonable, kind people."

"If my life works out as well as yours has, Mr. Carney, I will be pleased."

"I would hope better for you, Larkin."

"In what way?"

"I've been alone too long. For you, I would wish for more time."

"Thank you for sharing the picture with me." She offered it back to him.

"No, you keep that one."

Larkin reached out to give him a hug.

"Thank you," she said. "I will treasure it."

"I'm going to bed. It was exhausting work, being a financier and land baron."

The kids had cleaned up the family room and ran the dishwasher. They were deciding where to sleep. The consensus was sleeping bags on the family room floor. Larkin called the couch. When they were settled, Larkin went around the house and made sure doors were closed and locked. She placed her new picture on the desk by the poem.

With Bubba snuggled in the curve of her knees, Larkin looked at the lumps on the floor. If she never had children, she would have this. She saw a future of track meets and dress shopping, chess tournaments for Errol and trips to the emergency room for stitches. If something happened to Sukki, Larkin was to be their legal guardian and would finish the job Sukki started.

"I love you guys," she whispered.

"Love you, too, Emmy whispered back.

"Me, too," James mumbled.

Errol crawled out of his sleeping bag and knee-walked over to the couch. He leaned over to hug Larkin, his warm arms circling her neck.

"Love you, Tee," he whispered in her neck.

Larkin smiled in the dark.

When the light worked its way through the windows, Larkin awoke. She got up quietly and went to the kitchen to make coffee. When it was done, dark and fragrant, she took a cup to the computer.

Larkin,

Of course I know how to play Monopoly. Even though I do love you, I can't truly say I wouldn't fleece you in a game. Love is love, but a good game of Monopoly, well, that's a different thing altogether.

It's only a couple of weeks now until I come. I want to see where you live, so I can imagine where you are. I want to meet your friend and her children, and have a pint with Brynna's da. It would be nice to see Chicago. Mostly I just want time with you. I think it will be easier for you there, in a place where you are so comfortable. I wondered during your trip how it felt to be so far away from everything you know.

Deirdre says "hello" and wants you to know "It's working." So, that's all. I can't wait to get off the plane and have you standing there. I can see it in my mind.

Love,
Duncan

41.

The kids decided Saturday was to be shopping, finding pumpkins to carve, and a movie. Larkin was once again surprised at the different personalities of Sukki's children. They could have all been foundlings for the consistency in how they behaved.

James was impulsive. When they went shopping, Larkin had to talk him into trying on the khakis he wanted at Old Navy - he would have preferred to just buy them and worry about returning them later if need be. At the movie, Errol said James had his popcorn eaten before the opening credits were over and spent the rest of the movie trying to "borrow" some of Errol's. The pumpkin he chose at the pumpkin patch was the first one he touched, and when it came time to carve, he was the first finished. He cut his pumpkin without even drawing the face on it and barring the crooked smile, James was content with his efforts.

Emmy had to try on everything, whether she had intentions of buying it or not. Although her instructions were to find a long-sleeved turtleneck or two, she tried on an assortment of things, hopeful that she could talk Sukki into coming back. At the movie, she ate no popcorn until the first scene, then ate it with M&M's sprinkled over the top, careful to get popcorn and chocolate in every bite. At the pumpkin farm, she had to find a pumpkin the exact size as her head, as she wanted it to be a self-portrait, and cut it out with a stand-up mirror at the table to check her progress. When it was finished, she told Larkin in confidence that the eyebrows on her pumpkin were much too big. Larkin reassured her that she and the pumpkin bore little actual resemblance.

Errol behaved as Larkin knew he would. At the store, he hunted for a gray zippered sweatshirt with quiet diligence. He ended up with two for Larkin's inspection, one on clearance, and one full price. After discussing the merits of both, he decided on the sale item and said he would save the rest of the money.

At the movie, James complained that Errol ate his popcorn one piece at a time, never varying his schedule. One piece to his mouth, chew, swallow, reach for another piece, chew, swallow. Every ten pieces, he would have a swig of pop.

At the pumpkin farm, he prowled, a perfect size and shape in mind, and walked for rows before he found one that pleased him. He couldn't carry it himself, and so got a wagon and carted it back across the fields to where Larkin was buying pies. When it was time to cut it, he designed a face on paper first, then transferred the drawing on to the pumpkin. Larkin had purchased safety knives and Errol took his time, making a first indentation, then carving slowly so as not to destroy the careful lines he had drawn.

Larkin stood back to admire Errol's work. The cuts were clean, the face symmetrical, the top perfectly fitting its hole.

"That, Errol, is a fine pumpkin."

He washed his hands and joined James and Emmy in family room. As Larkin lined up their pumpkins on newspaper, glad no seeds had made their way to the ceiling fan, she noticed one thing the kids did have in common.

All of the pumpkins' faces were happy.

After returning the kids to Sukki Sunday afternoon, Larkin collapsed on the couch. Maybe she was already too old for children.

She did realize that every weekend wouldn't be like this one. Even so, she had even more respect for the job Sukki did. Somehow she found time in the day to fix nutritious food and read them articles on financial responsibility and plumbing that she'd found helpful.

She went to the computer.

Duncan,
What is the best part of fatherhood to you? And the most difficult?
L.

While at the computer, Larkin answered an email from Bunny concerning her father's coming birthday dinner. It had been her mother's idea that the sisters should all go in together on tickets to the opera as his gift, amusing the sisters, who knew it was their mother's preference, not their father's. In reply to the question of how the gift was coming along, Larkin answered that the Bulls' tickets were in the mail, nothing but the best, with parking at the United Center included.

Her eyes drifted to the picture of the Carneys and thought about their similar situation. What a small place the world was. She sat back in her chair. It was a strange notion, when she contemplated it, to love a man she couldn't see. She wondered sometimes if she was making it up; if she loved the man or the thought of him.

Then, they would talk on the phone and the conversation would become something authentic and solid, something she could hold out and say, "see, here we are." Surprising her at times would be flashes of a future; she could see it, a three-frame movie of their life together.

She shook her head. Not enough that she fell in love, she had to fall in love with a man an ocean and a culture away.

Her email bleeped.

Larkin,

Fatherhood is tricky business. Often the very things you love about it are the same ones that drive you mad. It is a responsibility unlike any other. I remember with Declan being nervous about everything. I worried about dropping him, giving him too much food or not enough. I calmed down by the time my daughter was born, but that feeling is still there. Now, it's how much freedom to give them, when to let them drive, even how they dress, as girls now dress much differently than when we were children.

Even with Kyla 16 and Declan 17 years of age, I still wonder if I'm doing it right. They must think it strange, the relationship Nora and I have. It's not a good model for marriage, I know. I can teach them what I know, but at the end of the day, they will decide what is right for them. I hope their decisions are good ones. There you have it. Not much, is it?

Now then, only 16 more days until I come. Is there anything you want me to bring? Have a lovely night. I'll be thinking of you.

Love,

Duncan

D,

I know just what I want you to bring. Find a shawl for me, something in a light color, warm and soft. Then, after you go home and I'm missing you, I'll wrap up in it and pretend it's you. And Whisp-a Bites.

L.

42.

Larkin fast-walked up the sidewalk to her door, her neck tucked down in her jacket to miss the wind. Mr. Carney was doing the last of his fall gardening, taking the mums out of the ground, and covering the roses with the white Styrofoam forms that would protect them for the winter. At Christmas, he covered the forms with garland and pine roping, making it look like a forest of tiny Christmas trees. The garden was a year-round affair.

"Mr. Carney, isn't it chilly to be out in your shirtsleeves? It can't be over 40 degrees."

"Ah, it's lovely. The sun is shining, there's a brisk breeze. You should get out in the air more, Larkin."

"You get out enough for both of us."

"Is everything ready at your house?"

"Everything I can think of. The only thing left is to make up the bed in the guest room. I wanted to wait until tonight so the sheets would be fresh tomorrow when he gets here."

"Tomorrow he comes, then. Does it seem like it's been a long wait?"

"In some ways, very long. It seems forever since I've actually seen him, but we email so much, it feels like we talk all the time. Strange, isn't it?"

"It is, at that. I wish Rose and I had the computer those years ago. The time would have gone faster." He used the shovel to push himself up. "Never mind, the man's almost here now. What have you planned?"

"The usual: Willis Tower, Millennium Park, the museums. Duncan has also expressed an interest in Chicago-style pizza. Having a pint with you was high on his list."

"You might take him to hear some music, if there's something you think he might like."

"You're coming to dinner later in the week, right?"

"I am, of course.

Inside, Larkin put away the things she'd bought, checked the larder for anything she might have forgotten. Opening the freezer, she looked over the meat supply, bought in pieces over the last weeks. There were small filet mignons, thick pork chops, a roast she would have to get someone to tell her how to cook, and a turkey. Duncan had never experienced a Thanksgiving meal, so Larkin had promised one while he was here. She had invited Sukki and the kids along with Mr. Carney, as she'd purchased a 20-pound bird.

She had Harp and Heineken - very popular in Ireland, Larkin had been surprised to discover – and the only Irish brown bread she could find along with some good cheese. Looking it over, she realized she may possibly have overbought.

Sukki popped her head through the door.

"How many more hours?"

"I'm not counting hours. It was hard enough counting days; I'm not torturing myself any further. I feel like a kid waiting for Santa."

"He comes in at five tomorrow, right? Are you going to work at all, or are you just sitting here staring at the clock?"

"No, to guard against the watched pot, I'm working until one, then doing any last-minute shopping before I come home."

Sukki opened the refrigerator. "Seriously, more shopping? How much can the man eat?"

"I know. I went kind of nuts. After work tomorrow, I'll shop for new running shoes. That always takes hours and then it will be time to leave for the airport."

"And then he'll be here."

"In this country."

"In your car, then in your house."

"Close enough to see."

"Close enough to touch."

Sukki played with a napkin on the counter.

"I was wondering if you had put some thought into decisions you will probably have to make."

"Yes, Mother Sukki, I have thought about it. We're still just starting here, so that part can wait."

"And if it can't?"

"It can."

"So, he's sleeping..."

"In the guest room. I've got it all ready but the sheets and I'm washing them fresh tonight."

"The guest room."

"Yup."

"You're aware it's right next door to your room."

"Sukki, we're adults. We have decided what to do. Give us a little credit."

Sukki smiled, twined the napkin in and out of her fingers. The phone rang and Larkin reached for it.

"Hello?"

"Larkin."

Her face split into a smile.

"Duncan. Are you packing?"

"Larkin, I'm so sorry, I can't tell you how much, but I can't come."

Larkin's face froze. She walked to a chair, and eased herself into it.

"What do you mean?"

"I can't come, Larkin. There's been an accident. My brother has been badly hurt at work. He works at the electric plant, and fell two stories off a walkway. He is in critical condition. If he lives, he'll most certainly lose one on his legs, but they're not sure he'll make it through the night."

"Oh, my goodness. When did it happen?"

"A few hours ago. He works the afternoon shift. I just found out. My oldest sister is calling all of us, and I have to go to Sligo right away. I'm so sorry, Larkin. The timing is terrible, but I have to go."

"Of course you have to go. Absolutely. I'm so sorry, Duncan. Is he married, does he have children?"

"Ah, of course. His wife's name is Ann, he has three little ones. The oldest isn't even ten years of age."

Larkin was shaking her head, one hand rubbing her forehead.

"Larkin, I feel awful about not coming."

"As do I, but there's really no choice, is there? You have to go. Give me a call if you think you might be able to make it later in the week, or next week, although I have to go back to work next week. Never mind, we'll work it out. Go see to your brother."

"Ah, Larkin, thank you for understanding. And, again, I'm so sorry."

"I am, too."

"I love you."

"I love you, too."

Larkin hung up and slumped in her chair. Sukki had come to sit in the chair next to her; aware Duncan wasn't coming, but not understanding why. Larkin explained.

"Now, there's some terrible timing," Sukki said.

"I'm fairly sure it wasn't intentional. It would seem extreme."

"Poor man. It's really serious?"

"Critical. If it was one of my sisters or you, I'd stay home, too."

"It's the kind of guy he is."

"One of the reasons I fell in love with him."

Sukki paused. "How badly do you feel?"

"Perfectly awful, and guilty on top of it for feeling so disappointed that he's not coming."

"What are you going to do?"

"I have no idea. I guess I'll call work to see if I can go in. No sense staying home."

"What you said about next week - isn't there a way to work this week and stay home next?"

Larkin shook her head. "I start a new group next week. It's all set up. I have to be there."

Sukki reached over and hugged her. "I'm so sorry. You have to be incredibly disappointed."

Larkin lay on Sukki's shoulder. After a minute, she raised herself, wiped her face with the napkin lying on the table, and sniffed.

"I understand. I really do."

"I know you do."

"It's just I've waited so long."

"You have."

"I hope his brother's all right."

"Of course you do."

"What am I going to do with the turkey? We'll have to eat it this week. It takes up way too much room. I'll probably need some ice cream to get me through this and I don't have room for a single pint."

"Ice cream therapy? Not very professional."

"Professional, my ass. I want Haagen Daz Vanilla Swiss Almond."

"Back to the store?"

"You bet."

The next day after work, Larkin came home. The only thing she really wanted to do was get in her house, close the door, and sleep until morning. When she woke, it would be over - the time for leaving for the airport, the time when he would have walked through the doors into the waiting area, the time he would have swept her up in his arms and kissed her...

Stop it, she thought. Enough.

She sighed, dropping her purse and laptop on the kitchen table. She went upstairs to get the mail. Outside, Mr. Carney was sweeping leaves off his front stoop. At the sound of her door opening, he looked up, put his broom aside, and came to her.

"Ah, Larkin, Sukki told me what happened. What a disappointment. Have you heard anything about Duncan's brother as of yet?"

"No, not yet. I didn't expect him to call today, really. Things must be very chaotic there. He said the whole family was going, so that's seven of them at the hospital, plus his brother's family."

"Yes, they'll all be there. It's a good family. Now then, what are you going to do with yourself this week?"

"I lined up some work. Really, my disappointment is small potatoes compared to what his brother is going through."

"True enough. Larkin. I was wondering if you might like to stop over tonight, either by yourself or with Sukki. I have a dessert I need to try and I thought you might not be wanting to sit home by yourself."

Larkin smiled. "How kind of you. I'd love to. What can I bring?"

"Some cider, if you'd care for some, but I have Guinness if you'd prefer, or coffee."

"Should I tell Sukki, or do you want to?"

"By all means, let her know. I'll get started on the dessert."

After dinner, Sukki got the kids a movie suitable for all of them then met Larkin in her kitchen. Larkin had a small bottle of brandy she knew Mr. Carney liked, and Sukki carried a bunch of freesia cut from the plant she was cultivating in her bay window.

"Freesia in the winter." Larkin bent down to take a whiff. "What a treat."

"Keep a sprig for you, then." Sukki pulled a bloom from the center of the bunch and reached for a small vase in the cabinet. "The nice thing about freesia is you don't need much."

They walked to Mr. Carney's, the wind whipping leaves around their legs. As they reached the door, Mr. Carney opened it, motioning them in.

"Come in before the wind lifts you up and out. Early in the year for this kind of day, isn't it?"

The women shook off their coats and ran fingers through their hair.

"Whew!" Sukki said. "If this is an indication of winter, we're in deep trouble."

Mr. Carney hung their coats. Each woman gave her gift and he led them to the dining room table, laid for three with lovely china: dessert dishes, cups and saucers, and shining silver spoons. Under each setting was a lace placemat, finely crocheted with silk ribbon flowers embroidered in the corners to match the china.

"What a beautiful table!" Larkin turned to look at him. "All for us?"

"Nothing but the best. Now have a seat. What would you like to drink?"

"I'd love coffee if you have it made. Or tea."

"The same for me please, Mr. Carney," Sukki said.

After serving their coffee, Mr. Carney brought a cake plate to the table. It was a bunt cake, creamy yellow with yellow frosting dribbled over the top. A scent of lemon wafted toward the women, making them lean forward to get another smell.

"Lemon cake! Mrs. Carney made me a lemon cake when Emmy was born." Sukki smiled at Mr. Carney. "Is this the same one? I still remember that cake." She turned to Larkin. "Lemon batter with fresh chopped cranberries; a hint of tang to it, but sweetened with the frosting. After the time I had delivering that girl, it was just what I needed."

"It's that very cake."

He cut cake for the three of them, then sat and motioned for them to start.

"Please."

Larkin took a forkful of cake. Putting it in her mouth, she caught the taste first of the lemon, followed by the sweet of the frosting, still lemon, but rich with sugar and cream cheese. The cranberries came through then, a different sweet with a different tang. At the table, they all smiled at each other.

"My mouth is a happy place." Sukki said, drawing the fork through her cake.

"This is lovely, Mr. Carney. Can I get the recipe, or is it classified?" Larkin had another bite.

"Of course you can, nothing secret about it." Mr. Carney cleared his throat. "Now, Larkin, how would you be feeling?"

"I'm all right. It's only disappointment. I hope to hear from Duncan tomorrow about his brother."

Sukki reached out, touched her arm. "Do you think he might be able to come for part of the week, anyway?"

"I wouldn't think so. It's so far and very expensive to come just for a few days. Probably we'll reschedule." She looked down at her plate. "I'm trying not to think of this as a sign. I don't believe in signs, but somewhere in my head a stupid little voice is saying he's not coming because he's not supposed to, that this isn't going to work, and if it hadn't been the accident, it would have been something else that kept him from being here."

"You're not listening to it, are you?" Sukki frowned at Larkin.

"I'm trying not to."

Mr. Carney shook his head. "Larkin, it was an accident. It didn't happen to Duncan, it only affected him. It didn't happen to you, it only affected you. It wasn't a sign, it was an accident."

"You're right." Larkin smiled at Mr. Carney. "Let's talk about something else. Will you tell us a story? An Ireland story?"

He put his index finger to his lips. "A story. From the old sod. I'm sure I can come up with something."

In bed later, Larkin thought again of Duncan. She'd been all right most of the evening. Mr. Carney's entertainment had kept her mind from it, but now there was nothing keeping her from her thoughts.

Larkin curled up in a ball. Bubba jumped up on the bed and lay in the curve of her knees, making a satisfied noise when he settled.

If he were here, she thought, he'd be in the room next door. I could probably hear him breathing, or, she smiled, snoring. When I got up tomorrow, I could wake him with a cup of tea or wait in the kitchen, knowing he'd come looking for me.

She had planned on showing him her town tomorrow then eating at her favorite diner. She intended on going easy the first day, then doing Chicago next week, going to different neighborhoods and seeing the Christmas windows on State Street. It didn't really matter what they did; he would have been here. They would have awakened in the same house and eaten off matching plates.

She felt hot tears in her eyes and said words out loud, causing Bubba to raise his head and come sniffing at her face.

"It's not fair."

Bubba nuzzled her. He took two steps, turned around, and fit himself in the circle made by her chest and stomach.

In the night, Larkin awoke from a disjointed dream. She forced herself into a sitting position, putting a pillow behind her head. She couldn't remember the details, but she was left with a feeling of restlessness. The question that woke her rambled around in her head.

How much of this is made up?

Was she designing something in her mind that wasn't real? Now that he wasn't coming, she had no way to know. She would be going forward on the little she had and a handful of faith in who she had seen him to be and in her own discernment. They had needed this week to fill in the empty spots. The fact was there was only so much to be wrung from the computer and the phone and she was so ready for more.

"It's not fair."

43.

Larkin had no work for the weekend, so busied herself with chores. She hunted cobwebs in the basement, swept out the garage, and threw away last year's Christmas cards. She shopped for running shoes. She put the turkey in the fridge to thaw, thinking she would cook it on Monday.

Duncan called on Saturday with news of his brother.

"He's alive, Larkin, but will definitely lose the leg. They say there's no way to save it as it was so badly crushed in the fall. His wife is holding up, but I wonder what it will be like for them when he comes home. She's not strong. It will be months before he goes back to work."

He talked about the fight going on already with the hospital and his brother's employer. At the end of the conversation, he stopped.

"Ah, Larkin. As much as is going on here, I can't stop thinking of what I'm missing there."

"Me, too. Do you have any idea when you think you might be able to come?"

"Not this week, that's certain. I'll be here a few more days at least, and at that point, it wouldn't make sense."

Larkin sat down and sighed. "I suppose not. I'd take it, though, even a couple of days."

"Wouldn't it be better if we made it for another time, in a month or two, when I could stay the whole week, or even two?"

"It would, I know."

"I know what you're feeling, Larkin. It's the same for me. When I get home, I'll check the jobs coming up, and the first time I can get away, I'll be there. All right?"

"Of course. I'm sorry I'm being such a wuss."

"A what?"

"A wuss. A ninny, a wimp."

She heard a smile in his voice.

"You're not being a wuss, Larkin, because I'm feeling the same way, and I'm certainly not being a wuss. Now, be looking for a package in the mail Monday or perhaps Tuesday."

"A package? What kind of package?"

"A surprise package."

"What's in it?"

"That's the part that would make it a 'surprise.'"

Larkin laughed. "All right. Please give my best to your family. I'm praying for you all."

"Thank you, Larkin. It's difficult here, but I think at the end of the day, it will be all right."

"Call again if you get a chance."

"I'll do it. If not, I'll call when I get back to Athlone, probably toward the end of the week. Good night, love. I miss you."

"You, too. Talk to you soon."

"Love, you. Bye, bye. Bye."

Sunday, the bird was thawed, so Larkin spent the day cooking the traditional meal. She roasted the turkey with apples and onions inside, putting it on in the morning to cook for hours, filling the house with its scent. She made stuffing with toasted bread, onions, apples, water chestnuts, celery, and spices. She put potatoes on to boil, then mashed them with sour cream, chives, and a little milk, seasoning them with salt, pepper, and a couple of tablespoons of horseradish. For salad, she made a Chinese blend of romaine, mandarin oranges, peapods, bean sprouts (which the kids would pick out as if they were poison), green and red peppers, and Napa cabbage. The dressing was a mixture of sesame oil and plum sauce.

Larkin took the top off the bottle of sesame oil. She took a deep whiff of it and smiled. There was something about that smell that made her think of ancient things, deep and dark. She poured some in a crystal cruet. It was important to be careful. Sesame oil could overpower even the strongest of tastes. She added the plum sauce, shook it up together, and tasted it with the tip of her finger. She added a pinch of ginger, shook it again, tasted. Perfect. When the meal was ready, she would toss the salad with the dressing and sprinkle chow mien noodles on top.

The salad was not traditional Thanksgiving fare, but the rest of the meal was so crowded with carbohydrates, Larkin made it for balance.

She washed sweet potatoes and put them in next to the turkey to bake. She liked nothing better than just baking them and topping them with butter and cinnamon. She found her grandmother's relish tray with sterling silver overlay flowers in each divided section. She pulled out black and green olives, a jar of tiny sweet pickles, and bright red crabapple slices. These she arranged in the dish, then covered it and put back in the fridge. She made cranberry sauce on the stove with whole berries and orange juice instead of water, and put it in a blue bowl, the colors working well together.

Now for bread. She flipped through her cookbook. Out of the middle, a recipe card fluttered to the floor. As she bent down to pick it up, she recognized her grandmother's thready writing.

"Hazel's Buttery Biscuits," Larkin read.

Well, a recipe for bread. She didn't know who Hazel was, some church friend of her grandmother's, perhaps, but it sounded perfect and the recipe literally presented itself. Even if they were terrible it would make for a good story.

She got out the ingredients and measured flour, baking powder, butter, and salt. She added the milk, moistening the mixture, then floured a cutting board on which she kneaded the whole sticky mess.

While she was kneading, she toyed with the idea of inviting her parents to the pre-Thanksgiving feast. The more she thought about it, the more she could hear her mother's voice questioning her choice of salad, the use of her grandmother's dish (beautiful things being made to look at, not use), the questionable wisdom of using apples in the stuffing.

Larkin shook her head. She just wasn't up to it.

When the biscuits were cut into shapes and arranged on the cookie sheet ready for baking, Larkin contemplated the table. She put a leaf in to accommodate Sukki's family and Mr. Carney, then pulled out a fall tablecloth. She put it in the dryer to fluff, hoping to erase the folding lines. She looked at her dishes, deciding to use the Spode set, colored all over in greens, browns and golds, with touches of red and periwinkle blue.

The dryer beeped. She got the tablecloth, flipped it up over the table to let it catch the air and slowly settle, like a beautiful parachute. One corner was still wrinkled, but she put it by her place and called it good.

She set the dishes, facing them all the same, and got out napkins in blue to match. She shined up the silverware and gave the salt and pepper grinders a swipe before putting them out. She placed a crystal candle holder in the center of the table, and found a perfect green taper. She put it in the holder so it sat straight, and covered it with the crystal chimney. She'd have James light it when he got here.

This was a good reason to have company on a regular basis, she thought. How often do I appreciate the pretty things I have?

She checked her watch and opened the oven to wriggle the leg of the turkey to check for doneness. It was a trick of Pat's mother - you grab a leg and move it, seeing if it's still tight or loosening. Larkin had several times pulled the turkey out too soon, the first cut showing pink still in the breast, the whole thing having to be put back in for another forty-five minutes. She grabbed the leg, gave it a tug. Still tight. She figured another hour at least.

She looked around at the kitchen. All the prep dishes were washed. There was nothing left to do until the turkey came out and the biscuits went in, her guests not expected for another half hour. She picked up a book, sat on the couch with her feet up under her, and turned on the light. Bubba raised his head from his bed by the patio windows, walked to the couch and heaved himself up next to her.

"Silly dog, you didn't have to move." As she talked, Larkin scratched his ears. When she finished, he curled himself into a ball with his back resting against her leg and fell back to sleep.

Larkin smiled. What a good day. There was food to feed her friends, a loyal dog, a lovely place to live, and a man in her thoughts.

In bed that night, Larkin stretched. Dinner was a success, but it never ceased to amaze her how long it took to prepare that meal and how quickly it was eaten.

Sukki brought Larkin's favorite pie, a fruit combination of blueberries, raspberries, and blackberries, so over dessert and coffee, the group watched The Sound of Music. Sukki and Mr. Carney had insisted on cleaning up and when they all left, the house felt empty and too quiet.

On Monday, Larkin got home just as the mailman was leaving.

"Left a package at your door," he called, waving his hand out the window of his truck.

Larkin waved and hurried up the sidewalk. She smiled as she grabbed the package with one hand, the other fumbling with her keys. The return address was Brynna's B&B, the postmarks and stamps unfamiliar.

Larkin went to the kitchen and got a knife, working at the tape on the long end of box. She took a breath, pulled back the wadded tissue paper crammed in for padding and reached for a wrapped package. It was flat and light.

In the tissue lay a shawl, tightly woven of cotton and silk, with a metallic sheen. It was hand-made, by the intricate look of it, mostly creamy beige with occasional white and tan threads. She shook it out and took off her coat. She draped it over her shoulders and drew it around herself.

In the bottom of the package lay a bag from Burke's, a grocery store on the outskirts of town. Five Whisp-A-Bites.

Sukki stuck her head in from the closet door.

"Got a package?"

Larkin turned, smiled. "Look." She turned, bringing the shawl out to the sides for Sukki's inspection. "And Whisp-A-Bites."

"Enough to share?" Sukki walked to the table and reached out to run her hand over the shawl on Larkin's shoulders.

"Of course. Want some now?" Larkin ripped the wrapper off one and broke it in half.

Sukki took a bite. "Let's not tell the kids you have these."

"I'll pick them up some Hershey Kisses or something."

Larkin sat down across from Sukki. "This was the surprise he told me about."

"It's lovely. Did he send a note with it?"

"I didn't see one, but maybe it's in the bottom." She looked inside the box. Taped to the side was an envelope with her name on it.

"There is a note." She opened it, read it, and smiled. She looked at Sukki over the top of the note.

"It says he's sorry he's not able to come," Larkin told her. "And it says he misses me."

"I'm sure it does."

"And it says he's disappointed he doesn't get to meet my very special friend, Sukki, who he knows means the world to me."

"Sure he did."

"He did. See?" Larkin flipped the note around for Sukki to read. "Right there. '...very disappointed not to be able to meet your friend, Sukki...' I told him all about you."

"It also says he wishes he had you close to him right this minute."

"You skipped a paragraph."

"I'm a speed reader from way back."

Larkin smiled at her. "Eat your candy."

44.

Duncan returned to Athlone from Sligo on Friday and emailed Larkin with his brother's condition. He was going to be all right, minus the leg, of course, and his employer was going to find him a different job in the plant, giving his brother's wife some peace of mind. Duncan was going back to work the next day and within a week would have some idea about rescheduling the trip.

Larkin mailed him back, thanking him for her treasures. The shawl was always in her sights, hanging over the back of a chair or draped at the foot of her bed. She was hoarding the chocolate, she told him, just eating it a bite at a time, and told him when he came, he should bring some for Sukki so she would stay out of Larkin's stash. He thought the end of December going into the first week in January looked good to visit, and said he hoped to get there in time to kiss her at midnight on New Year's Eve.

At work one Friday in mid-November, Larkin looked out of her window to see snow falling, huge flakes coming down close together. Her assistant, delivering papers to her desk, commented that the weather service was predicting three inches by 4 p.m.

"Should make the ride home a real treat," Larkin said, "but it is pretty, isn't it?"

The snow fell all day, stunning the town with a full seven inches, falling in bucketfuls. Larkin sighed as she got into her car, knowing that even though the Chicago area had been getting heavy snow all of its life, the first snow confused drivers. Larkin drove slowly, happy for four-wheel drive. By the time she got to her street, it was dark and beautiful, the snow dancing in front of the streetlights on its graceful way to the ground.

Turning onto her block, she slowed. Down the street at the entrance to the townhomes, an ambulance and a fire truck were pulling away from the curb toward her, lights on and sirens starting their squall as they neared the intersection Larkin had just reached. She pulled over to let them by and bit her lip.

After the trucks turned, she drove to the front of the townhomes, parked, and jerked the door open. The car still running, she ran up the stairs toward Sukki's door. On the porch sat Errol holding Bubba, both of them shivering. Tears had run down Errol's face, making white tracks, and his eyes were red in his pale face.

Larkin knelt down in front of him and grasped his arms. He looked at her, tears starting again.

"Errol, what is it? Where's your mother?"

"She went to the hospital."

"What happened to her?"

"Nothing. It was Mr. Carney. He fell over. Tee, I think he's dead."

Larkin stared at Errol, her grip on his arms loosening.

"Come inside. Where are James and Emmy?"

Larkin stood, reaching a hand down to Errol's. She opened the door to Sukki's house. The kids were sitting at the kitchen table until they heard the door, then ran to Larkin, talking over each other.

Larkin held up a hand.

"Stop. Sit down a minute, and you can each tell me what happened."

James started. "After I got home from school, Mom went to check the mail. When she opened the door, she noticed Errol coming up the walk and Mr. Carney shoveling his porch. She called to him that the association would be by soon to do it, but he said they took too long. Errol got up to his porch and he stopped talking, and leaned on his shovel."

Larkin took Errol's hand.

"Then what?" She asked him.

Errol looked at her.

"I could hear him breathe and it didn't sound right. Then he moved toward his porch, like he was going to sit on his step." Errol stopped for a moment. "The shovel fell over and Mr. Carney fell down on his knees. He grabbed his arm and looked over at Mom, waving at her to come. She came running over in the snow and he fell over on his side. Mom said a bad word and she told me to tell James to call 911 right away, that Mr. Carney was having a heart attack."

James nodded. "I called 911, gave them our address, and told them what was happening. They said they'd send someone right away."

Larkin turned to Emmy. "Then what?"

"We ran back outside and Mom was bent down over Mr. Carney, doing CPR."

"She did CPR?"

James nodded. "She knew how."

"Then what happened?"

Emmy continued. "The firemen came. One of them helped Mom and the other ones ran back to the ambulance to get some stuff." She paused.

James continued. "They lifted him on to the stretcher, and wheeled him down the sidewalk. When they got to the ambulance, the firemen lifted the stretcher up into it. A policeman had come, and was asking Mom questions. A fireman came out of the ambulance and asked her if she was in Mr. Carney's family. She told him she was as close to family as he had here. They put her in the front seat of the ambulance. She opened the window and told me to have you come to the hospital as soon as you got home."

Larkin sat back on her heels and looked back to Errol.

"Honey, why do think he's dead?"

Errol looked up at her. "I was standing with Mom by the ambulance when the fireman came out and the other one inside was saying, 'I can't get a pulse.' It's your blood, you need a pulse. If you don't have one, you're dead." His eyes filled.

Larkin reached for Errol. He was still shivering and she rubbed his back.

"We don't know yet what happened to Mr. Carney. I'll find out. It's possible he's not dead, so don't even think about that until we know for sure."

Standing, she gathered all three kids close to her.

"Here's what's going to happen now. I'll go to the hospital and see what's up, and at some point bring your mom home. You guys stay here and get something to eat. Even if you're not hungry this minute, you will be soon."

"There's frozen pizza," Emmy said.

"Good." Larkin pulled away and looked at all three individually. "Will you be all right until we get home?"

They nodded.

"We'll stay here together and wait for you to get back," James said. "We'll be OK."

Larkin started for the door. She turned back to James.

"Which hospital?"

"Alexian. In Hoffman Estates."

Larkin nodded. It wasn't the hospital where Pat died. One less thing to have to think about.

"All right, I'm going. Don't forget to eat."

On the sidewalk, she ran, skidding on the snowy concrete. She grabbed the railing at the stairs and slowed. Her car was still running, making it tropical inside. Larkin opened a window half-way and headed for the hospital.

Traffic had slowed to a crawl, snaking along. She took quick turns, avoiding the gridlock downtown, going through residential areas between main streets.

Her mind was scattered. She pushed aside the thought that Mr. Carney was ill, perhaps critically. She would not even visit the idea that he was dead. She hoped Sukki was all right.

If Mr. Carney was anything more than mildly ill, Sukki would be in pieces. Mr. Carney was part of the healthy world Sukki had created, a grandfather to her children and the closest thing she had ever had to a functional parent.

As she pulled into the parking lot of the hospital, Larkin found a space, turned off the car, and sat. Now, after running yellow lights, making illegal turns, and driving too fast on a snowy night, she didn't want to go inside.

Because she knew. She knew Mr. Carney was dead. She had known it from the time Errol first said it, the word flashing in her mind. He was dead.

In the cooling interior of the car, Larkin's face crumpled and she covered her eyes with her hands, hunched down in the dark. She couldn't contemplate it, hadn't warned herself of the possibility, but here it was. In the space of an hour, the world was again irrevocably different. It would be like when Pat died. She dreaded missing him, dreaded the hole she already felt in herself that would widen as time passed, as she realized just what Mr. Carney had been to her.

It would be a nightmare, and it was about to begin.

Larkin wiped the tears and sweat from her face with a napkin, and took a deep breath. Much would be expected of her in coming days. There would be complicated arrangements to get Mr. Carney home. Larkin would help. She'd make lists, go wherever, and do whatever was asked. She would be busy. She would take care of Brynna, of Sukki and the kids, of the neighbors. She would watch over them as they had done for her.

Larkin started to cry again, then shook her head. It would have to wait. She opened the door of the car and went looking for Sukki. She found her in a room off to the side of the Emergency Room, sitting at a table with a cold cup of tea. She had her feet up on her chair and was holding her legs with both arms. She looked up when Larkin opened the door, her face breaking.

Larkin got to her in two long steps and knelt down next to her.

"Tell me."

"He's gone, Larkin, he's dead, before he even got here, maybe even before the ambulance came, he's dead, oh God, Larkin, he's dead."

Larkin reached out to Sukki, pulled her into a hug. Sukki had been holding on until Larkin got there but now she let go, crying hard, her body shaking. At one point she pulled away.

"Do you remember what Mr. Carney said about Duncan's brother? That what happened to him didn't happen to us, it only affected us? That it really happened only to him, and to his family?"

Larkin nodded.

"Do you think this hurts enough to be happening to us?"

Larkin took a breath, steadied herself, and nodded again.

"If pain is the criteria, then we can definitely say this is happening to us."

In bed that night, Larkin curled into a ball. The evening had passed in a blur. They arrived home to the kids waiting silently in the hall. Larkin and Sukki told them Mr. Carney wasn't coming back. They cried, all of them together, then sat cuddled on the couch.

On the way home from the hospital, the women had decided it would be Larkin that called Brynna, her relationship so much stronger since the trip to Ireland, so Larkin left them to find the number and make the call. She sat down at her kitchen table with her phone book, looked out the window at the night, then dialed the number. Although it was the middle of the night in Ireland, she had decided against waiting until morning to call. The world had changed, and Brynna should know.

The phone rang and Des' voice came on, furry with sleep.

"'Lo?"

"Des, it's Larkin. I'm sorry to wake you, Des, but I need to talk to Brynna."

There was a pause. "Ah, Larkin, I'll get her, right."

Brynna's voice came on, thick with sleep, fearful.

"Larkin, what is it? Are you all right?"

"I'm fine, Brynna. It's..."

"Oh, dear God, it's my father, isn't it? Larkin, is it my father? Is he ill, was there an accident?"

Larkin's voice broke. "Brynna, I'm so sorry, but he's died. He had a heart attack this afternoon shoveling snow. There was nothing they could do for him, it was very quick, but he's gone, Brynna. I'm so sorry."

There was a pause, and Larkin heard the receiver drop to the bed and Brynna begin to weep. There was a soft scuffling, and Des picked up the phone.

"Ah, Larkin, is it her da, then?"

"It is, Des. I'm so sorry."

"Is he dead?"

"He is. He had a heart attack around 4:00 this afternoon."

"All right, all right. Thank you for calling, Larkin, for letting us know straight away. We'll be talking to you later in the day, I'm sure."

"Let me know what I can do here, Des. Anything."

"We'll call you later. Let me see to Brynna now."

"Of course. Please tell her again how sorry I am."

"I'll tell her, Larkin. All right, now, bye. Bye, bye. Bye." Des hung up.

Larkin sat at the table with the phone. She wondered who else she should call. She dialed one neighbor, gave her the news, and asked her to call the rest of the people in the complex.

She should probably let Duncan know. She looked at the clock. It was past 2:00 now, much too late to call. She couldn't make herself get up and walk to the computer to email. She just sat, the phone on the table in front of her, the house silent. She looked over and saw the shawl draped over the back of the computer chair. She forced herself to her feet and got to the desk. She picked up the shawl and drew it around her shoulders.

She pulled up email. There were three messages from Duncan. She didn't read them but pulled up "new mail" and typed a note.

Wanted you to know Brynna's dad died today. He had a heart attack after shoveling some snow. It went very quickly. We are so sorry here. We will miss him very much.

L.

She read it over. It sounded so impersonal.

Not far from the truth, she thought. Wasn't he mostly unknown to her and very far away?

She sent the email, then sat with her fingers on the keyboard. What was her relationship with this man, really? They emailed, they talked, and the rest she made up. What was she thinking, getting involved with a man thousands of miles away? Getting involved with any man, really, when there could be such complications. Surely, one of them would leave and then there would be pain, and if even if they stayed together, one of them would inevitably die, leaving the other old and alone, too late to start another life, too broken to do much of anything but wait and grow roses.

She lifted her hands off the keyboard, put them in her lap, and tried to slow her mind. All she knew for sure was Mr. Carney was gone and Duncan wasn't here. Both truths left her empty.

Without reading the emails Duncan sent, she closed down the computer, shook off the shawl, and laid it on the back of the couch. She looked over at it once, turned off the light, and went back to sit with Sukki and the kids.

45.

Brynna came that evening, staying at her father's house. Des stayed behind to run the B&B and get things ready to bring Mr. Carney home.

Brynna, Larkin and Sukki and organized the wake, the service, and a gathering afterward. Larkin had spoken to her before she got on the plane and had notified the papers in time to have the announcement appear in the next day's obituaries.

The wake was packed, the neighbors coming en masse, and colleagues and their wives along with the management from the railroad crowding the room. The cashier of the nursery where Mr. Carney bought his roses was there, as well as the bartender from the pub where he would sit and chat with his pint. There was a contingent from the Senior Center, well-padded ladies in dresses, and tall, thin men in sport coats with suede patches at the elbow. There was a scattering of Irish, known from home or met here, their accents turning Larkin's head.

Larkin's parents were there, Bunny for once not intent on being the center of attention. She had cared deeply for Mr. Carney and was frequently the recipient of the lovely Marie Louise roses she had once announced as her favorites. The two had developed a strong connection and would, at parties, most often be sitting together.

When Larkin questioned her about it, Bunny said he was very much like a man she knew when she was young. Just his manner, she had said, and the way his eyes looked when he smiled.

Brynna greeted them all, keeping Sukki and Larkin nearby. At one point, Larkin stole away. She eased her feet out of the black shoes she hadn't worn since Pat's funeral, remembering belatedly that these shoes had made that horrible day even worse.

She considered the coming days. There would be a short Mass at Saint Theresa's tomorrow, then she and Brynna would get on a plane for Ireland. Brynna had asked both Larkin and Sukki if they would accompany her back to Athlone. Larkin was able to go but Sukki couldn't, or wouldn't, consider it. After doing her best to alleviate any barriers to her going, Larkin concluded she didn't want to go and told her it was all right not to want to go.

"Stop with the psychology." Sukki told her. "You go for both of us."

Sukki was holding up, but Larkin worried about the long-term effects Mr. Carney's absence would create. When Sukki's parents had died together in a drunken one-car crash, she had been estranged from them for years, their alcoholism an issue since Sukki's childhood. Larkin had stayed the night with her, and Sukki told stories from her childhood, a veritable warzone of a home, with no place safe for a child. She grew up watchful and quiet, and spent as much time away from her house as possible. She was drawn to friends with stable homes, staring at fathers coming home from work in suits to eat at a table with matching dishes, no one smelling of old cigarettes and brown liquor.

The mothers of these families didn't like her, she told Larkin that night. They were nervous about her; they didn't want what was in her house to come to theirs, so she visited among them as an alien and for all real purposes, an orphan.

Still a teenager, she left the stench of her parents' house and made herself a life. Classically, her first husband an alcoholic, but after that she was more careful and even after her second divorce, constructed a home for her children based on what she wanted for them, not what she was used to.

Larkin knew she and Sukki would look to each other to help fill the gap the death of Mr. Carney would make. Larkin was grateful again for the blessing that put her next door to the best friend she'd ever had. They would be all right. They were not, either of them, unacquainted with grief.

Duncan flashed in her mind. She had not communicated with him, her excuse being the business of the past days, but would see him in Ireland. The thought gave her no comfort. She had not read the emails still sitting in her computer, had not even turned it on since the night Mr. Carney died.

She sighed, put her shoes back on, wincing, and went back to the wake.

46.

The flight was uneventful. Knowing the circumstances, Aer Lingus put Larkin and Brynna in First Class. Larkin stretched out in her comfortable seat and slept. Brynna had fallen asleep immediately, not yet recovered from the jet lag she'd incurred on the way over, and the two passed most of the trip unaware.

At one point, Larkin awoke. The cabin was dark and she was disoriented for a moment. She stood, careful not to disturb Brynna, and went to the bathroom.

When she was washing her hands, she looked in the mirror. The strain of the past days showed plainly, her face pinched and her eyes small. She had no idea what to expect in the next days. She was surprised to feel some expectancy. It was a mournful errand she was on, but there might still be enjoyment in it. She felt a flash of anticipation at seeing the women from the team, Paul from behind the bar at Sean's, and meeting Brynna's siblings.

She made her way back to her seat. Brynna was awake, rearranging herself in the seat.

"How are you feeling?" Larkin whispered to her.

"Not so bad. I'll be better when we get home."

"I'll bet. Your body clock will take some resetting after this."

"Oh, Larkin, I've been meaning to tell you. I got a letter from my da a few months ago. He was fine, he said, but he wanted me to add a paragraph to his will and have it notarized."

"Why would he do that? Do you think he had some idea he wasn't well?"

"Ah, no, I wouldn't say that. He was always one for being prepared. Anyway, that's not the important part. He said when he died, he wanted you and Sukki to split up the roses and my mother's dishes between the two of you, and he wanted you to have the medal you wore in the championship race."

Larkin stared. Brynna turned away to give her a moment, then turned back.

"He loved you, you know. He told me if not for the two of you, his life would have been a waste of time these past years. It was being with you two and Sukki's children that made him feel a part of things. I knew he wouldn't marry again after my mother, but I was worried he would just split his time between the garden, the telly, and the pub after she died. You gave him family to love."

"We loved him. I can't believe how much we're going to miss him."

"We will miss him differently. I didn't see him every day, but we talked and emailed so much, if felt like we did. You have that to contend with walking by his house and seeing someone else living there. It will be hard on the two of you, I think."

"And on Sukki's kids. They adored him, especially James. He remembers your dad from birth."

"Ah, well, we were all glad to have you there, my brothers and sisters and I."

"How many are you? I was never sure."

"We are five. Not large for an Irish family. The only one who won't be there is Mary, my sister in Australia. So, the others are Garvin, who you know, my sister Philippa, and my brother Seamus, Shamy, we call him."

"I don't remember Seamus. Have I met him?"

"Probably not. He doesn't go far from home, Shamy doesn't. Lovely man."

Larkin hesitated. "Brynna, about the dishes. I understand about the roses, you couldn't move them here, but perhaps you or your sisters should have the dishes. They were your mother's, after all."

"I won't hear of it. They were my father's dishes, to do with what he liked. He wanted you to have them and have them you will. There will be no talk from the rest of the family about it, I can assure you."

Larkin smiled at her. "I believe you."

"Now, are we almost arrived or should I go back to sleep? Ah, there go the lights. Won't be long now. Are you looking forward to seeing Duncan, then?"

Larkin shrugged. "I haven't thought about it much."

"You haven't? I thought after missing the trip earlier, you'd be counting the hours, even now."

"Actually, I don't think I told him I was coming. It's all been rushed."

"It has, at that. Des might have mentioned it to him, I don't know. Well, you'll see him one way or the other. I'm sure he'll want to sit with you at the Mass. You'll be up with the family, of course, and he's welcome as well."

Larkin made a non-committal sound, then turned to the window. Brynna unhooked her seat belt and struggled out of the seat to go to the bathroom.

"I'm sure he can't wait to see you, whatever the reason. It won't be long now."

When the plane taxied to the gate, Larkin saw a hearse waiting to take Mr. Carney's coffin to Athlone. It would wait until Larkin and Brynna got their bags and met Des, and they would follow it the two hours home.

On the way home, Des told Larkin Duncan had called, wanting to know if she was coming. When Des affirmed it, Duncan said he'd see them at the church.

When they pulled into Athlone the hearse went straight to the funeral home down by the river. Waiting was Garvin, a man who must be Seamus, and four nephews, ready to serve as pallbearers.

Brynna, Des, and Larkin stood by as the coffin was pulled out of hearse and taken inside.

"What happens now?" Larkin asked Brynna.

"People will come now, drop in all day. Then tonight, the family will meet here around six. More people will come and close to eight we'll go to the church for the first Mass. Tomorrow morning, there will be another Mass and then the burial."

The funeral director was opening the lid of the coffin. Larkin turned away.

"So now, we'll go to the house, freshen up a bit, and get things ready for people to come to the house after the service tonight. After the burial tomorrow, we'll all meet at McNeil's and they'll have sandwiches and tea and beer, but tonight, people will be stopping by and we need to be prepared."

The day rushed by. Larkin was sent shopping but was to call a nephew when she was finished to bring it back in his car. On her walk to the store, she was hailed by Mr. Murphy, sitting near the Castle on a bench.

"Ah, Larkin, is it you? How are you keeping yourself?"

"I'm fine, Mr. Murphy. How are you?"

"Not so bad, not so bad. Here for Brynna's da, are you?"

"I am. It all starts tonight."

"Ah, of course, I'll be there, he was a lovely man, Thomas was. And, now, lovey, how long are you home?"

Larkin stopped. How long was she "home?"

"I don't know, exactly. My ticket is open-ended. I wasn't sure how long I'd need to stay."

"Well, it's good to see you. Regards to the family."

Larkin smiled and continued on her way to the store.

'How long are you home?'

The question remained in her mind as she did the shopping. Paying, she chatted with the check-out girl, remembered from the summer.

"Now, Larkin, how long are you home?" she asked.

It was the same question asked by everyone she saw that day and the next, again and again. It reminded her of decisions she had to make; it brought her face-to-face with her choices.

'How long are you home?'

At 6:30, Larkin, Des, and Brynna walked over the bridge to the funeral home. They were the first ones arriving, but looking at the guest book Brynna counted forty people that had stopped by in the afternoon to pay their respects.

Larkin looked around the building. It was a miniature church. Small stained-glass windows lined one wall and there was a table-top crucifix, a bowl of holy water, and perhaps fifty chairs all together.

In the middle of the room was the coffin. It was up on a stand, waist high. At the wake in the States, Larkin had managed to avoid the coffin altogether. This day, it was not to be avoided.

She took a breath in and forced herself to walk the few steps. She looked down at Mr. Carney. Larkin had been afraid he would look as he always had, but he had changed in death. Larkin saw his skin was sallow, that his face had changed shape, had melted back into itself. She had never seen that suit and didn't recall the tie he was wearing. She was glad of the differences. She didn't want to recognize him here.

"Ah, look at him, now. Doesn't he look fine." A woman she didn't know came up alongside Larkin, leaned over, and kissed his forehead.

Larkin went back to join Brynna. She watched the people as they approached the casket, some kissing him, some sprinkling him with holy water from the bowl, a few reaching into the casket to put a hand to his cheek. Nearly everyone touched him.

The room was full by the time the priest arrived. He swept into the room and came directly to the family. He greeted each of them by name and shook their hands. When he got to Larkin, Brynna introduced her and explained who she was. The Father took her hand.

"Welcome, Larkin. Brynna has spoken of you often. How good of you to come."

When he walked to the front of the room, Brynna whispered that the Father and her dad had gone through school together, that he had married her parents and had baptized all the children and grandchildren. He was her father's favorite, she told Larkin, and had come out of retirement to do the service.

Larkin had been to funerals where the dead person's name was mispronounced, where facts were confused, and children's or grandchildren's names were left out. She thought it tremendously sad. That wouldn't happen now. Although the Carneys had been gone for many years, the bulk of their living had been done here, with this same man presiding.

Father Michael walked to the head of the casket. He looked at Mr. Carney, sighed, then made the sign of the cross over him. He reached for holy water and sprinkled him. He turned to the people assembled and motioned for them to sit. He raised his hands palms up and raised his voice.

"Praise be to God, the Father of our Lord Jesus Christ, the Father of mercies and the God of all consolation. He comforts those who are in trouble with the same consolation we have received from him."

He recited the 23rd Psalm, finishing with the blessing.

"The Lord be with you."

The people in the room replied, "And also with you."

"Lord, hear our prayers and be merciful to your son, Thomas Aidan Carney, whom you have called from this life. Welcome him into the company of saints, in the kingdom of light and peace. We ask this through Jesus Christ our Lord."

"Amen."

He invited anyone who hadn't to approach the casket. A stream of people made their way to the center of the room. When they'd finished, the Father announced that the family would be saying their last goodbyes.

Larkin sat for a moment, then quickly stood.

"I'll be outside," she whispered to Brynna.

Larkin walked to the head of the casket, paused a moment, then put her fingertips on Mr. Carney's icy forehead. She moved toward the door as the family stood.

As she left, the doors to the funeral home were closed and Larkin crossed the street to the railing to look out over the Shannon River. Minutes passed and the doors opened. The pallbearers brought the casket out and the people waiting outside came in closer, gathering around to watch the box slide into the open end of the hearse.

Brynna motioned Larkin to one side, took her hand, and took the hand of her sister on the other side. Family first, the entire group fell into step behind the slowly moving hearse, walking in rows of three or four.

The hearse and the people following began their walk through town. As they came into sight, cars stopped, waiting to resume movement until the hearse had passed them. People on the sidewalk faced the hearse and crossed themselves. The men took off their hats and mothers motioned children to hush. The atmosphere was one of deep respect.

As the group moved nearer the church Larkin saw others waiting outside for them to arrive. The hearse pulled up near the doors and the pallbearers took their places. The casket was brought up the stairs into the vestibule and put on a rolling stand that would take it up the center aisle of the church.

As the family took their places behind the casket, the bells of the church started to ring. The priest stood at the front of the casket, an altar boy on each side, one holding a hanging container of burning incense, the other a wand in a bowl of holy water. Father Michael called out to the group.

"The grace of our Lord Jesus Christ and the love of God and the fellowship of the Holy Spirit be with you all."

"And also with you."

He took the holy water, dipped the wand in the bowl, and splattered each side of the casket. Returning it to one boy, he took the incense from the other and wafted it toward the casket, walking all of the way around it, making sure every side was touched.

The scent reached Larkin. She knew she would never forget that smell or that sound: the heavy, spicy smoke coming from the silver pierced container softly clanging at the end of a long silver chain.

The priest said words of blessing over the body that Larkin didn't hear, then turned and walked slowly forward. Organ music began and someone sang in Latin, mournful and moving even to Larkin, the family moving in unison under the huge domed ceiling toward the altar.

The people in the pews rose as the casket passed, crossing themselves, reaching out to touch the wood as it went by. Words were whispered and hands patted shoulders as the family made their slow walk.

Larkin felt a light touch on her arm. She looked up to see Duncan, his face registering sympathy. Next to him sat two teenagers. Larkin had just enough time to see Duncan's height in the boy's stance and notice the brown curls on the forehead of the girl before the procession moved on.

The family took the first two pews as the casket was placed at the edge of the steps leading to the alter, the congregation still standing and speaking words they'd known since childhood.

"The Lord be with you," Father Michael intoned.

"And also with you."

The priest genuflected, then went to a nearby microphone. He spoke, asking those reading scripture to come forward.

Three grandchildren came to the podium at the side of the altar, each reading a passage. They were stiff and uncomfortable, one small girl losing her place and starting over, the others fidgeting on the bench where they waited. When they came back to the pews, their mothers smoothed their hair and whispered in their ears.

While they spoke, Larkin watched the Father. He sat with his hands in his lap, dividing his eyes between the casket and the altar boys. He was older, gray and slow-moving, and she wondered what it was like to have worked in this church for fifty years, christening children, marrying couples, burying the town one at a time. Did he know real sorrow over this death?

She watched his hands as they made the sign of the cross, watched as they spread wide, his arms out, sleeves billowing like butterfly's wings. He looked to the casket again and something passed over his face, something Larkin hoped was grief. He raised his hands to the congregation and spoke strongly.

"He who dwells in the shelter of the Most High and abides in the shade of the Almighty says to the Lord, 'My refuge and my stronghold, my God in whom I trust...'"

He spoke on, the initiated answering in unison. The people around her stood and she got up, smoothing her skirt and grasping the hand Brynna offered her. It was done for tonight. The morning Mass was at eleven.

They stepped back out to the aisle, walking to the rear of the church. Larkin kept her head forward but Duncan caught her eye as she passed.

"I'll see you at the house," he mouthed to her.

She nodded. She saw his look go puzzled before she continued walking.

At the rear of the church, Larkin looked back to see how far the casket had traveled up the aisle. Surprised, she turned to Brynna.

"Why isn't he coming?" After the words, she shook her head. "I mean, what happens to the casket now? Where does it go from here?"

"It stays in the church until Mass tomorrow."

"Here? Alone?" Larkin shook her head. "Doesn't someone stay with him?"

"No, Larkin, no one stays." Brynna looked at Larkin, questioning.

"I just didn't realize he'd be here by himself. I never thought of it."

Brynna smiled at her. "It's not him, Larkin, not anymore. It will be all right."

Larkin shook her head through the words. "No, I don't think it's right. I don't think he should be alone."

"Larkin, he's already with my mother, playing cards and smelling the roses." She took Larkin's arm and led her away from the doors of the church.

In the short walk from the church to the house, Larkin shut herself down once again. Since the night Mr. Carney died, she had often gotten to the edge of her emotions, then pulled herself back, holding on. She would grieve, but not yet. She wasn't ready to feel what price it would exact from the reserves it had taken so long to build.

The house swarmed with guests. Larkin asked Brynna if a general invitation had gone out.

"Ah, no, Larkin. People just know if they should go to the house. With the exception of Jimmy there, who goes to everything, there isn't anyone here I wouldn't have invited."

Larkin stayed busy, serving food and pouring beer, until Duncan put a hand on her arm.

"Larkin, stop a moment. Are you all right? I was worried when you didn't answer my calls or emails."

She looked up around him.

"Are your children here? It was them at the Mass, wasn't it?"

"It was, but they've gone home. Are you all right?"

She looked back at him.

"It's been so busy since it happened. There's been no time." She paused. "I'm sorry."

His brow creased. "It is just Mr. Carney or something more? I hardly recognize you."

She realized with relief that he didn't know her well to know what questions to ask. She forced a normal look to her face.

"Of course it's Mr. Carney. You know how fond I was of him. Sukki and the kids were hit hard, too. It's been a long week and I've been going non-stop. We'll talk after tomorrow." She forced herself to touch his wrist, then picked up her tray and went to the kitchen.

If nothing else, she'd bought a day of time.

Yesterday when they arrived at the house, Brynna had squeezed her hand and told her that her room was waiting.

"I don't have to have that one if you need it for someone else," Larkin told her. "I can sleep on the couch."

"Ah, no, Larkin. The room wasn't the same after you left. You'll have to manage your own bag, though. Des is up to his arse in cousins."

Larkin had lugged her bag up the stairs. She held her breath at the top and walked into the room. She smiled, in spite of the day, and walked up the steps to the window to watch the people walking the streets in the November cold. She opened the window a crack to take a full breath of turf-laden air.

Tonight, in the throng of people wandering the house and Duncan watching her, Larkin wanted the quiet of her room, where she didn't have to keep herself under such perfect, rigid control.

47.

The next morning dawned cold and threatened rain. Larkin sighed from her bed at the top of the house. Every funeral she could remember attending was overcast and uncomfortable.

The house smelled of food and tea, Brynna, Des, and her sister cooking for the many extended family. Larkin insisted on helping.

"All right, then, you know what to do. Here's bread for the table by the window - those are cousins from Cork. You'll have to watch your man nearest the door. Last time he was here, he nicked the pitcher right off the table." She shook her head. "That one, he'd take the eyes right out of your head and come back for the lashes."

Larkin took the basket out, came back in the kitchen to serve more food, fill pots for tea, and put sausages in the chipper. By 9:45 it was done, and she and Brynna had a quick breakfast in the kitchen before dressing for the funeral.

The walk to the church was cold. The wind was biting and mist hung in the air, hitting them in the face as they walked. Brynna sighed.

"I had so hoped for sun. My father loved the sun."

Larkin smiled. "He did. I'd watch him out there, working the roses in the heat, his head turning bright red." Her voice changed. "I am going to miss him, Brynna."

Brynna tucked her arm through Larkin's. "I know you will, Ducky. So will I. But you'll have the roses and I'll have memories, and the man will have what's he's been waiting for since my mother died."

"He waited with style."

Brynna laughed. "He did at that. Left some broken hearts at the Senior Center, is my guess. He was a fine man, Larkin, and I was proud of him. A good father, a good husband. More than most can say."

They stopped at the steps to the church and looked up. There was a crowd at the top, slowly filtering in the main doors. They made their way up, people stepping aside to let them through. At one point, Brynna stopped and hugged a woman in a blue shawl. They spoke for a minute and Brynna rejoined Larkin.

"Did you see her?" Brynna asked. Larkin nodded. "That's the one I told you borrowed my shawl and never returned it. And she wears it to my father's funeral! I should rip it right off her shoulders."

They walked to the front of the church and took their places in the second row with the rest of the family. Larkin looked around at the church. The ceiling must have been 100 feet tall, domed with marble arches. Marble pillars, carved into scrolls at the top, supported the arches. Behind the altar were more arches, inscribed in Latin.

Father Michael made his careful way to the front of the altar, genuflected slowly, pulling himself back up with his hand on the marble alter and faced the congregation.

"The God of all consolation in His unending love and mercy for us will turn the darkness of death into the dawn of new life. May we then go forward eagerly to meet him, and after our life in earth, be reunited with our brothers and sisters where every tear will be wiped away. We ask this through Christ our Lord."

The congregation murmured, "Amen."

Incense was lit and wafted toward the casket. That smell brought Larkin back to the reason for being here. She closed her eyes a moment, then opened them to the Father reading from a book he held in one hand.

"With faith in Jesus Christ, we reverently bring the body of our brother, Thomas Aidan Carney, to be buried in its human imperfection."

The congregation responded, "The Lord is merciful and kind."

Until that moment, Larkin had pushed aside the thought of the burial. Her breath faltered.

"Let us pray with confidence to God who gives life to all things, that He will raise up this mortal body to the perfection and the company of saints."

Larkin forced herself to whisper with the congregation, "The Lord is merciful and kind."

"May God give him a merciful judgment and forgive all his sins."

"The Lord is merciful and kind."

"May Christ, the Good Shepherd, lead him safely home, to be at peace with God our Father, and may he be happy for ever with all the saints in the presence of the Eternal King."

"Amen."

The people moved to the kneelers. Larkin knelt, twined her hands, lowered her head and prayed it was true, prayed he would be raised in heaven with his wife, prayed it was sunny there and he would be happy forever.

The altar boys came forward and lit incense. She stood with Brynna, tears on both of their faces, as Father Michael moved again to the microphone and called out words of intercession.

"Saints of God, come to his aid! Come to meet him, angels of the Lord!"

The congregation responded, "Receive his soul and present him to God the Most High."

The priest went on; exhorting the heavens to welcome Mr. Carney, to bring him to the hand of God. The amplified sounds bounced off the marble around her, becoming echoes in the air. She had the urge to close her eyes, to cover her ears, to run. It wasn't completely real until now; until the sounds were everywhere and she couldn't get away.

She clenched her hands on the pew in front of her and fought for control. Just another few minutes and she would just slip away to the house and meet them later.

The priest's voice echoed off the walls. She held on. Then the words caught her.

"Father, into your hands we commend our brother. We are confident that with all who have died in Christ, he will be raised to life on the last day. Help us to comfort each other in the assurance of our faith, through Christ our Lord."

"Receive his soul and present him to God the Most High."

"Take him now to be with you into eternity with the saints, Lord, and comfort us, who until our own day of judgment will be without his presence."

Larkin whispered the last word with the congregation, her eyes tightly shut, tears painting her cheeks shiny.

"Amen."

The priest moved to the rows that held the family and shook each hand. When he got to Larkin, he smiled.

"I was sorry when Thomas and Rose left us for America, but I'm glad you had a chance to meet him."

Larkin took his outstretched hand. "I will be forever grateful."

He smiled at her, his face becoming cheerful. For a moment, she could see what he'd looked like as a boy.

When he'd spoken to them all, he took more incense, wafted it around the casket, dotted it with holy water once more and moved to the front of the procession. The pallbearers took their positions and started the slow rolling of the casket down the aisle. Brynna and the family stood, moved to the rear of the casket, and followed.

Larkin stayed a bit to the back of Brynna. At the door, Brynna turned, her eyes red and swollen, and looked for her.

"All right. Just one more thing to do."

Larkin took a breath. "Brynna, I don't think I'll go to the cemetery."

"Why ever not?"

"I just don't want to go."

"Larkin, it's a beautiful place and I'm sure my father would want you to see him through to the end."

This is Brynna's father, Larkin thought, not mine. She nodded and moved behind the hearse for the walk to the cemetery. The flowers from the church rode on top of the casket and Larkin caught a hint of carnations and lilies in the cold breeze.

The weather hadn't changed and Larkin shivered. She felt movement behind her and a man's jacket was draped onto her shoulders. She turned her head, saw Duncan arranging it on her so it wouldn't slip off, then moving back in the rows of people following the slow-moving hearse.

The warmth of the jacket was welcome to Larkin but she was uncomfortable wearing it. She lifted the lapel of the jacket to her nose. Duncan's scent, so intoxicating to her in the past, evoked nothing in her now. It could have been the smell of a stranger.

At the cemetery, Larkin looked around. The gravesites were different than home, bigger spaces surrounded by short iron fencing. Looking at the stones on the way to Mr. Carney's grave, she saw the gravesites actually held many members of a family. The writing on the stones started at the top and other names had were added as spouses or children died.

Brynna motioned to a stone next to her parent's plot.

"Look at that one. Always fascinated me."

Larkin looked at the names on the stone. It started with a woman, 'wife of John,' then the husband some twenty years later, and after that, his second wife.

She looked back to Brynna, eyes wide.

"No!"

Brynna nodded and gave Larkin a quick smile. "It would be a bit too close for me if I was the first wife, buried with the second one, all stacked up there like bricks on a wall, but who am I to say? I told Des, though, if I go first, find a different place for the next wife. I want the spot next to him on my own."

They turned back to the Carney plot. Larkin looked over to the hole. The pallbearers slid the casket out of the hearse and carried it across the rugged ground to the grave.

Larkin watched as they got closer, watched as Seamus lost his footing on a rock jutting out in the path and the rest juggled for balance. When they got to the grave, they placed the casket next to the hole with straps underneath it, then stepped back and waited for the priest to begin speaking.

Father Michael raised his hands.

"Let us pray."

Heads bowed. Larkin kept her eyes open, her glance moving back to the grave. For a moment her eyes brushed with Father Michael's, and he gave her a nod before he bowed his white head.

"Lord Jesus Christ, by the three days you lay in the tomb, you made holy the graves of all who believe in you, and even though their bodies lie in the earth, they trust that they, like you, will rise again. Give our brother Thomas peaceful rest in this grave until that day when you, the resurrection and the life, will raise him up in glory. Then may he see the light of your presence, Lord Jesus, in the kingdom where you live for ever and ever."

Those gathered murmured once again, "Amen."

As the pallbearers lowered the casket down into the grave, Larkin reached for Brynna's hand and could feel her shaking. She put her other arm around her as the coffin disappeared from view and the weeping of the mourners joined with the sound of the casket hitting the ground out of sight.

At a sign from the priest, Brynna and the family moved forward, Brynna still holding tightly to Larkin's hand. At the head of the grave, Father Michael held out a small spade to Brynna's eldest brother, who dug a bit of earth from the pile that sat at the right, lifted it, and let it fall to the top of the casket. Larkin winced as the dirt and rocks hit the wood.

The spade traded hands down the line of the family, each stepping forward to put dirt in the grave, taking their time. After Brynna finished, she handed the shovel to Larkin and nodded. Larkin looked to the pile of dirt next to open hole. On one side, there lay a small wildflower, caught up in the digging. She took a bit of dirt on the shovel, then caught the flower on its edge. Tears streaming, she turned back to the grave, closed her eyes, and tipped the spade. She heard the dirt hit and looked in to make sure the flower was there, a tiny bit of yellow within the hard walls and quiet darkness.

Father Michael took the spade from her as she walked back to the family waiting silently. Brynna again took Larkin's hand. Together, they huddled in the cold and falling mist as the priest said his last words.

"Since Almighty God has called our brother Thomas Carney from this life to himself, we commit his body to the earth from which it was made. We commend our brother to the Lord. May the Lord receive him into his peace and raise up his body on the last day, making it like His in glory. Let us pray."

Larkin let her head drop, her tears falling on the packed dirt of the cemetery lawn. Father continued. "Lord, listen to our prayers for our brother, Thomas. Now, in love and mercy, give him a place with your angels and saints. We ask this through Christ our Lord."

"Amen."

The priest made the sign of the cross over the grave and lowered his head. Quietly, almost to himself, he spoke again, his voice breaking for the first time.

"Give him eternal rest, O Lord. And may your light shine on him forever."

At McNeil's later on, the mood was quietly festive. There were trays of sandwiches set out on the pool table covered with a pretty cloth for this occasion. People sat in groups, most with a Guinness, although some of the ladies opted for a glass rather than a pint. Larkin carried a cider. It was a full pint and not her first.

She was at a table with Brynna surrounded by neighbors and friends. They had all known Mr. Carney and each had a different story; stories of his kindness, stories of biscuits handed out the kitchen door, or a help with plumbing. One man reached in his pocket and handed Brynna a bill for the "fiver I borrowed and never paid back." Larkin was smiling with the group when she saw Duncan had come in and was scanning the pub. She excused herself, and made her way to where he was standing.

"Larkin." Duncan reached for her hand and led her to a stool in the corner. "Are you all right, then?" He brushed hair from her cheek, a small caress.

She made a tiny movement with her head and he let his hand drop.

"Larkin, what is it? What's happened?"

She looked up at him, her tone muddled but stern.

"Mr. Carney happened."

"It's a sad thing, but what has that done to us?"

"I don't know."

"That's not good enough, Larkin. This is a talk we need to have. Maybe not this minute," he said, looking at her bleary eyes, "but certainly before you go home. When do you leave?"

"Boy, that's Ireland for you," she said, taking a sip of cider. "First it's, 'how long are you home?' and in the next breath it's, 'when are you leaving?'"

Duncan sighed. "Larkin, do you know how long you're staying?"

She shook her head. "No, my ticket is open-ended."

"What would you like me to do? It certainly doesn't seem you're wanting my company here."

"Whatever you like," she told him, finishing her pint. She got up, walked to the bar, and ordered another. He watched her from the corner.

When she got her pint, Larkin moved to stand with Deirdre and the rowing team, blending into a knot of people. When Larkin looked up, she saw Duncan paying respects to Brynna and the family, shaking hands and kissing cheeks. She turned back to the conversation, and the next time she looked up, he was gone.

She felt a twisting in the pit of her. She could imagine her head in the curve of his neck and could feel his hands on her back. She stared at the door for a long moment, then closed her mouth. She took a mouthful of cider and turned her attention back to the group.

In the morning, Larkin was up to help feed the relatives before their drive home.

"Look at you, now." Brynna eyed her when she came down the stairs. She poured her a cup of tea, Larkin gratefully burying her nose in the heat and the scent. She took a sip and made a face.

"Sometimes it smells better than it tastes," Brynna said to her. "Let your poor stomach sit a while."

When the cousins were all fed and gone, Larkin helped clean up the kitchen. When the last load was being sloshed in the dishwasher, she sat at the table.

"Toast?" Brynna asked.

Larkin nodded. Brynna fixed bread for them both, along with a cup of tea for herself and coffee for Larkin. Larkin looked at her.

"You're doing very well with this," she told her.

Brynna sighed. "I had practice with my mother, Larkin. I've never gotten over that, really. It's a comfort knowing they're together again. I'll miss him dreadfully, of course, but somehow, it's different this second time around."

"Even though my father isn't Irish, I want to have an Irish wake for him when he dies. That was nice, the storytelling with a pint, even the very white-haired ladies sipping their Guinness. At home, it's not like that. The sandwiches are similar, but it's lot's more boring."

"He would have liked it, for sure. And now, what about you? Are you all right?"

"I'm fine. I do think, though, that I'll see if I can get out today."

"Today! Larkin, you've only been here 48 hours. Surely you can stay a few more days."

"I shouldn't really, Brynna. I need to get back to work."

"If you go today, I can't take you to the airport. We have a full house tonight, with the football in town. It will be all those wild boys from Sligo. I hope they don't rip up the place."

"I'm going to run to the travel agent on the corner of Pierce Street and Connaught now, and see if I can get a seat. I can take the 2:00 bus to Dublin and be there in plenty of time."

"Why are you in such a hurry?"

"I have to get back to work."

"Well, if you have to get back, I suppose you'll go. I wish it were different, though. Last summer was such a treat, having you here. We still talk about it. Maybe you'll come back again this summer? Then you and Duncan can have some time again."

Larkin swallowed coffee and forced a smile. "We'll see."

After securing a seat on the afternoon plane, Larkin walked down Pierce Street. As she walked, she thought of what she wanted to see in case she never came back. At the next corner, she turned right, passing the Palace and walked toward the Castle Inn. Today was Saturday, so she would be leaving again without seeing the Sunday session. She rounded the corner past Sean's, waving as he swept the front walk. She walked around the curve of the Castle, touching the centuries-old stone and running her hand along the damp surface, the moisture in the walls so deep it never felt completely dry.

She got to the bridge, and stood in the middle where she had thrown the flowers. She looked down from the bridge to the Strand, to a green door in a building a few feet from the river, bright against its dark gray background. She knew that door.

Toward the middle of her stay in the summer, Brynna had taken her to see a piece of property with the thought of opening another B&B on the river. They had walked to see it, meeting the realtor there on a bright afternoon. Brynna had pointed out the green door from the bridge where Larkin now stood.

"That's it," she told her. "And isn't it a nice location!"

They had gone in and walked the property, a three-bedroom townhouse. From every room, there was an unobstructed view of the river. Larkin listened to the realtor talk on about electricity and heat, watched her point out corners in bedrooms that would work for bathroom additions.

At some point, Larkin turned right when they turned left and explored the house alone. She walked the uneven floors, counted the churches she could see from one of the upstairs bedrooms and stuck her head out to see what flowers were planted in the window boxes attached by wire to the shutters. Coming downstairs to the kitchen, she saw another set of stairs, and walking up, found a room all to itself, not connected to the other bedrooms. It was big and square, with a fireplace in one corner and plumbing for a bathroom started in another.

This one would be mine, she thought.

She walked to the window and looked out. She would live here part of every year. She would study and write for professional journals. She turned. The bed would go there, she decided, across from the window, and her desk would sit here, where she heard the river lap up against the concrete wall that sat a short ten feet away. A four-foot counter top could sit on one wall, with a small refrigerator underneath and a two-burner "cooker" next to it. The counter would hold a toaster and a proper coffeepot with coffee in a pottery canister. A cupboard above could hold a few pieces of pretty china and the other minimal essentials.

A small table for eating could sit here, she thought, walking a step to the corner of the room nearest the window and a wardrobe would fit opposite for clothes and linens.

She paced the space, the worn linoleum cracking under her feet and thought of a hardwood floor with a big soft rug. She imagined the big wall by the staircase with one of Sukki's murals, and saw herself come up those stairs, red with the cold, to warm her hands over the grate and fix toast and coffee.

"I could live here," she said to the empty room.

She could buy it. There was money left from the insurance when Pat died, so she could pay cash for the place and come back and work on it, fix it up to rent; all the rooms but this one. Brynna could surely find someone responsible to live here and the upper room could be waiting for her whenever she wanted to come. Sukki and the kids would visit. They'd camp out on the floor, listening to the boats passing and eating Cadbury's chocolate and popcorn. She'd come alone and be able to work on the writing she'd put off.

Voices made their way up to Larkin. They were laughing as they found Larkin standing in the middle of the upper room.

"Ah, Larkin, have you ever seen such a mess? Holy Mary, it would take me a year to get it cleaned up enough to live in, and even then, it's laid out like a maze, what with two rooms on the other side and this one shut away over here. Look at the work! The plumbing would all have to be replaced, the walls are damp, and the outside needs pointing all the way round. The only thing it has to say for itself is the view, and that's lovely, isn't it, but not enough to make up for the rest." She turned to the realtor. "It would have to be someone with deep pockets and a lot of time on his hands to take this on."

Larkin blinked. She looked at Brynna, already making her way back down the stairs, calling over her shoulder, "Larkin, are you ready? I need a cup of tea after this."

Larkin did a slow turn, looked again at every corner of the room.

She nodded to herself. "I could live here."

As Larkin stood now on the bridge, the "For Sale" sign rattled in a gust of wind. It still hadn't sold, but she knew she was turning her back on the dreams the house implied. She continued her walk, counting the number of old men on benches dotting Church Street, and turned right to walk along the Shannon. When she got to the green door, she touched it in passing. Further down the Strand, she stood where she and Duncan had picnicked, then walked up the hill toward home.

On Pierce Street, she passed a bright yellow door, stopped, and went back. Inside, someone was playing beautiful violin music, sweet and sad, and Larkin stood there until it ended, letting her fingers drift across the yellow paint as she walked away.

From there to Brynna's, she slowed her walk, savoring her last moments in the country where the scent in the air alone was enough to make her want to return.

Brynna took her to the train

"I still can't believe you're going so soon, Larkin. Are you sure this is what you have to do?"

"I really do."

"Ah, Duncan must be heartbroken, just seeing you for these couple of days. What did he say when you told him you were going?"

Larkin shifted in her seat. "I really haven't had time to call him. I'll get in touch when I get home. If you happen to see him today, please tell him I'll explain later."

Brynna turned to her. "What does that mean? You didn't have time to pick up the phone for two minutes and call the man? You didn't want to, is more like it. Have you lost interest, then?"

"It's just not a good time. I'm thinking it might be better to calm down for a while until things get more manageable at home."

"And you couldn't tell him to his face, Larkin? Doesn't he deserve at least that?"

"There wasn't time or the opportunity in the last few days, and I really do have to get home today. Please, Brynna, don't make it harder than it already is."

"I think you're being selfish, Larkin. The man's been beside himself since you got here, don't think I haven't noticed."

Larkin was silent, then turned to her.

"I'm sorry, Brynna, but I'm not going to talk about this anymore. It's between Duncan and me and I'll talk to him when I get home."

Brynna swung the car into the train parking lot. She turned in her seat and looked at Larkin.

"Larkin, I think you're making a mistake."

"That seems clear."

"Are you certain of your thoughts?"

"I am."

Brynna jerked open the door. "All right, then." She walked around to the trunk, opened it, and pulled out Larkin's bags. She set them on the damp gravel and stood with her arms folded. "I don't know what I'll tell your man if I do happen to see him. I hope he doesn't come looking for you at my house."

Larkin pulled the handle out of her bag, and placed the smaller one on top to navigate the rough gravel to the depot. She reached in her purse for a sealed envelope and handed it to Brynna.

"What's this?"

"It's a check for the Rowing Club towards a boat. The rowing team decided after the funeral that we would raise money to buy a new boat and name it 'Mr. Carney.' I don't have time to get it to Deirdre so would you mind holding it until she can stop by?"

Brynna looked at the white envelope. "And whose idea was that? Was it yours?"

"It was a team thing."

Brynna softened. "He would love that. A shiny white boat with his name on it. And will you come back and row in it?"

"Brynna, I honestly don't know what's going to happen."

Brynna shook her head, then opened her arms for a hug. After holding her a moment, she looked Larkin full in the face.

"You'll be back, Ducky. I don't know what's going on in your head, but Ireland's in your blood."

She kissed Larkin on the cheek and waved away thanks for the ride.

Larkin rode the bus to the Dublin airport. She checked in and went upstairs to get a sandwich before the flight. Sipping her coffee, she winced. The only thing she wouldn't miss about this country was the coffee.

A few minutes before her flight, the chair across the table was pulled out hard and she looked up to see Duncan, red-faced and angry.

"Larkin, what are you doing? I called Brynna's to talk to you and she says you're already gone, you have a flight for today? What kind of shite is that?" He sat down in the chair.

"I was going to call you."

"Well, thank you very much, Larkin." Duncan's tone was scathing.

"There wasn't time to talk and I have to go home today. There are issues at work."

"For the first time since I've known you, Larkin, I don't believe what you're saying. You're running from me, and I don't understand it. Is it something I've done? Something you've done?" His voice got more intense. "For God's sake, what?"

"It's nothing anyone's done. It's just different now."

"Different, how? Something had to change your feelings. It's pretty clear you have none left for me."

The public address system announced Larkin's flight.

"I have to go."

"Not yet."

"They've called my flight. I have to go."

"I'll walk down with you."

"You don't have to. I can manage."

"I wasn't asking, Larkin."

He grabbed her carry-on bag and waited for her to stand. They walked to the escalator, Duncan stepping aside to let her get on first.

Even when he's angry, Larkin thought, still polite, still considerate. I'll miss that.

They got to security and Larkin reached for her bag.

"I have to go," she repeated.

"Don't go without saying something, Larkin," Duncan said, handing her the bag.

She faced him and looked up to his eyes. Even infuriated they were beautiful. Her gaze dropped and she fixed it somewhere near his shoulder.

"I don't think it's a good idea, what we're doing. It doesn't seem fair to either one of us to continue it when there's really no future."

"So you don't love me?"

His voice was harsh but she knew he would believe what she said; he wouldn't question her and he wouldn't follow her. In this moment, he couldn't tell her anything about herself that she didn't already know.

"It can't be worth it, Duncan. It's too hard."

"Are you really ignoring all we've put into this, all the feelings we have for each other?" He touched her arms, tried to get her to meet his eyes, rubbing his thumbs in the inside crooks of her elbows. His voice went lower, but still strong. "You can't, Larkin, not after what we've said and what we feel. You can't let it all go."

This would be a hard thing, but she had done hard things before. Larkin looked back up to his eyes and thought of sharp pain her body could endure; the way it felt to strike her shinbone, the feel of something tight around her wrist, how her thighs felt pounding on the pavement in a long run, and it was knowledge she could use. She stared at him, drank him in for a moment, then spoke to him gently.

"Watch me."

She turned, got on the plane, and went back to her life.

48.

When Larkin got in her car, the air smelled like snow. It hadn't snowed in the six weeks since Mr. Carney died, but today there was the deep chill in the air the Midwest can produce.

The wind whipped around her bare legs raising goose bumps, and Larkin shut her car door and started it up, letting it run for just a moment before turning on the heat. She pulled out of her driveway and drove the four blocks to the park district building where she ran every day but Sunday. She had kept up an exercise program she'd started with rowing, and was now to the point where she felt lazy if she didn't run as opposed to feeling virtuous when she did.

She trotted up the stairs to the running track, a circle of carpet that sat above the gym. She walked to an area next to the track to stretch. She waved as an older couple walked by. They were here every day, walking together at first, then the man dropping back as he tired. He'd had cancer the previous year. She watched him as he walked, one hand on the railing and his steps unevenly spaced. His wife caught Larkin's eye and smiled and Larkin wondered how soon it would be before she came here to walk alone.

After stretching, Larkin walked two laps to warm up, and hitting the start button on her watch, started running. She loved what happened to her brain as she ran. It was as if her body paid so much attention to running that it gave her mind free reign to go wherever it liked.

Finishing the first lap, her mind turned to Thanksgiving. Only two weeks ago, it had been decidedly sad. Mr. Carney had always been a guest for dinner, seated next to Bunny, and his absence was palpable.

A lull had settled in after pie, and one of Larkin's sisters asked about Duncan. In the time she'd been home, Larkin hadn't talked to anyone in her family about ending the relationship. She first looked at Sukki, always invited to holidays, then turned to her family.

"It was just too far away to have a relationship, so we stopped communicating." She kept it short, and to her own ears Larkin sounded as she wished: practical and believable.

"I'm sorry," her sister said, embarrassed. "I didn't know or I never would have brought it up."

"No big deal." Larkin smiled at her, picked up her coffee cup, and turned her attention to the conversation at the other end of the table.

Larkin knew her sisters and mother exchanged looks after she turned, but Sukki had reached under the table and squeezed Larkin's other hand, clenched in her lap and crushing her napkin.

On lap six, her thoughts went to her new group. Someone always surprised her and last week, one of the women was humming along with the music at the start of the session. She went from a hum to softly singing, then lifted her voice and really sang, the other women in the room stopping to listen. When she finished, she stood in the middle of them and cried. In the session, it came out that she used to sing in a band, but her boyfriend hated her singing and made her miserable until she quit.

"Why did I let him do that?" she'd said, her mascara running in streams down her face, "Why didn't I quit him instead?"

"Excuse me."

Larkin came back to the present and took a running step to the inside of the track. A woman behind her had come up fast, and Larkin hadn't realized she'd gotten so close.

"Sorry," Larkin said.

In her tenth lap, Sukki came to mind. When Larkin returned from Ireland after Mr. Carney's funeral, she told Sukki what she'd decided about Duncan.

Usually, Larkin could read her fairly well, but there was nothing telling in her expression, and Larkin frowned.

"What are you thinking?" She asked her.

Sukki made a noise and shook her head.

"I'm not sure. I'm wondering why you ended this. There has to be more of a reason than distance, or you never would have started it."

"It's probably more than that, but whatever - it's over."

"Are you sure it was the right thing to do?"

Larkin thought of Duncan's voice when he dropped his hands to let her get on the plane. There was shock on his face, but it was resolve she heard in his voice.

"I'm sure. Why let it go any further?"

Later by the sink, Larkin washed coffee cups and Sukki got ingredients from the fridge to make a salad. After getting a knife and a cutting board, she leaned over and put her head on Larkin's shoulder. Larkin looked down at her.

"What?"

"I missed you when you were in love," Sukki said.

Larkin tilted her dark head till it rested on Sukki's light one.

"Not to worry. We are the Lone Rangerettes once again."

It was always late in the run that her thoughts turned to Duncan. Her resistance was down, she supposed, and whatever loose control she held over her thought patterns was long gone.

She wondered how he was, and what he might be doing. She hoped he'd finished the house he was working on when she left and wondered if he was ever happy with that roof. She remembered his hands.

She let herself picture the Cliffs of Moher; leaning back on him with his arms around her, joined with hers at her waist. She saw the white birds.

For the next laps, she just missed him. She closed her eyes for a few steps and imagined him in front of her, and could almost feel his hands in her hair and his breath near her mouth. She opened her eyes, thought of Doolin, and the warmth of those nights. She remembered how it felt to turn and see him watching her.

She knew that he would not chase her. He believed what she had said. He hadn't called since she got home and she'd received no emails, though her heart still hiccupped each time she turned on her computer.

He was gone and it was completely her doing. In the two remaining laps, Larkin told herself again why it was the correct thing to do. She shook her head and ran the last lap hard. At the end, she slowed down and circled one more lap with her hands on her hips and the music turned off before getting her sweatshirt and keys and going home to shower.

She was dressed with her hair still damp when the doorbell rang. She made a face and ran down from the bedroom to answer the door. On the porch stood Bunny, dressed for the weather in a mid-length camel coat, a flowered cashmere scarf at her neck, and wool pants.

Larkin was surprised. Her mother preferred to be visited at her home, and had never before stopped by without calling.

"Mom."

"Good morning. Might you have a cup of coffee for your mother?"

Larkin opened the storm door wide and Bunny stepped into the hall.

"I just put on a fresh pot. What good timing you have." Larkin reached for her coat. "Can I hang that up?"

Larkin's voice was careful. Bunny handed over the coat, but kept the scarf, still draped around her neck. She arranged it over her, catching both shoulders and making a loose tie in the front. Watching her fuss on her way back from the front hall closet, Larkin noticed the raspberry color in the scarf perfectly matched the fitted turtleneck Bunny wore.

She is well kept, Larkin thought. No extra pounds and good attention to detail.

She got cups from the cupboard, reaching for the Old Country Roses mug she knew her mother would prefer, then filled a sugar bowl and poured milk in the creamer.

"I don't suppose you have half-and-half?" Bunny said from the table.

"I don't, Mom. I didn't know you were coming, or I would have picked some up."

It was as close to asking why she was here as Larkin would attempt.

"I didn't know for sure I'd make it today, or I would have called. Do you have a bit of time?" Bunny accepted the cup and put in a half-teaspoon of sugar and a generous pouring of milk. She stirred it carefully and placed the wet spoon on the edge of the place mat. She took a sip.

"Good coffee, Larkin."

Larkin got her cup and sat down. She reached for the milk, added enough to turn her coffee the color of caramel, and waited.

Her mother began. "I've been wanting to see you since Thanksgiving, but I wasn't really ready until now."

Larkin shifted in her chair. Bunny sat for a minute and took a breath. She started to talk, her voice gentler than Larkin was used to hearing.

"Do you remember," she started, "that vacation we took when you were around five? We went to South Carolina, to North Myrtle Beach. We stayed in a little place right on the water, and you girls lived in your bathing suits the whole week. You were out there in the sand from sunup to sundown. That was before we knew enough to be careful of the sun, and you all came back as brown as..." she looked over at Larkin's cup, "... your coffee."

"I do remember that. It was a great vacation."

"It was. Your father and I watched you girls out there, in the water up to your knees, just so happy."

Larkin could play that back in her mind, the sand and the water and the smell of her mother's sun tan oil shining on her skin as she handed them juice from the cooler by her chair. Larkin had loved the look of the sun glinting off her mother's shoulders like they were soft metal, beautiful and unique to her.

Looking at her now, Larkin saw she was still beautiful.

Bunny continued. "It was a good week. Toward the end of it, I was sitting in the sand with you. You were digging for those tiny clams. You'd find them, scoop them up, put them on top of the wet sand at the water's edge, and watch them dig their way back in. That fascinated you."

"I still do that."

"You were out there for hours. Then, you put down your shovel and walked over to where I was sitting on the sand. You were the cutest thing, all skinny and leggy, your bathing suit hanging off your little bottom from sitting in the wet sand so long, and your hair back in a braid. You got on your knees in front of me and crawled into my lap, facing me. You put your legs around my waist and your arms around my neck, and you just," Bunny paused and smiled, "melted into me. You laid your head right here," she touched the curve where her shoulder met her neck, "and I rubbed your back and you sighed, and fell asleep. I held you there and I could feel the warmth in your body and your eyelashes on my neck. You smelled like ocean water and juice and soap, and I could have sat there for hours."

"I don't remember that."

"I won't ever forget it. You woke up after fifteen minutes or so and went back to play. When you got up and ran off, I almost cried. If I had known then what I know now, I would have."

"What?"

"Thinking back, Larkin, that was the very last time you needed me."

Larkin stopped, her mother's words surprising her.

"What do you mean?"

"You are by far the most independent of my children, Larkin. Your sisters depended on me but when you were growing up, you did fine without my counsel. When you became an adult, you literally pushed away any input I might have."

It's true, Larkin thought

"Your sisters still call me for advice. It's not that one way is right and the other wrong. You just grew differently; you were fine on your own."

"What was that like for you?" Larkin asked.

"It was hard. I wanted to be more a part of your life but I couldn't fault your choices. It was almost like watching a movie."

Larkin shifted in her chair.

"How did that bring us to today?"

"Because now, for the first time in thirty years," Bunny told her, "you need me."

Larkin looked at her mother, gave her head a small shake.

"I do?"

Bunny picked up her cup, sipped her now cool coffee, made a face and put it down.

"Yes, Larkin, you do."

Larkin got up and poured them each a fresh cup of coffee. When she sat down, Bubba jumped into her lap and put his head on her thigh.

"In what way do I need you, Mom?"

"At Thanksgiving, when you said you weren't communicating with that Irish man any more, I knew instantly what had happened."

"What is it that you think happened?"

"Thomas died. No one close to you has died since Pat and it put you in a tailspin."

"I loved Mr. Carney, Mom." Larkin's voice took on an edge.

"Don't get defensive, Larkin, I know perfectly well you loved him. I loved him, too."

"What was it with you two? Sitting together at parties, always next to you at dinner?"

"We were very fond of each other, Thomas and I. For different reasons, but very, very fond."

"What was your part?"

"When I was young, I was in love with a man. Thomas reminded me so much of that man that the first time I saw him, I nearly fainted, until he spoke, of course."

"So it wasn't an Irishman that you loved?"

"No, he was from my own little town. But he looked like Thomas, acted like him, and had the same gentleness."

"What happened to the man you loved?"

"He died."

Larkin stared at her.

"How did he die?"

"It was an accident. He was learning to fly so he could do crop-dusting, and the plane in which he was training malfunctioned and crashed."

"Mom, how do you feel about flying?"

"I hate it. I do it because the options are limited, but I'd rather be anywhere but a plane."

"You've never said anything."

"No need to make the rest of you nervous."

"What happened, after he died?"

"I was devastated, of course. We were weeks away from getting engaged, and suddenly, it was gone. My life was shattered."

"What did you do?"

"I mourned. I cried and wailed and screamed into a pillow. Then I got tough."

You never know, Larkin thought, what a person has endured.

"Mom. I am so sorry. I didn't know."

"No one knows, except your father."

"Did Dad know this man?"

"No, they never met. I met your father later."

"What was the man's name?"

Bunny hesitated.

"No, I don't think I'll tell you his name. Anyway, when I met your father, I was sure I would never love again and would certainly never marry. Your father talked me into going out with him in a friendly way, when there was a dance, or a new movie. No strings attached, no commitment."

"How long did that go on?"

"It was a year or more. He was a patient man."

"What changed?"

"It was the Vietnam War. That morning, my brother had come home to tell us that your father had been called up, and would be leaving in two weeks. The minute I heard, I ran to find him." Bunny sipped her coffee, then continued. "He was at his house, just leaving for work, and I burst into the kitchen. I ran to him and stood in front of him, not knowing what to do or what to say. He took me into the living room, sat me down on the couch, and held my hands and I was babbling and he just sat and listened. 'You can't go,' I told him. 'Of course I'll go,' he told me. 'Why wouldn't I go?' I took a deep breath, and when it came out, I was telling him I loved him and now he was going to war and I was so afraid. His eyes got big and then he closed them for a second and when he opened them he leaned forward and kissed me for the first time. It was on that couch that he proposed to me with his mother in the next room listening, and we were married when he came home on his first leave."

"When she redecorated, you kept that couch until it about disintegrated."

"Even so tattered, it was hard to let it go. The night before it went to the trash, your father took me to the basement and sat me down on it, told me it was the smartest thing he ever did and he proposed again."

Larkin shook her head. "Who'd have thought he'd be so romantic?"

Bunny straightened in her chair and smiled.

"Your father adores me, Larkin."

For years, Larkin and her sisters had felt silently sorry for their father, Bunny being Bunny, but Larkin suddenly realized their sympathy was ill-placed. Her father quietly delighted in her mother and seemed to want nothing more than the life they had together.

Why was that hard for me to see? Larkin wondered. Because it's hard for me to adore her?

"Larkin, the point is there is life still in you. There is room for love and a family and growing old together. Why are you pushing it away?"

"Mom, you don't even know Duncan."

Bunny shook her head, impatient.

"It's not Duncan we're talking about, although I'm sure he's a fine man. You've always had good taste in men. You are pushing away the whole thought of love and involvement."

Larkin sat across from her mother, playing with the spoon she'd taken from her placemat. Her mother moved on her chair.

"Larkin?"

Larkin looked up and sighed.

"When Mr. Carney died, it was awful. It was the loss of another man I loved. I don't think I could stand losing another one."

"So your choice is to be alone? Intellectually I understand, but practically, it won't work for you."

"I seem to be giving it a shot."

"Larkin, what do you want?"

"I don't know."

"That's not good enough. What is it you want?"

"In relation to what?"

"In five years, what do you want your life to become?"

"I don't know. Pretty much the way it is now, I guess."

"Nothing risky about that. What else?"

"What are you trying to get me to say?"

"If you could have anything, Larkin, what would it be?"

"What do you want me to say?"

"I want you to say what you feel. What do you want?"

It came up from her heart and out in a breath before she could stop it, and Larkin was surprised at the strength the words still carried.

"I want Pat."

"Yes," Bunny told her, "that is exactly what you want. What about Pat do you want?"

"All of him. Waking up with him, going places, watching him eat, knowing he's on his way home. All of it."

"You loved him."

"Completely."

"You can love again."

Larkin tried to steady her breathing. She shook her head at her mother's words.

"I don't think so. Not like that."

"I did."

"That was different. Pat and I were together for ten years, married for eight."

"Love is love. You didn't love Pat more than I loved Lewis. You loved him longer. You are a very strong woman, Larkin." Bunny smiled tightly. "You get that from me. Right now, however, you are using your strength to keep from living your life, and that is not a good use of your ability."

"What would you have me do? Run off to Ireland with a man I hardly know?"

"Don't be ridiculous. My suggestion is to find out if that relationship could work. If not, then open yourself to another."

"It's not that easy."

"Of course not, nothing is. Let's talk about Duncan specifically for a moment. Is he kind?"

"He is."

"Fun to be with?"

"Yes."

"A gentleman? A hard worker?"

"All of those things and more."

"He is respected by his friends and his colleagues?"

"With good reason."

"Are his looks pleasing to you?"

Larkin nodded.

"It's worth mentioning that you're not the type to get involved physically with a man without commitment. Although it's none of my business, I assume you have considered what you would be missing out on if you didn't remarry. You are a sensual woman, Larkin." Bunny smiled again. "You get that from me, also."

Larkin shifted in her seat, waking Bubba, and leaned back to study her mother. It was another piece of Bunny she hadn't put name to, her habit of touching textured fabrics as they passed by clothing in a store, her fondness for velvets and cashmeres, anything with softness. At the dinner table, she would stroke Larkin's father's hand, smoothing the hair in the direction it grew and Larkin saw her own hand on Duncan's wrist, loving the feel of his skin under her fingers.

Bunny continued.

"He must be a fine man, or he would not have caught your attention. The fact that he lives in another country is an imposition, but you can work around that. So, the question to be answered is: do you want to love again? It is a choice, and I am asking you." She lifted her eyebrows and locked eyes with Larkin. "Do you want to love a man, marry him, and maybe, Larkin, because there is no guarantee, have to bury him?"

"I'm not sure."

"Is it your opinion that Duncan would be that man, if you were sure?"

Larkin looked off over her mother's shoulder to the family room. In her mother's gaze, she opened herself to the thought of Duncan and it ended as a nod of her head.

She looked back at Bunny.

"With all that I know of him and what I know of me, yes, it would be Duncan."

"Are you willing to take the chance, Larkin?"

Larkin got up and walked to the computer. She reached for the poem hanging there and walked back, placing it down in front of her mother. Bunny read the first sentence aloud.

"Who once has known heights and depths shall not again
Know peace."

The rest she read silently until the end. After she'd said the last line, "Who once trodden stars seeks peace no more," she looked back at Larkin with tears in her eyes, but in her voice sat the strength Larkin now recognized as the root of her own.

"What is your choice, Larkin? Now that you have 'trodden stars,' what are you willing to do?"

Larkin got up and knelt in front of her mother's chair. She studied this new woman and wondered how she could have missed it; how it was that she had stopped looking before finding the depths of the woman closest to herself.

"I'm sorry," Larkin said.

Bunny shook her head. She reached forward, took Larkin's hands, and rubbed the tops of them with her thumbs.

"You did fine on your own. Now, though, today. What have you decided to do?"

She waited a moment, looking down at her mother's hands - veined and wrinkled but still pretty, still strong - and she squeezed them, then looked back up to her mother's eyes, softer, but still firm.

"I think I have to go to Ireland."

Her mother smiled at her and closed her eyes for the second it took the tears to fall from her eyelashes to her cheeks. Larkin let go of her mother's hands and reached up to hug her, then laid her head on Bunny's shoulder, on the soft cashmere smelling of good perfume and her mother's own scent. Bunny's hands went to Larkin's back, rubbing up and down, and mother and daughter stayed for a long moment, rocking gently.

49.

On the train coming into Athlone, Larkin dozed, her head against the window. This was, she thought, the most impulsive thing she'd ever done. Yesterday, her mother made more coffee while Larkin called work and arranged to be off, then sat with her at the computer looking for a flight.

"It's a good thing you save your money," her mother observed. "You're going to need it."

"Another thing I probably got from you," Larkin told her.

She made the reservation. When she'd finished, her mother rose to go. They walked to the hall, Larkin getting and holding her coat for her, and when her mother turned back to face her, Larkin shook her head.

"I don't know how to thank you, Mom. I'm in awe."

"What a nice thing to say."

"It's true. I'm very grateful to you."

"It would be a good thing to remember the next time I annoy you."

Larkin laughed and they hugged tightly.

"Give my best to Duncan. Tell him I hope to meet him soon."

"I will."

She had gone, Larkin watching as she made her way down the sidewalk, stopping for a moment at Mr. Carney's to look at the rose cones, decorated in garlands and ornaments for Christmas. She turned back to look at Larkin. Larkin stuck her head out the door and called to her.

"Each of the neighbors picked one and decorated it. By next year, the townhouse will be sold, but we wanted it the way Mr. Carney would have liked it this year."

"Which one is yours?" Bunny called back.

"In the middle, with the green pine roping and holly, and the dried heather. I snuck that back from Ireland."

"It's the prettiest one. He would have loved it." She waved, then walked quickly down the steps to her car, her scarf whipping in the wind.

Larkin went inside, stood in the middle of the living room, and tried to decide what to do next. She had only four hours until she needed to be at the airport. She had to see if Sukki would watch Bubba.

Sukki.

Larkin walked down the stairs and through the closet. She knocked, then went into Sukki's family room, calling for her.

"Up here," Sukki answered from upstairs. "In the office."

Larkin ran up the stairs and stood in the doorway of the bedroom in which Sukki worked, smiling at the organized chaos in which Sukki seemed to thrive. Sukki was at the computer. She turned when she heard Larkin approach.

"Hey. What's up?" Sukki smiled and flexed her fingers.

"Do you have a minute?" Larkin asked.

"Absolutely. Want coffee?"

"No thanks, I'm floating."

They walked to the kitchen where Sukki got coffee and sat down on the couch in the family room. Larkin laid her head on the back of the sofa, then turned to her friend.

"I'm going to Ireland."

Sukki opened her eyes wide.

"When?"

"What time is it?"

"Today? You're going to Ireland today?"

"It's true."

"All right, spill. What happened? Did Duncan call?"

"No. Actually, it was my mother."

"Bunny?"

"She gave me a good talking-to."

"About Duncan?"

Larkin nodded.

Sukki whistled. "It must have been some talk."

"I've underestimated my mother."

"Really."

"I believe so."

"I don't know what amazes me more - that you're going to Ireland or that it was Bunny who talked you into it."

"So what do you think?"

"About Bunny?"

"About Ireland."

Sukki turned on the couch to face Larkin, and tucked her legs under her.

"Why are you going?"

"Because I still love Duncan and I want to tell him in person."

"Are you still afraid?"

"Of course. But unless I want to give up the thought of ever marrying again or possibly having children, or as my mother insinuated, never have sex again..."

"Bunny said that?"

"In so many words."

"Wow."

"She was good."

"And you're going to Ireland today."

Larkin checked her watch. "In six hours. I need to be at the airport in four."

"I'll take you." She looked up. "OK, what else? We'll watch Bubba, of course, and the mail and paper..."

"Sukki."

"What?"

"How do you feel about me being attached again?"

"What do you mean?"

"You missed me, you said. I don't want our relationship to suffer for the one with Duncan."

"Larkin, we will always have us. That won't change. After the kids are grown I hope to find me a hunk, too. Keep an eye out for a promising Irishman."

"Good enough for you? That will take some time."

"What did Duncan say when you told him you were coming?"

Larkin raised an eyebrow. Sukki's look changed to amazement.

"You didn't tell him you were coming?"

Larkin shook her head.

"Gutsy move. You're just going to drop in on him? Use the element of surprise?"

"That's my plan."

Sukki reached out her hand to touch Larkin's arm.

"Larkin, what happens if he was too hurt by your leaving to want the relationship back?"

"He has to. He promised."

"He promised what?"

"He said he'd wait for me until Christmas."

"Athlone! Athlone Town!"

The call of the conductor woke Larkin from her doze. He walked past her, calling the station, and she leaned back in her seat and smiled.

She checked her watch. It was almost five, the sky darkening to a pale purple with a dark blue line at the horizon.

When the train stopped, Larkin wrestled her bag down the steps of the train and dragged it across the gravel of the parking lot to the waiting taxis.

The first cab driver in line jumped out of the car to open the trunk and put her bag inside. When he turned to ask her where she was going, she saw it was Lara's boyfriend, Emmet.

"Larkin, is it, well, look at you! I didn't know you were coming back to us so soon!"

"Emmet, I didn't know myself."

"Well, it's grand to see you, Larkin. And, now, tell me," he said, "how long are you home?"

He kept up a chatter into town, but fell quiet when he heard her sigh at the sight of the river.

"There is it." she said.

Emmet nodded.

"Still here, just as you left it."

They pulled up outside Brynna's B&B, Emmet getting her bag out of the trunk and starting to walk it up to the door.

"I'll get it, thanks." She pulled money out of her pocket. "Thanks so much. Tell Lara I'll call her."

He pocketed the money and waved.

"I'll tell her, Larkin. She'll be pleased."

Larkin walked the rest of the way to the door, putting her hand on the warm stone of the house before ringing the bell. She heard steps in the hall, and the door swung open.

"Might you have a room at the top of the house for a tired traveler?"

Brynna stood with one hand on the doorknob and the other at her throat, her mouth open. Larkin started to laugh and Brynna exploded with, "Larkin! Holy Mary, Mother of God!"

"Can I come in? It's getting cold out here."

"For goodness sake, come in, of course, come in." She closed the door behind her, bellowing toward the kitchen. "Des! Look who just showed up on our porch! Des!"

Des came through the door, a towel twisted around a cup in his hands. He stopped long enough to drop it all on the dining room table before hurrying to Larkin, arms out.

"Why in God's good name didn't you let us know you were coming? We could have picked you up at airport, or at least the train!"

"I took a cab; in fact, it was Emmet, Lara's boyfriend."

"Oh, good, someone you knew, at least." Brynna shook her head, still astonished. "Now, Ducky, what in the world are you doing here?"

Larkin stopped a moment. She hadn't considered how she would explain her sudden appearance to Brynna.

"I need to talk to Duncan."

Brynna smiled. She reached out and hugged her.

"Ah, I knew it. I knew it all along. Does he know you're coming, then?"

"I didn't tell him."

"Didn't tell him you were leaving; now you don't tell him you're coming. You can only hope he's a man for surprises."

Des picked up her bag.

"Up to your old room, Larkin? Or would you like something downstairs this time?"

"Oh, no, my room at the top, please, if no one else is in it. I dream of that room."

"If someone else was there," Brynna told her, "I'd move him to another. Now, are you hungry, Larkin? Would you like a sandwich or some apple tart?"

"Thank you, no. I'm too nervous."

"Let me get you coffee while Des takes your bag up. Come to the kitchen."

As Larkin walked through the house, she took a deep sniff of the air in the house, scented with turf and laundry, just as she remembered. In the kitchen, the range was lit against the cold. Brynna sat Larkin in the chair closest to the flame and got cups and coffee, fixing a plate of cookies and bringing a small table to sit near Larkin's knee.

When they were settled with cups, Larkin reached over to touch her arm.

"Brynna, how is Duncan?"

"Ah, he's all right, I guess. Not too cheerful, but all right."

Larkin hesitated.

"Would there be any obvious reason for me not to go over there tonight?"

"You mean has he found himself another woman? Not that I know of, Larkin, and I think I would know. It's not that big of a town."

"Has he said anything to you about all this?"

"Nothing for him to say, really. With you going off like that, it seemed clear what you were doing."

"He came to the airport that day."

"Did he, then? He was upset when I talked to him on the phone but he never said anything more about it."

"I wasn't all that nice."

"Well, you've found your way back to apologize, haven't you?"

Des came down the stairs into the kitchen.

"There, now, Larkin, you have fresh towels in your bathroom and the bed is made up. Like to shower, would you, or take a rest?"

Larkin smiled up at him. She'd bet a ten-Euro note there were already fresh flowers in her room.

"A shower sounds perfect, Des. I can only hope" she looked over at Brynna, "it will help me think of what I can say when Duncan opens up his door."

"Take your time, Ducky. Get the words right."

She walked up the stairs to her room to find her bag on the bed and a vase of flowers on the dresser. Larkin took her coffee in the bathroom with her, and took a long, hot shower. By the time she was done, she had an extensive talk in mind. She would sit him on the couch and try to make him understand what happened. He was a sensitive man. He would listen, she was sure, and if he sent her packing it would be for good reason and fully within his right.

She dried her hair and put on fresh clothes, a white turtleneck with a black fleece and jeans. She checked her face in the mirror.

Larkin walked down the stairs to the kitchen, Brynna and Des sitting by the range with their tea. Brynna stood as Larkin walked down the last few stairs.

"Do you want me to run you over? It wouldn't take but a minute."

"No, thanks. I'll walk."

"All right, then." She squeezed Larkin's hand. "It will be fine."

"I hope so."

"So do I. Go on, now."

Larkin opened the back door and stepped off the porch. As she started the walk to Duncan's, she saw the Castle, staid and solid, and the clouds in the now dark sky. At the corner, she hesitated, then turned left toward town instead of right toward Duncan's.

As the darkness gathered around her, she walked the streets of Athlone. She wanted time for the town to feel familiar to her again, to remember the steps leading down from the bridge, to walk by the art store and see the print she'd meant to buy still hanging in the window, to touch the green door, the "For Sale" sign now plastered with a "Contract Agreed" sticker.

I should have bought it, Larkin thought. Whoever bought it will change it completely and that perfect room will be gone forever.

As she walked, she was aware that if things did not go well with Duncan she would most likely be leaving tomorrow. The smart thing would have been to call him, or e-mail; to open communication that way, and then visit. This wasn't just impulsive, it was foolish.

She turned around at the Prince of Wales Hotel and started the slow walk toward Duncan's. At the very least, she could apologize for her thoughtlessness in leaving without telling him last time. If nothing else, she wouldn't have to miss him for the few minutes she was there.

Nothing like throwing away a lifetime of good decision making for one ridiculous, impetuous action. And for what? Did she honestly think he would be thrilled to see her and instantly forgive her?

That would be nice, she thought. Not realistic, but nice.

Duncan was a kind man. Even if he wanted nothing more to do with her, he would let her in and let her say her piece.

Larkin hoped Brynna was right about there being no new woman in his life. She couldn't imagine anything worse than knocking on his door and having some beautiful girl open it; Duncan having to be kind to her while having a twenty-five year old supermodel hanging off his arm.

She passed Sean's on the opposite side of the street, noise coming from it in waves every time the door opened. She turned the corner to Duncan's house, visible at the end of the street. She slowed her steps but promised herself she wouldn't stop. At Duncan's door, she took a deep breath and knocked. As the door swung open to the light, she found herself face-to-face with a beautiful girl, tall with brown curly hair and gorgeous eyes.

You've got to be kidding, Larkin thought. Shit.

She stood there saying nothing until the girl spoke.

"Hello. Are you looking for my dad, then?"

His daughter, Larkin thought. Not a woman, his daughter. Kyla.

"Yes, I am. Is he here?"

"He is, of course. Come in, I'll get him."

As Larkin passed through the opened door she smiled at the girl, so much like Duncan. "You have your father's eyes."

"That's what everyone says. His hair, too, though that's harder to control."

She went to the hall toward the office. Larkin stood up straight, put her hands in the pockets of her coat, and waited.

Kyla came from the hallway, Duncan behind her. When he saw Larkin, he stopped.

"Larkin?"

Larkin cleared her throat.

"Hi."

He walked toward her.

"Is everything all right? Has anything happened?"

"No, nothing has happened. Everything is fine."

He stopped in front of her.

Kyla made a noise behind them and Duncan turned to her.

"Ah, Larkin, this is my daughter Kyla. I don't think you've met."

Kyla came forward with her hand out and Larkin shook it.

"Lovely to meet you," Kyla said. "My father spoke of you often."

'Spoke' of me often, Larkin thought. Not 'speaks.'

"It's good to meet you, too. I think I saw you at the funeral but only from the back."

"Ah, it was too sad, wasn't it? I didn't remember much of her father, of course, moving away when I was young, but I've known Brynna since I was a baby."

Duncan turned to her.

"Kyla, do you think we could finish your paper later?"

"Ya, of course, it's not due for a week. I'll go home and do maths. I have pages and pages." Kyla turned to Larkin. "I hope to see you again."

"I hope so, too."

Kyla got her coat and reached up to kiss her father's cheek.

"Thanks, da. See you tomorrow."

When she'd gone, Larkin turned back to Duncan.

"It's amazing how much she looks like you."

"She's a good girl, even for that."

He was standing a few feet away. Not overly glad to see her, it seemed.

She plowed ahead.

"Duncan, can I talk to you for a few minutes."

"Of course, Larkin, please sit down. Can I take your coat? There's a bite in the air tonight."

He walked to the fire and tossed in more turf, then walked back to the couch where she had taken the same seat as the last time she was here.

He sat at the other end, his arm up along the back.

"So, Larkin, what brings you to Ireland again so soon?"

His voice had lost all inflection. She took a breath.

"First, I want to apologize for the way I left last time. It was thoughtless, and no matter how upset I was over Mr. Carney, there was no excuse for treating you that way. I want apologize and ask you to forgive me."

"Don't tell me you came all the way here just for that?" Duncan's tone was impassive. "I would have forgiven you over the phone, Larkin."

"There's more." She paused, losing her nerve, and sidestepped. "By the way, how are you? Whatever happened to the house with the terrible stairway?"

"Finished, thank God. I'm starting a new project in a week if the funding comes through from the bank."

"What is it?"

"It's a terrace house on the Right Bank of the river, on the Strand."

The Right Bank. Maybe it was near the green door.

Maybe it *was* the green door.

No way, Larkin thought. Can't be.

"Which building?" she asked him.

"It's gray, with windows overlooking the river and a green door."

"You bought the house with the green door? The one next to the fishing boat place?"

"I'm trying. The bank isn't so sure. I'm thinking of fixing it up and living there."

Before he'd finished talking, Larkin was leaning forward on the couch, interrupting him. Once she started, she couldn't stop, and when it was over she would wonder if it was the copious amounts of coffee and no sleep, yet another flight over the ocean, or just being in the same room again with this man that made words tumble out of her.

"I'll make up whatever the bank doesn't want to lend you," she blurted.

"Larkin, what are you talking about?"

"I have money set aside. I want to own part of that house."

"Why?"

"I love it. I was in it last summer with Brynna. She didn't like it but I loved it, I wanted to buy it, I should have, really, but I wasn't smart enough then. I am now."

"Larkin, why would you buy a house in Ireland?"

"I want to live there, I always have, since the first time I walked up the stairs off the kitchen. I want an office in that wonderful upstairs room, with a real coffee pot and pretty dishes." She rushed on. "We could do it together, work on it and own it, but I would find somewhere else to live until we decided what to do about us, about being together."

The words flew out of her mouth, leaning toward Duncan, her face open. She started again.

"I don't know that I meant to say it quite that way..."

"Larkin, why did you come back to Ireland?"

"To see you."

"Why?"

"Because I think we have a future."

"You had convinced me you thought otherwise."

"I was frightened after Mr. Carney died. I couldn't take the chance on something else with no guarantees."

"There aren't any now."

"I know."

"What's to say you won't disappear when the next crisis hits?"

"I have a story to tell you, but suffice to say my mother would never let me get away with it."

"I don't know that I'm convinced. I had put hope in you and you left it easily, without even a look back."

Larkin wanted to touch him, but it was important that he first understand her mistake.

"Let me tell you how it was after I got home," she started, slowly. "Every day, including today, my first thought of the day would be you. Then, I would think of you while I ran. Off and on during the day, I wondered how you were and where you were. I was envious of whoever you were sitting with at Sean's. I could close my eyes and see your face perfectly." She reached over to where his arm lay across the top of the couch, and brushed the back of his hand with her fingertips. "I could have drawn your hands."

She continued, softer.

"It was awful. I don't know how you felt, but please don't think I left here untouched. I paid heartily for my decision."

Duncan hadn't moved aside from a change in his face when she'd touched his hand. As she took a breath to start again, he held up his hand and stopped her.

"Larkin, did you need me to know you suffered as well? All right, I know. Are you wanting absolution? I've already accepted the apology you've offered. What more do you want?"

She smiled. "Duncan, I want everything. The same as I'm willing to give."

She got up and moved a foot closer to him, carefully, and took his hand off the top of couch. She looked down at it and ran her fingers under his palm. She turned it over to find a cut in the thin skin between his thumb and forefinger, healing now, but still evident.

"How did this happen?" She asked, running her fingers on each side of it.

"I caught it on a sharp piece of steel, working on a roof." His voice had gone low.

"Did it hurt?"

"It did. It went deep."

"But it's better?"

"Every day, it gets a bit better."

"And when I left, did it hurt?"

"It did, of course. I'd forgotten hurt like that."

"And, every day, did it get better?"

"It never got better. When I woke this morning, it was still there. No, Larkin, it didn't get better."

She still had his hand, one of her hands twining his fingers and the other smoothing the hair on his wrist to the outside, as soft as she remembered. His fingers moved in hers.

"The question becomes, Duncan, what do you want from me? Do you want what I can offer?"

"You haven't said why, Larkin."

"I love you, Duncan. I never stopped."

"I know how that feels."

"I've decided how to fix it. How about you?"

"Did you fly in today?"

"Yes. It took an extra six hours with delays. I came here after a shower and a walk."

"You came just to see me."

"I did. It wasn't something to do over the phone."

"To bring us back together."

"Yes."

"You took a big chance."

"I still am."

Duncan spoke slowly.

"It is still so unusual," he said, his other hand covering hers as it encircled his wrist, "even after all the times it's happened, to hear my own words come out of your mouth." He turned his eyes to her and let her see into them. "Everything you said... it could have been me. You have been my first thought of the morning and my last before sleep. I see your face; I can hear your voice. You've never been gone from my thoughts."

"Why?"

"You know why."

"I need to know it's going to be all right."

He moved gently toward her and she drew in part of a breath and then the rest as he came to sit close to her, his leg bent underneath him and touching hers. He reached his hand to the side of her neck under her hair, as light as a white feather, and her thoughts went to the cliffs and the white birds, circling in the dangerous winds because they had proven themselves, and she felt brave and sure and sanctified by fire.

He brought his face close to hers and she reached up with both hands to touch the corners of his eyes. It came from him as it had the first time: naturally, with no apology and no flamboyance.

"I love you, Larkin."

Hearing the words from him stilled her, as it had before, and in that stillness, she knew there would be color in their lives. It would not always be bright, but there would be color: light and dark, dashing and opaque, pale and brilliant; color to break up their days and heighten their nights. As he leaned forward to kiss her, she knew with certainty that at the base of the cliffs in the rogue winds, fearless and calling them home, the white birds flew.

Mrs. Carney's Lemon Cake

2 sticks of butter, room temp.
2 C sugar
4 large eggs
1/3 C lemon zest, grated larger than usual
3 C flour
½ tsp baking soda
½ tsp baking powder
1 tsp salt
¼ C plus 1 tbs fresh squeezed lemon juice
1 C chopped fresh cranberries
¾ C low-fat buttermilk
1 tsp vanilla extract

Preheat oven to 350 degrees. Grease and flour Bundt pan or 2 cake pans.
Cream butter and sugar until very light and fluffy. Add eggs and lemon zest.
Mix together flour, baking powder and soda and salt in a bowl.
In another bowl, combine the lemon juice, butter milk, and vanilla.
Add flour and buttermilk mixtures alternately to butter and sugar mixture.
Bake for 45 minutes to an hour, depending on pans, until a toothpick comes out clean.
Cool and frost.

Cream Cheese Frosting

1 stick of butter, room temp.
8 oz reduced fat cream cheese
2 ½ C powdered sugar
1 tsp vanilla

Cream all ingredients till very well blended, then frost or drizzle.

Acknowledgments

This has been a journey and as such, there are many people to thank. I gratefully thank my husband, Lee Plate, for his consistent and unending support and the ability to keep a straight face when I want to try something outlandish. I thank my children for adding such color to my life.

Thank you to the Irish contingent, who took me places I never would have found and told me stories I never would have heard. To Eileen, Padraig, Callaigh, and Ciara Broderick, my eternal thanks. To Anne Lyons and Albert Austin, thank you for letting me see the inside of the B&B business. Tony Maguire, may he rest in peace, let me sing in his bar at 4am. Dinny from Sean's and Tommy Curley told me important stories, and Anne Flannery told me the truth. Mr. Coady sat me down in the best chair next to the fire and taught me about roses. Anthony and Vinny from The Bastion gave me the best room in which to work and let me make my own coffee.

The American contingent was fabulous as well. I received assistance from the University of Wisconsin Rowing Team, hospitality from the Fowlers, encouragement from Barbara Butler and Ed Rossini, and the ravioli recipe from Mike Ryan. Many people related stories difficult for them to tell concerning hospitals and death. I am grateful for their time and willingness to share their pain with me..

I thank the early and recent pre-publication readers for their honest feedback and the push to finish. An incomplete list is Laura, Marcia, Rainey, Stacy, Bethany, Karen, Keith, Deb G., Jerry, Tracie, Sue, Suzanne, Jane, and the Moms.

My thanks to Erin Brooks, who edited the original manuscript. Without you, it would have been twice as long with far too many commas. I thank Bryan Keadle, who saved my sanity by doing all the things he's good at and I'm not.

I thank Tex, who laid next to my desk for the first writing of this book, and to Mighty, who sat in my lap for the rewrite.

.

Made in the USA
Charleston, SC
10 October 2015